FREKE WYRD VOODOO

BOOK 3 VALHALLA AWOL

STEVE CURRY

Amazon print edition

ISBN -

Steve Curry, Author

Lubbock, TX 79413

https://www.facebook.com/MyWyrdMuse/

https://MyWyrdMuse.com

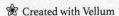 Created with Vellum

ACKNOWLEDGMENTS

To my team.

My family, the daughters that help me proofread, develop dialects and set up the odd Book Signing events, my mother, aunts and cousins for reading the early labors; thanks for the support and every scrap of help. I couldn't do it without you.

Also thanks to the artists and professionals on Fiverr.com for amazing cover-art, formatting and promotional efforts.

And finally, a huge thank you and appreciation to Cindy for pushing prodding and encouraging me with only the occasional reminder that I should have started writing twenty-years ago when she first told me to.

FREKE~

"Avaricious" in old Norse, Freke was one of two wolves who could normally be found at Odin's side to do his bidding.

1

NEVER DID any dragon-prowed Longship full of my brothers a-Viking look so good to me as did that single rider on her jet-ski. My excitement had nothing to do with how well she filled out her colorful swimsuit. Nor did it concern the beautiful weather or the gorgeous scenery. It didn't even have anything to do with the thought of New Orleans just ahead and around the marshes off of our port, or left rails.

Maybe the nearness of New Orleans and the supposed end of our little charade had made my "companions" complacent. After all, I had behaved like an innocent little lamb thus far. Why would they think I wouldn't walk right into the slaughterhouse with the same vacuous look on my face?

I saw one of the women on board get annoyed when the much smaller watercraft buzzed so close to our bow. The men seemed preoccupied with the cute and bouncy lass on the seadoo or whatever it was called. When she cleared our bow by yards and circled the boat laughing and waving, the red-blooded males on board responded with perhaps even more enthusiasm than the adventurous rider.

That meant almost nobody was looking when I dug a duffel out from under my chaise and moved to the rail. Almost nobody is, however, not the same as nobody. I heard one startled profanity followed by a flurry of motion. Before I could make good on my escape one meaty hand grabbed my bicep and spun me around.

That was almost a relief. I hadn't been sure about my instincts concerning these people and their handling. For all I knew, it was all in my imagination and the crew was just being efficient and professionally distant.

The grip on my arm changed that from professionally distant to intimately aggressive. I might not have been comfortable with my guesses, but I was *quite* comfortable with intimate aggression. When he used that errant paw to jerk me towards him it was just too opportune to ignore.

I let his own impetuous step forward collide recklessly with the punch that came around courtesy of the spin he'd imparted by jerking on my arm. My fist felt like it sunk to the wrist in his middle. His breath came out with a spray of spittle and halitosis. An instant later my arm popped free of his abruptly less enthusiastic grip. I took a few seconds to dig under his windbreaker despite a weakly protesting hand or two. I dragged out two glaring corroborations. First was a sleek compact Glock in a leather holster clipped inside his belt.

The second was his wallet. It didn't have any official badge or law enforcement ID. But it did have a driver's license with a name different from the one on his nametag for the last few days. That was evidence enough of under-cover status for me. I took the opportunity to relieve the agent of a modest wad of cash before dropping his wallet in the gulf.

By the time his nice leather hit the water I was clambering over the railing. It took just a second to drop my duffel an instant before I let go of the rail and let gravity take over. I hit the water in an awkward feet-first dive right after the duffel. Both of us went down together and I got lucky enough to grab it with minimal floundering underwater.

We broke the surface just as the girl on the two-person watercraft came around the yacht's stern and zipped over to drop her speed and idle right up to me. That's when the spectators started to show any sign of alarm. I heard two or three voices shout out in surprise and then one, more authoritative voice, started shouting orders like. "Don't just stand there. Stop him!"

By then I was on the back of the little motorcycle turned boat. Almost before my butt hit the seat, we were skipping over the waves. I found myself with one hand holding onto a trim and muscular waist while my other hand secured the duffel by the expedient of stuffing it between our torsos.

"YeeHAW!" Her shout was almost as fun as watching her bounce around on the waves had been. It matched the excited laughter that came bubbling over the lady's shoulder as she gunned the boat and headed straight for what looked like impassable mangrove swamps.

The swamps weren't impassable, but they proved to be pretty decent concealment from small arms fire. We saw a handful of small geysers erupt around us but only one lonely round bounced with a whine off of the skipping little boat.

After that, we had a screen of hanging vines and trees that looked like they were anchored on floating islands of moss or weeds. The crew back at the yacht managed to fire a few more rounds searching the swampy area but probably realized that a fusillade of gunfire into a wildlife sanctuary so close to a major American Metropolis might draw attention. Good luck on my part or some very good planning by someone else.

We dropped to an idle as my pilot carefully picked her way along twisting waterways for a very long time until we came to a rickety dock in the seeming middle of nowhere. My companion had to know this place like the proverbial back of her hand. We'd turned so many times that I wasn't sure of north or south since the sun was well down on the horizon by the time she stopped.

An old man in insulated brown coveralls and high waders came out to help moor the seadoo while the girl jumped ashore to top off her tank. She handed him cold hard cash rather than a card. I tend to approve of that kind of behavior. I normally opt for simple, virtually untraceable, cash myself.

"There's an old jeep Comanche pickup behind the convenience store." The girl spoke her first complete sentence in the time we'd been together. Of course, the noise of the marsh and the little engine had discouraged a quiet conversation. I for one didn't want to risk yelling a bunch of questions at her while we might be pursued by some of the folks from the Arr Guile, my old friend Eachan's yacht. At least I had been told it was Eachan's boat, back before things started not adding up.

She continued speaking as I unwound myself from the bobbing motorcycle-style seat. "Tell Angie she owes me a big favor. Gas, time, inconvenience and a hazard pay bonus, not to mention incidental damage to my baby here."

Her grin told me she was only half-serious about the whole gig. Her next statement reinforced it. "Or maybe you can take me out for dinner and dancing and we'll call it even? Or would my girl object to me stealing her new beau?"

This time I joined her in laughing. There was no point

in trying to explain that I had never met "her girl Angie" in my life. That particular relationship was brand new and based on something a lot more solid than chemistry or physical attraction. We had friends in danger and that was a lot more cohesive than romantic entanglements.

I had to be chivalrous though. This complete stranger had risked herself to help me out of something that I wasn't even sure about. All I knew was that those people on "Eachan's boat" weren't the kind of people he would employ. There was a lot of secrecy going on and I was supposed to be the clueless innocent lamb.

I hadn't bothered to tell them that I had a phone they didn't know about, or that I had used it to find out a few bothersome details. Nor did I ask a lot of stupid questions to let them know that I wasn't as completely ignorant as they seemed to believe.

When the girl turned down my offer of cash for her gas and time I thanked her heartily, and surreptitiously slipped a couple of the twenties into the little side saddle pouch on her boat seat. They'd been in a wallet someone considerately dropped right before I escaped the yacht. The money seemed a lot more useful to my rescuer than the recently unconscious and somewhat shady character that had imprisoned me with good scotch and cigars.

I stopped on the way down the docks to shake her hand for one more round of thank yous. "Look, I don't know why you did it, but I'm pretty sure you saved me from something pretty nasty. So thanks again, and I'll give you a raincheck on dinner and dancing."

She flashed another of those dare-devil smiles at me and then seemed to think of something more serious. "Yea that was weird alright. Angie told me where to meet you and when it had to happen. She only had me waiting out there half an hour or so. But she mentioned the old NSA facility as one probable goal. That's kinda funny and not like a mediocre joke. That place hasn't been a military facility for a decade or so. It's mostly private businesses now but there are a lot of empty warehouses and secluded docks that nobody uses. It sure ain't someplace I'd want people I didn't trust to tie me up and get down to some serious interrogatin'."

It was a sign of my confusion that I shared a little more information in response to that. "She told you all of that? How the Hel would she know so much? I barely talked to her about the boat and the situation I was in."

Normally, I'd be considerably more security-minded around a stranger. Maybe it was the way she'd handled my escape, but it also might have been the effect of being held against her warm torso in that thin and clinging swimsuit for so long.

She shrugged her shoulders which did interesting things under that same clinging swimsuit. "You know Angie. We didn't call her Sister Wizard for nothing."

I filed the nickname away with the rest of what very little information I had about this new player in my personal adventures.

"Yep, good old Angie. Thanks again." When I went for one last handshake she just grinned and leaned in to give me a good old fashion country hug. That girl was cute as hell, handy enough to rescue me, and about as friendly as a spotted hound. It wouldn't be much of a chore to take her up on that dinner and dancing date if I weren't so worried about the whereabouts and safety of another young lady.

The jetski whined to life and then zipped away as quickly as it had shown up. I just had to hope the lady driving it had remained anonymous and managed to get away scot-free.

I was in the jeep and unzipping my duffel by the time I remembered that we'd never even exchanged names. I pondered that, while I cranked shut the small emergency oxygen tank and reached into the jury-rigged compartment within the duffel. I had to wonder if it had been an intentional distraction that kept me from asking about her identity. Despite the adrenaline-junkie attitude and aww shucks Texas slang, that young lady seemed like a pretty smooth operator.

In fact, she kind of reminded me of another smooth operator with a Texas drawl. The aforementioned Sister Wizard Angie. I knew her as Angel or Knave. I'd only talked to her a couple of times and both of those had been within the last forty-eight hours. I still wasn't sure if she was an ally or just another jailkeeper.

The coal-black feathered head and redly glowering eyes that popped out of my duffel bag did not seem impressed with my problem. Whether for good or bad, my mysterious pet raven Rafe passed a summary judgment on my doubts and thought processes."Dumbass."

I NEVER INTENDED to talk to the lady I'd now heard called Angel, Angie, and Knave. In fact, she called me out of the blue a short while after I left a coded message for an anonymous person at a private number with a secure answering machine. My original phone call had been on a different private number I'd been given to get in touch with my favorite hacker of all time. William "Wild Bill" Wooly had been one of my first contacts when I moved to Austin several years back.

Some clandestine, as well as a few not so secretive, queries, had netted me the email of what I had been told was the best hacker anyone from around the Longhorn campus could find. His appearance had been the first surprise when we met at a coffee shop with free wifi. Instead of hippy attire or some wild west Buffalo Bill costume, he was wearing preppy casual. Khakis and a business shirt with tie.

The size of his laptop had been the second surprise and one that almost screwed the pooch for me. I was under the impression that all the newest toys were sleek, lightweight and fairly quiet too operate. His toy was thick, cumbersome looking and loud enough to drown out our conversation from just a yard or two away. I almost gave up on him for having inferior gear. It was only later that I found out the differences were because his computer was about eight times more efficient and capable than anything on the market. The noise came from all the fans it took to keep the beast operational.

Over the years we developed a very firm business relationship as well as a rare form of friendship for two people with a paranoid obsession with security and their own secrets. I guess shared paranoia is one of those ties that bind. Since getting me out of trouble a few months earlier, Bill had become even more security conscious. He did some work with spooks and alphabet agencies on the side but kept a private number for only a few very trusted customers.

That private number was the first one I dialed when I decided to do something about suspicions concerning my boat crew or guards if that was what they were. My previous sea-going calls from a covert cell-phone had been more personal in nature but that's a different story.

Normally, Bill picks up that phone within three rings.

He's used to us needing his particular kind of help in a hurry. This time it rang six times then went to a voicemail I'd never heard but had been told about. "This is Bill Wooly, I'm sorry I missed your call. Please leave your name, number, and the problem with your computer. I'll get back to you as soon as possible."

Alarms, claxons, bells, and whistles all clamored in my imagination. That message was a red flag that had to be deciphered. The problem with your computer meant to call a second number. Do not use a computer to message or email. Do not text or come in person to his computer shop. Just follow the previous instructions and call the number I'd never considered actually needing.

I scrolled through a few apps on my phone and found the custom software Wild Bill had installed with a gaming icon instead of anything serious looking. I'm not a techno-geek so he'd broken it down for me. "This will mask your own number, bounce your signal a few times and scramble anyone poking their nose into our business. It should give us up to three minutes of snoop free communication but keep it under a minute just to be safe."

This time the phone picked up after the second ring. "Woolco communications. Please enter or speak the number of the person you wish to reach."

Instead of numbers, I spelled out his nickname Phoneti-cally in a clear and concise military manner that would make any drill sergeant proud. "Wilco India Lima Delta, Bravo India Lima Lima."

The phone had gone dead immediately and left me feeling deflated and more than a little worried.

Three minutes later my secretive little phone buzzed in my pocket just as I was asking one of the yacht "stewards" for a fresh scotch, neat, please.

I faked a coughing fit and clutched at the phone in my shirt pocket as if catching my breath. That quick grab hit enough buttons to hang up the phone long enough for me to fetch my whiskey as well as a bottle of water for my "choking". I excused myself to dart down the passageway and find the tiny cubicle head or bathroom in my cabin. I had water running in the small sink when I answered the phone the instant it buzzed again.

"Magnus, aka Eric, aka Donal, also known as Mouse. I am your new personal guardian Angel. Let's start with your current situation," Her tone was crisp and professional but there was a hint of the familiar Texas drawl in it. It wasn't the east Texan to Mississippi Forrest Gump style southern drawl, but the mid to west Texas cowboy twang that always reminds me of Sam Elliott.

By comparison, I barely have any Lonestar accent at all. "Stick with Magnus, please. Situation, currently at sea on private yacht *ARR GUILE*. Alpha Romeo Romeo, Golf Uniform India Lima Echo. Supposedly registered to Professor or Doctor Eachan Currie, current whereabouts unknown. Last reported to be sailing in a new yacht somewhere off the coast of Mexico. May be same yacht as previously mentioned. I am being held supposedly incommunicado by eight personnel operating as boat crew. Suspect military or police training for most crew members. I am unarmed and showing no sign of suspicion. Please find information on the whereabouts of Professor Currie. Also, locate and verify condition of one Maureen McKinnon, citizenship is Irish I believe. The last known whereabouts were outside of Mexico city. Look for any indication of why I might be held for questioning. Any chatter on official or government forums regarding myself or disturbance an hour or two drive outside of Mexico City involving Cartel and archaeological sites. Our minute is up. Best to end the call before anyone can eavesdrop.Will call back for updates in..."

She cut me off with a voice that sounded more amused than concerned. "Sugar, we got as much time as I need. They ain't about to bust my encryption and masking in a little ole minute. Hang on though."

I was sweating illegal armor-piercing black talon bullets twenty or thirty seconds later when she finally spoke again. "Mexican officials are congratulating themselves on a successful military operation that took down a major cartel facility for storage and transportation of drugs and weapons. All cartel members opted to go out in a blaze of glory but the officials are claiming seizure of several million dollars worth of contraband."

I grunted at that one. It wasn't really a surprise but I'd been hoping for something a little closer to the truth. Then again what newspaper was going to run headlines about a centuries-old semi-divine being and his score of supernatural Aztec Jaguar warriors that were defeated by a couple of Odin's Chosen warriors along with a Valkyrie and immortal wolf. Not to mention the aboriginal American deity and last but not least my favorite Catahoula Leopard dog. I guess it might get an inside story in one of the sketchier tabloids.

She continued as if my grunt was not entirely clear and concise. "Professor Eachan Currie has been called back to a last-minute conference on some neolithic ruins near Lake Austin...hang on. Let me bookmark that for later. That sounds interesting. The professor's Last credit card transaction was for an airplane ticket from Belize City, Belize dated..."

This time it was my turn to interrupt her rapid-fire delivery of a pile of information that I would have still been looking up three days after I asked the questions. "Hang on. Let's skip my incredulous questions about how the hell you're doing this info thing. Tell me what kind of ticket did the prof buy?"

She clicked away for all of ten or fifteen seconds before answering. "It was a coach class ticket on Southwest Airlines. Do you need the tail number or flight information?"

"Don't bother." My voice was probably as grim as the face I saw looking back at me from the small bathroom mirror. "The professor wasn't on that airplane. He's never flown coach in his life and would walk back to Austin across the length of central America rather than expose himself to all of that frustration and inconvenience."

Her voice was still professional but I thought I heard a trace of regret for me. "Alright then, want me to do a search and see if I can spot him with facial recognition on anything since then? He did make a large cash withdrawal prior to the flight. Several ATM's gave him two-hundred-fifty dollars each until he reached his daily maximum."

I shook my head at the spontaneous birth of some nasty suspicions. Wild Bill Wooly was the best I'd ever heard of at the kind of thing I used him for. This lady made him sound like a high school kid on his first home computer. Bill might offer a search to include facial recognition but he'd also clarify that any such search would be hit or miss with his current software and access to government databases. My "New Angel" sounded like she just might be sitting at a console in a certain government building at Langley, Virginia.

I decided maybe I'd pointed enough sniffers at the professor already. Maybe he was in trouble and maybe he wasn't. The fact was that I couldn't be sure I wasn't buying him more problems by talking about it with a stranger. It didn't matter that she was using Wild Bill's numbers and info. As he himself had often said, any network can be hacked. Toss in my own experience to add, any man can be broken.

It was entirely possible that Bill had been captured and compromised despite the assurances he'd given me concerning his new and hyper-paranoid security measures. Just because you're obsessed with the thought of being spied on by espionage agencies and various superpowers doesn't mean the Illuminati aren't listening to your phone.

"Negative on the professor. Or put it on the back burner at least. The ship I'm currently on is about seventy or eighty-foot long with..." Again I was interrupted.

"Not bad cowboy. The Arr Guile is a seventy-six-foot Jongleur yacht. Recently purchased and refurbished by one Eachan Currie. She needs a minimal crew of two or three but usually operates with twice that. The current position is about two-thirds of the way from Veracruz to Louisiana. You ain't exactly practicing for the America's Cup in speed, are you? Give me a little time and I can plot the course and predict some destinations. In the meantime let me see what else I can find out. Are you secure right this minute honey?"

It took me a moment to remember that she couldn't see my shrug. "Uncertain, I haven't seen any hostility yet but these people just don't add up. I'll keep playing along while I see if there's anything I can find out on board. I sure hope you're on the level lady. If you're not, then it's likely to get real ugly around here. If you hurt my buddy Bill, all the computers and techno-babble in the world won't keep me off your trail."

This time I could practically hear the smile and picture a flash of teeth, "Why sugar britches, that's plumb sweet. I'll be sure and tell Billy boy how concerned you are for him. Just as soon as I find out what happened to him. If you're involved in *that* then I'll use more computers and techno-wizardry than you could imagine to make you pay...over and over again, pilgrim."

That didn't seem like a profitable avenue to explore. We could both go on making threats at each other but with me at sea and her at a computer someplace else those threats felt a little empty. A sudden tension in her voice brought me back from those thoughts. "Alright chief, I just got a warning flag that someone is tickling my security programs. You go ahead and hang up. I'll lead this buckaroo on a wild goose chase on the interwebs. Might even buzz a couple of politicians that I don't care for. See how they explain a government snooper on their phone lines."

My "Angel" sounded somewhat devilish to be so amused at the prospect of raising alarms and suspicions between politicians and government snoops. That didn't mean she *wasn't* part of an alphabet agency. It did make me want to give her the benefit of the doubt though. I mean, c' mon, who hasn't wanted to raise a little misfortune for a senator or presidential candidate?

2

I MANAGED to put the hours between the first and second phone calls to good use. A few tools found their way to my room as well as everything from oxygen tanks to waterproof diver bags. There were even a couple of diving knives I managed to hide. The spearguns and bangsticks in the diving locker were very tempting. I decided they would be hard to hide and even harder to explain if anyone found them.

Finally, I settled for part of a bangstick. They're used to discourage sharks. It's basically a short spear that has a shotgun shell instead of a pointed spearhead. I took about a third of the spear and rigged a shorter trigger than the original spear had. There was also a box with a few shotgun shells left in it. I took those and hid them under the socks someone had thoughtfully provided for me.

After that, there were a couple of double scotch glasses, neat, for my nerves. Then a dinner of beef wellington done passably. The filet was overcooked and the foie gras seemed more like a garlic butter but beggars can't be choosers. I hadn't had to pay for anything for a couple of weeks now between one thing and another. Which was a good thing since I hadn't had any cash of my own since I was mugged by bikers who left me for dead in a desert.

That was before the run-in with the shamanic version of a date rape drug, multiple relationship mishaps on my part, a scrape with cartel bigwigs and a stint in a Mexican prison. At least the last one ended with a rescue of sorts.

I mean if a rescue includes blowing up your cell then I hardly count it as a total success. Come to think of it that was one of three explosions and a vehicle collision I caught myself in all within a couple of days.

Mexico had not been a vacation for me. By comparison, my apparent kidnapping was both unique and blissfully indulgent. Maybe not the part about using a friend's name, but the whole ploy of keeping your victim complacent via copious amounts of alcohol in a luxury setting was really creative.

After a brief nap and another nerve numbing scotch, I went to my cabin and pretended to nap more. In actuality, I was hard at work trying to keep busy and still be available when the phone buzzed again. It did so around ten that night.

"Evenin' there sugarplum. Anything critical to report?" Her voice was cheerful but I imagined I could hear the slightest hints of fatigue and stress under the banter.

"No major changes from my perspective. Your end?" I hadn't shaken the urge to keep our communications brief and to the point. For one thing, Wild Bill had been well past paranoia when it came to security and communications. For another thing, I still wasn't sure whose side this lady was playing for.

"Yup. Do you want to take some notes? Got a pen and paper handy?" This time I definitely heard a sigh and fatigue in her reply.

"Sounds too much like evidence. I'll grab stuff if it seems like you've surpassed this poor country boy's memory capacity." I tried to sound at least as cheerful as she did. Maybe there was a touch of empathy too. I found myself reverting to a Texan drawl of my own, though not quite as colorful or "country" as her own charming dialect.

Her quiet chuckle was reward enough for my attempts to adapt. The amusement was still in her voice when she started to report. "Alright sugar, your professor popped up on my visual search. He was in the company of two fellows wearing casual attire that might as well have been black suits and sunshades. Certain types of feds just never learn to relax and wear jeans right. First, they were tailing him at a couple of ATMs. After that, I spotted them all getting into a Taxi."

I heard her take a drink in the pause before she continued. I could only imagine that it was either coffee or an energy drink. She sounded young enough to want something to give her wings. "Taxi was not registered with any agency or company in that whole damned country. The license came up dry too. I did spot the vehicle at a private airstrip outside of Belize City. Records indicate it has been used by both drug smugglers and a few spooks from various countries and agencies. None of which sounds encouraging for your educator."

She cleared her throat and continued. "I found one mention of your Celtic damsel. Her name was listed in the initial report of people recovered from the "decisive victory" of law and order over those rapacious cartel devils. No further mention of her in any subsequent reports or documents. Your Maureen seems to have vanished as effectively as the professor. Query; Is it possible a friend agent or agency has vanished them for you?"

That was thought-provoking enough that I wanted longer to consider it. For now, I wanted her to continue the flow of info though. "Let me think about that one. Continue please?"

"That is all I have for current info on your two names. I could probably get some bank balances and such but that didn't seem germane. I already peeked anyway. The girl is practically a miser. A few hits for groceries and gas along with one budget car rental in Arizona. No major changes in expenditure for either of them except the professor's ATM withdrawals and one transfer of a large sum from one of his accounts to an offshore bank. That one was less than a week ago. It could be germane."

It felt good to know something she didn't. I broke into her narrative just long enough to relish it. "Negative. I know what that was about."

After a pause long enough to make sure I wasn't going to elaborate she cleared her throat again. This time I thought maybe there was a hint of disapproval or disappointment. Score one for the guy with maybe ten percent of the information she had dug up. Finally, she went on with the report. "Your ship is nearing the Gulf Coast of Texas or Louisiana. Your course seems to rule out anything south of Corpus Christi. My bet is for Houston or somewhere in Louisiana. Of course, considering the private airstrip, I did a search and discovered too many private docks and anchorages to count. The Jongleur ain't exactly a supertanker. It could land anywhere. I've got a hunch it's going further east along the Louisiana coast though. Hell darlin', I can't even rule out a stop at one of the dozens of offshore rigs out that'a'ways."

Sarcasm was much easier than cheerful for me considering that last news. "Check. Maybe we can figure something out to get me off this boat before they have me someplace with a blow torch to some of my favorite bits and pieces."

"Well don't you worry a hair on your little head honey, momma's gonna work that all out before it gets that bad. Why your situation is plumb promising compared to where I've gotten on Bill. I've got nothing on him since his panic program notified me. But I'll get him out too. Compared to that, you'll be easier than bagging deer at a salt lick."

It was my turn to chuckle at her attempts towards levity. "Fair enough, *momma*. By the way, what do I call you other than ma'am, missy or disembodied voice on the phone? I can hardly stick with Momma."

I could practically picture the friendly smile when she replied. "It's a little soon for first names or dinner with the folks there, cowboy. Call me Knave."

It sounded like a military call sign or maybe a gamer's sign-in. But at least it was something to call her. "Alright, Knave. If there's nothing else I'll sign out for now. I'm working on some contingencies. Found scuba gear but the tanks aren't charged and I doubt can use the compressor without getting caught. Right now the swim is too far and I have no idea where I'd go if I even made it to shore. Keep searching for news on my friends, please? All three of them. If I get out of this mess I'll see about helping Bill too. Call me around two tomorrow afternoon. That's central time. If you get something critical before then just text me an insurance salesman pitch and I'll get someplace private."

"Sure thing sugar britches." This time her voice was as grim as it usually seemed amused. "Not that I think there's an insurance salesman out there that would give you the time of day in the current situation."

That had been two days ago. Since then, we'd talked twice. Just enough for her to tell me when to look for the jetski and what to do about the arrival of my ride. Now I was traveling down what barely passed for a road in what seemed like miles and miles of swamp with a profanity prone raven as my navigator. The old jeep bounced along on a suspension that reminded me of a world war two halftrack for comfort. I only hoped it was as good in off-road conditions as the aforementioned halftrack.

It might not have matched a tracked vehicle but the jeep pickup was adequate for my trip. We came out of the swamp to see the Big Easy spreading out before us. Rafe cocked an eye and hopped once or twice on the vinyl seat before looking at me. "Shiny."

I couldn't remember the damned bird ever using that word. But then again I still wasn't sure where he'd learned to call me a dumbass at oddly appropriate times. Now was not the time for that investigation though. I punched an address into my phone and made a note to get a charger ASAP. The battery was down to twenty percent after a handful of terse phone calls when time, privacy and reception at sea would permit it.

The phone app led me to a small shotgun style house near enough to walk to the popular bourbon street area. A little longer stretch of the legs would get me to Jackson Square and some coffee and beignets that I'd been assured was a treat not to be missed. I parked the old jeep in a battered single-car garage with a manual door. Inside it was dark but the gaps between a couple of boards let me find keys hanging near the side door just as I'd been told by my telephone angel.

The keys let me into the narrow house where I could see from the kitchen back door to the front door out of the living room. Upstairs were two bedrooms and a single bath right off the stairs. It wasn't large but the place had all the necessities including no requirements to show my Identification. That was probably more necessary than even the bathroom which I put to immediate use.

After some timely relief, I'd indulged in a long hot and private shower with little fear of the prying eyes and cameras that I'd half suspected were all over the ship. Then again for all I knew Knave had this place wired to transmit my vital statistics and a hologram to wherever she wanted. Hell if she wanted a peep show she could do better in plenty of places around New Orleans. Whether she did or didn't have me under surveillance wasn't really an issue. I didn't mind either way. The hot water was too heavenly to cut short or worry about voyeurism.

I got out of the shower and changed into a jogging outfit I'd liberated along with the purloined cash from the boat crew. I still had enough money to get a meal or fill up the Comanche gas tank. I couldn't accomplish both though. Come to think of it, if I bought a phone charger I could only get maybe half a tank of gas.

I was still weighing go-juice over gumbo when there was a knock at the door. I fished the jury-rigged bangstick out of my bag and held it behind my leg before I opened the door with the chain still on.

"Delivery for a Mister Mickey M." The guy at the door was maybe twenty years old and lean to the point of concern. I tried not to groan aloud at the name he'd been given though. People who know me sometimes go with the nickname Mouse. Hence Mickey M. I could only guess at what self-amused sadist had made up that Mouseketeer surprise code to get my attention.

"That's me." My reply prompted the delivery boy to produce a package that looked almost too large for the bicycle leaning on the rail down the porch steps.

"Sign here." He produced the obligatory clipboard and pen then waited while I scrawled an illegible name with a fairly prominent duo of M's. His hesitance in leaving finally made me fish a few soggy dollar bills out of a pocket and give him a tip I couldn't afford.

Service people work for a living though. I didn't begrudge him the cash. I just had some concerns about where I was going to get the funds to operate effectively or even survive in a place as expensive as New Orleans can be.

My material concerns were made immaterial a few minutes later. Inside the brown paper-wrapped package was another duffel and a couple of plain brown envelopes. One envelope contained a tidy stack of cash as well as a handful of prepaid cash cards. The other had a worn driver's license and other obviously aged identification that listed me as Dalton Garrett. I just shook my head. I'd seen Roadhouse.

Finally, there was a new "burner" phone with a single open text message. "Good hunting. I'll be in touch. PS call uncle N.M Rod. Here's his number. "

The number that originated the text had been blocked. It was signed Angel, though. Maybe Knave was a name that could be traced too easily?

I shrugged and tossed a salute to any hidden cameras in the room. The duffel had more clothes in it. They were all my size, which is unusual. I hadn't really been paying attention to the jogging outfit since there had been no choice in the matter. Now though, I glared at the pants that hugged me tight from hips to calves and bunched up awkwardly around my canvas shoes. Even worse was the t-shirt that fit me like a snug cocoon on a fat caterpillar.

That probably deserves an explanation. I suffer from what I call an atypical height to width ratio. While my stomach does not ripple with washboard abs it also fails to roll over my pants in a muffin-top. I'm not so much out of shape as I am differently shaped. I've been told I might be taller if they measured across my shoulders rather than head to toe.

It had always bugged me when I was younger that I had to look up to others whether on a long-boat or inside a long-house. Over the years, and I mean lots and lots of years, that stopped bothering me so much. Occasionally, I still got annoyed by an aggressive jackhole looming over me but it was much less common. I guess repeated professional barroom thrashings of just such towering asshats had tempered my resentment.

I pulled on a heavy-duty t-shirt built for taller dwarf-like people such as myself, not that I'd seen a dwarf in decades. Still, my dimensions bore a passing resemblance to such folk. Black cargo pants just like some of my older favorites went over clean and comfortable boxer shorts. Finally, I replaced sodden canvas shoes with army surplus boots over thick woolen socks and foot pampering insoles. Thus armored and prepared I considered my options.

My first problem was to remain unincarcerated or captured by officials or spooks or whoever the Hel had been holding me. After that, I had to find out *why* they had been holding me. Somehow there had to be time to figure out what had happened to the professor and Maureen since Mexico. That went for Wild Bill as well. I might not be a rocket scientist but even a dumb old ex-Viking can figure out that so may abductions, disappearances and oddities at the same time were probably anything but coincidence.

And finally, I needed to figure out if my enigmatic "angel" wore a white Stetson or black one. She'd been so helpful that I really wanted to believe she was a white hat. My most recent experiences though were enough to make anyone suspicious, even an obsolete relic like me.

That would have been a great time for a long intense phone conversation if we couldn't meet in person. With her number blocked on the phone though, I had to wait for my benefactress to make the first move. Which really sucked. Patience has never been one of my strong suits. I'm much better at tenacious, bullheaded, stubborn forward momentum.

I suddenly had a clear picture of Andrew Jackson laughing as he looked down at me laying in the middle of a handful of unmoving or at least feebly moving redcoat soldiers. With another laugh, he waved back towards American the troops moving into the area. "Son, do you ever wait for the signal to *Charge* or do you always just go on a whim? Not that I'm complaining soldier. You might have got shot and cut a little less if you'd had a few friends with you though."

The problem was, I didn't recall ever serving with Andrew Jackson. But there were indications that there were a great many things I didn't recall. An old Yaqi shaman had fed me some intoxicants and hallucinogens before showing me some visions and claiming I was plagued by magical amnesia and some major tinkering amongst the neurons and softer parts of my melon. The fact that he had the hots for my girlfriend maybe colored my skeptical reception of his information.

On the other hand, Odin had been known to scramble

an egg or two for folks before. Read up on his idea of a fun prank with Brunhilde. I also had reason to believe that my own Valkyrie was capable of and prone to cracking a few shells to make an omelet if you get my drift. Honestly, there wasn't much I would put past Kara the Stormy. She was strong-willed, supernaturally skilled, and more than a little psychotic by any modern standards.

But finally, I'd found out recently that I spent a little time with a divine trickster without knowing who he was. For all I knew, he had planted some fun little seeds in that melon of mine. For the time being, I didn't know if some of my sudden flashbacks were real or a trickster's idea of practical joking.

When it came down to it, I didn't have time to worry about whatever bad seeds had been planted. Worrying wasn't going to get me away from spooks or help Maureen or the professor either one. All the cute little jokes with names and messages from my mystery guardian gave me an idea though.

The first thing to do was get some more supplies, including a phone or two that nobody would know needed to be bugged. I ought to be able to operate without even Knave knowing if I was careful enough. The second thing would be to figure out where the other two missing and presumably abducted people were.

About that, I had a shaky theory. I don't think it would be too egocentric to say that the common denominator in this whole mare's nest, would be the friend of the professor, boyfriend of the missing redhead, and blower-upper of that whole cartel secret underground facility. I went with blower-upper because "blower" just makes people do the butthead laugh.

Since I was the key character in all three of those roles,

then I thought maybe my own destination meant the others might be somewhere close at hand. The main reasons I could think of to capture all of us would be if we all knew something about the same adventure, or if somebody planned to use some of us to make one or more of the others talk. The old torture by proxy extortion scheme has only lasted so long because it works so well.

Maureen and I knew about the ruins, but the professor didn't. The professor might know something about my prison escape and other things that his money had made possible, but Maureen didn't know those same things. When it came down to it, I was the one with the most connections to everything that happened since my life as a nice uncomplicated bar security manager had gotten very complex.

Maybe it was egocentric to think that way. Other than me though, the professor and Maureen had no common ground except their shared ancient Celtic ancestry; not even the same branch of the germanic tribes really. She was Irish and he was Scottish. I vaguely suspected that each felt smugly superior to the other due to that heritage, but so far that had not manifested in anything worse than a snarky joke or raised eyebrow.

Back to the assumptions though. If our various woes were all tied together as suspected, then it was likely that both abductors and abductees were supposed to come together for a meet and greet. I was looking forward to my own little tete-a-tete with whoever was in charge. I just wanted to make sure such a conversation was on my terms and not a situation where I had various physical restraints and painful encouragement to bend my will.

That's where my little Knave-Angel had given me an idea. I set off to retrieve my phones so I could put that plan into action. Afterward, I might have time to look up the weapons and gear guy, our "Uncle", the hunter or Nimrod. She really did like the cute little obscure phrases and nicknames.

On the other hand, there were definite kudos involved for little-known bible history. Nimrod has such a negative name these days that few people know it was originally the name of a mighty hunter credited with all manner of things. Among them were the founding of many ancient cities including the tower of Babel. Then there was that trivial little rumor that he was, in fact, a giant.

Having met a few Jotun here and there, I wasn't too worried about any mention of giants. I mean sure they can be tough and mean, but no worse than a troll-born. Then again, chances were, she was just using the name to indicate a mighty hunter. I would probably need a good "hunting" guide not to mention someone to procure me a few toys that I didn't have a license to carry in Louisiana.

3

THE PICKUP TRUCK SEEMED UNNECESSARY, not to mention trackable, for my little excursion. Rather than worry about garage doors or New Orleans traffic, I struck out on foot. I figured if I put an electronics store into my phone, any nosey lurkers might try and keep an eye on me. An all-night pharmacy was a different matter though.

In just a quarter-hour or so I had my phones and was headed back to the shotgun style rental house. It started to feel like things were looking up. I had the beginnings of a plan. Now there were resources to help me with that plan. And for once I felt like maybe I was ahead of the game rather than reacting as the punches landed. It was a nice feeling and put me in a pretty good mood.

Of course, that might also have been a result of the groceries and other purchases I'd made. Foremost on the list of absolute necessities I'd found was coffee for the furnished kitchen that Knave or somebody had supplied. I found a decent brand, medium blend, good coffee without any of those nasty corruptions that some people call "flavoring". It would do until I could pick up my favorite Big Easy blend of coffee and chicory the next day. Maybe I'd even splurge on some warm beignets buried in an avalanche of powdered sugar at the same time.

In the meantime I had enough supplies for a day or two, not to mention some cajun take-out I discovered between one place and another. My mouth was practically watering at thoughts of crawfish, andouille, and red beans with rice. Those plans were derailed when I got within sight of my temporary quarters.

I got back just in time to see Rafe starting to peck at the ancient wire screen covering an upstairs window. He was still in the room I'd locked him in, but the raven was apparently bored and trying to get out. Or maybe he'd spotted a cat. I've learned, over the years, that my bird, along with his amusing antics, possesses a keen interest in feline hunting.

Nevermind that the bird is smaller than many domestic cats and even a few oversized kittens. On more than one occasion I had noticed an upsurge of cat disappearances when he escaped his captivity. In Austin he had a whole room converted to an indoor aviary with large hurricane windows that he couldn't break. Here I had made do with a closed bedroom. Maybe if I relieved some of the boredom he'd settle down while I tended to more important matters. If he'd been my dog Grimmr I'd have arranged a kennel. I haven't ever heard of bird boarding though.

I tossed a couple of phone books from the pharmacy on the floor for Rafe. He'd spend hours shredding such "toys". For variety, I dropped a couple of cheap classified ad papers down for him as well. To finish his confinement I had to cover the window out of his bedroom and then supply the little criminal with some nuts and dried fruits as well as a little cheese. It wasn't the best diet but it would hold him for a while. Two bowls of water went down since I was well aware that he might choose to foul one as an impromptu bathing bowl.

As I started to leave, the bird grabbed one of the newspapers and shook it violently at me. Before I closed the door he repeated that action and threw the paper at me before uttering his relatively new and awkward catchphrase. "Dumbass."

Shaking my head, I started to close the door. Just before the gap closed completely I caught a glimpse of the paper he'd thrown. It was a page of personal ads. Men seeking... Just like that my glimmer of a plan solidified.

I grabbed one of my burner phones and a pad of paper with a pencil from the desk. *Fun-loving but wyrd Bartender seeking a redhead. From groupies to school teachers I'm open-minded. Scottish and Irish alike are encouraged to reply! Built like a bear but meek as a mouse for the right girl. Let's go howl at the moon.*

I looked it over and changed a word or two before making the call to put it in two or three ads in trade papers and news journals as well as a craigslist personals ad. Maybe it was a long shot, but if these people employed Knave or someone like her then I was betting it would ping an alarm and I might get a call on the shiny new untraceable phone I listed.

There was my job, the professor's job, nationality or cultural identity for each of them, and then some of my nicknames. My waitresses in Austin called me Mouse. To some of my older brethren in Valhalla I was the Storm Bear. And just on the off chance this was tied to my previous adventures, I'd run into both of Odin's wolves traveling in human form. There had been Freke in Austin and Gere in Mexico.

Freke had left with the intention of losing his memories

of me. Last I had seen of Gere had been an extreme close up of his chest right after I rescued him, and right before an explosion knocked me out via an abrupt impact with his broad and immortal chest.

With the ad listed and out of the way, it seemed like a good time to contact ole Uncle Rod. If Knave was on my side then it wouldn't hurt anything for her to overhear the conversation. If she was playing good guy while working for the opposition then she would expect me to make the call anyway. Either way, it seemed best to use the phone she planted on me. If nothing else it might keep her from guessing I had a new number.

For that, I used the phone Knave had sent me. First I had to replace the memory card and battery. I don't know about anyone else, but I've never thought it was a coincidence that my search engines mysteriously pop up with advertisements for things I discussed around my seemingly innocent cell phones. I had rendered the thing more or less inert before I left it in the house for my shopping spree. Now it was time to let anyone listening have an appetizer.

After four rings, the call went to messages. I didn't get any clues there since whoever owned the number had opted to use the premade robotic message for voicemails. I got the canned "please leave a name and number" spiel but opted for discretion. If they were expecting my call then I would no doubt get a reply just from my number on their caller ID.

After that, it was a matter of waiting. I checked on Rafe and then went down to enjoy my dinner. The whole time I had the phone close at hand. Which is probably why they waited until I was washing my dishes from dinner to return the call.

I tucked the wine glass away and gave my hands a quick dry before answering. "Hello. Mouse speaking."

"Mouse is it?" The voice that came back at me was deep and exotic. There were hints of the islands in it. Maybe it was Jamaican or the Bahamas I heard. Whichever accent was coloring his voice, they were faint enough that he had been in the states awhile.

"So, Mr. Mouse. You are a very long way from home." He pronounced his V more like a B, it might have sounded like Castilian Spanish if I hadn't already detected the islands. There was also a soft blurring of the lines between vowel sounds in 'are" "long" and "home".

"Not my choice mister." I wasn't going out of my way to insult the guy with derogatory names or titles. No Buster or Mac even. On the other hand, I saw no reason to be too respectful with the sirs or "friend". After all, I still wasn't sure where everyone's' loyalties lay. "Mister" was about as good as it got for now.

"I would suggest, sir, that you would be much more at home...at home." Apparently, he didn't have the same reservations about the "sir" appellative. Any hint of respect from its use was buried under the threat as he continued. "Out in the Big Easy, it can be dangerous. Sometimes while you are seeking the big bad wolf, something meaner comes and gobbles you up."

I was starting to worry about my guardian angel's judgment in guides and procurement personnel. Wasn't old uncle Rod supposed to help me out and get me the tools to figure out this little predicament? I was still wondering about that when I noticed that the phone Knave had given me was still on the counter. I was holding the phone with a number recently listed online and soon to be in newspapers.

While my thoughts scrambled with the new information, my caller continued. "If I am wrong about you then my apologies. Consider this an eccentric phone call and forget about it. If however you are seeking a wolf to howl with, and your name is Mouse from Austin, then I suggest you return to your Lone Star State. The wolf no longer holds your secret, and he is no longer your concern."

The caller hung up without waiting for a reply. Which was probably a good thing because I had no idea what the Hel I would have said anyway. I wasn't entirely sure I even understood the intended message. Apparently, my clue about one of Odin's wolves had hit pay dirt and hit it deep.

After very little consideration it became apparent that the wolf in question was Freke. I had encountered him not that many months ago as the aftermath of a problem I had to deal with. He had taken it upon himself to dispose of a body or two and divert attention from what the professor, Maureen, and I had done along with the help of a police officer.

Suddenly I wasn't sure that this particular knot was tied around my presence. Maureen and the professor had both been in the house when I met Freke. He had promised to erase his memories of me. The theory was that Odin might be looking for me, or maybe my old Valkyrie Kara was on my trail. Neither of them would be happy that I had avoided them since a mishap or maybe a miscalculation left me unaccounted for in Vietnam.

In return for my help with some trouble his brother was in, Freke promised to make sure our encounter didn't come back to bite me in the ass. I never bothered to ask how an immortal wolf with connections to multiple gods and goddesses planned that. I just assumed it was something he could do or he wouldn't have made such a promise.

Promises mean a lot to people from our era. In modern society, they seem like nothing more than a cheap means to stress a statement or position. To people from ancient Scandinavia, a promise could be so binding as to cause physical stress if it was broken. As a chosen warrior from Valhalla, I could expect a loss of focus, mental strength, physical fortitude, and might or worse from a broken vow.

For the life of me though, I couldn't see any reason he would drag the professor or Maureen into this. Nor could I see why anyone else would involve us. Maybe someone could try and blackmail me with the info, but Eachan and my lady friend were normal people with normal lives and connections. Well, normal for the most part.

I mean both of them studied "magick" or pursued it from a spiritual angle. But it wasn't as if they were hiding from gods and Valkyrie. Nor did either of them seem to suffer from a memory that had several hundred years worth of gaps in a lifetime that appeared to span over a millennium. I'd gotten a couple of those memories back recently and planned to dig for some more. There just hadn't been an opportunity. Since discovering that my head had been tampered with, it seemed I always lacked either the time or the proper environment to see about recovering more of my wayward experiences.

Searching for kidnappers and missing friends didn't seem very likely to give me either of the above. Time was definitely going to be a problem. A gauntlet had been thrown down. No matter how civilly he'd said it, my caller had still offered a threat. So I really only had a couple of choices.

I could back down and go back to Austin, hope for the best for my missing companions. Without knowing what was going to happen to my friends or by whose hand it might occur that option was less than attractive. For all I knew they were part of some sacrifice or ritual that they couldn't get out of. Or perhaps some of the Cartel leaders had allies expecting revenge. Those weren't things I could allow to happen.

The second option was to move fast enough to keep my threatening phone caller off his feet. That could be done with some misdirection, or by getting to him before he could cause any more damage. The problem there was, I had no idea who I was dealing with or how to find him.

I was contemplating a feint to get some breathing room. If I got on a plane out of town, or even a bus, maybe that would throw the guy off my trail. If I planned it right I wouldn't have to be gone long. The bus would be best. Buy a ticket for Austin and then get off at the first stop and come back to New Orleans. Easy enough, but would he buy it?

The buzzing of a phone interrupted me again. What the hell? Was the guy reading my thoughts and already telling me not to try?

That was obviously not the case. I saw the other phone vibrate and skitter on the countertop. It was my phone tether to Knave the mysterious guardian angel. It was also the phone I had thought I was already using. That meant...

"Good news Cowboy." Knave greeted me with a note of victory in her voice. "My facial recog software got a hit. Your girl was spotted on camera getting into a vehicle a couple of country miles from you. Two fellows moved her from a private plane to an SUV It was earlier today so no imme-diate help but its a start. I ain't seen hide nor hair of your professor though. The vehicle she got in was a spook car. SUV I mean. One of those Toyotas the government likes. This one had bogus tags but I've tracked it down anyway. Don't ask how."

I took a deep breath and let it out in a ragged sigh. That must have carried over the phone because Knave answered it. "I hear ya sugar. We'll get there. Now about that tracking I did. The truck belongs to an agency I can't find anything about. There's some indication it's CIA, another lead went to the NSA, and there was even an FBI flag for it. I don't know who is using it for sure but it's gotta be an American spook. I did get a hit off of one of the guys with her though. An agent Dixon, branch of service unknown. This guy is super-secret clearance level. I have a first initial but no name."

I interrupted her with a growl. "The A is for Andrew. And I'm not sure who he works for either but we've got a past."

For once Knave was not on top of things. I heard her typing pause for a minute while she let that info sink in. "Mouse, why do you have contact with top-level spooks and I haven't had so much as a whiff of it from any of my sources? Are you involved with government level stuff I am not aware of?"

I could almost hear the wheels turning in her head. I'd probably be suspicious too if a hacker I obviously cared about had disappeared and been linked to someone that was now revealed as an associate of spy types who operated at unheard-of levels of secrecy. She was probably thinking that I might be the mole in the equation.

I heard even more in her voice a second later. In addition to a lot of anger, I thought I heard the kind of emotion that comes with fear for a loved one's safety. "You son of a bitch, if you're behind what's happened to Bill there's no place you can hide. I'll stalk you, haunt you, terrorize you, and at my leisure, end your miserable existence."

That explained a lot. If she was Bill's girlfriend she probably had access to some of his best toys now that he was missing. I'd never known anything about his personal life but it didn't stretch the imagination that he could have found some pleasant little nerd of a girlfriend to share his obsessions and paranoia. It also went a long way towards easing some of my own concerns about my Angel being a plant to gain my confidence.

The new problem was, how did I convince her we were still on the same side. But that answer was easy too. If she was working with Bill's toys then she had his files. If she was as good as she said, breaking the passwords to get some of my info wouldn't be beyond her skills.

I decided to take a chance on her. "Hang on Knave. I'm not with the G-men. They're after me. Look you've got Bill's files. Look up the file he called Valhalla Awol. It looks like a game file but it's not. You'll have to break the code to get in but it should help clear some things up. I just hope you're on our side and a little open-minded."

There was a space of maybe fifteen seconds where we both sat and thought. Breathing was audible from her end but that was all. There were no clacks of a keyboard or tapping of nails. Just silence while she thought.

Finally, the Angel rendered her verdict. "Okay, Mr. Mouse. I'll check all of that later. Right now I'm going to take a chance because I don't know anything else that might help Bill. That vehicle took a route that gave me a few more hits. At my best guess, it was headed to those same abandoned warehouses and docks that I thought the yacht was going for. I lost it the night after you escaped. Once it was dark they disabled any comms or electronics I could track. Then they doused the lights before sailing invisibly away. But they were within five miles of the old Naval Support Activity base. I'll send you a GPS for the base and mark some of the more suspicious looking docks and warehouses for you. Give me a few minutes."

I hadn't realized I was holding my breath until I let it out upon hearing her decision. After the burst of information, I let her know I appreciated it. "Thank you, Knave. I'm not forgetting about Bill either. I promise you I'm as much on his side as I am on the professor's. They've both been...very good friends."

I had started to say worthy allies or something like that. It would have been great a thousand years ago. People just don't put the same level of respect into worthy allies or trust or honor that we used to so long ago. Whatever I said to Knave seemed to have been good enough for now though.

"That's good to hear sugar. Now you just keep acting like that and I won't have to find someplace creative to hide the pieces of your corpse. Don't forget to make contact with the guide I've arranged for you. I assume you'll want more than a diving knife or speargun for protection. Unless there was something better than that for you to requisition on the professor's boat?" For once I thought I could hear the line of concern that gave away the false cheer in her voice. The girl was confident and maybe even arrogant, but something was eating at her as badly as my concerns were eating at me. I made a promise to get Wild Bill out of this whole and intact if at all possible. I owed both of them that much.

The phone in my hand beeped to indicate a message. A second later I was looking at a copy of a digital map showing the old Naval base. There weren't more than half a dozen docks and warehouses marked as points of interest. It appeared that she had mostly stuck with places large enough to hide a seventy-six-foot yacht. There were also closer shots, maybe satellite images or something. The images were grainy but you could identify vehicles and some blurry people in a few pictures. That gave me an idea.

I broke the silence that had developed as I looked over her images. "I've got a zip-gun made from one of those shark bang-sticks. But any further help with gear would be widely appreciated. But I have another thought. Someone else might be part of this. Keep an eye out for a biker. I don't know his name. He's close to seven feet tall though. Shouldn't be impossible to spot. Long greying hair last time I saw him and a rough salt and pepper beard. I have reason to believe he's caught up in this somehow too. Maybe someone saw us together briefly back in Austin. Come to think of it...he was part of clearing me from the case that Dixon..."

I caught myself abruptly. This girl was sharp. I'd already given her so much that it was just a matter of time before she peeked at cards I usually keep close to my chest. Still, I saw no reason to give her even more information to track down those awkward parts of my past.

The fact was, that biker was Freke. We'd run into each other at the end of a little excursion into violence and supernatural oddities a few weeks back in Austin. He was helping track down someone for what I suspect was an ancient South American divine being. It turned out that I had killed everyone involved, including the wayward vengeful creature and the person responsible for her being wayward.

Rather than blame me for the death, the old god or whatever he was, had forgiven me, and Freke had disposed of some evidence for me as part of a deal. He got rid of a body or two and promised to erase current memories of me, and I went down to Mexico and helped his brother Gere out of a jam. I still shudder to think about what that little adventure had entailed. I really hate being played with and blown up repeatedly by tricksters.

All of that was behind me though. Then again I thought Freke was no longer a concern. The weird phone call earlier though changed all of that. Now I knew Freke was here in New Orleans and involved in something dire enough to earn me warnings and threats. Maybe I could use him to track down the others?

A second later I was glad I'd only shared a little. Knave's voice came over with a curious and considering quality to it. "Well now. We'll have to talk about that case you share with Dixon. In the meantime, though I've got something on your biker buddy."

I heard the keys clacking away before she continued. "It's older though. He's on a sheriff's report for disturbance a couple of weeks ago. Witnesses described someone that fits the description in a scuffle outside one of the old private plantations near Lake Pontchartrain. Not quite in the city proper. But close enough for my search to find. He left the scene with several dark-skinned men in a plain white van. Nobody got the plates. Should I put on a wider search and keep looking?"

I had to think for a moment before responding. "Yea keep looking. Where's the plantation though? I might check that out as well as your naval base. I just have a hunch that he's tangled up in this somehow."

Knave didn't bother giving me an address. Instead, she shot me another map with the location marked. I made a note of it and thanked the girl for her help. "Look I may not have said it, but you've saved my ass. You didn't have to step up for Bill, but I appreciate that you did. I also promise to help you find him if he doesn't show up with everyone else. I'm going to find my "Uncle Nimod" now. Anything else before I hang up?"

I heard her chuckle at my acknowledgment of the old Greek mythology. "No hun, I got enough to work with for a while here. You go get me some more bread crumbs and we'll make this dog hunt."

She hung up still chuckling. I wasn't sure if she was

laughing at me or calling me a dog or what. But I was pretty glad she was on my side. And truth be told a little jealous of Wild Bill for finding a girl who was not only smart and useful but adaptable enough to take some of my odder revelations in stride. Even Bill himself seemed to take even the mildest stories I could give him with the proverbial grain of salt. Now I just had to make sure I got him back to repay her for all the assistance.

Step one was getting some gear. I was only mildly better armed than she knew. As far as I was aware, nobody knew for sure what happened to the firearm once I knocked out my guard on the boat. I didn't see any reason to change that. I've seen more than one occasion when a little ace in the hole came in very handy. And this wasn't just one hold out card, it was seven little forty caliber aces.

4

———

UNCLE RODDY DIDN'T CALL me back. Instead, I got a text message to meet him in a club not too far from where I was staying. Once more I left the Comanche in the garage. It was tempting to take it in hopes of stockpiling weapons and gear. Without having even spoken to this guy though, I couldn't think he'd give me a huge arsenal to play with just yet. Just in case though, I slung an almost empty duffel over a shoulder before I left the house.

I hadn't been to New Orleans in years. It wasn't quite the same as my last visit. Everyone seemed desperate to enjoy themselves rather than relaxed and having a good time. I don't think I recall quite so many sex shows and nude bars either. There were gift shops by the score and dozens of places offering you three beers for the price of one. Over it all was a tawdry, commercialized grasping urge to profit off of the ancient city's history.

I saw a half dozen shops offering "authentic" voodoo materials and pirate booty. Those were almost as confusing as the ghost and vampire tours. In my experience ghosts and rarely go on tours or stand around to sign autographs for people seeking them out. I'm assuming vampires are the same but I haven't met one to ask.

Underneath all the greed and neon though, there was still an energy I'd felt before. There's a certain spirit of New Orleans that I perceive as an exotic, earthy, sensual, primal female energy. She's wanton and free-spirited with larger than life appetites and no apology for filling them. Underneath the glitz and the phoniness, she still lays there, ready to embrace anyone looking deep enough to find her.

Unfortunately, there are other people more than willing to give you a different experience. I saw one pretty decent pickpocket. He wasn't great, or else I'd never have caught on to his act from across the street. That meant there were probably a handful of others that *were* good enough that I never noticed them. I saw predators trying to locate a target for the night. You can usually tell by the way a predator moves or how his eyes sweep a scene. Most of them were probably looking for no more than a chance to spend a night with some young girl too naive to no better.

There were others too though. Grifters and panhandlers and bored ladies trying to squeeze a dollar out of men who thought maybe they were the one she was looking for. Not all exotic dancers are the same, but there are enough to make a skeptical man be wary around the majority of them. I imagine some of those street wolves saw a bit of the predator in me as well. Just the fact that I knew what I was looking at was probably clue enough. Maybe the presence of an occasional horse-mounted policeman kept them at bay too. Whatever the cause, none of them tried their hand in my pocket or attempted to pull me in for a brief scuffle down an alley.

After a while, I ducked out of the stream of humanity and into the bar where I was supposed to meet this Uncle

Rod. I'd barely got in before a harried but smiling waitress snapped her fingers at me and asked what I was drinking. I went with Abita Amber. She nodded and pointed to a table near enough to the music to keep anyone from eavesdropping on any conversation I might have.

The bar was small, maybe a dozen tables and another dozen chairs at the bar. There were two waitresses hustling around the room. Periodically one of them would walk out onto the sidewalk and try and corral another customer or two. For the most part, they were busy keeping glasses full and fresh bottles of beer circulating.

On the tiny stage, a handful of musicians were keeping the mood light. They had drums, guitar, bass, keyboard and finally skinny guy in jeans and a t-shirt playing spoons back up and down on a shiny old-style washboard hanging down his chest. The singer was a substantial sized woman with black hair and chocolate skin that went with the smokey southern blues of her voice. From my ringside seat, the band was much louder and clearer than any conversation even a few feet away.

Which was a good thing because I had barely sat before another man sat down with me almost as if we'd entered the bar together. He beamed just as big a smile at me as the waitress had before gesturing at her to bring him two of something. Apparently, he was familiar enough that they knew his flavor of choice.

Once the drinks were ordered he leaned back over and spoke just loud enough for me to hear over the music. "So Mr. Mouse, I've got a picture to identify you. But a certain young knave of a lady told me to mention Professor Billy Mars to you. That's the only thing I have for credentials. Are we good?"

There she went with the cutesy code names and phrases

again. I nodded and tried to hide my grimace. Which got another beaming grin from my table companion. "I know man, she loves her little jokes does sister Wizard. What can I do for you though? She just told me you were safe to do business with and sent me the pic on my phone."

His accent was completely neutral. The guy could have been a newscaster for any midwestern tv station in the country. It was kind of jarring. In the big easy you get used to a mix of accents, but the folks with that caramel-colored complexion and amber eyes are usually natives of the city with a long history of mixed-race relationships and children. A hundred years ago he would have been called a quadroon or maybe a metis. Now he was just a New Orleanian who had won some kind of genetic lottery.

The amber eyes were striking and I caught more than one lady casting her own lingering gaze at them. His shirt was a white linen "poets" shirt with the neckline unlaced and open to expose a smooth and muscular chest. The loose sleeves were pulled up to his elbow and exposed thick wrists and muscular forearms that ended in large hands and artistic fingers. He kept his hair shorter than mine. What little there was of it seemed black or maybe a deep rust color that would probably be fairly attractive if he wore it longer.

I saw him give me a similar appraising glance; taking in the breadth of shoulders and thickness of chest that most people notice first. My eyes got only a casual glance, as did the rest of my face. I could get to like a guy that didn't go around memorizing faces for police to ask questions about later. He lifted an eyebrow at the barely noticeable bulge of a pistol behind my belt. That made him pretty much of a pro. Even a couple of cops had missed that as I walked past them on their horses. Finally, his eyes fell on the empty duffel hanging from the back of my high bar chair.

"I take it you're looking to buy something?" He asked the question and responded to my nod with one of his own.

"No drugs, no explosives, nothing that's going to get me on a terrorist watch list. Verstehen sie?" A nod had worked for me before so I kept my mouth shut and nodded again.

My new buddy grinned that perfect smile again. "Damn I love a discrete customer. You're going to have to give me something to go on though. Are you shopping for weapons? A little smuggled liquor? Duty-free cigs or something? Maybe you need some "lost" electronics or pre-release movies eh? What can Raphael do for you?"

That last question accompanied an expansive gesture. My hunting guide leaned back and spread his arms in an all-encompassing motion as if to indicate the world was mine for the picking or his for the selling. I felt myself grinning back at him though without the perfect smile and glaring white teeth.

We were interrupted by our waitress. She gave him two highball glasses with dark amber liquid and a single round sphere of ice. I'd heard of those. They melted slower than a drink on the rocks. They were supposed to keep the beverage chilled but didn't dilute as fast as crushed or cubed ice. For me, she had a trio of the Abita's stuck in a bucket with enough ice to keep them all cold as long as I didn't dawdle.

I decided to play it fairly straight with this guy. As long as he didn't ask the wrong questions I'd stick to the truth. After all, my guardian angel had sent me to him, right? "Mostly I need information. The *Big Easy* ain't my normal stomping grounds. I'm trying to find some people. A couple of them are friends and I'm guessing there are more than a few people holding them someplace. Once I know what I'm up against we can discuss the right gear for the job. Are you good for more than a stolen shotgun and some pirated DVDs?"

His eyes all but twinkled as "Raphael" gave me an identical silent nod to one of my own earlier versions. I chuckled back and pushed a little harder. "Are we talking army ordinance or something a little less lethal? I can make do with whatever we have but it's always easier to start with the right equipment from the beginning."

This time he unwrapped a toothpick he dug out of a pocket and worked on a gleaming incisor while he looked me over and thought about the request. Finally, he came to enough of a conclusion to leave off of the amateur dental work. "I can get some good "equipment". It's at least as good as what your average infantry marine carries. *Can* and *Will* are two different things though. I wouldn't even be talking about this if you weren't vouched for by someone I trust a whole lot more than I trust you. It's going to take more than one go-ahead text from the Wiz-kid though. For now, let's focus on the information. What do I have to work with? What can you tell me to help find these friends of yours?"

I hate giving out information about myself or information that can lead back to myself. Call it a side effect of living under the radar for half a century, not to mention looking over one's shoulder for the likes of angry one-eyed gods, ravens, or vengeful valkyrie. To compound that distrust, I wasn't entirely certain about the very person vouching for both of us. There was still something unsettling about how quickly "Knave" could accumulate information and make informed guesses with it. Is it odd that I would be more confident if she was using cards or stones to divine these things rather than a computer?

Still, this Raphael, aka Nimrod the hunter, could not assist me if he didn't know what he was looking for. I went for an initial disclosure. I could always give him a little more or less depending on how things developed. "Well Raphe, you might wish you hadn't asked."

All I got for an answer to my pause, was a raised eyebrow and another of those wide grins. If appearances did not deceive, this guy felt confident to handle any trivial matter I could come up with. I got the feeling that I'd get little more reaction if I announced we were hunting for a giant mutated irradiated Japanese lizard.

So be it, if he was feeling froggy I gave him something to jump on. "One is a professor of some kind of history and such from Texas, well okay, he's actually from Scotland but he lives in Texas now. Professor Eachan Currie. The other is a tallish knockout of a redhead from Ireland named Maureen McKinnon. Until recently she traveled around with her brothers who were going to be the next Metallica. Finally, they are probably being held by a shadowy spook from an unidentified alphabet agency with enough clout to sneak people out of Mexico. Someone who can waltz into an embassy or government facility and *"disappear"* private citizens."

Maybe all of that got his attention. My new ally dropped his dramatic eyebrow and leaned over to put both elbows on the table. Lowering his left hand to grip the edge of the table he gestured to "circle the wagons" and get us another round.

Only when he was sure that some alcohol reinforcements were on the way did he actually speak. "Government spooks, who can disappear people out of an embassy huh? And the Wiz sent you to me. I can't wait to show her my appreciation."

His rueful grin took a lot of the threat out of that statement. I sympathized with him though. I mean if they weren't *my* friends I probably wouldn't be super keen on pursuing this thing either. Part of me wanted to find a nice rock to crawl under, maybe somewhere in the Rocky Mountains, high up, above the treeline, under a couple of feet of snow.

Ever since this thing started back in Austin I'd been living on borrowed time anyway. It seemed like just a matter of time before I was found by some of the people who I sincerely didn't want to see again. With what Agent Dixon knew, I could foresee being plugged into enough wires and monitors to make Neo jealous. Considering some of the things I'd heard of "agency" people doing, I figured creative torture would be just part of the agenda to see how I ticked and what made some of my little "tricks" work.

Maybe I could fool them into overestimating my regenerative abilities. If they thought I was even more resistant than I was, maybe I could merrily expire on one of their tables while they still thought everything was under control.

Of course, that would just lead me to the *other* people I was avoiding. It had taken some doing but I was kind of used to being autonomous ever since I'd wound up unsupervised after a battle in Vietnam. Usually, Kara was good about rounding her warriors up after a mission. Sometimes we got the easy ride back through one of her nifty Valkyrie portals, and sometimes she just snapped a neck or chopped a foot or so off the top if you get my drift.

No matter if we died in battle or as part of her "services" Kara always got us back once we were in Valhalla. After Ia Drang though she'd missed her count I guess. I was left under a pile of troops while the rest of my mission group went back to feasting and fighting in Asgard. A few swapped dog tags and some serious chicanery with bandages kept anyone from ever figuring out I wasn't another walking wounded.

Cue ahead through decades of sneaking and maneuvering to stay in the shadows until I had a nice little gig settling down unruly partiers in a Goth/Metal bar in good ole Austin Texas. Keep Austin Weird! Just like the bumper stickers say. But one vengeful witch with a cheating husband and some occult secrets later made everything turn to crap.

It felt like I'd been doing little else except responding to the punches for weeks now. If I ever found myself in a place where I actually knew what was going on, who was behind it, and what to do about it, I might just pass out from the excitement.

A few of those punches had landed too. Maureen and I were on shaky ground even before she got kidnapped, and beat up, and shot a little, and kidnapped again. That doesn't even count losing a brother or being poisoned by ancient vengeance-minded tree spirits with venomous claws.

To counter all of that, I had also been beat up, and shot, and poisoned, and blown up two or was it three times? Oh and shot some more. Only one of those had been from Maureen though and I'd forgiven her pretty soon after. I mean it was mostly a misunderstanding that prompted her to put a load of shotgun shot from my own pistol into my neck and back. See? I'm adaptable and understanding for the most part.

But now, I found myself looking at it from the outside. There was absolutely no reason for this street hustler to get tangled up in my miseries. Hel I'd be tempted to walk away from myself if it was an option.

Imagine my surprise when he enlisted without hesitation. No sooner had his new drinks arrived than he downed about half of one and nodded before speaking. "Okay, so I never liked some of those spooks anyway. They always hold back information that might get you killed. Secrets seem like cocaine to them man. You got any idea what agency? Who or where or he reports to?"

It was my turn to mull and take a big draught of my Amber beer. "I know his uncle was a cop in Austin. Jackson didn't' seem to know any more than necessary about who the kid worked for though. The guy had enough clout to overturn a murder investigation and get the prime suspect released. He was also able to push his way into a Mexican prison and get a few minutes alone with me in an interrogation room. I'm not up on American Alphabet Agencies, does that sound like CIA or someone else?"

Raphael waved that away with an impatient gesture. "Department of Defense could do that. Since it's Mexico a few others could muscle their way in. It's a friendly country that shares our border and likes a steady influx of Uncle Sam's greenbacks. We need to focus on the earlier stuff. Someone in Austin probably saw a badge and made a record. I'll talk to Sister Wizard about it. For now, you keep your head low. Make a list of things you think you might need. Make it basic though. We won't know the big stuff until we know where they're being held and who by. If we can do anything at all."

I was still dealing with the surprise of his assistance. Before I could formulate the words to thank him though, the song cut off in mid-note and switched to something just as "Zydeco" but faster paced and noticeably different. I saw my table mate look up and then shake his head wearily.

He cut off my thanks with a wave of the hand before leaning close to give me instructions. "The hall behind us holds the restrooms and a supply closet. The supply closet has an outside door on your left as you go in. Outside you'll find yourself on a patio. Take a right there and hit the alley for another left and then a final right-hand turn at the street. That will get you clear of this."

I looked over my shoulder and saw that "this" was a handful of men dressed alike in white polo shirts and khaki pants. All of them were focused on our table as they entered the bar by shoving a waitress and two customers aside. The dance floor was directly between us. Though it was a tiny space, the spirit of New Orleans and a great deal of alcohol kept it packed.

The four or five look-alikes got tangled up in a drunken laughing crowd. Most of the dancers didn't seem to realize anything unusual was happening. Two of the shoving guys even got dragged down for some steamy looking kisses by reeling girls in crop tops and tight shorts or even tighter jeans and t-shirts. One fellow got well ahead of the rest though. I'm not sure if he was just that focused, or if he lost track of his allies. It turned out to be a bad choice to come at my new buddy Raphael all by himself though.

Raphe stood in a single sinuous movement and walked toward the other guy with his hands outstretched palm up as if asking what the problem was. Apparently, the problem for him was, he barely had room to properly perform the snap kick he used to drop the lone thug like a log. Just like that, the entire bar erupted into mayhem.

Girls were screaming. Others were flailing and biting and kicking and in one unforgettable case, pile-driving, people. The guys in white were throwing punches but weren't getting anywhere. As I turned to make my escape I notice the reason for their lack of progress. Although the mayhem seemed widespread, the only real fighting was centered on and around the guys on the dancefloor. In fact, I'd bet a week's bar tips that nobody else was getting targeted for real punches by the clientele and employees of the bar.

I mentally added the band to the list of defenders when I saw one polo-shirt suddenly stained red after a washboard vest came crashing down to break his nose and probably loosen several teeth. The grinning cajun spoon player gave me a thumbs up before turning around to deliver several face level kicks from his elevated stage. That made me think things were well in hand. The sudden arrival of several policemen told me it was also past time for me to leave.

I ran down the hall to escape as something about the cops entering tickled my memory. Just like that, I spun around to look again. In all of the other excitement, I hadn't really noticed the other guy towering over the police on the sidewalk. At least I hadn't *consciously* noticed Freke standing out there watching the whole scene impassively with his arms crossed on a chest as wide as mine but a foot higher off the ground.

I struggled through a ring of non-combatants to get a closer look. In the time it took me to make it back to my table, two of the invading force had reached it as well. I saw Rafe do a couple of professional looking boxer weaves to avoid the first two punches thrown at him. That second punch had too much behind it. The puncher got his arm extended too far. That left the punchee time to grab said arm and over-extend it further before turning his back to *hyperextend* the elbow as well. I heard the protesting carti-lage over the screams of the crowd.

Curiously, I didn't hear the attacker scream. Most people will give a very loud protest at such abuse of their appendages. This guy just grunted and then used the now dangling forearm to impede Raphe while another punch came in to land solidly on the hustler's cheekbone.

At the same time, the second approaching polo shirt lifted a very sturdy and heavy-looking pub stool overhead to deliver what might actually be a Mortal Combat level killing blow.

Well, I couldn't allow that. With both hands on the stool, my little duckling had no means to block the absolute haymaker I brought in from the bleachers. My fist hit him right below the ear just as he began his downward arc with the stool.

I heard the rotten melon sound of wood on a skull. It made me want to look away, but there was still an attacker to deal with and possible victim to rescue. I let the momentum of my punch carry me around to launch my own shorter but almost as impressive round kick.

My foot went through the space where I expected to connect with a bad guy. Instead, I saw a caramel-colored forearm come up and barely block the kick. Both of us staggered over the fallen twins. My victim had an odd jut to his jaw. It looked like he might need a surgeon and some hardware to get it back right. The other guy was in worse shape. In addition to his separated elbow, there were signs of another punch that had put him in the path of the descending bar stool. The mess that made was not worth describing.

Raphe gave me that amused eye-brow and grin again. "Watch who you're kickin' there, grumpy. I'm confused though, weren't you supposed to be down the alley by now or even on the next block over?"

I shrugged and gave him back a straight answer. "Yea, but my oversized biker buddy is over at the street."

I turned to point, but Freke was gone. In his place were hefty cops moving in with nightsticks and one loud whistle. I saw the rear doors of a van being closed by another guy in the white polo uniform. Before the door closed completely I saw what were probably size seventeen boots sticking up from where someone close to seven feet tall was laying on the floor. It was a white van, just like I'd heard Knave describing not that long ago.

"Shit, they have him." I pointed for Raphael, who immediately focused on the white van.

"I know that van." His reply was less amused than I'd heard him utter before now. He didn't elaborate though.

Instead, he grabbed my arm and spun me around to face the hall. "Left wall, right turn, left turn, right turn. Just like marching right bro? Now get out before I have to try and explain you as well as....this."

The last I saw of Raphael, he stood with both hands on his hips looking down at what was obviously a corpse after the barstool finished its work. One of the cops caught sight of the corpse and barked some orders to the effect of "raise your fucking hands."

That was enough for me. I was down the hall and marching to the beat of my fleeing drum. Once outside, it didn't seem prudent to dawdle so I sprinted across patios and down alleys before I slowed down to act calm and touristy while my lungs were aching for air and urging me to bend over and draw in copious amounts of oxygen. Epic exertions were nothing new to me though. Nor were the need to maintain appearances despite the pounding heart-beat and aching lungs.

I managed to avoid attention until I got back to the little rental unit. Instead of going straight in, I circled the house from across the street. I was tired of things sneaking up on me or events unfolding while I was still reacting to the previous surprises. This time I was going to scout around and...

I never finished the thought. A pair of dark Toyota SUVs circled in like sharks to park with one at the front and one at the back door of the little walk-through house. The guys that got out did not have the nifty fashion sense that I'd seen on Dixon. They were almost palpably "G-men" in their dark suits and glasses.

I shrunk back behind an ivy-covered post that was shadowed by the balcony overhead. Like many of the homes in and around bourbon street, this one had the wrap-around porch that let homeowners sit above the hoi polloi and enjoy their juleps or cosmopolitans while they watched the unwashed masses below. An added benefit was that it added concealment for lurking chosen warriors as they watched a government raid.

I saw one of the guys get out and slip on one of the lightweight protective vests I'd heard about but never worn. It was light and flexible enough to wear under your normal clothing. This guy just put a blazer over it though to make a nice disguise, as long as nobody saw him from the front. He was the last of a trio of the gents who approached the front door.

I was half tempted to keep on walking. Okay, I was maybe way more than half tempted. The problem was, my new clothes and some of the goodies Knave had got me were in there. The other problem was my bird. I'd be damned before I let some agency goons steal or even worse, kill my long-time buddy who had begun exhibiting some really interesting traits lately.

I'm not certain that Rafe was some kind of supernatural familiar or something, but I never taught him to say Dumbass or drive his beak through the eye of a witch that was about to kill the keeper of keys and provider of prey, namely one Magnus, aka Mouse, Gustaveson. So apparently we were back to square one, where I impetuously rush into a situation in response to someone else's provocation. It was really getting old.

Turns out I wasn't the only one feeling impetuous. I heard an engine rev and then the overhead door swung open on the garage concealing my borrowed Jeep pickup. Despite encroaching darkness, there were no headlights visible or even an overhead bulb in the garage. For a brief minute, the weak dome light within the truck glimmered. But only bright enough of long enough to show two indistinct human-looking shadows. Then the truck was bouncing over the twin lines of concrete to take out a small garden fence before racing into the street.

I saw my rescuer from the jetski in the passenger seat. She leaned out of the window to yell at me. "Get your ass in the truck. Andale chief, as in pronto!!"

She jerked her head back inside as the first gunshot rang out and sent a bullet whining away off of the street surface. That was all the incentive I needed. I only banged one shin on the side of the truck as I went over. And maybe my forehead on the raised part of the bed over the wheel. Part of me wanted to tell the girl that windshield glass wasn't going to protect her much.

The rest of me was burrowing as flat as possible in the beat-up old truck bed. Truth was, bullets weren't going to stop with that thin metal tailgate either. My best chance was in taking advantage of the concealment offered and hoping none of the shooters got a lucky hit in despite the invisibility of their target.

Shooters was definitely the right word for it. I heard all three of the guys in front of the house firing. One of them had a shotgun because I saw the pattern of shot around the rear of the back window just before the window itself exploded inward. Glass scattered all around the two women inside. I could tell they were both females because all of the profanities coming out of the cab were colorful country colloquialisms in a pair of cute cowgirl accents.

That was the last shot the g-men got. Our driver spun the wheel to put buildings between her and the pursuers and then shifted gears before she stomped on the gas. That crazy beat up little truck took off like the proverbial bat outta hell. I heard a pair of "yeehaw"s in stereo as the near escape got the better of both ladies.

The familiar face of the two looked back and down through the shattered window. "How ya doin chief? Got any holes leaking enough to need an emergency stop?"

I rolled over on my back and looked back at her from a somewhat upside-down position before answering. "Even if I was down three or four quarts I'd say no. Just get us out of here."

For an answer, she passed a cold beer back through the new service window of the pickup. "He's good Angie, didn't even get nicked but there's a nice goose egg growing in the middle of his forehead, unless his horns are about to pop out."

"Don't even joke about horns popping out. Remind me sometime when we're drinking and maybe I'll tell you about some of the weirdest shit that ever followed a country girl home from the way off desert lands." It was different in person, but I knew for a fact that the new voice belonged to "Knave" or "Sister Wizard". Now I just had to hope she really was my guardian angel. Otherwise, I'd just obliged the government goons by jumping right into their net while the bait was banging on my front door.

Other than jumping out of a vehicle doing a smooth forty miles an hour, I didn't have a lot of choices though. I mean I *could* bail out. Even an every day non-combat white-collar office schmuck could probably do so with no more than a few broken bones and maybe a transfusion for the various scrapes and wounds acquired by high-speed acquaintance with asphalt. Due to my previous employers, I was a touch tougher. Such an act of valor or stupidity would probably bruise the bones but not break them. I'd also recover from superficial scrapes and your minor wound before the blood level dropped too low. But it still stung a little.

I also wasn't sure what the driver might opt to do in the event of my premature departure from her moving vehicle. She'd already displayed a willingness to run over lawns, gardens, and ornate fences. For all I knew she'd merrily add an einherjar to that list. I considered those options for all of a second or two before making a decision. I opted to drink the beer.

_____

5

By THE TIME my beer bottle was down to suds and back-wash, we had eased out of heavy traffic and into less tourist-oriented parts of New Orleans. We talked in brief snippets through the broken window while my enigmatic guardian Knave drove us deeper into seedier areas of the big city. Finally, they stopped at a very disreputable-looking motel.

The place looked like it was normally paid by the half-hour or maybe quarter-hour stretch. If the couple of folks I saw leaving were any consideration, then it probably took a hardy soul to willingly spend much more than thirty minutes at a time within. I jumped out of the pickup and looked over a shoulder. The driver was still just a shadowy silhouette under the flickering low voltage lights. The lighting was probably kept that way to hide some of the worst visual aspects of the motel.

While I was tossing various skeptical and dubious glances back and forth between my ride and the hostelry, a couple of bags came out of the window to drop near my feet. Finally, though the passenger whistled to get my attention.

The nearer and more familiar-looking lady tucked her

chin atop an elbow hanging out of her open window. "If you'd like, Angie and I can look after your bird."

She hefted a cage large enough to require both hands. Even at that size, it was more like a carry crate than a living cage for Rafe. He looked me over and bobbed his head in greeting. After that, though he looked past me at the shabby motel. After tipping his head both directions as if not trusting his eyes, the bird shook himself all over and then turned away. I heard him use another phrase that was oddly appropriate. In fact, it echoed my own feelings about the idea of staying here.

Of course, it was kind of cute when spoken in the bird voice. "*No Way, Jose.*"

Apparently, my saviors found it more amusing than I did. Peals of laughter erupted from the truck cab only to be joined by the raucous Rafe mimicking the girls. Finally, the still-unnamed passenger leaned back out of the window and gave me a serious look and some advice. "One of us will be in touch with you in the morning. Before you waltz on in and get a room though, I'd hit up that drugstore on the corner. Some disinfectants, odor spray, and maybe a couple of antibiotics wouldn't be a bad idea. How current are your shots?"

Her renewed laughter had to substitute for any answer I might have made. They pulled out of the parking lot and drove away while she was still enjoying my predicament and her own witticisms. After another long look at the motel, I decided maybe her joke wasn't all that funny.

A few dollars later I had some fresh sheets and sanitizer in a big bag. Hefting the new purchases along with my duffels from the rescue ladies, I managed to get a room with a wad of cash all too disproportionate to the quality of the room. Then again it wasn't the quality I was paying for. It was the willingness to accept cash without any identification.

The room was everything I anticipated. I was curious about what manner of bodily fluids a blacklight might reveal. On the other hand, ignorance is sometimes bliss, or at least less anxiety. Once more I put my trust in those special perks that come along when a Valkyrie has chosen you.

As tough as we are to trauma, we're just about as resistant to disease and toxins. I'm not saying a face full of nerve gas won't take one of us down. We're fully capable of dying from poison or even disease if it's bad enough to wear down our energy and rejuvenating resources. Even trauma can get us if it's massive enough or we keep taking damage without any chance to recuperate.

I decided, that barring superbug STDs, I was probably safe for one night. Even if it was the largest version of a roach motel I'd ever encountered, one night probably wouldn't kill me, or make anything important rot off. I kept telling myself that even while I stripped and disinfected the bed, then changed my mind and disinfected the little vinyl bench that didn't look sturdy enough for two active people.

The bench creaked under the weight of a short stocky guy and clean sheets, but it lasted through the night. I declined the shower and the worn and chipped tub. Instead, my morning started with a sparrow-sized sponge bath out of the worn and chipped *sink*. Fresh clothes made me ready for coffee and a hearty breakfast.

I found both beneath a familiar yellow sign just across the street. That's also when I noticed the truck stop that would have taken a lot less money for much cleaner resting and shower areas. I sat down in the Waffle Shack with an eye on the motel parking lot.

You can say what you want about inexpensive breakfast food, but you'll never curb my enthusiasm for a budget-priced plate with eggs, bacon, sausage, potatoes, and a waffle as big around as a basketball. Real butter would have been good, but the warm syrup and fresh strong coffee went a long way towards making up for butter-flavored spread.

I was considering a third cup of coffee when a sexy full-throated rumble drew my attention to the street between my breakfast table and the shoddy environs of my previous night's "rest". When I caught sight of the bike, it was to smile in appreciation. In a world of Harley's, I ride a vintage-looking Enfield that might have come straight from a world war two battlefield rather than a factory in India.

The rider approaching was on her vintage Indian Chief that looked as new and shiny as it had coming off a show-room floor in the fifties. The seat had been upgraded to something more comfortable looking, but as far as the eye could tell, the rest was pure original American engineering. She cruised into the parking lot and pulled out a cellphone. Seconds later my "secure" phone beeped a message alert.

My previously unnamed rescuer turned at the sound as I crossed the street a few yards away. She beamed me a smile and then focused on where I was coming from. "I guess I don't gotta find a breakfast taco for you. Grab what you won't miss and toss it on the saddlebags."

She pointed back to where tie straps crisscrossed her bags. It was readily evident that my limited luggage would fit on with the straps to keep everything in place. I followed her directions and got the duffels strapped in place. She produced a second helmet and waved it at me before letting me on the back of the bike. "No helmet, no ride chief. You're already enough trouble without anyone getting traffic citations."

With a very unbecoming bulky helmet atop my squat shoulders, I leaned forward to wrap an arm around the girl's waist for the second time in just a day or two. "We really need to stop meeting like this."

The quip got a little laugh out of her as she started the bike and patted my hand. With the motor growling beneath us, she patted my hand and leaned back to reply over her shoulder. "Keep a good grip, but watch the hand placement mister. We haven't had that date yet so don't get too friendly."

I tried to nod as I chuckled back. The helmet limited such movement. Instead, I got one last reply in. "Dated? Hel we haven't even been introduced. I'm Magnus by the way. Or you can call me Mouse. It's a nickname. Long story."

She laughed again while the engine revved up and took us thundering out of the parking lot. With one last pat at my arm around her waist, she leaned back just long enough to yell over a shoulder. "Mouse huh? Well, they call me Lynx. So play nice and I won't have to show you what the barn cats do with rats hmm?"

The ride was only mildly less dangerous than the previous one that had included flying bullets and urban offroad events. Lynx stayed off the sidewalks and lawns, but I wasn't entirely sure we were on the streets for more than half of that ride. She seemed to delight in both speed and random bursts of flight depending on the road's contours.

Eventually, we left the city behind. Judging from the sun's position, I'd say we were heading mostly north. East of true north or west of true north were beyond my navigating skills with nothing more than a sun position though. We ended up out of the low lying areas though and someplace with fences and fields that would have been right at home back in central Texas.

We turned into a gravel drive that led us bumping over a cattle-guard with a typical ranch gate entrance overhead. This one seemed to be dominated by horses and trees. As we wound down the lane and past the screen of trees I could see why.

Straight ahead of us a corral already held an older gent who was pacing a horse around in circles at the end of a long lead. The barn behind him was big enough to hold a couple dozen of the sketchy hoofed beasts.

Don't get me wrong. I don't dislike horses. As a matter of fact, they were part and parcel of life for most of my existence. That didn't mean I *trusted* horses though.

In my experience, they are not only larger and stronger than I am, but they are also equipped with multiple outlets for mayhem. I've narrowly avoided those horrendous chomping teeth myself. As a matter of fact, I've seen a fellow chosen warrior lose two fingers to those giant grinding weapons. His Valkyrie was so entertained that she left him that way for close to a year before relenting and letting him have the digits back.

I've also been thrown, stepped on, and trampled. Now the last was, admittedly, not a surprise but rather the end result of poor decision making when it came to cavalry charges and infantry. In my defense though, his rider didn't get to celebrate the victory due to a large and sharp spear all the way through his guts. The point though is that I don't really trust horses.

Lynx didn't seem to have a lot of faith in the beasts either. She idled down to a very low rumble on the bike and skirted the area to keep from startling the hoofed menaces.

I found out about her real name at one of our brief stops for traffic and conversation. It was Roberta Lee Katte, so, Bob-cat aka Lynx. That was the same time that she told me we'd be joining Knave and my bird to discuss what went wrong and what to do next. I was almost of the opinion that the lady was a tad off of center plumb to put it in a country vernacular she'd understand.

Very few people in this world merrily go out of their way to get shot at and bounce around on dangerous vehicles for a complete stranger. Then again, from the way she drove, I'm guessing she enjoyed the adrenalin more than most folks would consider, well, stable.

She drove us stably and sedately around the livestock and back into some more screening trees that hid a small cottage or cabin. It had some features of both. Rustic logs made up the front face of the little house, but tough siding covered the other three faces. The windows were nice storm-resistant models with long narrow flower boxes hanging just below them. The boxes were a riot of colorful flowers that were probably picked for color and a tolerance for the humidity and gulf coast weather.

In front of the house, a redwood deck was dominated by a barbecue grill and some seating. There were even big umbrellas sticking up out of the middle of two circular tables. I noticed that *Lynx* seemed to be moving deliberately slow and quiet as we approached.

I reached back and slid the handgun from my belt and held it down concealed by my leg. It always seemed best to be both fore-armed and fore-warned so I whispered at her. "Do I get a briefing before we engage here?"

Lynx stopped dead in her tracks. I was scanning for threats all around when I noticed her shoulders shaking as her head went from side to side. Only when she turned around was I certain that she was laughing at me. "You're briefing is to be quiet lunkhead. Angie's sleeping. She was up most of the night. I got her to take my bed just before I dragged Cynthia-Anne out and rode down to fetch you."

I had to guess that Cynthia was the motorcycle. It was beginning to sound like I'd fallen in with some world-class nerds. I was almost willing to bet some serious money that these people all played computer games together, with the weird nicknames like Knave, Angel, and Lynx. Hel even Nimrod would fit in. Those were not thoughts that gave me a lot of confidence.

I was interrupted from those musing by Lynx's sharp glance at my drawn sidearm. "You want to holster that chief? I'm pretty sure a shot would wake her quicker than your loud assed stomping boots."

It wasn't easy to look cool and nonchalant as I tucked the weapon back out of sight under my shirt and behind the belt. In fact, from the look on her face, Lynx didn't think I'd managed to look cool at all. Her eyes didn't twinkle so much as flash bright neon amusement at me. She let it go with a shake of her head and beckoned me forward while maintaining her whisper.

"Your bird is in the back bedroom. He's been a very good boy. I'm not usually a bird kinda girl but that raven is about as cute and cuddly as a ginger tabby cat. Anyway, I bet you'd didn't get a lot of rest last night either. I know I'd have been awake and on perimeter guard against roaches, rats, and the odd slithering gelatinous STD sneaking up on you. Not to mention all of the...festivities, that usually go on in those places. Why don't you catch a nap until Ange awakes and we can talk about everything that happened." Once more she tossed me a glance that was entirely too entertained by my misfortunes.

I discovered that she was right. I was too tired to want to spar with this sadistically amused adrenalin junkie. I followed her through the front door, which involved not only a lock but some tricky jiggling of the doorknob. I made a note to work on that for her when I woke up. I'm not a professional when it comes to home maintenance, but when you've been around as long as I have you pick up a thing or two.

That would have to wait though. I didn't dare risk the ire of "Lynx" or "Knave" by dropping a tool or making an inappropriate noise. For now, my best bet was to lie in bed and think my way through some things. I still wasn't sure which side of the aisle everybody was rooting for though. I slid the pistol under my pillow with a hand on it. There'd be time to apologize for oil stains on the pillowcase later.

When I woke up, the first thought was surprise that I'd fallen asleep at all. My intention had been to lay there and think. Something about the ranch, the rusticly tidy house, and just being away from a city, was enough to lull me into relaxing more than was probably advisable.

I rose and checked the two open doors in my room.

Rafe was hiding in the closet. He was in his cage, but there was nothing to keep him there. Apparently, the bird had lulled his current sitters into thinking he was well-behaved. Hopefully, there hadn't been any cats or kittens in the house. Such creatures had a habit of disappearing around Rafe. I usually tried not to think about why that was.

With a weary sigh, I slapped the closet door almost shut and blocked the remaining opening with the cage and other materials. It ought to contain the miscreant and at the same time give him a little more room than the small travel cage. I couldn't be upset with the ladies for not knowing better. In fact, I was just amazed that they'd been considerate enough to save him as well as any incriminating evidence in my bags.

The other door was a small "half-bathroom". While there wasn't a shower, there was a sizable rose-marble sink and plenty of soaps, lotions, and more importantly towels. I stripped down and gave myself the best wash possible in the circumstances. It wasn't too unlike my early life. Back in our old Viking longship days, there were no showers. We managed with saunas and a bowl bath just like my present circumstances. Still, there was a lot to be said for a nice, long, hot, shower. I worked with what I had though.

There was a change of clothes in one of the duffels. I opted for blue jeans and a grey hoodie with a discrete lopsided A that represented some current comic book hero or another. I'd seen the symbol but didn't follow the movies. If I remember correctly, I watched the first one. The rendition of Asa Thor and Asgard was so preposterous that I couldn't focus on the rest of it.

Let's just say, I've met Thor. He's not that pretty. I mean he's got a lot of raw magnetism but then again he's got a strong fertility theme in some cultures. That doesn't mean he's pretty. Thor never works out, he doesn't have chiseled and defined muscles with a surfer's blond hair and perfect facial features.

In fact, at first glance, with his shirt off, you might mistake Asa Thor for a red bear with a bad fur condition. I saw a film with Robin Williams naked once. Make Thor look the same except a foot taller and about five or six stone heavier. For non-relics, that's seventy or eighty pounds. It's hard to think of the old Gods using modern terms sometimes.

The Thunderer would also be meatier than Williams. He's pretty massively slabbed with muscle. As I said, it's not chiseled but think working muscle under a furry layer of softer padding. I'm not sure he didn't have some polar bear somewhere back in his bloodline. As horny as some of those old gods could be, I wouldn't put it past them.

That didn't mean I wouldn't wear the hoodie though. That A might as well have been a runebind for all I knew. I could definitely fit Raido and maybe Tiewaz into such a configuration. Come to think of it, the "Road to Victory" wouldn't be a bad logo for a superhero movie. I shrugged inside my new and fresh attire and moved quietly into the next room.

Earlier I'd barely got a look inside as my tour guide had ushered me straight past any possible diversions or accidental noise making. Now I came out to see a cozy dining nook right off of a compact but well-equipped kitchen area. The living area was more spacious than I remembered. There was plenty of room for furniture to seat close to a dozen people. One of them would have to be at the computer desk to reach a full dozen though.

Just like someone was at the computer desk right at that moment. I waited a minute for them to turn and acknowledge me. When she didn't move, I looked closer and saw the slimline headset she was wearing. If she was the nerd and gamer I suspected, then that headset would be noise canceling and probably surround-sound. In my opinion, that meant I was not obligated to make conversation.

I edged past and found an almost full pot of fresh coffee waiting. A clock above the sink showed that it was well past noon. That went a long way to explaining the beginning pangs and rumbles in my belly. Breakfast had been good, but that was several hours ago. Beside the coffee was a service set with cream and sugar, a large stoneware mug, and a note.

The note was in a no-nonsense print that didn't indicate masculine or feminine either one. The message was fairly simple as well. "If Ange is busy don't bug her. She'll let you know when she's ready to talk. In the meantime, make yourself to home. Coffee is fresh, food in the pantry and fridge."

It was signed, "Lynx". Under that was a more typical comment from the lady in question. "You can call me Bobbi though. That Lynx thing is just a funny nickname the guys gave me at the same time Angie was called Angel." That seemed to bolster my theory about gamer nerds. Although I'd heard that gamer nerd lasses that were curvaceous, intelligent, adventurous, and funny, were irrefutably a mythological creature. Hot gamer girls are the unicorn of the twenty-first century. I shrugged off that line of thought for now.

With permission in writing, I went to work. There were plenty of groceries around. It was well enough stocked for me to decide this wasn't a rental at all but probably someone's full-time home. Whether it belonged to one of the girls or was simply someplace they were borrowing, it felt very warm and comfortable.

In fairly short order I had shrimp and spicy Cajun andouille sausage sizzling in a buttered skillet. A splash of cheap white wine joined them as well as some shallots and peppers of various colors that I had sliced into "battonets" that were about a quarter inch thick and maybe two or three inches long.

Fortunately for me, somebody believed in shortcuts and bought par-cooked rice. All I had to do was drop a bag of it in boiling water for a few minutes. That was perfect. I have a bit of a love-hate relationship with rice. I love eating it but hate the way I muck it up about ninety-five percent of the time.

While I was working, I glanced over at the mostly oblivious other party in the room. She never spoke loud enough for me to hear, but it was evident that she was chatting with someone over the headset.

I was guessing that this was "Knave". I'd barely gotten a glimpse of her in our harried rush through the city and later she'd been mostly hidden in shadow. This was my first real look at the lady who had saved me twice now, or at least that's what it seemed like for the moment. I still wasn't convinced that she wasn't trying to get more info out of me for whatever agency had spirited away Eachan, Maureen, and apparently Wild Bill.

Now, I took the opportunity to take a long hard look at the lady. It was hard to get a precise height because she was sitting with one leg drawn up into the chair with her. She wasn't particularly tall, perhaps a scant few inches over five feet. Her skin was bronze with maybe a hint of honey to it. Dark hair hung in a thick curtain around her face and down to mid-shoulder-blade. Her profile showed a narrow almost hawk-like nose, cheekbones so high they almost met her eyes, and a mouth that was full and generously wide from my angle.

A muscular and broad-shouldered frame made her seem even shorter than my initial estimate. I was sticking with the first guess though. She had the build of a gymnast or maybe an ice skater. The leg I could see was neither long or slender but was instead well-muscled and shapely for all of its difference. The shadows hid her eyes, but I was betting on dark brown or maybe even black.

Knave turned her head and spotted me pouring my second cup of coffee. With a pause and a hesitant smile, she pointed to the cup in my hand and mouthed, "please". That was easy enough to interpret. I pointed to the cream and sugar containers in turn. She shook her head at the first but nodded at the second before turning her attention and her quiet voice back to the computer screen.

When I delivered her cup of coffee, Knave flashed a smile and adjusted her oversized sleep-shirt to cover the raised knee and make a concealing tent from her shoulders down. With the cup in hand, she divested herself of head-phones for a minute and gestured at a nearby chair for me to sit.

For an awkward moment or two, we just looked at each other, then as if by pre-arrangement we both took a long draught of hot coffee. I was wondering where to start. Judging by her expression so was Knave, or Angie, or what-ever she was being called at the moment.

Finally, I broke the ice with a safe topic. I pointed to the computer screen over her shoulder. From my vantage, it looked like some video game taking place in a bar or lounge. Most of the characters strutting through the club were too good to be true. Typical hormonal representations of impos-sibly beautiful bikini models and the kind of men you see wearing parts of firefighting equipment on calendars prowled around a dance floor with the kind of lighting that makes people want to try the recreational drug my own bar patrons called "X", or ecstasy.

It was just a computer screen to me though. Gamers pretending to be something they weren't. Kind of like semi-divine warriors pretending to be plain vanilla bouncers and security managers at a goth bar. That took the steam out of any prejudice or judgment I might have been inclined to indulge.

As Eachan had said more than once, people in glass castles shouldn't lob stones. Everyone else I knew usually went with glass houses. Then again I'd heard that Eachan actually grew up in a Scottish castle so I guess he got to say it however he wanted to.

Anyway, at my gesture, she turned and glanced at the screen before turning a challenging raised eyebrow at me. She didn't need to say a word for me to clearly hear her taunting me to make some kind of disparaging remarks about her hobby.

Instead, I just asked a simple question. "Whatcha playin?"

You'd have thought I'd questioned her heritage and personal habits all in one. She sat up straight and let the shirt slide over her knee to drop, right after I got a glimpse of a taut but feminine tummy that had just enough padding to cover any heavy muscle.

"Playing?" She asked.

With her head tilted to one side, she answered her own question before I could get a word out. "I guess you could call it playing. The platform is a game. I discovered it when...well, a while back. It helped me through some tough times before I went back to school. It's an escape, even though some people claim to make a good living with the virtual market. You'd be surprised how many people are willing to pay real-world money just for a creative design of clothing or accessories for their character or avatar. I've even heard of people leaving their families for someone they've never met except through a computer-generated image."

She turned back and surveyed the parade of super-models appraisingly. "The funny thing is, you have no idea who you're actually talking to in there. But staying tethered on the uglier side of reality isn't always easy when you'd much rather the world worked like it does in the Role Playing rooms."

I saw that the avatar her screen was centered on had

been dancing with another character. The dance partner was tall and devilishly good looking, with long blonde waves of hair and a physique to make Fabio green with envy.

Knave hit a couple of buttons, and I saw that her character responded with a casual dismissal. She simply waved her hand as if the peasant could go about his business now that she did not require his entertainment. Then the shorter female avatar, which looked a great deal like it's operator behind the computer screen, strolled through the crowd which parted around her as if the force of her will was a wedge to push the common folk aside. Once she made it to her table and sat down, Angie hit a few more keys that sent her character into what must have been some kind of preprogrammed routine. At the same time, a faint blinking "AFK" appeared above her head.

"There we go. Now we can talk and I won't have to worry about someone looking to talk to me, or Knave rather. If it's important, there's an alert that will let me know I need to check-in immediately. But to answer your question, yes it's a game, but it's also a communication hub. I can arrange to meet people in there and discuss topics under better security than I can devise for a cell phone. We meet in that virtual bar and handle...well, business."

A ping from the computer caught Knave's attention. She put up a finger to pause any questions from me while she turned back to the keyboard. Rather than put the headset back on, she hit a few keys. A minute later the computer pinged again. After a couple more messages back and forth, Knave let out a tremulous sounding sigh, followed by a couple of earthy phrases that good country girls weren't supposed to use.

"Dammit, this is not good. I've been doing some discrete digging. After you left the bar last night, I got one message from Raphael. After that, he stopped even looking at text messages. So I hopped on here because we often meet in the club rather than risk a face to face." Knave turned back to me at the end of her statement. I could see that she had been biting her lip.

Suddenly it became apparent that she had also not rested as well or as long as she probably needed. Her eyes looked incredibly tired on top of being full of worry. I wanted to reach out and pat her on the head or give her an avuncular squeeze.

Instead, I just waited until she spoke again. "Nobody has seen him since he talked to the police after that brawl. Normally it wouldn't be a cause for concern. Raphael tends to march to his own beat. But he would never leave my messages unanswered for so long with the kind of trouble we've been seeing."

Another voice broke in from a doorway I hadn't seen open because it was around the corner from the kitchen nook. "Which is why you're both here and not hiding out at other locations we'd considered. Right miss trouble and her big buffoon?"

An audible rumble from her stomach overrode the conversation as my apparent hostess entered the room. Bobbi, aka Lynx, took a deep breath full of inviting peppery and sausage aromas with that particular addition that only comes from well-sautéed shrimp. "So we need to set down to a war council, but not before I make a pig of myself with that skillet sauté I smell."

6

OVER LUNCH, we did some casual planning. At least Bobbi and I did. For her part, Knave sat at her computer with food and a coffee refill provided by her subservient companions, Lynx and Mouse. I got her at least two coffee refills despite my own reservations. When I mentioned that she might get more use out of sleep than caffeine I was rewarded with an icy glare that cut straight through any defenses I thought I had against female magic.

Bobbi appeared from nowhere to rescue me with a hand guiding me back to the table as well as some good ole country advice. "Just back away sugar, don't make eye contact or turn your back. Can't be too careful about triggering those maneaters and their predatory instincts."

When we were both seated with our own drinks rejuvenated, she reached over and patted my hand before continuing in a low voice. "Neamh Ange is too wound up for any common sense cowboy."

She pronounced the names "Nev" and "Ange". The second came with a sound closer to "aw" or "aw" than "A". I suddenly got the connection between Knave and Angel despite the French-sounding accentuation. Couple those natural names with a tendency or character quirk and you got the kind of names we used to give our squadmates in the last century or two.

If you went back to my original memories we did something similar. Back then though, we might add a nickname that was the complete opposite of the trait involved. For instance, a particularly skinny gent might be called Ivar the Fat.

Bobbi distracted me with a gesture of her coffee cup towards the lady in question."She's not sleeping well or really eating either. Nev Ange Wooly is one of the smartest folks I know, but she ain't real good about taking care of herself when she's focused on something. Five bucks gets ya ten that she won't eat more than a few bites no matter how good the food on her plate is."

That caught me by surprise. I knew Wild Bill was paranoid and private, but it seemed like he'd mention dating and then marrying a cute and exotic looking brainiac with hacking skills to rival his own. It's not like we hung out at barbecues or cruised for women together, but we did talk more than many of his customers. That paranoia could be a bond of its own when you meet someone as secretive as you yourself are. My feelings were almost hurt by the exclusion.

What the hell was that though? When I was a youngster we didn't go around getting in touch with our feelings. If someone upset you, they were more likely to get a punch to the throat than any puppy dog eyed disappointment. I knew my eggs had been scrambled by Odin himself and that, according to one shamanic counselor, I had more memories blocked than accessible.

Now I was beginning to suspect the modern values and

perceptions were doing their own twisting of my gray matter. Now wasn't the time for those worries though.

"Wooly huh? So she's all knotted up looking for Wild Bill?" I suppose the relief was in my voice. It seemed like maybe I finally had the answer to my worries about which side this guardian "Angel" was on. Unless they weren't on normal speaking terms for a married couple.

That was a concept that had taken some getting used to when I awoke in the twentieth century.

Say what you will about my brother *barbarians* and me. We took oaths seriously. A wedding vow was pretty hefty mojo back in the day. Of course, there was as much legal consideration as religious or moral heft to a marriage. But you usually kept a good relationship with the mother of your children, future or present. And you didn't really want to give her a reason to lock you out of any home that became her jurisdiction upon marriage.

I knew more than one gent that went raiding just because he had been matrimonially banished to his ship. If you're going to be sleeping onboard anyway, you might as well get some work done. Maybe if you were lucky she'd take you in when you got back. Some gold usually helped make her happy and we all wanted to keep the lady of the house happy. After all, they had the right to divorce you and keep the farm just like today.

I looked over at Nev Ange and dismissed those worries as Bobbi Lee replied. "Knotted up is a good word for it. Ever since we rushed over here she's been on that computer looking for clues about Bill and about that fellow Raphael."

That gave me another avenue for questions. "So what was it you said about Raphael being the reason we were all here instead of other places?"

Bobbi Lee clucked a tongue and gave me a rueful smile.

"I swear sometimes my head's screwed on backward. I forgot all about telling you that part."

She paused to take a deep draught of caffeine as preparation for what I imagined was a long story. She didn't disappoint.

"Well after we dropped you off, I popped Ange over at her...place. She took your bird for the night and I got em both settled in before heading this way in the Comanche. I guess I'd gone maybe five or six blocks when my cell started ringing. Well, when I saw it was Ange calling already I just turned around and shot back. With the phone on speaker mode in my lap, I asked her what was going on. She told me Raphael had been taken and that there seemed to be someone staking out her place."

That brought a couple of questions to mind but I waited while she continued. "Well, she told me about the suburban the fellow was in so I injun'd up and got a look. Sure enough, this fellow was watching her place through one of those little video camera things with the zoom lenses. He and his partner were watching hard too. Didn't even notice when I eased about three-quarters of the air out of his back tires and then low-crawled my cute little butt back to the pickup and told her to be out the back door and hunkered down in five minutes.

After that, I came roaring in. We loaded up and tore outta there like old Smoke himself was on our tails. There was a god awful racket when the peeper tried to drive away and couldn't make his turn. Those flat tires are hell on traction when you're trying to do a high-speed U-turn in a topheavy truck ain't they?"

My grinned answered her wicked smile at the prank. It also made me take the cowgirl a little more seriously. It took nerve to crawl up to a probable hostile and sabotage the vehicle right under their nose. I was also well aware that most bumpkin girls don't use military-style nicknames and phrases like low-crawling.

Maybe my initial guesses about computer nerds and gamers was a tad off base. It started to sound like I was in with some veterans or special ops people. They often used the same squirrely nicknames or callsigns. It also might mean the Bobbi Lee "Lynx" wasn't a crazy and vulnerable adrenaline junky gamer. Instead, she just might be a very sharp and dangerous adrenaline junky and recon scout. I decided to ask her.

"So where'd you learn to sneak up on bad guys and low crawl around?" I punctuated the sentence with a casual lift of my coffee cup and a polite slurp or two of high-octane elixir. I didn't realize my coffee making was weak until I saw what Bobbi considered a proper ratio of grounds to water. I wasn't entirely certain how strong and tough the lady was, but her coffee was brewed for dragons or at least superheroes.

"Whoa, now cowboy. Remember we ain't even been out for dinner and dancing. You can't get all the secrets without the price of admission. Besides, Uncle Sam didn't want me talking about us genteel ladies serving in forward combat positions." She made her eyes wide and innocent looking with a few big blinks for accentuation. I wasn't buying it.

Any woman who served alongside combat troops had to pass the grueling physical training and testing for the role. For females, it was usually much harder since a large number of men didn't want them there. The training and testing were made as difficult as possible to "prove" that women didn't belong in those roles.

That was something that seemed to have gone very far backward since my first time in combat. Women regularly

served alongside men on the battlefields of ancient Scandinavia and Europe. Celtic women even led whole armies.
Hel, there were even women in Valhalla, and we all heard
the story of Freydis Eriksdottir driving off native Skraelings
in Vinland. She was eight months pregnant and beat a
borrowed sword on her bare breasts then charged the
Indians who broke under her crazed attack. So why do
American men feel like their women aren't competent
enough to fight using modern weapons and tactics? Let me
know if you find an answer that makes any sense.

Our conversation was overridden with a loud and
naughty word from the computer desk. Nev's visible leg
thudded from the chair to the floor as she leaned forward to
stare intently at the screen. Bobbi Lee and I rose at the same
time, with my question only partially answered. When we
got close enough, I could see the tail end of some
surveillance footage that just showed tail lights going
around a corner. At our request, Nev Ange started the video
over. We watched as Raphael found himself confronted by a
shadowy figure at the end of a sidewalk just ahead of him.

Against a lone opponent without visible weapons, I'd
give Raphael the edge in most confrontations. He seemed to
think the same thing. There was no sign of hesitation or fear
in his posture as he apparently spoke to the undefined
person standing well out of the light. That conversation
went on for several seconds before a familiar-looking white
van rounded the corner behind them and sped forward to
bounce up on the sidewalk and form a barricade behind
Raphael with the shadowy menace blocking him in the
other direction.

As I had seen before, Raphael was not a man of slow
decision making. He leaped forward and delivered a series

of quickfire punches that had to have altered some topo-
graphical features for his initial target's face.

Before he could take advantage of that, the van erupted
with white shirts. They all crowded around the procurement specialist and began trying to "subdue" him. That
seemed to be going badly for them. After a flurry of
exchanges, I saw more of them subdued or at least semi-
conscious than were erect.

That's when the initial battered victim rose to his feet
and pulled something from his coat. I tensed and expected
the flash of a gunshot. It never happened. Instead, a slender
stick about two feet long shined in the light and seemed to
flare briefly. Raphael went down like he was shot despite the
lack of a gun.

Even through the computer screen, I thought I felt a
surge of energy like the ones I put into my runes. If I was
able to do something like I'd just seen that is. That changed
things dramatically. Unless I was terribly mistaken, there
was someone down there who worked with magical energy.
Call him a sorcerer, practitioner, wizard or energy-worker.
The title didn't matter, but his presence changed the
battlefield.

Some of those figures who had been down rose to shaky
feet and half a dozen hands grabbed Raphael and tossed
him roughly into the back of the van. An instant later it sped
away until the last thing we saw was those flashing taillights
again.

"I know that van." My statement drew two pairs of eyes
to bear on me. Anger and concern were at the forefront of
those eyes, but there also seemed to be some questioning.

I tried to answer at least some of the questions. "Those
were the guys that showed up to cause trouble at the bar

when I was meeting your guy. They also grabbed my biker contact and drove off with him."

Those four eyes didn't lose any intensity. If anything, they burned a little deeper. Finally, Ange cleared her throat before speaking. "And this just now occurred to you? The fact that someone knew enough to kidnap a random seven-foot biker? Or do you think he's involved in this."

"Not a chance in Hel." I didn't even have to think about it. There's no way Freke, an immortal wolf who could take human form, would ever willingly get involved with federal intelligence agencies. In my experience, the supernatural community tends to avoid contact with people who might want to put them in cages and study them. That doesn't even count the ones like me with secrets that some people would merrily extract with forceps and scalpels.

I could see that my answers didn't do much to bolster Ange's confidence in me. Lynx didn't look as concerned. She looked more amused and maybe condescending. It's the kind of look I was used to seeing on skeptics. As far as I knew, she wasn't related to any of the currently imprisoned people in our lives though. Both ladies studied me for a long moment before looking back to the computer screen.

Ange was the first to speak. "What bothers me is how they tracked Raphe. His phones have the best encryption and avoidance apps I could put on them. I'd have sworn he was safe from anything except a full CIA surveillance force."

I was getting up to speed. It didn't take me more than a second to realize she wasn't talking about my raven. She was talking about her missing purveyor of exotic goods. It also indicated that their relationship wasn't new and untrusted either. She knew him well enough to install some of her super top-notch anti-surveillance goodies on his phones.

If she hung around with Wild Bill for long, then some of

his paranoia had to have worn off. Besides, hacker types all seem to be fairly secretive out of necessity. Very rarely do they want anyone prying into their business while they pry into someone else's business.

I had a thought that seemed worth sharing. "What if we're looking at this wrong? What if the van had nothing to do with us?"

The idea started growing on me, so I continued. "Doesn't that police report you mentioned about my biker mention a white van and some dark-skinned individuals?"

I punctuated that question by pointing at the screen where the video was replaying. In it, we could clearly see that the people pouring out of the vehicle were darkly colored beneath the white Polo shirts.

"Your buddy seemed to know these guys. In fact, someone in the bar knew enough to warn him through the music. That sounds like they have a history with him and nothing to do with us." I was starting to feel more and more certain of my new theory.

Nev Ange was not as quick to believe as I was. "Then why have they been seen going after your biker buddy twice now? You think it's just a coincidence that one of your acquaintances has been kidnapped in a city where your other friends are being held after being kidnapped?"

That one brought me up short. Just like other paranoids, I have a hard time believing in coincidence. That didn't mean I was indecisive though. I gestured back to her computer. "Didn't you say the police report listed a plantation? Maybe it's time to go visit the region's colorful past."

It turned out that it wasn't quite time to go on my plantation tour. First, there were plans to make. Fortunately, I was with some world-class planners. They found the plantation maps from satellite images and google earth of all things.

While Ange did that, Bobbi Lee took me to a beaten and worn storage shed that she opened to reveal a bunch of beaten and worn tools as well as a beaten and worn storm cellar door.

Beneath that door, was another door. This one was neither worn nor beaten. If anything, it resembled a bank vault laid flat on it's back. Bobbi Lee made me wait in the cool shadows of the aged shed while she punched in the code to open the cellar.

The peace and quiet in that shed were too good to pass up. I dropped to my butt and achieved as much of a "lotus" position as my thick and not entirely limber frame could manage. Just a few seconds with my spine aligned and mother earth underneath me was enough to ground myself and clear away a lot of the mental and emotional detritus I'd been carrying.

Don't get me wrong. I'm not a yogi or a new age Reiki master. But both of those disciplines have something to offer. Grounding one's energy is an ages-old concept though. It allowed those who work with various energies and magicks to "reboot" themselves so to speak.

It also let me drop some of the concerns that weren't really material at the moment. I heard Bobbi Lee clear her throat with a hint of hesitation or question behind it. She was patient enough to give me just a little longer though. I didn't get a thorough job of it, but things seemed a great deal less chaotic afterward. It also left me a little unsteady and disoriented while I climbed awkwardly to my feet.

"Okay Gandhi, can we carry on now? Or were you ill? You certainly stumbled around like a punch-drunk for a minute there." Bobbi's words were more impatient than her voice. That didn't mean we needed to dawdle though.

"Right as rain Cowgirl. Lead on." I figured if she could go with the weird nicknames so could I.

We went through the door into a reinforced concrete tunnel that went perhaps twenty feet before opening up into what was probably a converted bomb shelter. Back in the nineteen-sixties, anyplace within a long shot of Cuba had feared a nuclear strike. Underground shelters sales took off at that time like home monitoring services started to blossom in the twenty-first century.

This looked like a deluxe model of one of those. Or maybe it was two of them hooked together consecutively. It was stocked for a fairly lengthy stay. One half of it was devoted to living quarters and a giant pantry of staples with long shelf life. I was betting a woman had been involved in the stocking of those shelves. One whole section was devoted to toilet paper and such.

The back room though was right up my alley. It had been converted into a beautifully stocked workroom. It was also a nice private arsenal. I found myself asking aloud what popped into my head. "Why the hell did she send me to Raphael when you two were sitting on this?"

Bobbi Lee did not seem impressed by any implied criticism of her friend. "Because she hadn't asked me if I wanted to play nice and share. This is my little hole-card. She helped me with some of the fancier bits but I've been putting this together ever since I ETS'd.

From my own very short stay in Uncle Sam's army, I knew that she was talking about her End of Term of Service. I had one too. It was half a century old and said I was released due to debilitating wounds suffered in combat. I bet they'd be surprised to see me now without all that melted skin from napalm. The funny part was, it wasn't even the Vietnamese that got me.

I was working for Kara. We were holding a riverbed to cover the flank of some American troops that didn't know we were there. Once the Vietnamese hit, we engaged them and stopped what would have been a massacre. It devolved to my kind of a brawl. A bayonet on a rifle is enough like a spear to give me an edge in close quarters. I was happy as a clam until Colonel Moore saw us and decided to drop that strike there.

Some people claim the plane missed with the napalm strike and got us by accident. I'd heard someone who was there tell it differently. Upon seeing a bunch of what looked like American troops being overrun by the enemy, Lieutenant Colonel Hal Moore had decided that if his men were doomed, they'd go out his way with a pyre of enemies to lie on.

That's when Kara lost me. I guess there was just too much burned and broken meat for her to be sure of us all. Whatever the reason I was left behind and woke up in an army field hospital. It took a few dog tags swaps and some convincing acting, but they eventually ETS'd me with a bus ticket to the Texas Hill Country.

That's old news though. The current situation indicated that I needed to mend a fence. "Oh no. You've got me wrong Bobbi Lee. I was just admiring the collection. No offense to you or the Angel."

I was hoping for complete reconciliation, what I got were a considering look and a correction. "Just "Angel", don't call me "The Lynx" either. It's Lynx, as in a dangerous little predator named Bobbi-Lee Katte."

She emphasized that statement by lifting a nasty little MP5 submachine gun off the wall. The magazine she stuck in it was an extended version and was clearly filled with lethal nine-millimeter rounds rather than the civilian fun gun's smaller twenty-two caliber ammo. The selector on the side also proudly declared that this was a fully automatic weapon. Unless someone had a very special federal license, that gun was as illegal as half the other weapons I saw on the wall.

"Lady I don't know where you shop but somebody needs to get me a credit app for that store." My admiration was not lost on Bobbi.

Her cool reserve melted with a wicked grin and a quip of her own. "No credit necessary. You just have to pass the group initiation. We got all sorts of friends in low places."

Any replay I would have made was cut short by a flicker of the lights and one almost innocuous-sounding beep. Bobbi's reaction said it was anything but innocuous.

She practically leaped over the worktable in her rush to get to the other room. From there she opened a cabinet to reveal several computer monitors that were just then coming to life. The main screen showed a text message in huge letters.

Perimeter breach. Large force incoming. Stay locked down. I'll try and lead them off.

It was signed, Knave.

Bobbi Lee growled and rushed back to the weapons. She slung the submachine gun over a shoulder along with a bag full of magazines. To the mix, she added an M24 sniper rifle derived from the civilian Model seven hundred. This one was tricked out with what was evidently a competition-grade barrel, specialty stock, and different scope from the army issue Leupold. It also had the bipod, a sound suppressor and a bag full of short fat magazines full of .300 magnum rounds.

My respect went up for the girl in leaps and bounds. Not only was she obviously competent with the weapons, but she also didn't show the faintest hesitation in fielding that brutal rifle with its shoulder punishing magnum round. She gestured to the wall while barking at me. "Grab something that goes bang, troop. Or else hide down here whilst I..."

A soft thump and hiss at the front of the shelter cut her short.

"Dammit, Angie, No!" Her growling anger turned into instant fear for a friend. I saw the computer screen flashing again. All around it different cameras hidden in the trees gave us angles to watch every side of the white van that crunched across the gravel driveway. Behind that, at least two more vehicles were obscured by trees.

A different camera showed the back door of the little cabin bang open. Out flew a bag followed by a lurching figure that resolved itself into Nev Ange. The problem was, I'd never seen Ange's offside. Which meant I never noticed that her leg ended just below the knee on that side. She was moving extremely fast for someone on a crutch and one foot. That didn't mean even a moderately fast person with two feet wouldn't catch her.

My heart rose into my throat when I saw that in addition to the tossed bag, she had that damned miniature birdcage rocking back and forth in her free hand. She almost fell when she released the crutch to grab the bag and toss it in the back of the Comanche truck hidden behind the house. Then she had to juggle cages and bags and crutches until she got it all straight and made it into the cab of the vehicle.

That turbo engine must have sparked on the first try. In a split second the truck was throwing turf behind it as she sped off directly at a wall of trees. At the last instant, she swerved through an all but invisible gap and then became hard to follow from our cameras.

The van didn't fall for her mama bird ploy. They didn't

chase the wounded prey but slid to a stop at the cabin. Seconds later the other vehicles arrived similarly in screeching brakes and torn turf.

I counted a full dozen men erupting from the two vans and one luxurious looking BMW.

The last out of the beamer was our fellow from the video. He was obviously a practitioner of some sort of magick from what we'd seen. What we hadn't seen is that he did not look as dark-skinned as his fellows. Perhaps it was all of the white polos that made them look darker. In his darker colored suit, he almost looked Caucasian. Maybe it was the Louisiana vibe, but I'd been expecting a Haitian or Jamaican voodoo priest.

My memory snapped back to the phone call warning me back to Austin rather than seeking the wolf. That had probably been it. My anticipation of this guy came from that soft islander accent. Maybe somebody else made his threatening phone calls for him.

If that was the case, it wasn't the same for his frontal assaults. This fellow marched to the front of his troops and pushed the door of the cabin open with a cane he held in his left hand. When nothing happened he nodded to himself and then gestured to two of his minions to go in and clear the house.

I was perplexed. Nobody that was approaching had any weapons. They entered the cabin like fully armed and armored commandos. A complete lack of fear showed even from the vantage of the cameras. They swept through the place and came back with a few articles of clothing and a plate that one of us had used for lunch.

Cane-guy nodded at the offerings and yelled something over his shoulder. At his command, the van door opened and out stepped the towering form of Freke wolf in his biker skin. I saw the guy with clothes and dishes approach almost within arm's length of the biker. The fellow with his cane came closer and leaned forward to speak to Freke. When he was done speaking, he had the minion lift the clothes up until Freke leaned forward and took in the scent from close range.

He closed his eyes and looked around. His hands lifted towards the house, at which point I saw the large and heavy looking manacles that were wrapped around his wrists then attached with a loop around his waist by what looked like freaking loggers chain. That restraint had to weigh the better part of a hundred pounds but it didn't seem to bother Freke much.

He pointed at the house for a minute. Then he turned and waved his hands at the path we'd taken on the bike earlier in the day. He pointed the bike out under a canvas cover. Then he looked around again. I saw his eyes linger on the little shed. A frown furrowed his forehead but he cleared it with a shake of that enormous noggin. He finished the performance with a shrug and what looked like a word or two growled at the smaller people around him.

At his words, the fellow in the suit switched the cane to his right hand and poked it at Freke like a cattle prod. There was a visible arc of electricity and the big man shuddered and favored that side for the briefest of moments. He glared at the apparent boss man, then sneered at all of the minions in their white shirts. I saw his neck tense and he lunged to snap inhuman looking teeth at the hand still holding my worn shirt towards him

A second shot from that cane produced a much larger zap and actually sent the immortal wolf stumbling backward. His knees buckled but he got control of them before he actually hit the ground. I saw the cane wave back and forth a few times and the anger on Freke's face dissolved. He went as still and emotionless as the proverbial wooden Indian at a cigar store.

"What the hell?" Bobbi's voice almost in my ear startled me. I had thought she'd still be trying to get out of the shelter and lay down some fire on these assholes. Instead, she was beside me watching the cameras. That didn't change the level of anxiety in her voice or in the jittering hands and feet that kept turning to the door and then back to the camera.

She let out a long sigh and settled down with an effort. She wasn't settled enough to conceal the growl in her voice though. "I can't do anything right now. Angie locked us down remotely. Which we're gonna have a long talk about the good Lord willing. She never told me she could do that when she worked out my security measures and software. That little bitch."

I would have sworn she was livid, but the tears running down Bobbi's cheeks told a different story. "That stupid, self-sacrificing little bitch better make it out of here."

That sounded more honest than the earlier anger. I wanted to comfort her somehow. A pat on the back or the "I'm sure she'll be fine" rote. The problem was, I was as worried about the girl as Bobbi. I was also worried that any such gesture might get me a face full of angry special ops scout. It wasn't that I was worried too much about her damaging me. As I said, those things tend to slow me down less than most people. But I needed her. I needed her help and her trust. Come to think of it, I wouldn't mind her friendship, and not just because she was just as cute as she often joked about.

7

I DECIDED to get some info and hope that it helped settle my companion. "So question one is, do you think she can get away? They don't seem to be in a hurry to chase her. Question two is how long are we stuck down here?"

Bobbi stared at the camera's helplessly until I thought she hadn't heard me. Then she turned and gestured for me to join her at the compact dining nook. She stopped at a cupboard and produced some snacks, then joined them with a six-pack of beer from a fridge that seemed to be connected to a radically new looking battery panel.

She saw me looking at the panel and then gestured overheard. "It's connected to some solar panels hid around the place. Keeps enough juice to run the whole shebang and it's completely off the grid. Angie built it after reading some articles about that Tesla guy."

I couldn't argue with the results. The beer was just the right temperature. I popped my can at the same time Bobbi popped hers. She reached over and clinked the cans with mine. "We won't drink a lot of it. Two or three each ought to be okay. We're down here for at least half an hour. That's the limit we set on the emergency lock. Anything less and Angie thought it might be sidestepped. Anything more and I was afraid someone might have a medical emergency we weren't equipped to deal with."

We both took a long drink or seven and thought about the situation. Bobbi spoke first and answered my first question from moments ago. "She'll get away. None of those vehicles are gonna follow her along the route she took. Even the Comanche will have to switch to four-wheel drive. The weather lately has left some of that road slicker'n snot."

She toasted the general direction of her friend with a raised beer can then turned back to me. "This thing has me boogered. How the hell do they keep finding us? Is it something that fellow in the beamer can do with his cane? Is it something with that big guy at the van?"

Her frustration was evident in a growl as she asked her questions. Another clue was in how fast she drained that first beer and pulled another out of its plastic ring. I stuck with drinking mine in a more casual manner. At the same time, I kept going over any information I could think of. Which prompted something I could have said earlier when we still had the brains of the operation around.

"You know, I may have spoken to that guy on the phone." My statement brought another of those head swiveling stares to bear. She didn't say anything at first. She just let those deceptively wide and innocent blue eyes bore into me.

When I didn't cough up any more information quickly enough she cleared her throat to get my attention. "You want to expand on that a little bit, sugar? We have some time in here so feel free to share with me. Remember it's a minimum of half an hour before the locks release. After that, we have up to eighteen months of supplies without going into another shelter and rigging up the aquaponics and long term sustainability systems."

I wasn't sure that was a threat. If it was, she needed to work on her technique. In other circumstances, I could get invested in the idea of spending a few quiet years hidden away with a cute button of a lass who wasn't a shrinking violet.

Anyone who does the kind of things she did for Uncle Sam, and I did for Kara and Odin, usually learns to embrace life in a number of ways. I was willing to bet that this deadly young woman was "no better than she had to be" in the opinion of some of those judgmental church ladies she probably knew by the hundreds. The south is full of them.

These weren't normal circumstances though. We had normal people looking for us as well as threats from the less mundane aisles of the creeper section. The guy with the magic cane wouldn't let up just because he didn't get us on the first pass. A true wizard was said to be able to do some incredible things with the proper amount of preparation time, and with a link, like maybe my clothes or a dish with my saliva on it.

I continued my previous thought aloud after another long pause that seemed to do undesirable things to Bobbi's blood pressure and that murderous baby blue gaze. "After you got me off the boat, I drove to the safe house, then made a quick jaunt for necessities like food and a couple of burner phones.

At the mention of phones, her gaze incredibly enough got more intense. For a minute I thought I could feel the heat of her eyes scorching my forehead. That was probably just my imagination though. I mean months ago a woman had tried to combust me with just a word and a gesture. She'd been mostly a magical tree though so I thought it unlikely that her spellcraft and Bobbi's burning stare were related.

Then again I've noticed that a number of women have a similar ability with glares or words that can quite handily scorch the face and or confidence of a fellow to ash. I pushed through the heated glare and continued. "Anyway, one of the phones was used to put an ad in a couple of trade papers to try and stir up some attention. I made oblique references to some nicknames and facts that someone like Agent Dixon would know. Those references included subtle hints concerning the professor and my...and Maureen."

I wanted to say, my girlfriend. But the truth was, I wasn't entirely sure about that still. We'd had a warm reconciliation after the events in Mexico. There hadn't been time though, to really go into everything that made me think she might be second thinking our relationship. So whether I wanted to call her that wasn't material. Her identification was.

"I think it was something about the big biker out there that got someone's attention. Before the ad even had time to run I got a phone call. It was someone with a faint islandy accent that warned me off of hunting said big bad biker." This was firmer ground. I'd be more accurate to call him a big bad wolf. The predator in front of me though would have probably caught onto that and asked some probing questions that weren't mine to answer.

As I've said before, we supernatural types try and play our cards real close to the chest. The cards about Freke were his though and I didn't want to lose any appendages at over-reaching too close to his chest. We'd seen how that could work out when he almost bit the polo shirt that was a little too much in his face outside the cabin.

Or rather, we'd seen an attempt. I'd seen his brother do

something similar and remove a guy's hand and another's face. There was no reason to doubt that Freke was just as dangerous as Gere in wolf form or in their current human disguises.

Another soft clearing of her throat got me to look back at Bobbi. With an exaggerated gentle motion, she put her beer down and cocked her head to the side before asking, in a patently soft voice. "And after you got this phone call, what did you do? And why didn't you think it was something to mention back before my best friend had to hobble out of my cabin on one leg? If I recall she was carrying your damned bird, and fleeing for her life from some guy that has a dozen fashionista gangsters and a cattle prod hidden in his cane."

Part of me wanted to vent my own frustration by matching her sarcasm with my own. All that would accomplish though was a shouting match at a minimum. At the other extreme one of us would have to dispose of the other one with that aquaponics and sustainability system.

So with a herculean effort of restraint, I answered evenly and without any reaction that her acidic question seemed to demand. "The phone is in my bag. It looked like the duffel she was carrying to the trunk. I hadn't had it quite so full as she did though. It's probably safe to assume that she added some stuff to it and took the whole shebang to keep it out of that fellow's hands."

A drumming of short-cropped but well-kept nails on the table joined those twin blue cannons in expressing Bobbi's current opinion of me before she spoke up. "Magnus, Mouse, dear, has anyone ever bothered to explain why we call them "burner phones"?"

She leaned forward and poked at a finger at the air to punctuate the next words. "It's because we burn the damned things when we've used them. No wonder you had people following you all over creation. You sent them a damned smoke signal then kept waving the blankets in the air so they could follow the smell."

I didn't really have an answer for that one either. But it was starting to give me some ideas about building a better, or at least a bigger, mousetrap.

The rest of that afternoon went into avoiding each other's fraught nerves. Well, that, and making some preparations from within the shelter. I'd done a little work with my runes and some supplies out of the workroom. As a result, I had a makeshift and magical faraday cage built into a little silk pouch that held the offending "non-burner phone".

I was also geared out with a few items I might find useful in the event of another attack or a foray of our own against the forces of darkness and evil. Or maybe it was just a foray against the guys starting to really piss us off.

If my gear seemed complete and very generous. Bobbi Lee's collection seemed, well, excessive doesn't quite cover it. She'd put together a grab bag of firepower, explosives, recon gear, and other goodies that were too esoteric to identify even by someone who'd seen everything from spears and shields to prototype assault rifles in action. The half dozen claymore mines clamored for my attention. I just had to hope she had the skill to use them, and the inclination to be discrete with the things around allies. That was assuming that she still considered me an ally.

I wasn't really sure if I was a guest or a prisoner by the time night fell. By her own description, we'd been free to leave for hours. She hadn't responded to any of my hints that we might need to go out and look for Nev. Instead, she'd just offer me another beverage or tell me where I could get some rest.

We ate MRE's, the Meals Ready to Eat that I recalled

from years past. It wasn't as entertaining with just two people. In a squad or platoon-sized group, MRE's had been the basis for a social time. Jokes, complaints, bragging and some fast dealing, usually went hand in hand with the opening of those brown plastic bags.

This time I got lucky with Beef stew. Bobbi made do with Chili and cornbread. We used the microwave to heat up water for the coffee packets. I let her have my cheap, cardboard-based brownie. Neither of us was tough enough for her cheese-filled snack food.

As the sun started to set, I couldn't take it anymore. "So do you have a plan, Lynx, ma'am? I mean, shouldn't we be out looking for Ange and making sure she's okay?"

She snapped the slide back and chambered a round in the Submachine gun she'd just broken down and cleaned meticulously, only to put it back together again in almost the same pristine condition it had started in. "With the burn, I got in my belly right now Mr. Man, you prolly oughtta think about being real quiet and not making too many sudden moves. That lady out there is a friend. She's got me out of some nasty scrapes and done more for me after we got back than all them therapists and feel good doctors combined at the VA. So right about now, my dainty little trigger finger is just itchin to empty rounds into folks until she turns up safe and my nerves settle down. You don't want to keep jumping up and down on them nerves by asking fool questions do ya?"

She leaned forward and rested her head against the cool metal of the weapon. It didn't seem to bother her that the fresh lubricant would leave unsightly streaks on her forehead. As a matter of fact, I don't think she ever looked like she bothered much with makeup and other feminine tricks and wiles. That was okay, her fresh-faced charm was just as appealing as most high fashion models with their tiny waists and fabricated complexions. Her willingness to deal with sketchy sounding men on their own terms was even more appealing though.

She moved onto a tactical shotgun and started stripping it down as well. That seemed to settle her nerves a little more, at least enough to talk to me without any offers to put high-velocity openings into random bits of my anatomy. "Right now, I have to hope she gets free and gets back in touch with us. We hadn't set up a safehouse or fallback position yet because we weren't sure how serious things were. She was about ready to do all of those things after Raphael disappeared."

She paused in her speech to blow at the breech in the shotgun. For a change, I was smart enough to keep my mouth shut and let her focus. Only after she was sure any dust that might have been in the gun was gone, did she continue speaking. "Fact is, she was probably working on that stuff when the polo gangsters out there showed up. Now I don't know which way to go unless she gets in touch with us. So I'm giving her til about midnight. After that, I'm going to that plantation you two talked about in the police report. She downloaded that information to my email. I checked it when we got stuck down here."

Another pause inserted itself while she concentrated on reassembling the shotgun before finishing her speech. "Now, with any luck, she'll send me another message to let us know she's safe and where to pick her up. Without that kind of luck, I'll go asking ladylike questions from those white polo guys one at a time until one of em is smart enough to answer me before he stops breathing, and screaming."

There didn't seem much to say to something like that.

This Bobbi Lee might sound like a sweet old country gal, but she reminded me of the kind of woman the Israelis were fond of leaving with prisoners for a while. I'm not sure Bobbi would enjoy the work as much as rumors said those others ladies relished the job. I had no doubt she'd be just as effective though. That was even more likely after she watched them chase her handicapped ex-teammate and best friend like hounds after a fox.

I was just hoping our fox was smarter than the hounds. From what I'd seen so far, there weren't going to be many hounds smarter than her, but none of those hounds were missing most of a leg, now were they?

As luck would have it, brains seemed to trump a full complement of appendages. A little before midnight, a signal told us there were incoming vehicles again. Bobbi snatched up a couple of her lethal accessories and ran back to watch the cameras. The Escalade was a deep gleaming blue in color. That alone made me cautious about stepping out and starting a firefight.

So far our foes had stayed monochromatic with white vans, and black SUVs or BMWs. My hopes of a peaceful visitor were rewarded when a young-looking woman in business casual slacks and blouse stepped out of the driver's door and hurried over to help Nev Ange out of the rear seat. We saw them speak briefly and smile at each other over an obvious exchange of cash. At least I saw that much.

Bobbi was already at the door keying in a complicated string of symbols. She didn't even admonish me to look away. Maybe it wasn't a big deal. If that combination would only let someone out, then it was a little less private than one that would allow entry to the hidden retreat. I shrugged and followed her out.

On the way, I gathered up the various gear we'd both

worked on. My shiny new gift of a Kabar knife was enhanced by runes such as Teiwaz for victory, Kenaz for fire and creativity, Uruz for the connection to strength and earth magic, and maybe a couple of others. I'd used a beat-up soldering iron to burn the runes into the wooden rings of the grip.

With the amount of energy I had chanted or galdored into the working, that blade should be extremely sharp and preternaturally durable. It also had the potential to unleash a surprise or two if I could focus and release the energy in some of those runes in various creative endeavors. I often added little touches to weapons and gear with runic magick. I rarely put as much variety and thought into a simple knife as I had with this one though.

Normally I'm not expecting to go up against what looked like a major practitioner of one or the other forms of magical art. The presence of the gent with his mysteriously charged cane upped the ante. It also left me with several unanswered questions.

Why would someone with that kind of background work with the very people other-naturals tended to avoid? How was he out and commanding his own strike team without Agent Dixon watching and pulling his strings? And where was Dixon in all of this?

So far I'd only heard him mentioned by Nev Ange. I hadn't seen any sign of him myself. Then again judging by his actions in the previous meetings, he was quite comfortable in the shadows and behind the scenes even when operating on a federal or even international stage. It bothered me that the slick-looking, groomed and atypically fashionable spook was involved.

He had displayed an entirely unreasonable attitude about his uncle's death. He blamed me for killing the old man. I guess in some ways he was right. I hadn't anticipated the aging cop's assistance at just the right moment to keep us all alive and help end a very bad creature responsible for multiple gruesome deaths. I also hadn't figured out that the Woods Wife and her cousin La Llorona were just puppets for someone else. That someone else was directly responsible for Sergeant Jackson's death.

That didn't mean that I was clean of blame or guilt though. I'm a chosen warrior of the Norse people. Picked from the battlefield by one of the most fearsome Valkyrie I'd ever heard of, I had apparently earned my own reputation for ferocity and an ice-blooded pursuit of success in her name.

The last people I'd talked to who might know about me had all but blanched at the mention of the title I'd earned in her service. They called me Stormbjorn or the Storm Bear. It probably had more to do with my build and Kara the Stormy's title. But another Valkyrie had recognized the name when Gere uttered it and had been prepared for all sorts of dire catastrophe if I were any judge of her reactions.

The point though is that I should have been better. I should have prepared more, known more, protected the cop. Sure we all made it out of that fight alive. But why hadn't I figured out that we had one last loose string? Even worse, it was a string that could kill the old man and dispose of the body as her first act of revenge for the defeat of her supernatural arboreal vengeance spirits shaped like women.

I was still considering all of that when I caught up to the women. They exchanged a couple of hushed whispers but started talking more normally when I got close. They were lurching to the door as a team when I arrived. First I dropped Bobbi's bags at her feet, then offered her another weapon or two to sling and attach here and there on her combat harness.

With my hands free, I started to lean over and scoop Ange up to carry into the house. I don't know where the little warning bell came from, but it stopped me before I was quite in a position to lift. From my awkward position bent half over, I looked up at the icy glare of a girl with pride enough to hate needing anyone else's help. With a weary sigh though she leaned over and laced her hands around my neck.

"This is just because we're in a bit of a time crunch here fella. Don't get any ideas and don't think I need you. It's just easier." She was working to project a strong and competent voice. She managed that much, but underneath it was just a hint of the fatigue she must have earned evading the sketchy folks in their vans and luxury cars.

"Lady," My response was heartfelt and meant to reassure her of my very real respect. "You've been helping me since before we even met. Hel if it weren't for you I'd probably be with our friends as a hostage and lab experiment. Just let me return a small part of that favor by getting you into the damned house."

8

Inside the house was not an improvement. The only initial benefit was in that, once Bobbi Lee set it upright, I could put Ange into her favorite computer chair. The main problem there happened to be a missing computer. That seemed to cause me more concern than it did the computer's owner. She was upset, but I suspected there was information on that system that I didn't want in the wrong hands.

Over the years I've had to feed Wild Bill a few facts here and there which he had used to compile a tidy little file on me. It was by no means the complete and unabridged story of an Einherjar out on walkabout without "supervision". But there was enough info in that file to cause me considerable trouble if someone like, say, Dixon got their hands on it.

I interrupted Ange's litany of unladylike swearing with a profanity of my own. "Son-of-a-bitch, does this mean the bad guys have all the info we've been researching as well as the older files of Bills you'd been looking through?"

Maybe it was the anxiety in my voice or just the insult to her forethought, but my question shut Ange's rant up instantly. First, she shook her head and then cranked it around to stare me right in the eye before asking. "You are kidding, right? I haven't left a computer open to outside tampering since I was old enough to know roosters don't lay eggs. They can't break the password. If they open the case wrong there are a couple of surprises inside. If any storage component is taken out of the system it will erase itself. No busybody snoops ain't the problem chief. The problem is, that's the best computer I had available down here in Louisiana."

She slumped in her chair and bit her bottom lip in a manner which I found inappropriately charming. After all, I was only sticking around the "Big Easy" to rescue someone who might or might not be my significant other or at least a candidate for the position. Secondly, I was still divided about the wisdom of having a romantic relationship at all. I mean a physical relationship? Sure. But romance means emotions and feelings and sharing secrets. Some of my secrets are enough to get someone killed, or at least kidnapped it seems.

And aside from the danger issues, how do you explain to a modern, sophisticated, logical lady, that you were born over a thousand years ago and have died dozens of times but somehow you're still around and hanging out at a low-risk job in Austin Texas? Do you avoid the whole thing? Because keeping secrets or lying about stuff like your very identity seems a bad way to approach your love life.

I dropped my ill-timed musings to hear what Ange said when she turned to face Bobbi Lee. "How about you Bobbi? Who do you call for help with computers or phones or even the internet?"

Bobbi turned an embarrassed eye back to her friend to answer. "Umm, I call you Ange. Everything here from the phones to the internet to the security and computers in the shelter was all your work. I mean I did some manual work, but you sent me all the instructions in short words suited to my country upbringin'. I guess maybe your buddy Rafe would have access to some good stuff but he's part of the problem now instead of an asset."

I for one didn't understand the problem. "Look I can get some funds transferred around and we can just go to an electronics store, right? Presto, we're back in business."

This time the pause was longer. If anything her voice was sweet and reasonable, if you were immune to sarcasm. I'm resistant to sarcasm but not immune enough to completely miss it in her voice when she said "Well sure sweetheart. We'll pop over to Wally Mart and grab stuff off the shelf and get right back to hacking through government firewalls and security measures. Oh and while we're there can you get a state of the art custom-crafted cooling system off the shelves? Don't forget the limitless algorithm security system. It also runs hot enough to fry any normal system."

I suppose her tirade was supposed to put me in my place. All it did was make me think outside of the box a little. In fact, it moved me completely out of normal boxes and into someplace that I really didn't want to go. It didn't sound like we had a lot of choices though.

"No, not Walmart. We just need to go to the right basement. There's someone that I'm betting can help us. We just have to find him and hope for the best. He's not exactly happy with me these days."

It was my turn to earn the look of blank surprise. Nev Ange was first to find her voice. It just seemed like that same voice had picked up a hint of disbelief while it was lost. "You? Know somebody in Louisiana that can get their hands on a state-of-the-art high-security custom made computer that can handle the kind of software I use?"

People don't use the word "scoff" that often anymore. I was pretty sure that whether she meant for me to hear it or not, Ange was scoffing at my naive assumptions. Then again, she wasn't the only person with connections and secrets. I decided to save any explanations for later. If she had a hard time believing I even knew someone like that, she'd have an even harder time swallowing the rest of the tale.

Instead, I focused on getting us there. "Okay, so maybe he's not as good as you, but this guy has his own tricks and if he can't get you the system he'll know someone who can. So can we hit the road? Even if we go with a different plan, anything is better than sitting here waiting for the goons with Mr electro-cane to come back."

At least we all agreed with that. Ange went into a bedroom and started gathering some of her stuff. Bobbi Lee directed me to make some sandwiches and round up provisions. For her part, she took our gear outside and said she'd get the ride ready.

By the time Ange wheeled herself out in a space-age looking wheelchair, I had a large sack full of snacks and sandwiches as well as beverages and some dry goods we could use with just a heat source and water. I stuck my head out once to ask why we couldn't just pack more of the MRE's. Bobbi Lee was nowhere around though.

Maybe they wanted to save those rations for a more pressing need. I couldn't argue with that kind of discretion. We weren't locked into the shelter and had options even if they were sandwiches and cold fried chicken. I heard the engine before I spotted her coming around the stable area at a sedate pace on the motorcycle again. Even in a hurry, she was considerate enough not to startle the livestock.

When I did get a good look at the motorcycle though I understood how she planned to transport all three of us.

The rear of the seat had been cleared off and a padded extension added. That would account for two of us. But the odd sidecar she had attached didn't look like anything I'd ever seen before and I have a sidecar for my own Enfield motorcycle.

Ange knew what it was though. She wheeled down a ramp at the side of the cabin and rolled right onto the platform of the odd sidecar. Her chair fit like it was made for it. It was more likely that the sidecar was made for the chair though. Bobbi jumped off the bike and pulled a hidden panel around to enclose the wheelchair completely. To any observer, it would like a "normal" sidecar. For Ange though, a couple of quick-release clasps would release her and open the rear of the vehicle for a speedy exit.

She shifted a couple of bags around in the forward area of the sidecar. Apparently, all of our new gear was stowed just out of the way for the hacker and her chair. The ladies both got into their respective places and then looked at me in tandem and spoke in stereo. "Get on the back bitch."

We made it across town without any white vans, or black SUVs or even random gunfire. I had to use my "Secure" phone to access an address and locate it via GPS. Eventually, we found the place I was looking for. The apartment building looked to have been abandoned after one of the many storms and hurricanes had its way with the already aged and vulnerable building. The corners of the brick building were crumbling, the roof was missing enough material to fall through, provided the roof would support the weight of anything bigger than a malnourished pixie anyway.

Both of the girls took turns staring at me to see if this was some kind of prank. I didn't acknowledge those questioning expressions though. Instead, I gestured to a side yard with parking under some rusty awnings that leaned at an alarming angle. "Park there. It ought to keep the weather off until I can come back and flag you in."

I had to pause to think about how to phrase the next part. When Bobbi started to say something I gestured at her to give me just a minute. Surprisingly she waited for me to organize my thoughts. "Look, ladies, you need to stay out of this. No matter what happens, just stay with the bike until I call for you. If nothing else, he'll just let you drive away as long as you don't get involved. Cool?"

Both of them looked perplexed by my request. But it was Nev Ange who asked for clarification. "What exactly do you mean? Don't get involved in what? I mean, what do you think is going to happen?"

I unwound my stumpy legs from the bike and wandered out of the shadowed parking area towards a sagging cellar door. "I mean don't get involved when he tries to kill me. I told you earlier, he ain't particularly fond of me at the moment."

Both of them sat back with a thump. I saw Bobbi's hands go for one of the bags in the side-car. I just shook my head at her and waved a finger. "No guns. Don't shoot him. He's already mad enough without that. Right now I can probably handle him. If you shoot him then all bets are off. One of us would have to die at that point. And to be honest, if you piss him off anymore I'm not real sure whether it would be him or me."

I had the satisfaction of knowing that if I did manage to die in the next few minutes, at least I'd have the memory of those two appealing ladies staring at me with their jaws hanging. That satisfaction lasted all the way to the cellar door and an old fashioned door knocker on a wooden post beside it. That's when satisfaction was replaced with a cold uncertain knot in my stomach.

Maybe this wasn't one of my brightest ideas. To be honest, that's saying a *lot*. I've been known to pull some real boneheaded stunts. Fortunately, even before I was Valkyrnized, I was tougher than your average stump. Unfortunately, I was built like your average stump too. Low to the ground, gnarled and almost wider than I am tall. Between my innate toughness, stubbornness, and some boosts from the Divine Sisterhood of the Ravening Fanatics, even boneheaded stunts can succeed, albeit with an unplanned amount of blood loss and mayhem.

That thought was enough for me to square my shoulders and thump the door knocker again. An almost inaudible whine drew my attention to the eaves of the decrepit building. I couldn't spot it, but I was willing to bet there was a camera up there telling the occupant who exactly was at his doorstep.

A faint thud resounded somewhere underfoot. That was followed by a tension-building minute or two in which I imagined a rumble of heavy footsteps shaking the earth as my old "acquaintance" got closer. I was pretty sure it was my imagination at least. Or maybe it was rumbling from the dark horizon I saw approaching from seaward. I heard the ratcheting sound of a heavy lock somewhere near the cellar door.

A moment later I thought I heard another thud from down the underground corridor. Had he gone back to his lair? That didn't seem likely, all things considered. I turned to see if the ladies were getting impatient. It turned out that they were, but not with me.

Our arrival at the unusual location had brought out a few curious folks from the lower end of the economic spectrum. Most of them kept a fair distance away. At least one or two had approached and held out a small box to beg a little cash for the next meal or at least a drink or two.

I strained my hearing to its limit. Although my ears remained clueless, I felt a tingling along my spine that had proven trustworthy in the past. Ask anyone who pursues war and conflict for a living. We learn to trust our instincts even when there's no apparent basis for those feelings.

That was warning enough to brace myself. It didn't seem likely that he would invite me in for tea and crumpets. In fact, if Stige recognized me from the camera, I could expect anything from a contest of escalating insults to an impromptu rush of a very strong cousin of the giants themselves.

That instinct was my first warning, the gasps of my two companions and a rush of feet were my second and third warnings. I managed to get turned around just as the bundle of rags with its box of coins hit me like a tidal wave. Coins, rags, and stench exploded around me as the grubby clothes felt like they were leaving a trail of grease on my skin. I was too busy to worry about skin discoloration though. In fact, I was more concerned with skin removal, either one painful strip at a time, or in one fell swoop like a grape being peeled.

Still, those multiple warnings had allowed me to brace myself. When Stige hit me, he probably expected to bowl me over and land on top to deliver a vicious beating that would have him banned from any MMA circle. Since I was at least partially warned though, I managed to divert part of that charge. I spun and managed to turn his rush into the impetus for a hip toss that sent my attacker sailing towards the rickety building.

I had forgotten just how strong he was and how long his arms were. Stige managed to wrap one improbably beefy hand around my bicep as he flew past. That one meager grip was enough to take me tumbling with him until we exploded through the door and into a building with floors crumbled away to nothing. We found ourselves sprawled in dank earth and straining against each other.

Stige headbutted me across the bridge of my nose. If I hadn't ducked just when I did, he probably would have temporarily blinded me with pain and a spray of blood from the broken cartilage that held said nasal appendage out from my face. Instead, he got me right between the eyes. Which still blinded me with pain, just not the blood. I'm pretty acclimatized to pain though.

I felt his thumb reach up and jab into my cheek when I ducked into it. He missed my eye by inches but left a bloody furrow along my cheekbone. That told me what kind of match this was. We weren't sporting under the Marquess of Queensbury rules. This was a good old-fashioned holm-gang. So far he hadn't produced steel, but since we hadn't really discussed the rules, that was probably on the table.

Since we were apparently *not* playing like good little boys and girls, I drove a knee up between his legs while we were both struggling to get our feet under us. In retrospect, that was probably not the best way to make friends and gain his assistance. It was, however, the quickest way to break his grip and back off a bit.

We both took advantage of the respite. I drew in deep breaths and wiped the blood from my cheek. Stige clutched his nethers and spat a choice curse or two at me. "Dit elendige krapyl. Hvad har du at gøre her ved Stiges dør? Jeg har set frem til dette møde." *You worthless bastard. Why do I see your face on Stige's stoop? You know I have waited for this.*

I couldn't argue. I won't specify where the bad blood originated, but we had run into each other a handful of times since I awoke in that modern army hospital. Every time started like this, and every time we'd been broken apart before it got too far.

That wasn't likely to happen any time soon. Police didn't respond to areas like this with any alacrity. And the other homeless people that had been around were prudent enough to disappear when the battling and bleeding started.

Since we were separated for a minute I decided to try some diplomacy. "Åndsvage læs lort. Det behøves jo ikke ende sådan her, hver gang vi mødes. Du har jo, for Helvede, tævet mig sønder og samen. Tror du ikke snart vi står lige?" *You dumb pile of shit. We don't have to do this every time we meet you know? Hel you've beaten me half to death repeatedly. Don't you think we're even yet?"*

His answer was another roar and a charge. This time I met him partway. My hand came up not like a fist, but with the rigid edge extended and held taut while my thumb safely tucked itself out of harm's way. It struck him between his nose and lip with a meaty thwack and a spray of blood. In the shadows of the ruined building, that blood was dark and thick.

For his part, I caught a brick-hard fist to my rib-cage. A few inches to the left and up would have put that shot into the potentially fatal triangle below my sternum and between the lower ribs. I'd heard of people rupturing lungs, hearts and other organs that way. All I got from it was a breath-stealing pain and the audible snap of a rib or two, maybe even three.

The blow also drove me back a full three steps while robbing Stige of almost no momentum. He came on with a windmilling attack of haymaker swings. All it would take was a solid connection from one of those wide sledgehammer blows to put even an Einherjar out or at least ring his bell loud and clear.

I ducked, twisted and sidestepped all of them and stopped the assault with a simple straightforward sidekick to his gut. I may have insinuated or baldly stated that I am broad, stocky, stout, maybe even portly. My musculature isn't chiseled or defined, it's just slabs of meat with a little softening from things like waffles and red beans with rice.

That being said, there's a lot of muscle under that soft coating. I put it all into that kick. Any other time I would have expected my opponent to end up face-first on the ground with some severe breathing difficulty and possibly organ dysfunction.

Stige was not a normal opponent though. The kick brought him up short, and I'm pretty positive he gulped down a mouthful of pain and nausea. He didn't fly backward or fall down though. Instead, he reached one impossibly long arm down to brace himself like a sprinter in the starting blocks. With his spread fingers buried to the middle knuckle in dark, musty smelling earth he growled.

"Vi er ikke lige. Endnu. Men se nu her." *We're not even yet. But we're about to be."* That last word was like the shot of a starting pistol. He shot off the ground at me too fast for anyone that size to move. I expected it though. A sidestep brought me in line to deliver a clothesline that would all but knock his block off if it connected. It connected. But so did he. One of those long arms wrapped around my waist even as I felt him lose some momentum from the shot that he took on the chin rather than across his neck or chest.

For a second I had some hope that Stige was knocked out. That was short-lived though. His arms tightened around my waist and lifted me off the ground for several feet before we exploded out of the splintered window behind me. To be accurate, we exploded out of the wall and the lower window sill. Stige used me to make a suitable opening then widened it with his own silhouette as we emerged back into the waning sunlight.

Flashing lights made me hope for the police. Alternately I was afraid I was seeing stars from the multiple blows of an old enemy and rotten wood, not to mention the impact of mother earth along my spine and the back of my head. A blink of the eye showed me flashes of lightning almost upon us rather than police cars or my own individual stars and birdies.

Stige was up before me. He wrapped both hands around the arm I was waving to regain my balance and my feet. With a heave, he tossed me a good three or four yards to crunch into the rusty body of a pickup truck that had been left in the weeds at least three or four major hurricanes back.

I didn't get to judge the dent I'd put in the truck. I was pretty sure my head was dented worse though. I got my feet under me just as Stige closed. I may have failed to mention it, but despite the abnormally long arms, Stige himself was only an inch or two taller than my own slight height. Also, like me, he had shoulders that belonged on someone a foot taller.

That was what made his name so entertaining. Stige is Scandinavian for Ladder. This example of the name was, however, anything but long and lean like a ladder. His fuse was even shorter than his stature. Spittle flew in my face along with his fetid breath as the stumpy figure wrapped those long arms around me. He locked rough oversized fists around the frame of the truck on either side of the window.

"Så fik jeg dig." *Now I've got your ass.* He punctuated the statement by driving his entire body against mine like a hammer on hot metal with the truck as an anvil. I wanted to fold over like the horseshoe in such a plight. The body of Stige against mine prevented that. With another surge of his shoulders and arms corded with muscle, he slammed me against the truck again.

I felt my ribs creak and protest at the abuse. The ones that already had cracked or broken sent searing pain throughout my torso. They didn't seem to pierce anything vital though. Despite that, my breath left in a rush and I was reeling and all but helpless in his grasp.

I saw teeth unlike any normal human just inches from my eyes. They weren't relatively even and flat like my own. Instead, these teeth were more like a serrated blade or a saw, suitable for ripping flesh off without the benefit of civilized cutlery. His voice all but crooned in my face as I struggled to regain my balance and my senses.

"Jeg har ventet så længe på at få hævn. Hvornår var det nu vi mødte i Paris? Kan du huske forsamlingerne? Faklerne og hadet? Jeg fandt en vej ud, men der var flere fra klanen som ikke klarede det, ikke? Alt sammen fordi du hjalp forsamlingen til at finde vej til os." *I've waited so long for my vengeance. When was it that we met in Paris? You remember the mobs yes? The torches and the hate. I made it out, but some of my clan did not. Did they? And all because you helped the mob find us.*"

I didn't deny it. I couldn't. He was right. In my pain I switched back to English, at least we weren't speaking old French...yet. "They had to blame someone. Some of your clan was stealing children instead of livestock. The more people dug the more they got close to things I was charged to keep secret."

His crushing embrace stopped my voice for a second,

but I gamely continued. "It wasn't personal. Necessary Sacrifices. I...did...what I was told."

The last three pauses were for more blows, this time it was his fist slamming into my less damaged side over and over while his other hand closed inexorably over my throat and windpipe.

That wouldn't do at all. It might take longer, but he could suffocate me just like anyone else.

He knew it too. "Jaja. Jeg har dig nu. Jeg smadrer dig, dræber dig, æder dig, bruger dit fjæs som vaskeklud og skider dig ud med badevandet så du end ikke husker din plads på Moder Jord." *"Yea. Got you now. I'm gonna crush you, kill you, eat you, take your face for a cleaning rag, and shit you in the ocean so you never know the mother's embrace."*

That made the connection for me. Stige gained his strength and much more from a connection to mother earth. With his bare feet planted in the earth, he was stronger, tougher, and infused with earth magic. I thought maybe I could fix that though.

On his next surge forward I didn't try and hold him off. Instead, I rode the pain while I wrapped my arms around his waist just like he held mine. I had my knees bent though where he was hunched over. It gave me the advantage of leverage. With my own muscles screaming in protest I lifted the struggling figure in its filthy rags off the ground and held him in a bear hug.

Now it was his turn to sweat and swear between bouts of breathlessness. I locked my hands at his spine and slowly tightened every applicable muscle. Stige bent away from me, his face contorted in pain. I also caught a hint of fear. That might have been hope and imagination though.

I tightened my grip further and felt his torso begin to give. I might not be able to crush him like a can. I also had no interest in eating him or even blowing my nose in part of his face. But given his strength and connection to mother earth, I'd merrily dump him into the Gulf, preferably in the middle of a shark frenzy.

Stige wrapped both hands around my throat and began choking the life from me. We were stuck in that moment, striving to be the last one aware while the other choked, or had his spine broken. The blood was pounding its pulse in my head, trying to force more oxygen into my carotids and feed my struggling brain. For his part, Stige was bent far past what most people would tolerate. His spine was creaking and grinding under my fists. It was just a matter of time before that spine snapped, or I blacked out from strangulation.

That was when a roar of sound preceded a shower of glass over both of us. We separated just far enough to both look at the pattern of holes and odd bits of metal sticking out of the hood of the car not a yard from us. I squinted at the nearest metallic bits until I identified a flechette.

Sighting backward from the spread of flechette rounds, I saw the ladies at the motorcycle both pointing weapons our way. Nev Ange lifted her shotgun and pumped a new round into the chamber while Bobbi just casually waved a submachine gun at both of us. It was Ange who caught our attention, but Bobbi Lee kept it with her sweet southern drawl.

"That's about enough macho bullshit for the moment boys. If you don't let go each other and step back, well, Angie was never that good a shot. I imagine she's likely to shred both of you with those tiny little razor blades if she fires again. Nasty wounds those flechettes make. Enough to turn my stomach I tell you."

9

I THOUGHT SHE WAS LYING. Not about us both getting shot. Both women looked pissed enough to put a number of holes in either or both of us. I thought she was probably misleading us about Angie's accuracy though. That first pattern of shot had come within inches but hadn't hit either one of us.

I felt the hands around my throat slacken marginally and a quiet voice whispered near my ear. "Er det dine venner? Dem kan jeg li." *"Friends of yours? I like them."*

For my part, I slowly released my grip with the same exaggerated care Stige did as we both decided to behave under the snouts of the ugly weapons. "Tog du dem med som en forsoningsgave? Jeg kan ikke rigtig finde ud af om jeg bare skal æde dem eller først fjolle lidt rundt med dem. Måske lidt af hvert. Hvad synes du? *"Did you bring them as a peace offering? I don't know if I should eat them or play with them some first. Maybe one of each. What do you think."*

Almost as if she understood him, Angie swung the wide bore of the shotgun to center on his face. "What did he say, Magnus?"

I growled one last thing under my breath in the language Stige would understand. "Vær rar. De er mine venner, ikke legetøj eller et måltid. Og pas på dine manerer. Som vor vært, må du hellere begynde at tale Engelsk og forsøge at huske hvordan man opfører sig i høfligt selskab." "*Play nice. These are my friends, not playthings or meals. And mind your manners. As our host, you should probably start speaking English and remembering how to behave in polite society.*

"I said I like you. You are both delightful looking." Stige spoke the words without any hint of deception. He also managed to avoid looking to see if I'd play along. He needn't have worried. I wanted his help far too much to encourage Ange or Bobbi to spatter him with bullets or shot.

I played along with my new "ally" but scowled at my only slightly older allies. "What happened to *No guns. Don't shoot at him?*"

I got a double eye roll from both girls followed by their simultaneous replies. Nev Ange went with, "I shot near him, not at him. Come to think of it, I shot near both of you."

Bobbi Lee answered with her own counter-question. "What happened to, *it'll just piss him off and one of us will have to die?*"

They had me there. The situation was suddenly diffused. I'm not sure why the anger drained from Stige when it did. I was just glad we weren't bent on mutual annihilation any more. Just to be on the safe side though, I stepped away from him while manfully trying to ignore the hitch in my side when those cracked ribs protested.

For his part, Stige straightened most of the way up and came near to convincing me that his back was aching abominably. Once the danger was past, and he'd been reminded of old-world manners, Stige stepped up like a champ.

"Ladies, if you will swear not to attack me or cause me harm until the sun sets tomorrow, I shall offer you hospitality and see what extraordinary circumstances prompted this visit."

He really spoke like that. I think it had to do with growing up during the Renaissance. Of course, his delivery was mildly awkward since the words came out in a voice better suited to mixing concrete or grinding gravel from large rocks.

The ladies gave me a questioning look to which I responded with a firm shrug. "You can trust him or not. I'll tell you that creatures as old as...him, are usually good for their word. Especially about things like hospitality and old-world values. That being said, one of his favorite uncles has been verified as a kidnapper who liked the taste of children."

Bobbi Lee tossed her head back to reveal the length of her smooth throat while laughter bubbled out. Her response did not indicate that she took me seriously. "Sure thing honey, I had an uncle Ray that used to howl at the moon sometimes. Come to think of it, momma always said he was a lady-killer when he was young."

For her part, Ange just gave Stige, and then me, very direct looks with something vaguely suspicious behind them. She apparently made up her mind to give us the benefit of the doubt. Even though her expression still looked uncertain, her hands went to the releases that would allow her chair to exit the mother-ship as I'd heard her refer to the sidecar.

The two of them approached Stige's cellar door with some trepidation. I'm not sure if it was fear of my foe or uncertainty about the safety of whatever was behind that door. The trouble was, I could not in honesty reassure them on either front. Stige had offered them hospitality which meant he was obligated to offer them the best he could provide on short notice. That being said, his home did not have to be safe for them, and some things a troll could eat with impunity would not be good for a human at all.

I'd also noticed that he had very carefully worded his invitation and hospitality to the two ladies only. That meant if I went in I was taking my own chances. Considering the sheer length of our animosity, it didn't seem likely that we were going to be best buds just because we swapped damage and the girls' courage had entertained him. It seemed best not to mention that to the ladies though. Their expressions indicated they would welcome any excuse not to pass through that rickety door.

As soon as Stige turned his back and fiddled with some secret knocks or locks or trickery out of our sight, the cellar doors opened. Waning light from the cloud cover conspired with the occasional flash of lightning to reveal a dank and dirty cave that perfectly fit the battered wood of its doorway and the rotting building above it.

My shoulder blades ached with the anxiety and tension built around expected ambushes or knives in my back. I went first as a sort of encouragement to the girls and an act of defiance to Stige. Showing fear to someone like Stige would have been tantamount to an invitation. If he thought I was afraid he would gleefully restart the mayhem that we had just postponed outside. Which also meant that I didn't want to transmit that fear to the ladies.

That fear was not overly evident though. At the sight of steps leading down at a steep angle, Ange cleared her voice. "This might mean I need to stay with the bike. In our hurry, I didn't grab any of my crutches."

The stumpy figure in his greasy rags tilted his head to the side and appraised her. If she'd shown fear or revulsion, then he could interpret that as a rejection of his hospitality and a slur upon his honor. That would almost definitely end badly. If he read fear in her before she had actually entered the abode, well that could go almost as badly.

As I said though, their fear was not particularly evident. Ange tilted her own head in a faintly mocking gesture as Stige regarded her. That seemed to settle something for my recent mortal enemy. He bowed to her in a motion at odds with his thick outline and shabby clothing. "If the lady would permit, I will most tenderly convey her inside?"

Ange looked surprised but covered it with her own formal bow of the head and a gesture to proceed. I had to hope that it wasn't all bravado. I saw Stige lift her chair as if it were empty rather than filled with a brave and athletic-looking genius. With her in his grasp, and practically brushing his face with her hair, any fear she felt would be as clear to him as a wounded deer's scent to one of the local favorite Catahoula hunting dogs.

Even if she was quivering with fear, Stige's invitation should prevent him from any act of hostility. *Should*, was the operative word. If his sense of vengeance outweighed his honor, or if any reactions drove his instincts past normal control, then all bets were out the window. I'd gotten lucky fighting him outside. Most of that had come from being able to break his contact from Mother Earth. Down in this hole, we'd be surrounded by that same earth.

I was so distracted with my thoughts that it took a few seconds to notice when the root cellar walls turned into worked stone. When I say worked stone, we're not talking bricks or even concrete. This was actual fieldstone cunningly shaped and fitted together in such a way that it was hard to tell if there was even mortar involved or whether the fit of stone on stone was in itself enough to hold the walls in place.

The much nicer section of tunnel was out of sight of the entrance because of a gentle curve of the path. Right in the middle of that stone tunnel was another portal, rather than the high-tech bomb shelter at Bobbi Lee's place, this looked like something out of Arthurian legends. The door was oak, bound in what I thought was probably bronze. Steel and iron don't necessarily bother all trolls, but a number of "alt-natural" creatures have serious reactions to the presence of iron.

Considering his reputation, I was betting that Stige kept his environs safe for all sorts of creatures that didn't do their shopping at normal retail stores. Stige was an enigma of sorts. He was huge, tough, strong, brutal-looking in a ruggedly handsome way, and sharper than an obsidian scalpel.

Despite his rough and physical appearance, he was actually one of the smartest people I'd ever run across. I was withholding any opinion on whether his gray matter was any better than Nev Ange though. So far this lady had impressed me even more than Wild Bill. I wondered if she had the same reputation as her brother in the underground community though.

"Stige, I wonder if you've heard of Wild Bill in your hacker forums?" It seemed like a decent enough approach to see how everyone would get along. Maybe I could get some praise for Bill to make Ange feel better, or impress Stige with the "Net-cred" of his new visitor.

His reply was everything I hoped for. "Wooly Bully? The Wild Bill that cracks into federal databases for fun? Oh yes, we've chatted a couple of times, always through several layers of buffer and security though. Lole."

He actually articulated that last word. LOL for laugh out loud had apparently evolved to replace the actual act of laughing out loud. That almost made him more droll than troll. He didn't require any translation for the current company though. Nev Ange caught on instantly.

She tossed him a winning smile. "Why that's sweet of you to say. My baby brother has come along way since I taught him how to build his own system. He's not half bad these days. I hear he got some nice toys from Uncle Sam that made him even better. These days he hardly ever has to call me for help with security or a build question."

I saw Stige's eyes widen at either her expertise or the sheer braggadocio involved with her claim. She just smiled back and gushed some more southern sweetness. "I declare, when he was in Junior High and a few years after, I was worried the boy was a touch addled. But he came along pretty nicely."

I decided maybe it was time to balance that scale a little. "Stige, this is Nev Ange Wooly and her friend Bobbi Lee. I have yet to decide which scares me more. Ange's brains, or Bobbi's driving. Ladies, this is Stige Landson. He's as good as Wild Bill in a different manner, and he's a troll."

Bobbi Lee laughed again while a light of dawning comprehension began to spread itself across Ange's face. "Right, one of them internet trolls. I didn't know there was a career in that. Though the whole living in a basement sure fits."

"On the internet or in the dark of night either one." Stige's voice was amused as he finally removed the patch-work cloak and homeless rags. The anachronistic LED lights in the anteroom we had just entered revealed a muscular man of only medium height but with arms better suited to someone a foot taller. Despite that oddity, his features were appealing in a rough-hewn kind of way. It was only when he smiled to reveal the shark's teeth that all the other little differences kind of focused themselves.

As I said, he was kind of attractive. Picture an ageless Sylvester Stallone with blond locks. Now replace that mouth with a few dozen serrated teeth. Put pointed ears under the surfer boy locks, and make the fingers long even for those disproportionate arms. And make it look like maybe each finger had an extra joint somehow that made them even more articulate than your best piano player or artist.

Sly didn't quite look like he was carved out of oak and granite, but the resemblance was close enough to Stige's appearance in the artificial lighting. I saw Bobbi's eyes linger appreciatively over the broad shoulders. Ange, however, took in the whole picture.

I saw her hand dip down below the side arm of her wheelchair. It was likely that she had a grasp on one weapon or another. I caught her attention with a firm shake of the head and was relieved when the offending hand rose to grip the chair again.

Her voice didn't show much of that reaction though. "In the night huh? So is it true about sunlight and trolls? And that means Magnus wasn't joking about your uncle either doesn't it?"

Stige flashed those shark teeth again. "Uncle Kelbad had a great weakness. In fact, it is what led to the first meeting between my clan and...him." He hitched a thumb in my direction while the smile contorted itself into a grimace.

I suppose a similar expression was on my face. I don't have all of the memories of my time in Valhalla or some of the missions between. Kara and Odin are the most probable culprits behind some magical holes I'd found within my head. Both, Valkyries and the monocular menace have a tradition of enchantment and mind-muddling. The mission in which I'd had to divert a slavering mob onto the trolls was still in there though.

At the time it had seemed clever, after all, the mob was only slavering because someone had started preying on them like sheep. It seemed like a trollish thing to do, and I couldn't risk my mission or our warriors being revealed by the rampaging mortals. I left a trail of breadcrumbs so to speak that led right to the troll lair under an old cathedral. I doubt whether any magic could wipe the smell of burning flesh and the screams of the dying. Even trolls die hard and ugly if you pay attention. Especially the younger ones.

While I was still wallowing in guilt, Stige mastered his emotions and brought out the disquieting carnivorous smile again. "The sunlight thing is, let's just call it situational. Sometimes it works and sometimes it doesn't. But it is generally poor taste to bring it up in polite situations. Much like asking if there is anything that you are dangerously allergic to while in the middle of meal preparation."

Her question had caught me by surprise and I tensed up for possible repercussions. The troll had responded with a remarkable amount of restraint though. I had to wonder how much of that was due to his offer of hospitality, and how much of it was due to his respect for Bill and curiosity about the girl and her lofty claims.

I spared a glance for Bobbi at the same moment Ange did. We both saw the same thing. She'd gotten around to seeing more than broad shoulders and beefy biceps. The country girl had wandered into the twilight zone and wasn't adjusting as well as her buddy. She simply gaped for the length of the previous exchange. When she did finally find her tongue, the tone was one of disbelief. "Ange, are you seeing what I am? Cause if you are then I'm gonna need to hear that this is a case of some really good special effects makeup."

Ange made sure her voice was quiet and unprovoking. "It's okay Bobbi Lee, I don't think he's going to hurt us. At least not right now. So don't get twitchy okay? We're going to talk to him and see if he can help out. If you want, you can go back to the bike. You'll be safe out there right?"

Bobbi absentmindedly reached up to scratch her head. It seemed likely that she wasn't even aware of the semi-automatic pistol that had materialized in her hand and was scraping at her temple. "You mean this is real? I thought hobgoblins and bugaboos were just stories made up by grandmas to hush up little annoying toddlers. How can you be so calm about this?"

Ange tossed a look at both of us male types over a shoulder. That annoyed glare told us we should give them some room. There wasn't a lot of room for such a concept within the small anteroom so Stige inclined his head towards the next carefully crafted door in its stone frame. "As much as I hate the thought, this would be easier if I offer you hospitality as well. Do you promise to do me no harm or betray me within my home?"

I was almost too stunned to reply. After the shock wore off, I found my voice. "I promise I intend no harm to you or yours through this visit."

The weight of the promise settled on my shoulders with an unavoidable firmness. Promises are like that for some of us. It's bad enough when we make such a deal with a normal person from the current time. The effects can be much worse when a bargain or promise is exchanged between two creatures of a different time and ties that are much less "natural" than most people ever experience.

It was a double-edged sword now. If I broke my word, bad things were all but inevitable. Anything from losing part of my non-human abilities to losing control of my senses or even my mental well being. The same could befall Stige if he broke the rules of hospitality. Even worse, if word of a broken oath got out in the alt-natural community, then the offender could no longer make a bargain or even travel in safety since we would be fair game to a number of creatures who take notice of such things.

Stige shuddered in tandem with my own reaction and then blinked to shrug it off. "Let us go inside so the ladies may speak. I will start tea while you decide how to address the dire circumstances that brought you to my door. For I can think of nothing less than dire, that would make you dare show your face at the seat of my power and security."

The last sentence, spoken over his shoulder, was followed by almost inaudible murmurings and flashes of magick that were strong enough that even my very simple skill with runes responded with a tingle of identification. Maybe tingle isn't the right word. The magick he used was strong enough to make my teeth vibrate. Whatever his stone and oak defenses were, they were bolstered by magick that would beggar anything I had personally seen outside of a Valkyrie's company or in Valhalla itself.

We passed into a decent-sized living area. There was a feeling of pressure in the place. At first, I thought it was more magick. Then I realized, it was nothing more than the subconscious awareness that the earth surrounded us completely and pressed down from above.

I'm not necessarily claustrophobic. But I had a hard time with the thought of living down in this hole without any sunlight to brighten my windows or the knowledge that the whole wide world was outside just a few inches away past thin modern walls. Down here, there might be a foot of earth above us or we might be several yards below the surface, it was hard to tell in tunnels with gentle slopes.

Stige motioned me over to a table that would hold perhaps a dozen folk even if they were as broad across as the troll or I. For an uncomfortable few minutes, my host attended to making tea and setting out snacks and such. For my part, I tried to remain silent and hopefully inoffensive.

Inoffensive is a complex concept. For some, remaining silent means respect. Others can take silence as a form of snobbery or even outright rejection. Fortunately, this time, Stige seemed no more inclined to converse than I did. He set places for four. I suppose it would only be polite to include Bobbi just in case she decided to rejoin us. Or maybe he had a touch of foresight because Bobbi Lee followed Ange through the door after just a few minutes for their own conversation.

"We want to thank you for your invitation." It seemed that Ange was going to talk for both of them. Bobbi kept her lips sealed and nodded in time with her friend's speech.

Ange didn't waste any time once she started talking either. "I am sure we can all use a cup of tea. Sandwiches and such are unnecessary and I would hate for you to trouble yourself. To be honest, we're on a bit of a schedule. So let's get down to it. I don't know why, but Magnus seems to think you can help me with a hardware problem."

While Ange was speaking, the troll served tea all the way around. When she got around to mentioning her hardware problem, he lifted a thick eyebrow and rolled his hand at her to continue. Oddly enough, he also ignored her directions about snacks and pastries. He set a couple of sandwiches in front of me and a platter of cookies and danishes in the middle of the table for everyone to serve themselves.

I wasn't arguing with his initiative. The smell of roasted turkey and cheese on the rustic artisan bread had latched onto my stomach with a vengeance. I grabbed one and started in on it even as Ange continued. "I'm gonna be upfront here. I don't know anybody anywhere who can come up with what I need. Not without a week or two of preparation time."

She took a deep breath and started spitting out words in a language I was only vaguely familiar with. I like computers and devices but anything much past Wikipedia and the fringe of the dark web is well beyond my comprehension. Nev Ange was obviously fluent in nerd speak. "I need a portable computer, probably in an older laptop case with state of the art power to accommodate cooling needs. It has to be capable of cooling a system protected by AES 256 encryption. I handmade my own system with internal pressurized coolant and multiple fans as well as a computer desk that was really just a phase change cooling unit. I could achieve 512-bit encryption on that without frying it, but we don't have time or space for a phase change cooler, do we? It also allowed me to overclock the system to speeds that the Department of Defense would love to achieve."

This time it was her turn to cock an eyebrow at the troll. I suppose she thought she'd stumped him. Get it? Stumped? He was a short, thick, guy who looked rough-hewn from wood, maybe even petrified wood. So...stumped? Nevermind, it was funnier in my head.

Whatever her expectations, Stige didn't fulfill them. Instead of shaking his head in denial, or staring goggle-eyed at her request he just nodded. "Nice, you humans are so creative sometimes! Let's look at what I'd suggest though."

He pushed aside a door that was disguised to look like a wardrobe. Behind it was another room. This one was as spotless as a research lab. The floors and ceiling were stone, but it was almost like one hollow cube of granite. There were no seams even between wall and ceiling. It wasn't concrete either. I took the time to look at one corner with my nose almost on the cold stone. It was seamless and perfect. Maybe the troll was better with stone than even I had guessed.

If he was good with stone though, he might be shite with computers. The shelves he directed Ange to obviously did not meet her expectations or approvals. All of the systems were laptops but the cases were obviously high-tech and much thinner than the systems I'd seen her and her brother use. To Ange that must have meant they were incapable of her power and cooling needs.

"I was afraid of that." She sighed her disappointment. "I need something though so we'll take the best you can offer. I'll just have to use some less reliable security."

Stige answered her with a good-natured belly laugh. "Miss, do you have a memory stick or portable drive with your encryption software?"

Ange nodded and dug out a slim case with a USB cord attached. "Yes, it's right here. Also an innovation of mine. Quite a bit better than most solid-state drives you can get on the market. But the software would fry such a small system within minutes."

Once more Stige laughed and gestured her to choose. "Pick any of them. Some have LED accents and other upgrades, just tell me which one suits you. If it burns up then that is my fault no? Let's just give it a try though."

At the same time, he very gently took her hard drive and unwound the cord. Ange shrugged and pointed to a slim case in a matte black finish. It seemed to absorb light and was, in fact, one I'd hardly noticed amongst the others.

Stige seemed surprised by her choice. "That one? Interesting. Most people do not see past the glamour. Let us hook it up though."

That made sense on one level and was confusing on another. How had Ange seen through a spell that befuddled me? Was she a practitioner as well? And if so, why hadn't I sensed it?

I watched as keenly as the lady did while the troll powered up the system with the portable drive plugged into an external power source as well as the laptop. I immediately decided my own desktop computer was obsolete. When I hit the power button on my pc, the screen stays black for long seconds or even minutes.

This one came on immediately and almost inaudibly whirred to life while a bar on the screen informed us it had identified the connected device and initiated a download. I watched the loading bar race across the screen while Ange's eyebrows raced towards her hairline. The entire loading bar filled in just under a minute.

A second later a pair of figures appeared on the screen. One was the popular image of a ninja in a black mask and outfit. The other was a knight in full plate armor with a gleaming heater shield held protectively in front of him. Under them respectively were the words, stealth mode, and defense.

The hushed tone of Ange's words did not go with the earthy string of profanities and amazement. "Mother Mary, and Hay-sus fuckin H. How the hell did you do that crap? I don't barely even hear the fans or power supply and this downloaded faster than my own computer."

She turned to glare at the troll as if he was responsible for some truly evil shenanigans. "That is inherently impossible. USB 3.1 maxes out at around 10 gigs per second. Mine is tinkered up to 15 gigs and I've never seen anyone match it. So how did your system get info out of my disk quicker than the disk is capable of delivering it?"

By the end of her statement, the computer hacker was bent low over the system with her nose practically in the various ports and docks visible along its slim frame. She raised astonished eyes to the smugly grinning troll. "You want to explain?"

She also caressed the case with a possessive and appreciative reflex. I was pretty sure it would take more might than Stige had to separate her from this new toy with her own brainchild already installed.

He didn't try. Instead, he beckoned her over to a case that was open and obviously only half constructed. "Easy, I used magick."

At her renewed glare he just chuckled and waved a condescending hand. "You genius humans are so funny about things like a consistent flow of the timeline. Even that German with the bad hair found it a difficult concept that time can be a mutable variant in certain situations."

At that, Bobbi Lee in the doorway let out a strangled giggle and then backed away to go back to her tea and cookies. We had obviously gone well outside her own comfort zone. The surprising thing was that Ange did not even blink at the statement. She just waited for more.

Stige obliged. "I did most of the work myself. Some of the parts I contracted out though. A small branch of dwarvenkind has ventured from traditional smithing to more...modern concepts. There are also some bits and pieces I had to trade from Svart Elves. The big innovation was in the heatsink."

He moved a couple of wires and pointed at some random piece of laptop anatomy. "Rather than a bunch of big and noisy fans, I put in a diamond matrix the dwarves carved for me connected to an Ice Core powered by runic magic. It's at least as cool as a liquid nitrogen bath but fits right there as you can see. Don't touch it though. Breaking the containment around it would be...bad. I'd guess the components are as effective as when I first built it. The point is, it's smaller, quieter, and it will not lose efficiency over time as any mundane system must. The magick will not degenerate. It would destroy a normal chip with the energy involved. However, Svart Elves make very good components that are innately resistant to most detrimental magick."

Nev Ange Wooly never batted an eye. Instead, she stroked the laptop and if I weren't mistaken, she actually purred at it before speaking over her shoulder to Stige. "I'll take it."

An instant later she seemed to rethink the possible terms of such a transaction. "Um, this ain't gonna cost me my soul or anything is it? Or make me deliver people up to barbecue at your next family reunion?"

That earned a hearty laugh. "No miss, I gave up on man-flesh quite some time ago. Too often it brings attention and misery in its wake. Since I am guessing you have no excess of gold with you, we might work out a trade, a favor for a favor, or I can accept most major credit cards."

I could see her mulling over the "trade" and "favor" concepts with commendable caution. Trolls and other creatures from that side of town tend to make very good bargains. They're usually good for them and bad for the other side. Something about that thought made me stop and review the entire exchange since Stige and I had stopped fighting.

Something was wrong there. My instincts had proven right far too often for me to ignore the sudden uneasiness that I felt. What deals had we made? Or maybe there was something about the current deal that rang a subconscious alarm.

Ange didn't hear the alarms. If anything she seemed relieved about the credit card option. "Okay, so what kind of credit limit do I need for this purchase? I've got some decent cards but I'm no secret billionaire."

Stige grinned again. "Well, I was hoping for some stolen credit card information. But we can probably make a deal anyway. I'll charge you for the physical components. As for magick, if you're really as good as Wooly, then we might work out a trade. I'll make you a gift of the system, and you owe me a favor. Every once in a while I meet security I can't crack or find some unwanted snoops that just won't go away."

Before she could reject the idea outrightly, the toll lifted a gnarled hand with those odd extra-jointed fingers. "Hear me out. You don't have to accept any of them. You choose. If you have not helped me with any such requests in say, five years, then you owe me five times the already high price I am about to ask just for components. Take it or leave it."

I could tell that she wanted to think it over. Such a deal sounded simple on the surface. On the other hand, for all she knew, he might pit her against creatures even worse than man-eating primal beasts from legend. I didn't know if she believed in demons and devils or angels and old gods, but I could personally assure her that some of the above were very real.

Well, they were real unless I was completely cuckoo for cocoa. Hel, if my most recent experiences were any basis, then the world was even crazier than I had believed. And I believed I was a centuries-old chosen warrior with a vengeful Valkyrie on his tail.

The vengeful thought is what triggered my sudden apprehension and refocused my thoughts on deals made. That was also when Stige sprung his trap. "Whatever you decide, you and the lovely lady at my table are free to go at your leisure."

We both noticed that my name was not included in that statement. Ange tossed me a questioning glance as my own anger began to build. I let the rage stoke itself and prepared to throw down with a vengeance. Fortunately, my promise had been made in such a manner as to make Stige forego his own precautions, like disarming me.

I reached for the rune-enhanced combat blade sheathed along my belt in back. No sooner had my hand gripped the hilt than a faint sizzle could be heard along with the scent of burnt meat. I jerked my hand around to stare at the red and blistering fingertips.

Stige just smirked and showed me the full array of his shark's teeth. "No, no, now Magnus. You promised me no harm for your entire visit remember? And you did it surrounded by my own power within my own wards. You can't think to just break such an oath at any old whim can you?"

I itched to go for the knife again with its runic surprises and silver oxide blade. That had been a surprise I managed with the help of Bobbi Lee's extensive first aid collection. Among many other items, I'd found a few vials of powdered silver that could be used in conjunction with various other compounds and ointments for a variety of purposes. For me, it had been an easy choice to adhere to the blade she'd given me. It had taken some time and liberal use of Kenaz, or the fire rune, but I'd more or less heat forged the silver along the blade without losing its temper or edge.

I wasn't positive what effect it would have, but silver was

just as widely feared as cold iron in certain circles. If I couldn't even hold the blade though, no runes, cold iron, silver, or even a blessing of the white Christ himself, would do me any good. But I wasn't sure what the problem was.

"Okay so I promised no harm for the visit but you promised old-world hospitality. If you break your word then how can my own oath hold?" I was confused and royally pissed at the implication that he was not allowing me safe passage as he was the girls.

"Oh but I am not breaking my oath, Magnus." He almost spat the name at me before continuing. "I offered the girls hospitality for twenty-four hours and required their pledge for the same amount of time. My offer to you made no mention of a time limit, nor did your oath of nonaggression."

Yea, I knew my instinct was trying to get my attention over something pretty important.

10

STIGE WAS GRINNING at me with a mix of hate and joy at having outsmarted his longtime foe. For my part, I'm pretty sure the snarl on my face had plenty of hate but none of the joy. I was about ready to risk burning the fingers completely off my hand if it meant I could pull that blade and take this miserable piece of dirt and dung out of existence.

Ange reached a restraining hand across to grip my own in her warm fingers. "Hang on, big guy. Let's talk this out before you go to gettin' all impetuous. Why don't we meander out to talk this over? Bobbi ought to be about settled down now. This is all just real new to her."

Ange's voice was calm and soothing as she put my hands on her wheelchair and made me push her out towards our waiting not-so-hot tea. Apparently, we made our way close enough to the table for the subject of that statement to overhear.

At least she didn't sound as stressed as she had when we first came down. "Real new ain't the right words for it hun. But I need to know why you ain't freakin out right along with me. I mean, you used to lose your shit if the road was too bumpy or the freaking sand reminded you of Afghanistan. How are you dealing with something out of the brother's Grimm living in a cave and trying to trash your mercenary bud?"

Ange motioned for me to push her closer to her friend. Once they were side by side at the table, she locked her fingers with Bobbi. "Why don't we see if our host has some-thing stronger than tea, that is still safe for you and I, right?"

She shot her previous question at Stige with calculating look for me. "We are still under his promise of safe passage until tomorrow aren't we, Magnus?"

I nodded as did the troll. He produced different cups. These were taller, handmade from clay and were delicately shaped to resemble fantastic creatures that would have been appropriate in Narnia or classic works from Tolkien.

Besides the cups, he placed a platter of cheeses and fruits along with more of the rustic bread. Lastly, came a couple of decanters. "The deep red is mushroom wine. It has been known to be both soporific and hallucinogenic for humans so beware. The white is a simple dandelion wine. There is also brandy or a single-malt whiskey I trade from the dwarves." The last two beverages were produced in ornate silver flasks about the size of a large canteen.

Ange very thoughtfully poured herself a modest glass of the white wine. For Bobbi, she rationed out a good double jigger of brandy and regretfully declined the potential drowsiness of the mushroom wine. I imagine she was just as reluctant as I was to see what even a mild hallucinogenic would do to Bobbi's anxiety. The fact that she was probably heavily armed just made any chance of a bad acid trip less appealing.

Bobbi squeezed the hand she was offered gratefully and then downed the oversized brandy in a quick convulsive gulp.

That seemed to settle her down enough for Ange. "Bobbi hun, you remember my hallucinations and the visions and anxiety I used to experience along with my PTSD?"

At Ange's words, her friend glanced at us guiltily. I suppose she was blaming herself for the revelation of her friend's troubled past.

"Don't worry about it, hun. I had some issues and I'm not particularly ashamed of them. But what you don't know, is that it wasn't all in my head."

She nodded reassuringly at Bobbi's widened eyes. "No ma'am I ain't kidding. While I was at that school on the veterans dime?" She made a question of the last as if asking Bobbi if she remembered.

"Well, something from back in Afghanistan showed up for a little payback. Blamed us for everything from assault to religious grievances, sought out all the survivors and killed em. I was the last. Long story short is; the evil genie critter underestimated me and my friends. It got sent to wherever they go in the afterlife and I got rid of a ton of that anxiety and self-doubt. It's probably what made me pretty damned functional in normal society and my new little career niche."

Maybe it was the brandy or the sincerity in her friend's voice, or maybe it all just slipped into overload and Bobbi's brain decided to deal with it later. She blinked once or twice, poured another hefty dollop of brandy and slugged it down, then cleared her throat.

"Alright, fair enough. For now...So what's the next step?"

The brandy or pent up emotion made her voice a little rough, but the combat experience and training seemed ready to exert themselves as she adapted to the situation.

Ange's next statement might have come close to derailing that remarkable adaptation. "Well, we have us a situation. The troll seems to have Magnus by the short and curlies. They made a deal that lets our "*host*" here keep short and wide over there under lock and key indefinitely. We're free to go. But if I want to take this little beauty of a laptop with us I have to make my own deal and hope he doesn't have any nasty surprises in the fine print."

Bobbi Lee's potential derailment never occurred. Instead, she focused on, let's call it the adversarial component, of Ange's statement. "So the mutant over there wants to start trouble? That's right up my alley."

Her eyes grew wide again as she reached for her own weapon, and discovered it would not come out of its holster. "What the actual..."

Stige cut her off with a shrug. "I invoked a little sympathetic magick earlier. Our deals are equally binding. I could no more harm you than you could draw or fire your weapon. Both outcomes are impossible under the limits of our agreement."

This time the heat in her glare was palpable. She probably could have heated up our lukewarm tea with some decent focus. She let go of the weapon though and drummed her agitation out with fingertips on the tabletop.

Everyone sat silently for several long breaths, at which point Stige sighed and said a word in Old French, I think it meant "Open Oilseed" or at least something close to that. Apparently, it was the verbal command to open another set of hidden doors on the wall across from his hearth table.

Inside those secret doors was a bank of monitors attached to cameras with a panoramic view all around the building above us.

"You may stay if you wish. I would not be here when that arrives though." He pointed to the dark line of clouds far off across the gulf. Those clouds seemed particularly dark and flashed with a constant barrage of lightning. It looked like the kind of storm that spawned skull smashing hail, city-leveling tornadoes, and enough lightning strikes to depopulate a small third world country.

He gestured to a different camera and we saw a few of the local urchins loitering around the motorcycle outside. They weren't necessarily close enough to warrant a reaction. But they were close enough to be wary of when anyone went back out to the bike.

As we watched, Stige spoke again in a whispery tone. One of the "kids" tossed back his hood and turned to face the camera with darkly red glowing eyes and razor teeth showing through a misshapen grin. The raggedly uneven tops of his ears were both pointed and tufted. A flash of lightning in the distance gave me the distinct impression that the face we were looking at was a black so deep as to appear almost purple.

Stige helped me with that identifying feature immediately."Dokkalfar. Less civilized and much nastier cousins of the Svart elves. For the next twenty-four hours, you are safe from them, unless you leave my home with trouble in your thoughts. They will sense such duplicity and it will release them to sate their, darker, appetites."

Both girls stared at the monitors with varying degrees of disbelief and anger. Maybe there was some fear in there too. If so it was well hidden. I thought I saw those seeds of anger grow into a resolve that made me want to cheer and warm them away at the same time. Unless I missed my guess, the ladies were getting ready to fight this battle for me.

While it was a heartwarming thought, it was not one I was comfortable with. It was my own stupidity that got me in this mess. I didn't need Ange or Bobbi either one to suffer from that lack of thought on my part.

"Hang on ladies." This time it was my turn to advise patience and diplomacy. Somehow that didn't bode well for us. I'm not really accustomed to the role of diplomat. I'm more of a "diplomacy through subdual hold" kind of guy. "Stige, I doubt you want to feed me and wait around while I figure out a loophole or someone comes looking. So that means you have a plan or at least a new deal in mind. So spill."

Okay so maybe it wasn't diplomacy so much as desperate dickering. It kept anyone from getting shot or incinerated by bad troll joojoo though.

Stige paused to give me a considering look. "Maybe you are not as stupid as I believed. Of course, I don't want you in my home any longer than necessary. I could, however, torment you enough to break your promise and let me exact most satisfying revenge, followed by a highly unusual feast and one I've denied myself for quite some time. Long pig can be so tasty."

He bared those teeth at me again. That particular ploy was fast losing its effect though. "Yeah, yeah, you're gonna torture me, kill me, eat me, and shit me out in the ocean. I got it the first time. So let's skip the threats and posturing. What's this about and what's the plan?"

Stige actually pouted his disappointment at my reaction. If you've never seen a roughly carved piece of petrified wood with serrated teeth pout, well I can assure you it's disturbing. He eventually broke down and offered an explanation though. "Very well, I have two main options for consideration. The first is, I could hold you for leverage with some people who have been causing problems and snooping around. For the last few days, a number of "personnel" from your neighborhood have been around town. They have also been rather *abrupt* with some of my community."

By "his community" I took Stige to mean members of the alt-natural group. Call them Fay, spirits, sprites, or supernatural beings. I've even heard that the new term is cryptids and encompasses everything from the Sidhe fairies to an Abominable snowman, or Nessie. And by abrupt, it sounded like someone from the neighborhood of Valhalla was playing rough.

I hazarded a look at the two women, they were oddly content to remain silent for the moment. In fact, they seemed fascinated by the speech our host was making. I did notice that they seemed to communicate with a series of minuscule shrugs and other gestures as well as a sparse few silently mouthed words and phrases. I didn't catch any of the meaning though. I was probably too chromosomally challenged to interpret their fem-speak.

"Okay, so there are people from my past causing trouble. How does catching me help? Are you planning to sell me to them?" I kept my tone even despite the fact that I was considering a surprise or two of my own. I wouldn't better my position by waiting for someone to sell me out to "my kind". That almost had to mean that Kara was out looking for me.

The presence of that ominous line of storms heading straight for us suddenly took on new meaning. In my shrouded memories, I faintly recalled arriving on a battle-field amidst just such conditions. Kara would be waiting, with the rain and lightning making her look like a shining purple-black vision of retribution.

Those flickers of light would writhe up and down her dark spear while she held it atop her steed and then pointed forward for us to attack. I even seemed to recall bolts of violet energy, eye-searing strikes of lightning so intense that they left serpentine after-images on one's eyes.

"Wait, you said...My kind." My voice sounded raw even to me. "A wolf-maiden? In shimmering mail with a dark ominous spear."

I felt all three pairs of eyes lock onto me with a hint of confusion. The girls seemed completely bewildered by my reaction. Stige just looked confused. "No, one of *your kind*, a warrior, in a leather jacket and dark turtleneck. The guy looked dark with curly hair, maybe even Latin."

That eased a knot of tension in my back, and neck, and shoulders, spine, groin, toes. Hel even my hair follicles had bunched up at the thought of Kara hot on my trail while I was incarcerated by a tricky troll. I was consoled by a different thought. The description fit the only other Einherjar I'd run across in quite some time.

If Luis was here, then I could bet that his Valkyrie Heather was as well. He was her only Chosen, and I had never seen them apart. If her appetites were anything like Kara's, then I had to imagine the reason Luis spoke so rarely is that he was too exhausted to muster the energy for speech. Let's just say that Kara had no problem keeping up with a dozen of her favorite warriors on any given week.

As if my previous thought about Luis had been a summons, I saw an indistinct silhouette detach itself from shadows down the street. Even walking down the middle of the sidewalk he was just so, average, that it was hard to take notice. Luis was of average height, average build, with medium brown hair atop an unremarkable face. In short, there was nothing about the guy that screamed: "Nigh unstoppable immortal warrior Chosen by Valkyrie."

Then again I'd seen him stopped. In all fairness, it had taken a handful of similarly sacred jaguar warriors on their home stomping grounds. They'd stopped him though and only the intervention of his Valkyrie handler had saved him from ending up right back in Valhalla at a most inopportune moment.

Which brought up a new question. If Luis was walking down the street by himself, where was Heather? It looked like I might get the answer to that question myself. Luis walked right up to the door and banged authoritatively on the brass knocker.

I hope Stige was perplexed by my lack of concern. The plain wrapper gunman and I weren't exactly at odds though. He was probably the only einherjar that I wouldn't automatically hide from. As far as I was concerned, we both owed each other respect or maybe even a favor or two, like life-saving kinds of favors.

I pointed him out on the screen. "That the guy you talked to who was looking for me?"

Stige squinted at the screen and shrugged. "Could be. The hair is right, and the clothes. I can't tell for sure though."

When I shook my head in disbelief, the troll got almost defensive. "Hey, what can I say? You guys all look the same to me. Smug, self-satisfied, and offensively sure of yourselves. Hair color and stuff like that doesn't make much of a difference. You're all the same, like the guy that got half my family burned as demons in Paris."

We'd hashed this over before. It usually led to another session of mutually attempted dismemberment. For once, I was ready to offer an olive branch. "Stige, I am sorry for your losses that day. I could point to official excuses, that my Valkyrie would have ordered it, that your uncle brought it on you, or that it was just a job. I don't expect forgiveness for my actions. But I think you should know, I stayed and watched in horror as they torched the building above your folk. I am just glad some of you got away."

We stood there staring in uncomfortable silence until the demanding knock came again. Stige cleared his throat, "Well, we can talk about that another time. For now, I better let your brethren in before he summons more help and we have a repeat arsonist style assault."

As he passed me, I saw him stop and fiddle with another cabinet which swung back to reveal a bolt hole. He cleared his throat again and spoke over a shoulder. "That's for me in case I have to make a run for it. I'm not offering you people any escape there. If you got away I'd be very vexed. I might even make a post-it to come looking for you in a century or two. Always losing those post-its though."

The last sentence was barely a rumble as he passed out of sight. I took the opportunity to gesture at the escape tunnel. "You girls might want to make a run for it. I don't know what's going on here. And I think maybe I can get some answers. If you want to run though, there's the path. I can meet you at the bike or call you later with an update."

The truth is, I was torn. Part of me wanted us all to stick together for mutual protection. But another part of me wanted to get out and hunt some people down for an old fashioned whuppin'. And then there was the third little voice that thought just maybe the ladies would be targeted less if I wasn't part of the equation.

Ange looked at the secret door consideringly. Bobbi Lee just stood and waited to follow Ange's lead. Finally, the tough and resourceful lady in the wheelchair must have come to a conclusion. She reached over and nudged the secret door shut within an inch or so of latching.

"I think we'll stick around a minute. I'd rather get the information from the horse's mouth so to speak. Who knows what might get lost in translation on its way through that thick skull of yours." Her smile took away most of the sting. The fact that even I considered some of my actions boneheaded took away most of the rest.

I appreciated her gesture but didn't get a chance to tell her. She didn't stop talking long enough since she seemed to have questions of her own.

"Besides, maybe you can answer some questions for us. Like what exactly is your kind? And why would you get all lily-livered and pasty colored at the thought of some bimbo in cosplay clothes with a spear? Or even more intriguing...care to explain what and how you were in France at a time period when villagers would form up with pitchforks and torches? Don't try and tell me it was just a phrase either. I was paying attention to both of you."

A new voice joined us in time to save me from answering any of those questions. Luis stood in the doorway with a very sleek little semi-automatic pistol in his fist while he deliberated. "Well Strombjorn, do we answer their questions and shoot them? Or let them go without any of those intriguing answers in their grasp?"

I felt my shoulders slump along with the sigh that erupted. Strombjorn, that was a name I'd forgotten until just recently. It was also another link in the chain or at least a brand new question for these women to use in pestering me.

I could all but hear their heads cranking around to eye both of us speculatively.

It didn't seem worth looking for confirmation. The threat from our newest arrival didn't seem to worry them though. I'm betting I was the only one who didn't take his question as anything other than a joke. But I learned a little about Luis the last time we met. It didn't seem out all out of line for him to be light and bantering while planning which head would receive the first bullet.

I addressed him first. "I need them, Luis. So let's not start shooting holes in each other. Besides, I'm not sure. They might send you to Valhalla before you could get the job done."

Luis was a thoughtful enough Einherjar to actually think that exchange through. That meant he was young as chosen warriors go. Odin hadn't meddled with his head too much, yet. I don't know if his Valkyrie would change and start wiping his mind anytime soon either. She was young for Valkyrie just like he was young for being semi-immortal. From the lady's conversational stylings, I was guessing they'd been chosen for the job in the eighties. Heather was fluent in Valley Girl.

That thoughtful streak of his was what I was counting on at the moment. I was hoping he'd paid close attention to the part where I'd said he'd get that job done. Him, not we or us. In other words, he didn't need to count on me chipping in during the firefight. In fact, knowing that he would just wake up back in Valhalla, I'm pretty sure I would be actively engaging from the other side of that conflict.

It turned out that I was not the only one with those inclinations. A low rumbling voice boiled out of the small entry chamber behind him. "I would take it amiss if you were to attack my guests Einherjar. They are under the protection of my hospitality. If you were to become hostile then I would be sure you did not leave this demesne in the current century. The door is closed, so to speak. You are surrounded by nigh unbreakable trollstone layered with enchantments. Test them, and test me, at your peril."

11

IT NEVER BECAME apparent whether Luis had meant the threat or was simply joking. He made his pistol disappear under the leather jacket and spread his open hands to show himself disarmed. "Of course master Troll. I would not abuse your honor or hospitality."

The trim little "chosen" turned back to me with an exaggerated exhalation. "As if this wasn't shit show enough. Do you care to tell me what Kara is so interested in around this city?"

I felt the air leave my lungs at the same time a bundle of energy left my middle. "Oh Hel, is that what you were asking Stige about the last time you were here? Kara's in New Orleans?"

I was prepared for snark or deception. I was even prepared for a little spontaneous violence. I may not have mentioned it, but being an Einherjar isn't like being in a social club. We're more like the fraternal order of homicidal assholes. It probably comes from all of those countless entertaining days where we try and kill each other only to wake up for a feast sometime after "death".

What I was not prepared for was the blank look on his face. "What last time? I've never seen this troll before today. We got his location from G...from another Valkyrie. She said he was as likely to have the relevant news as anyone else in the area."

I was pretty sure he'd been enunciating Gon as in Gondul before he caught himself. I remembered her fairly well. Gondul was one of the few Valkyrie with a reputation as old and respected as Kara. She wasn't feared like Kara, because Gondul wasn't as psychotic as my own handler had been. But she was definitely respected for her age and power as well as a certain insane wisdom.

That wasn't as important as Stige's reaction and next word though. He gestured at Luis and tilted his head to the side like a large, gnarled and dangerous dog. "This is not the chosen warrior I spoke with before." Luis and I both jerked straight upright as if red hot poles had been shot through our spines.

My question was first. "There's another one?"

Luis followed right on the heels of my query with his own. "Someone else has already been here?"

Before Stige could answer, Luis had his cell phone out and was texting away. He stopped after only a few clicks. "*Mierda*, I got no signal."

Stige spread his hands in way of explanation and then pointed all around us. "Trollstone. I locked the enchantments once you were in. No signal will pass this except one of my own devices. Give me a minute to disarm the wards."

Luis was already showing agitation. By the time the troll was headed for the entryway, the little gunman was right behind him. I called after him while gesturing for the girls to get into the escape tunnel. "What's going on Luis? Why the sudden panic?"

I was lucky the girls were fast into the tunnel. Luis appeared back in the doorway with his teeth clenched in a snarl and his gun clenched in a fist. The gun was pointed directly at my left eye. "The panic is because my lady is out there waiting to be ambushed. And I am locked down here with Kara's secret psychotic hitman who has been something of a mystery for half a century. If anything happens to Heather, I'm going to do my best to make sure you die without a return ticket to Valhalla. It might take a while, but I'll find someone who knows how. So why don't we go out together, you and your…"

For the first time, Luis seemed to notice the women were gone. "Call them and let's get out of here. You're going out with me to call off whatever trap you set up."

I tried to spread my hands as convincingly as he had to prove my disarmed innocence. "The girls are hiding. You scared them with that talk of killing. I'll go with you though. We better hurry if you want to surprise any ambushers."

I didn't bother trying to convince him that I wasn't orchestrating anything. In his current state, he would never believe me. And if he was right, if there was an ambush waiting, then I'd have yet another spontaneous grudge-match death-cage fight when I didn't have time for all of this. For all I knew somebody was taking a blowtorch to Maureen's toes or maybe the professor was having his game knee worked over.

Luis didn't bother disarming me. I don't know whether it was a sign of trust or just a clear indicator of his agitation. I took the opportunity to free up the pistol behind my belt and hold it down alongside my leg as we exited Stige's tunnel.

It was still something of a question in my mind whether the troll was bluffing or could actually lock us away undetectably and with no chance of escape. The speed with which he "unlocked" the wards and front door argued against any complicated spellcraft. We were up in the yard scanning for trouble within a minute of Luis' first panicked reaction.

Trouble was easy. We followed the sounds of gunfire that erupted just ahead of us. Outside, Bobbi and Ange were at the motorcycle. Bobbi was prone with a long-range rifle barely visible in the grass around her. Ange had her chair wheeled in close to the bike and was using it both as cover and rest for her hand holding a long-barreled pistol instead of the ugly shotgun.

Both of them were firing carefully aimed shots at retreating headlights ahead of us. Luis had his gun up and pointed in their direction in an instant. It was a brief instant. I chopped the gun out of his hand with my own weapon while Stige tackled him to the ground with a snarl.

Apparently, the troll had come to enjoy the ladies' company more than I had guessed. I made a note to shoot a shotgun near his face the next time he was annoyed at me. The problem was, I'm not half as photogenic or eye-appealing as the two females. What can I say? I'm supposed to be tough. Pretty is optional.

At the sound of our little tussle, both women fired another couple of shots then turned around. It was easy to see that they were both amused and annoyed by yet another bout of masculine wrestling so soon after the last incident. Nev Ange reached into the sidecar and pulled out the shotgun she'd swapped for her heavy revolver. She hefted it with a considering glance and an eyebrow arched rather suggestively in our direction.

"Nope! No need to shoot anyone." I was quick to derail that thought. Bobbi might actually have been right about

Ange's aim. I didn't need a few flechette rounds in any sensitive anatomical locations just to check out the theory.

I waved a hand to get Luis' attention. "Right Luis? No need for anyone to get shot."

I saw him at war with his emotions but a brief moment later he jerked a nod. "Right. No shooting. At least not right this minute. But somebody probably ought to tell me what the gunfire was about and where Heather is."

Bobbi casually tossed her rifle to a shoulder and kind of squinted at the question. "Heather, was she the kind of girl that wore a lot of pink and had a giant pony-tail growing out the side of her head? If so she just got grabbed by a bunch of guys with guns and a black SUV. We ran into em ourselves a while back. This time we were ready to shoot back though so they didn't stick around."

I took an urgent step forward at the news. It wasn't quite what I was expecting though. "The Men in Black SUVs and not the white van with the Polo party?"

Almost on the heels of my impetuous step and question, Stige mimicked me. "White Van with guys all dressed alike? Not those assholes. I've been meaning to look into them. Lots of rumors on the streets about them abducting people. Not alt-norms like us. Regular people. But you know how it gets. A bunch of people go missing and then authorities move in and start digging. Then you get torched and burned down buildings. Right, Magnus?"

His interest had turned into a glare for the offending van cavalry. By the end of the statement that glare had switched from a distant vision to something much closer. In fact, I was staring straight into that glare from about a good swift punch away.

We were interrupted by Nev Ange and a loud snort of derision. "Before you two, or even you three, go back to your testosterone fest, maybe we should get inside and stop being so obvious. I mean some of us are apt to draw attention and be easy to describe. And some of us have honkin big sniper rifles sticking up over our shoulders."

At the polite reminder, Bobbi almost blushed. She did get a sheepish look about her eyes and lower the firearm to cradle it less noticeably in both arms. "Inside sounds good. Might do to get out of the rain too."

Lightning illuminated us all in the growing darkness. It wasn't just night falling, but the heavy cloud cover moving in made the night even darker and heavier. A roll of thunder followed so closely in the lightning's wake that it had to be fairly close. In unison, we turned and followed Stige back into his lair.

With the previous oaths given, Luis and the girls went right in. I hesitated at the door though. "Stige we have a problem. I am not going in there with our present deal in place. Either you set a time limit, or I withdraw any promise of peaceful behavior."

He grinned that shark smile at me again. "I was hoping you forgot. But since you are not quite as stupid as you look, I grant you hospitality until nightfall tomorrow if you promise me no harmful intent within my home for the same time period."

"Done." I actually felt a grin start to stretch my mouth. That wouldn't do at all. If we started acting as if we liked each other, who knows what might happen next. Instead, I offered a deep nod of agreement. "After you master Troll."

We entered the little foyer or cloakroom I guess they're called. There we had to wait until Stige removed his wards and let us all back inside. Once inside there was the whole ritual of tea making and settling in to get past again. At least most of us settled in and settled down.

Luis, on the other hand, was a spastic mess. He knew the importance of ritual in such situations and was doing his best. The abduction of his Valkyrie had to be eating him from his core outward though. Come to think of it, I don't even know how the MIBV's could have taken her. Heather might be new to the gig, but she had some of the most intense gifts I'd ever seen in someone not as old and steeped in lore as Kara or Gondul.

She had a real talent for shifting the odds. All Valkyrie have that to a degree. Their jobs are both to choose the slain, and to help decide the course of battles. Shifting the odds is just part and parcel of that role.

Heather was unique in that she could deflect the course of a bullet in flight. Not by magical wards or shields, but by making a random bit of wind pick up a random twig and divert it into the path of the bullet at just the precise moment to alter its course. If she focused, she could even plot the course of the bullet to hit an entirely new target. I'd seen her do it. It was scary as Hel.

"Luis!" I decided to go to an expert. "I can't figure out how any mundane government spook could get the drop on Heather and take her. I mean she could make their guns jam, or the van flood out. Hell for all I know a frozen poop bomb from the crapper in an airliner could fall through the windshield at her whim."

He gave me an exasperated look and let some of that nervous energy out in his reply. "Obviously she let them take her. She is too abrupt. Sometimes I think when they chose her so young, they locked her in that level of maturity."

His scowl bespoke affection more than it did proper respect of an Einherjar for his Valkyrie handler. "Heather would let them take her so that she could find out what was going on. She thinks like you, that her luck will always get her out. But you saw that it doesn't always work. You don't think she allowed me to be gutted like a fish in Mexico just so she would have to expend all that energy healing. Healing is hard for her. It took her days to recover all of that."

Apparently, since I'd broached the topic, Luis felt free to vent some of his own frustrations and questions. He continued without letting anyone interrupt. "A bullet isn't always likely to hit her. If she's not paying attention though it can happen. I've seen her hurt before. Usually, it has to be a surprise and she has to be distracted or tired or something. So what do we know about these jerks in the black vehicles?"

"MIBV's" Nev Ange answered while I was still thinking about what to say. "We've started calling them the Men in Black Vehicles."

Bobbi Lee exchanged a chuckle with the wheelchair-bound brainiac. Ange had managed to get down on her own this time, but only after Stige opened the secret tunnel and let her back in that way.

With the chair pulled close and her elbows on the table she just looked like a healthy and kind of cute country girl just back from college. I was hoping she'd leave Luis with that impression. She didn't need the attention of people from my neighborhood. Most of us were dangerous to each other. A girl forced to struggle with a wheelchair might be even that much more vulnerable.

Ange just couldn't leave well enough alone though. She leaned forward and went into her research and report voice. "They belong to one of the national agencies. I can't uncover which one. Frankly, that's amazing. I don't think it would be this hard for me to track down a nuclear launch code. These guys had someone good doing the work on their security and the red herrings though. I've broken through a dozen false fronts."

Luis didn't seem to find that much of an answer. He posed a new question for her. "So what would a bunch of clever government spooks want with my handler? And how did they track her down?"

This time Ange had an answer. It wasn't one he liked. It wasn't even one I liked. But it answered the question. "They didn't track her down. They were looking for dipstick the naive and incompetent there."

She turned and pointed at me with a cup of tea. "So tell me, Einstein. What happened to the burner phone you were supposed to burn?"

From the alcove behind me, I heard Stige rumble. "Yes, that was his name. The funny German with the wild hair. Einstein. He wrote some really quaint things about time and energy. Some brilliant, some very naive. I waited years to talk to him but he was always being watched."

His interruption didn't last long enough for anyone to look away or forget the question I didn't answer.

Finally, I broke down. "I turned it off and stuck it in a protective sleeve I made. They couldn't have tracked it. I'd swear by my runic work. The signal was blocked."

Once more Stige interrupted. He strolled over and dug in the pocket of his hanging cloak of rags, then turned back to me. "Do you mean this phone? I found it on the ground after our little disagreement. Meant to give it back to you but forgot."

I didn't plan to add much when Ange snorted at the sight of the phone laying in his long fingers with no sign of the runed pouch I made. The right words sprang unbidden from my lips though. "Well shit."

Somewhere in the back of my head, there was a reason I still had the phone that could be traced. In fact, even as I was thinking that thought, something else was wiggling just out of reach in my subconscious. I wanted to track that thought down, but everyone else was too vocal for me to focus. Luis was all about getting his girl. I was lucky that Nev Ange was wise enough not to blurt out that we had an idea where they might take her. We still weren't sure if our own hostages were being held there. It seemed like a fair bet that any move on our part would result in retaliation against the professor, Maureen, and Wild Bill.

That didn't even factor in the new information about an unknown Einherjar in the area stirring up the locals and making the alt-norms nervous. Luis focused on that identification while I was reintroducing my phone to its signal inhibiting holster.

He sat with Stige and urged the troll to concentrate. "Okay Master Stige, you said he was dressed like me. Was he taller than me?"

Stige squinted for a minute and then in a clear voice stated. "Yes, at least a head taller. His skin was lighter. The hair was redder. Except for his beard. His beard was almost blond. Yes, now it's coming to me. He had a tattoo on his wrist, one of those funny crosses that is all off-center. A Brigid's cross yes?"

I felt a fire begin burning in my chest at the same time Luis made the identification. "Lorcan." We said it in almost the same breath and tone.

"Do you expect me to believe you didn't know your replacement as Kara's crazy killer was in town?" The smaller gunman spun to face me with rage in his eyes. At least his hands were empty of weapons, so far.

Luis probably had a right to accuse me. But then again, I

guess we'd never discussed why I hadn't been seen in Valhalla in years. He had stories and rumors to go on. Luis had been Chosen long after I was left forgotten on a battle-field in Vietnam.

He had no way of knowing that I hadn't seen Valhalla, or Kara, or any of them for decades. I'd worked very hard during those decades to avoid any possible contact with the beings who had made the einherjar what we were. Maybe some of my brothers didn't mind the manipulation, the mind-wipes, the incessant and often unexplained violence.

I like to think that I am more free-willed than that. The years of the same fighting day in and day out had palled on me. Decades and even centuries of time lost to mind-fogs and long sleep was no way to exist. I'd say it was no way to live, but by definition, we were all dead anyway.

"Believe it or not buddy, I had no idea. I haven't seen Kara or Lorcan in years and don't care if I never do again. I don't think I've caught a whiff of any of her chosen since she left my dumb ass for dead in Vietnam."

What the Hel? Things were so far out of my control at this point that I was tired of trying to remember who I was hiding which facts from. Luis was sharper than a lot of us though. I saw his eyes widen and he whistled sharp and low under his breath. "Sangre de Cristo, that's why she's here. Kara's looking for you. That's why she never talks about you and just lets everyone think you're off on secret missions. She doesn't want anyone to know she lost you."

I guess that makes him sharper than me even. I had never considered that Kara would be so embarrassed that she kept my escape a secret.

Hel, I've been paranoid about way too many people for way too many years. Odin had no reason to send ravens after me. He apparently hadn't been told I was missing.

"Ah! Yes, that's the other one. The one that was here before." Stige's voice in no way indicated the importance of his statement. Luis and I were still too fascinated by the theory he'd uncovered to pay attention at first. The troll's tone really was that plain and unremarkable. The words, however, did sink through our thick skulls eventually.

"Wait, the other one? Lorcan?!" Our words came out on top of each other, but that was what I said. I have no idea what Luis was saying. We both spun around and rushed over to watch the closed-circuit camera. Our view wasn't ideal since we had to impatiently loom behind the ladies who had been paying closer attention. They beat us to the monitors by a good half minute or so while we were standing around being proud of coming up with the new theory about Kara's motivational embarrassment.

Even from yards back, and with the weather starting to impede, there was no doubt that we were seeing Lorcan cross the parking lot to stop and check out the bike. He fished out one of Bobbi's weapons and looked it over while she sputtered and snarled a really cute southern profanity. At least it was cute in her voice with a southern drawl.

Lorcan must have approved of Bobbi Lee's taste in weapons. He tucked an FDE or "flat dark earth" colored handgun behind his belt then took a few steps to the middle of the yard. He was still a few steps from the cellar door. He also knew about the cameras. We watched as he deliberately turned to face one under the eaves of the abandoned building.

In a combination of gestures and exaggerated mouth movements he clearly said, "Send out the Einherjar." Or at least something close enough to understand.

The chair under my fingers creaked in protest at the crushing grip I hadn't noticed applying. Some of my allies might have thought it was fear. The truth was, I don't like Lorcan. I *really* don't like Lorcan. Loathe is not even a strong enough word for how I feel about Lorcan. But none of that really mattered.

If I threw down with my old nemesis in the rain and mud, it was even odds who might win. But the odds were better than even that he could summon Kara quicker than I could escape from her. I was bracing myself for the inevitable when Stige flipped a switch. He hadn't bothered with an intercom or speaker for me. Then again he was trying to ambush me. "Please forgive. What were you saying? I have a hard time reading man lips. The lack of tusks mangles the words so badly."

He turned away from the monitors and took his finger off a button. "I can stall a few minutes. Figure out what you want to do. I am not going to start a pissing match with this guy while that is moving in."

Once more he pointed at another camera which showed an even more violent storm beginning to form much closer than before. It seemed to be heading straight for New Orleans. In fact, it seemed to be on a collision course with our present location. I understood his concern completely. It might be a coincidence, or it might mean that the storm was Kara's way of announcing her arrival. And with my luck, she was announcing her mood as well.

I was thinking fast. Which is not to say smart. I can be witty, worldly, even cunning. Nobody ever offered to hire me for any think tanks though. At the time everything always seems to make sense, but it's alarming how often my most incredible plans end up with broken bones and internal bleeding. It's just a good thing that I take internal bleeding and broken bones like a champ.

My speeding thoughts came spilling out in a rush of words. "Okay, we get the ladies back in the escape tunnel. You two stay armed and stay ready. If trouble erupts, you go away from it. This isn't your fight and somebody has to find our friends, right? If I go down or get captured, the rescue is all in your hands. And I'm not going to pretend that this one will be easy."

I scowled over my shoulder at the monitor showing an impatient Lorcan arguing with Stige safely out of range of our voices. "I am pretty sure I could take that guy. But his boss is another matter. If that storm is any indication she's almost here anyway. It's fairly certain that she will be keeping an eye on her men, and Lorcan is one of her top guys. So once I am out there she will probably show up and take me whether I've whipped her boy out there or he's taken me."

Both of them were remarkably quiet while my rapid-fire plans spewed around them. Nev got her thoughts in order first and had just started to speak when Luis forestalled her with a raised finger. He pursed his lips and then gave me his best alternatives to my plan. "You were not paying attention Amigo. He did not say send out Magnus, or Mouse, or even the infamous Strombjorn. He said send out the Einherjar. So I will go out."

Stige's voice rumbled over the tail end of Luis' declaration. "Whoever is going out, should probably be ready. I can't stall much longer. Oh, and the girls should not hide. He has seen the motorcycle with the funny sidecar for a wheelchair. If he does not see who that belongs to he might dig further."

Stige lumbered over to yet another secret panel and thumbed it open. "You promised me no ill-will or harm chosen warrior. That applies to my kin as well. Now get in.

The safe-hole is immune to scrying or divination. It's why you haven't sensed it or them yet."

On that enigmatic note, he gave me a shove and slammed the secret panel shut behind me. The complete darkness closed in and impeded any movement without risk of a faceplant or worse if there was any kind of drop or dangerous obstacle around. The time it took for my eyes to adjust was just enough for me to swear creatively about Stige, his intentions, stubborn women, and of course, this crazy new generation of Einherjar.

12

MY EYES finally adjusted to what I came to see (pun intended) was a soft ambient light. It had just seemed like pitch black after all of the fluorescent level of lighting in Stige's computer lab and kitchen. That's also when I noticed I was not alone. There had to have been two dozen trolls in the large cavern at the bottom of two or three stories worth of steps.

Those steps were just as cunningly cut or crafted as the walls of the home above. The pitch was a little steep for my stride. Stige must have very long legs for someone of medium height at best. At worst, well, trolls can be upwards of seven or eight feet tall. Even the trollborn cross between a human and a troll was usually basketball player height. At worst? Stige was a midget of his kind.

Most of his kin below me did not fit into the same category. Any one of them would have towered over me by a foot or more. Strike that, any of the front ones would tower over me. The more my eyes adjusted the more I saw that not all of the inhabitants were trolls and not all of the trolls were adults.

Behind an impressive bulwark of seven-footers, was a mass of smaller folk. Some of them were *much* smaller. But even the littlest ones had eyes that were wide and disbelieving as they stared at me. Finally, the center of the front line guards took a step forward and spoke while hefting a weapon.

"What has happened to Stige and what are your intentions here undead man?" Maybe the statement and brandishing of arms was supposed to be intimidating. But when the weapon is a rolling pin, and the voice is something like Jessica Rabbit, what you get is less intimidating and much more jarring.

That voice just didn't go with a creature near seven foot tall with curving tusks visible from her lower lip. This was one of the less human variants too. She even had a pair of ram horns curling back over her ears like a Princess Leia hairdo. My delay in answering her got a reaction that ratcheted up the intimidation factor by a wide margin.

She lifted her rolling pin and smashed it down, reducing the chair in front of her to several component pieces and a brief burst of wooden shrapnel. The sound was also not what one would expect from a typical store-bought rolling pin. A quick glance, maybe paired with an impulsive gulp, showed me that the implement was troll-sized, and typical troll material. It looked like it was made of granite or marble.

As a rolling pin, it probably made very fine crusts and layers of pastry dough. As a braining implement, it would undoubtedly make just as big a mess of my head as it had of the chair. I might not always use my head to its full potential, but I've grown fond of having it in place atop my thick neck.

A quick answer seemed in order. "Stige is fine for the

moment. He shoved me down here to keep someone from finding me. Now I think he's up there trying to talk his way out of the situation along with a couple of, well, I guess they're friends of mine."

The weight of all of those stares was uncomfortable. It took a while, but finally, the main guard and breadmaker let her rolling pin crack heavily down onto a marble countertop. She motioned to one of the medium-tall trolls who darted over and opened another of Stige's endless cabinets to reveal another bank of monitors.

In addition to all of the ones he had shown us before, this one had cameras in the rooms above, including a half dozen rooms we hadn't seen or even guessed were around us. The important views though were, the entry-way, the yard outside, and the kitchen where Bobbi and Nev Ange lingered over cups of tea hot enough for steam to be visible even over grainy closed-circuit cameras.

Through the grainy image of the cameras, I got a sense of tension despite their attempts at casual demeanor. That sense of anxiety wasn't present in the view of Stige striding confidently out of his entryway. The third vision though was different.

Like I've said, my brother Einherjar and I don't really get along well most of the time. We can be arrogant, violent and fiercely competitive not to mention brutally cruel. Lorcan was the epitome of our worst traits. He was even older than I am and almost as free of mental manipulation.

That probably requires some explanation. I am well aware that my neurons have been fiddled with. I can't trust my own memories and I have seen first hand the dreamscape that hides dozens of things that have been hidden from me.

Compared to most of other Einherjar though? I'm a

trustee of the psych ward we called home. Part of the client load but trusted to operate on my own sometimes.

Maybe it was some potential she sensed in me, or maybe I was just too damned stubborn for it to be worth her time, but Kara had always left me with a great deal more free will than most of the others.

So many warriors succumbed to the brainwashing, the alcohol, the cult of violence and sex, and the mental whammy of their care-takers. I can't give you percentages, but a majority of my kind were all but zombies. They had enough will power and skill to use their weapons and follow directions. That's about where it ended.

Lorcan operated independently as well as I did, just more brutally and with a sadistic glee I've never embraced. Or at least I don't remember ever being that way. Damned amnesia magick.

Luis was new enough, as was his Valkyrie, that he didn't seem to have any mental deficit at all, yet. Which meant he was bright enough to know how fierce an opponent Lorcan could be.

You could all but smell the caution even through cameras, encroaching darkness, and turbulent weather. Luis knew better than to let a predator sense fear, but he knew just as well what kind of trouble the older beast of a warrior could be. His shoulders were visibly tight with his emotions.

He'd barely gone into his denials, indicated by the shaking head and spread hands. Lorcan stomped forward and I knew his growl well enough to imagine what the younger man was hearing. It would be profane, threatening, and above all mocking. Lorcan always had to make fun of anyone he thought he could take in a fight.

Luis seemed ready to placate the older warrior with more gestures to indicate compliance. A nod of the head, those empty hands spread wide in deference, and a very regretful looking shake of the head at another question conveyed respect and disappointment that he could not be more helpful. Through it all, the younger warrior showed fear and worry in every line of his posture.

He wasn't worried enough. His reply did not come from Lorcan, but from the heavens themselves. A pair of lightning bolts struck the earth between Stige and Luis. They were so abrupt, and so blindingly bright purple, argent and white, that even through the monitors, everyone in the chamber gasped and looked away to blink vision back into their eyes.

When we turned back, Luis was on the ground and smoking from the near-strike. Stige was down, but only to all fours. He crouched in a runner's start and shook his head like an old bison. Those two weren't what riveted my attention though. Between them stood a Valkyrie almost as tall as the troll with her rolling pin.

Kara wasn't armed with a marble cylinder. She held a weapon made of blackest night. At least the metal was dark enough to mimic night itself. That darkness was accentuated by the ripples of purple and silver electricity that rode up and down its length. That same energy sparkled and rippled along her chainmail, crafted in darkest grey. Her hair was the color of my raven's wings and her eyes could have been holes into deepest space for all of the humanity they showed.

One of the trolls flipped another switch and I felt my spine turn to jelly as a voice resonated. It was a voice I had only heard in dreams or nightmares for half a century. My nightmares didn't do it justice. It was even colder and harsher than I remembered.

"Lorcan, my trusted hand, this is not he. Why have you

called me?" Kara's words evoked in her warrior the same rippling fear and respect for her as I held myself.

"No my lady, but this one reeks of the Bear. I don't have the power of you or even the Bear, but I can smell his stink all over this one."

Lorcan strode over and rolled Luis to his back to better see him.

Kara didn't bother. If anything, her voice grew harsher and more annoyed. "Of course he does, dog. He and his mewling valkyrie were with Strombjorn in Mexico. Everything I've heard confirms that much. Odin is livid with them over the intervention. Whatever they did down there crossed lines. Other gods and their followers were involved. You know how the all-father likes being caught out by surprises like that. So they were with him recently enough for his magick to linger around them. But I see no storm bear?"

Her tone was mocking, sickly sweet, and to anyone who knew her, deadly dangerous. Lorcan answered promptly albeit with a thick and stumbling tongue. "No my lady, but he was there as you said. Perhaps he knows enough to help us. And perhaps he needs to disappear as well. You said he was down there with the bear. Does he know enough to cause you any embarrassment?"

We all saw Kara nod appreciatively. "That was not ill-thought-out my chosen. It would make things much easier for me if I could make him disappear. Without his Valkyrie though, that is most unlikely."

Lorcan was on top of that idea. "Then take him with us. She would have to come for him eventually right? She is young, and weak compared to my Mistress of the Storms. Make them both disappear. She has no other chosen and Odin might not even remember her."

Her reply was as mocking as his own. "As long as he has those damned ravens, the one-eyed will forget nothing. We might get lucky enough for him to miss seeing what we do though. If we are careful, if we hide our movements, perhaps it can be done."

By the end of her comments, that voice had gone to just chilled and contemplative rather than icy and merciless. I wanted to rush out and do something. I had no idea what, but there had to be something to do. Except there never was an opportunity. She gestured for Lorcan to gather Luis, which he did as if he was handling a small child.

He turned with one hand holding the slighter einherjar over a shoulder and gestured with his free paw at Stige. "And what about that vermin? He is aware of what we said and what we planned."

Around me, a collective growl mingled with a few gasps and even some fearful sobs. That was all in reaction to Kara stepping forward. It was that menacing. Anyone watching could not fail to believe they were seeing the final act of something like one of those hunts on nature shows. The lioness was about to make her kill.

No feline I've met kills with fire and lightning though, or with a spear made of both of the above plus blackest night and glacial cold. Kara kicked Stige into a backward stumble just as he rose to both feet. His back hit the wall just a fraction of a second before her spear pierced the same wall along with his torso.

The pain and glacial cold must have taken his breath away. We saw him struggle to scream, and then he struggled just to get enough breath. Kara stopped that with a remorseless hand that closed over his lower face with bone-crushing force. We saw blood spurt between her fingers. It was not hard to imagine a ruined mouth and broken teeth beneath that cruel clawed hand.

Almost as if she was caressing him rather than reducing his face to paste, Kara leaned over and kissed Stige's brow. "The young these days, they play games that tell them the only way to kill a troll is with fire."

She twisted the spear inside Stige's innards. From the angle, it looked like she was tearing his intestines up. Her hand still smothered any cries he might have made though. She continued in her quiet voice that was barely audible even though the microphone seemed to be just above the two of them. "We both know that is not true though, do we not? I could reduce you to nothing with my bare hands and none of the powers which I command. But fire seems like a...fun choice."

Power surged along that spear. This time scarlet and gold mingled with the silver and purple lightning. The wall behind Stige erupted in flames that spread to engulf the entire room in a split second. Kara's hand on his face provided the finishing move. She shoved him through the flaming wall into an inferno as the rooms above him began to collapse into a funeral pyre.

The world collapsed on me a second later. I never heard the female troll creep up behind me. Just like I never heard her retrieve the marble club that she smashed down on my thick and rocklike skull.

13

I CAME to with a bunch of ugly just inches from my face. The tusked and horn crowned female troll was front and center above me. Around her were several other trolls and what I took to be a wendigo or other nature spirit. As I tried to focus my thoughts, tiny footsteps seemed to patter right up to my ear followed by a vicious pain in that earlobe.

"What the Actual Hel?" It was my voice but I don't recall initiating the bellow. Then again I was barely aware of anything. Except for a lot of hot halitosis in my face and the scorching heat of more animosity than I'd seen outside of a moment with Kara. That awareness was followed by a sense of vertigo until I figured out that I was on my back. The cold underneath me said it was probably the marble counter I'd seen earlier.

Multiple hands slammed me back down on the counter as I struggled to sit up. There were so much growling and cursing and crying around me that I couldn't single out any one voice to make sense of. Until the door opened and a second later a shotgun spoke louder than the other voices around me.

I craned my head around to get an upside-down look at the stairs and the dauntless southern rescuer standing hipshot atop them with the shotgun angling up from her waist. "You folks need to calm down a bit and get your priorities right."

I felt enough slackening of various grips to roll off the table and turn to face them. The hand that went to the knife at my back sizzled again and jerked away of its own volition.

"No time for all of that fussin' and fightin' kids. Ange is trying to use the troll's fire suppression system but we need someone to open the doors so we can get out there before he stops screaming." Even in a crisis, Bobbi's voice had that lazy drawl you get from cowboy movies or any time Sam Elliot is speaking.

The hands stopped grasping at me as the largest trollish woman shoved everyone, including me, out of her way to bound up those oversized stairs three at a time. Bobbi managed to get out of her way before the troll flattened her into cute southern roadkill. Somehow I managed to beat everyone else up the stairs after the running boss lady.

That probably had more to do with the shock and horror I saw on the faces that blurred past as I ran. We could all hear the screaming now. It was coming from speakers all over the first floor of troll apartments, undoubtedly piped there from a camera or microphone somewhere near where Stige was enduring a highly personalized version of biblical style hell.

By the time I got to the main chamber where our host had been entertaining us as guests, the female from the hidden chamber had the outer door open and was out of sight. What was very much in sight, was an almost catatonic looking Nev Ange. She was at the computer that controlled the monitors and microphones.

The monitor directly in front of her showed a cloud of white that completely obscured any kind of detail inside the room. The only things even remotely discernible were a few flickering glows where the fire had not quite surrendered to whatever safety measures the troll had in place.

Ange let out a low terrified sounding moan and went from catatonic, to hysterical sobbing that wracked her frame. Bobbi took one look at her friend and the monitor and then let out her own anguished cry before running out of the room to help Stige. I started to run after her, but another heart-rending cry came from the previously fearless lady at the monitors.

It suddenly seemed to me that the two outside were plenty to recover a charred corpse. I changed my course from the door to Ange's side. I turned her face towards me only to see wide vacant eyes. Wherever she was, it wasn't in the same room I was seeing. I couldn't fathom what kind of horrors would make someone as tough as this warrior in a wheelchair so distraught.

"Ange, Knave! Nev Ange are you okay? Can you hear me? C'mon lady. We're gonna need you to get our friends back. I don't think we can do it without you."

When I got no response, I ran to the kitchen area and flipped open cupboards until I found a stoneware mug. Then it took a few moments to figure out the exotic trollish components of a sink and faucet. Either Stige had a new type of sensors, or his sink was operated by hand movements to draw water out of the sink. I must have gotten lucky and "pulled" water from the cold pipes.

If he even used pipes that is. I got ice out of the stone "fridge" nearby and topped off the water before running it back to Ange. She was making some odd mumbling sounds.

They might have been words but were low enough that I

couldn't discern them over the beeping of a computer system that seemed unhappy about flames overhead. Despite the new sounds coming from her, Ange's eyes were still wide and staring in horror at empty space.

I was trying to get her to drink or speak to me or do anything except that terrible panic when Bobbi opened the door and allowed the troll from downstairs in. The unnamed female had a scorched and stinking mess in her arms that wasn't even remotely identifiable as Stige. She passed us along with the smell of burnt meat and took him through one of the other hidden Doors.

Bobbi didn't follow this time. Instead, she stopped and took the glass of ice water from my hand. With a firm hand, she pushed me back and then splashed a good quarter cup or so of the water at her shuddering, hysterical companion.

Just like that, the color came back to Ange's face along with awareness in her eyes. I suppose I gasped in shock at the apparent lack of compassion from Bobbi. In return, Ange gasped at the shock of cold water. Then she collapsed forward onto the computer desk for more tears and sobbing. At least it no longer sounded hysterical or frightening. Now she just sounded scared and weary.

Bobbi put the glass on the table and then used both hands on my shoulders to point me back towards where Stige had been carried away. "I've got this. We've worked through it before. You go lend a hand with the victim back there."

I resisted her push for all of two or three seconds. I didn't want to see the horror's inflicted on even a long-time foe's corpse. I'm uncomfortable with death since I hadn't truly experienced it as many others had. Oh, sure I have sent more than a few to whatever afterlife awaited them. That doesn't mean I'm at all good with the grieving process or all of the emotions that go along with death.

The fact though, is that I am even worse with most crying females. I'm not sure if it's the sound or some premonition associated with unhappy women and dark consequences, but female tears almost always evoke more anxiety for me than say, gunfire, or supernatural face-eating creatures.

I found my way back to where a face-eating creature was laying on a table under the fierce gaze and flowing tears of a skull-smashing member of his clan. "If you come in here, then you help, or you stay out of the way, or I make soup with whatever is left of you. The soup would help to feed him to his health."

I was more shocked than intimidated. The shock was because I did not know anything that would have survived what I thought I'd seen. Despite the husky and admittedly sexy voice she growled in, the troll *did* manage to be intimidating this time, not by the growls themselves.

No, it was the calm and detached manner in which she confidently stated my options and potential consequences. This wasn't threatening banter. It was a cool discourse with only a fraction of her attention while most of her focus was on the patient she was attending to.

Stige had stopped thrashing, screaming or even moaning in pain. Now that he was flat on a stone examination table, the damage was gruesomely apparent. His entire torso had been bared for the work being done. That meant I could see the gaping wound that seemed to start just under his ribs and reach down to where a navel would be on a normal man.

Blood so dark it was almost black welled out of the wound. It didn't spurt or even gush but rather spread out like a balloon with several leaks. I couldn't even be sure his heart was still pumping. A second later that barrel chest rose in a shuddering breath, so he was still alive at least.

"I've got some medical training. Not with trolls but with humans. Let me wash up and I'll help." I was proud that my voice was cool and professional. Because professionally speaking, I wasn't sure he stood a chance. A wound like that would come close to taking me down and I cheat when it comes to trauma and healing.

Throw in what looked like second and third-degree burns almost everywhere you could see. Such burns weakened the body, reduced its ability to recover, and left so much surface open for infection. I was really hoping that Stige was even tougher than I had previously thought he was.

The next words from the trolless made me hope even harder. Once more they were all the more chilling for the detached manner in which she so firmly stated them. "If he dies, you will wish you had gone first. We know enough to make sure you hurt for a long time. To keep you on the screaming edge of death but not far enough that you just die and go back to that treacherous bitch."

I was trying to look nonchalant about her threats and searching around for someplace to scrub up when she snorted and stopped her own work to stare at me like I was a less than stellar pupil.

"You're worried about dirt in his wounds? What part of stone-troll does not translate? Come hold his arm down while I get this needle in."

Look I've started IVs. I mean after mercenary work and combat pay got tiresome I used someone else's GI Bill to go to school and get a paramedic license. It wasn't hard. Most of my brothers had some experience with wounds and trauma. But I'll gladly admit that when I start an IV, the needle doesn't look like something you knit with, or maybe use to hold down railroad ties.

I grabbed his arm with both hands while the needle was steadily advanced by the competent hands of his, I couldn't decide whether it was a wife, girlfriend, sister, daughter or great grandmother five times removed. Alt-naturals don't age like you and I and their family trees can be mystifying.

"You can call me Lola." Her sudden introduction bordered on magick. I was tempted to add mind-reading to her resume of bread making, furniture demolition, fire and rescue, and now medic. It was probably just good logical thinking about easing up our communications. We could hardly go with doctor and nurse considering I was a Warrior with a capital and mystical W and she was a Troll with a capital T. T as in Torture, Thrash, Throttle, Tear limb from limb.

"Thank you, Lola, you can call me Magnus, or Mouse if it amuses you," Maybe I could defuse the situation a little and join her on the detached professional but courteous level.

"What would amuse me, little mouse, would be to toy with you like a great cat with that little mouse and then squeeze your guts out like cheese-whiz to eat on crackers." Apparently, I had misread her introduction. Rather than reply, I tried to remain as quiet and unobtrusive as my namesake, that dormouse, while Lola the troll worked like a team of doctors and nurses to stabilize a creature that wasn't used to needing any such help.

Even without knowing troll physiology, I could tell she was losing the battle. Her next words confirmed that she knew it just as well as I did. "This isn't working. I will need you to be very still, very quiet, and think nothing but good thoughts Magnus. If you can not do that then go below with the others. You might even voice an opinion in their arguments."

"What arguments?" I was curious but quickly amended that. " Of course I'd rather stay here and help anyway so forget the question."

She growled her answer anyway. "They are arguing about who gets to kill you and who gets to prepare the feast they make of you afterward. So either go down and make a recipe suggestion or shut up and quit jarring my elbow."

After that, I was quiet and still. For at least a quarter of an hour, I watched her strain harder and harder, not with medicine, but with magic.

Symbols glowed as she sketched them on and around Stige with her talon-like fingernail. A litany of words that sounded harsh even behind those sultry tones rattled from her throat and fueled more whorls of visible energy.

Still, Stige's breath became more labored. It started to sound wet and gurgling before he began coughing up the dark red blood in thick loops. At that moment I became aware of how the room echoed his heartbeat. It was as if the table were a drum skin and the heavy beat of his troll heart played the tune of that drum. It had gone from a steady primeval thud to a dubstep techno soundtrack. Light beats of that heart were going at a rate of two or three beats a second instead of a second or so between each beat.

"I am losing him." Lola's voice was blurred with tears she choked back. Her head snapped up and those granite eyes locked on mine. "Do you truly want to help? It might save not only Stige but your life as well."

"Lady you need to stop trying to threaten me. The worst you can think of doesn't really match up to what I can expect from the "person" who did this to Stige. I want to help the troll because he didn't deserve what just happened to him. Not because of any threats from you and the meta-physical menagerie down there." Part of me wanted to say more and ask a few questions.

I wanted to ask why everyone wanted to kill me, but I suspected that the answer was self-evident. If I had to guess, they were all gathered here under the protection of a strong and cunning leader because of recent events. Things like Einherjar wandering around asking questions in the typical belligerent manner scared many of the not so natural side of things. Toss in a bunch of spooks in their tuxedo-themed black and white vans. To make it worse, the head spook was fascinated by paranormal folks and creatures.

These folk were all hiding and nervous before I ever showed up. A short time after I do show up, their leader is in the process of dying painfully and gruesomely. That seemed like the clearest answer to why they wanted me dead and digested. The worst part was, I couldn't really blame them.

Lola confirmed my guess and also said something to make me think I was mumbling my thoughts. "Yes, the black van men have been everywhere stirring up the little folk more than my own kind. We have dealt with Papa Beaufort in his white van for a while now. He is an evil man but easily avoided. But was it not your Valkyrie that showed up right behind you with her second most feared henchman to do this?"

She looked up from her work to gesture at the slowly dying troll on the marble slab. The strain of her work to keep his huge heart beating was apparent in every line of Lola's body. She already looked as drained and weak as a surgeon after a procedure that took all night.

"So make your choice. Help him or leave. If you leave now I will not alert the others. You can escape New Orleans before the little ones decide your fate and stick you and the women in their bellies."

The women too? When had that been added to the equation? It didn't really matter. I would be a chore for these "little folk" to take down face to face. I also suspect that they were seriously underestimating the women, to nonchalantly state they were going to eat them. Like it was a foregone conclusion.

I was willing to offer good odds that there wouldn't be enough of the "folk" around to finish off even me. Not after Ange and Bobbi got through reducing their numbers. That didn't change the facts though. Maybe their conclusions weren't one hundred percent accurate, but these folks were right that I bore some responsibility for Stige's injuries. It was very likely that I was the cause of all of those Einherjar asking questions. I was also the reason the black vans were in town.

The information about this Papa Beaufort was new. It also meant I wasn't behind his presence. But he was still someone I'd have to deal with. It seemed like Freke had gotten involved with him while looking to live up to our previous bargain. So now I had another immortal freaking wolf to rescue.

Maybe I needed to get business cards printed up. "*Demi-gods and immortal creatures rescued or eliminated. Reasonable Rates. Inquiries welcome.*"

"Okay let's do this. How can I help you that won't stop me from helping my other friends?" I decided it was best to do what I could and worry about the rest after we saved the stupid troll that wanted to shit me into the gulf.

Lola's answer did not encourage me. "I never said that this might not stop you. In fact, it will increase your risk manyfold, outside of these chambers. I need you to open your magick to me. Let me use your special abilities to heal Stige. You will be drained. Weak. Your enhanced healing will be gone so that he may use it to recover. Without those protections and abilities, it is very possible you will be killed by something that would normally be of little concern."

That took the wind out of my sails. The whole reason I was in New Orleans was to save some friends from my own hunters. The fact that those same hunters were causing problems for the alt-natural community of the Big Easy made it even more important to stop them. Was giving up my own advantages the right thing to do?

I mean sure I felt responsible for Stige's injuries. In so many ways this was a result of nothing more than my presence in the area. But was it fair to everyone else to give up those things that made me more capable of facing the current threats?

Then I started to get mad. I was mad at the abusive government people stirring everyone up. Mad at this Papa Beaufort for hunting down my possible ally, Freke. Mad at Kara the Stormy for too many things to list. I was even mad at Lorcan over a dozen incidents between us over the centuries.

Mostly though, I was mad at me. Was I not a warrior? A proud member of my old bloodline stood on his own feet. He met setbacks with determination and grit. My forefathers did not rely on magic or a gift from the gods to do what needed to be done. They strapped on uncomfortable leathers, hefted crude weapons and heavy shields, and did the job.

"Do it." My voice sounded tense and even angry. If it sounded the same to Lola, she did not show it. Instead, she spoke to the stones and watched as another table rose out of the floor itself just on the other side of her from the table already present and full of cooked troll.

"Get on the table. This will not seem to hurt, at first. No needles or lines. Just calm yourself and focus on projecting your power. I don't suppose you have studied Reiki or energy projection through spellwork?"

She was too focused on Stige to give me more than minimal attention. Maybe that would be alright though. Surprisingly enough, I *had* studied some of those esoteric principles of energy work. My own runic abilities had prompted some curious research.

"I'm not a master of any of that." I was a touch hoarse with the latest escalation of what seemed like days or weeks of near-constant tension. "I mean I don't have a black belt in Wizard-Fu or anything. But I can pull energy from a strong enough source and project it a very short distance. The effects might vary, but I can get the juice out there."

She snorted before answering. "Don't even think about any effects. I will direct the course of this. You just project. Which hand do you use for drawing and which for projecting?"

I decided this was probably a test to make sure I wasn't falsely bragging. The occult community at large feels like you pull through one side of your body and project from the other. The consensus is that the left hand is used to draw in energy, while the right expels it. I suspect it has something to do with the course of life fluids out of a human heart.

I also know for a fact that it is not a universal truth. For whatever reason, my left hand is dominant for both purposes. I can both pull or project weakly from my right hand. But for more potent work, my left is the draft horse to the right's reluctant donkey. Despite my reservations, I told the troll medic just that. I didn't get denial or skepticism though. All I got was a thoughtful glance aside from her focus on keeping that other heart beating.

"How unusual. Then place your left palm against the tabletop and try not to pull against the flow. I need your energy. I do not need you taking from the patient or of my own energies for that matter. If I feel you begin to draw, then I shall terminate the connection and summon the cooks and butchers from below."

14

THERE'S a drug I used to give for people with bad flu or other infections. It was by injection to the meatiest muscle we could find in a haunch. That was because patients often described it as having hot lead injected only to spread in a truly painful lump of hot liquid in your butt. I never had to have the shot so I never had any context for those statements.

That was no longer the case.

No sooner had my hand touched the tabletop, than that cool marble surface seemed to warp and embrace that hand. A single heartbeat later, the blood in that hand turned into hot lava being run through a two-twenty volt outlet. I actually looked down in expectation of seeing the skin bubble and burn or at least sizzle around the pain.

When I started to clinch the hand to relieve it, Lola hissed a warning. "Don't block it. And remember, do not draw, just project."

With her warning alongside visions of a still twitching side of Magnus hanging on the hook, I focused all of my will on keeping that hand open and pushing my own crude energy out of it. It took a lot of focus and will. The more I pushed, the more it hurt. The more it hurt, the more I wanted to pull back. But for all I knew, trying to pull my hand away might send the flow of vital forces the other direction. Such an act would surely doom Stige, and raise my own odds of being the main course for dinner.

I've seen a few different alt-naturals eat. It can be everything from a formal dinner to make Louis XIV envious, to a scene from a, particularly disturbing nature documentary.

Considering that some of the denizens below sported teeth and other sundries that would fit on a fierce predator, that image was more than apt and a great deal more than uncomfortable. I'm sure it would *feel* even more primal and uncomfortable than the image.

With that in mind, I put every bit of focus and willpower I could into quelling any reflex that might be construed as "drawing". Have you ever willing held a fingertip to a hot surface or tried the childhood foolishness with a battery on your tongue? Your nervous system is built to reduce such harm before you ever have time to think about it. Your finger jerks away, your tongue recoils. All of this happens without, or sometimes in spite of your own direction.

That's what I was fighting. Every nerve and muscle in my hand and entire arm wanted to recoil from the pain. I've been told, *"you got more stubborn in you're blasted pinky finger than most full-growed adults"*. This was five such fingers arguing with me. If my fingers are stubborn though, my head is hard as a rock when it comes down to stubbornness. I've heard its solid as a rock for other reasons as well but I choose to go with the stubbornness.

In the struggle that ensued, my hand and arm put up an impressive resistance. It took enough focus that I lost track of time, of my surroundings, of anything except the pressure to push that hand into the stone suckling at it.

With those thoughts of pushing, the trickle of lava became a torrent of magma all charged with bolts of lightning that made my fingers curl into claws against the stone. But I didn't pull away.

Maybe it was a desperate attempt of my conscious to escape the situation, but I found that I had completely blocked out the room until all that was left was the present but distant searing agony of the energy transfer. That new absence of thought or pain was too tenuous to rely on. I put my mind to another task. *How do these people keep tracking us down?*

Applied logic is not always my greatest gift. It promised to be a decent distraction though. It takes some real focus for me to work through problems sometimes. Alright, more than sometimes.

Most of the time my initial reaction is to rush at a problem and overcome it with sheer tenacity and aggression. I can temper that reaction with some rudimentary tactics and fast adaptability to surprise and changes. That works well on most battlefields and barroom brawls. It is not a great habit for someone getting involved in the mysteries and conundrums I'd been facing recently.

So applying every bit of focus I could, while dealing with the external agony, was an exercise that required more of me than I was sure I was capable of. While I was still struggling with the problem, I noticed that two overheard lights sprang up over the exam tables. It seemed like maybe there had been one over Stige the entire time but the one above me was new. It also seemed very distant in my altered state of mind.

In fact, the distance and bemusement made the two

lights appear as a pair of golden eyes. They seemed to pulse in a lurid blue and purple glow as I stared. The pulse matched my own laboring heartbeat. I could no longer concentrate on my logic problem or even what I needed to do to overcome it.

Instead, I was trapped in the glow of those pulsing lights. And then they swooped down at me. At the last instant, the ceiling seemed to separate into twin rows of sharp teeth each about the size of my stubborn fingers.

I didn't have time to react, not even long enough to draw a breath for battlecries, or warnings, or screaming like a three-year-old. For the second time in my life, I was swallowed by a great wyrm that I now knew was an entrance to the shadow world, the other side, never-never or the faerie courts.

There were many names for where I went, but I knew them as the land of shamanic visions and the domain of witch doctors and medicine men.

The first time I had found myself in this weird quasi-plane, was a result of several factors. Among them was my very recent near-death experience at the time, as well as feeble attempts to please an angry girlfriend. In fact, it was the same "girlfriend" I was currently searching to rescue. The last component of that previous "trip" was my underestimation of a Yaqui shaman and his alcohol-laced plant-based little hallucinogenic doorway to my inner self.

That visit sucked. It sucked a lot, but it also taught me some things about myself and the world we live in. Or maybe it's the world we don't quite live in. It's really confusing even when you aren't hopped up on powerful drugs and booze.

Then again maybe I was close to meeting the whole "near death" component of my earlier vision quest. I don't recall thinking long and hard about the possibility of being vampired completely dry by the troll saving her clanmate. When I did consider that possibility, well, what could be expected if you let someone drain off your lifeforce and the odd bits of divine help that have kept you alive for ages?

This time, I had a little idea of what to expect down the dragon's gullet. Instead of being crushed to pieces and having my flesh stripped away by burning agony, I curled up into a tight ball and exposed as little of myself as possible to the grinding surfaces and cruel juices burning at me.

That little bit of precaution meant I didn't land in a stripped clean pile of all two hundred some-odd bones. Nope, I landed in one messy jumble of partially articulated skeleton with a few shreds of scorched meat attached. Once more, I landed in a scary old hag's cooking pot. And once more the "Bone mother" came cackling over with an obvious intent to "crack some marrow" for her soup.

Most fortunately for me, that tattered flesh included most of my respiratory tract, and a goodly portion of my facial, umm, meat. "Most respectful greetings do I bring thee, Mother."

I was trying to be as suave and urbane as the shaman, Tio Guillermo, or "Uncle Bill", had pulled off when he guided me through this hall of horror. Suave is hard to pull off when your voice is sloppy and bits of facial, stuff, falls off your, face, in mid-sentence. Even in my bewildered state, that last idea came across as awkward.

Then again it wasn't really surprising that odd random thoughts were popping into my head about the current state of things. After all, a giant dragon chomped and burned my body up at the same time a stone-sorceress troll was sucking the life-force and assorted mojo out of my body in another dimension. That kind of thing can be distracting.

It also seemed quite surprising and annoying to my current hostess in the other-world. Her reaction was not as encouraging as I had hoped, but at least she wasn't breaking my bones when she made unintelligible sounds that slowly morphed into words. "Gaahhh, Wotha, Aagh, ye frightened me old withered dugs off boy!"

Her recovery was immediate and far less frightening than the last journey. At that time Tio Guillermo had started her humming a song instead of snapping my femurs. We snuck out while she was distracted. I didn't know any of her favorite tunes though.

She didn't go straight back to bone breaking and soup stirring. Instead, she gathered me up and rolled the ball of bone and gore along the floor of the cave until bits of everything around began sticking to the muddy and bloody mess. She started humming her own tunes without any prompting from me. It was an old tune that seemed familiar. I couldn't put a name to it though. In fact, after just a few notes I doubt I could have put a name to myself or what was happening.

The old lady crooned and rolled and talked to herself until she was happy with whatever her goal had been. At that point, she picked me up and took me back to the soup cauldron. The flames sprang up just as she stopped crooning and lifted me to drop in the pot. It seemed like a helluva bad way to make stew. I've never been fond of cave detritus in my food.

The last vestiges of lassitude from her song wore off just as I hit the steaming broth in which I could see bits of bone and meat and maybe even an eyeball. I got out about a quarter of a decent *shout* of anticipation before the vile mess closed over my head. It might have sounded high pitched to anyone near enough to hear, but I'll blame that on the acoustics of the dream-world cave rather than any terror that might make a stalwart warrior scream like an infant.

Once more, my terror, or rather, my *concern* was misplaced. It felt like emerging from a dip in a sauna or exceptionally warm swimming pool. I came out of the soup whole and with more energy than I'd had prior to draconic consumption.

When I tripped over the lip of Cauldron and sprawled on the floor (that was clean enough to eat off of), I also discovered I was naked as the proverbial jaybird or newborn.

"Oh such fine muscle with just a hint of juicy fat." The mother's sigh of regret and longing was not enough to encourage any dinner invitations. I feared that any such invitation would make me prone to more consumption right on the heels of my most recent digestive adventure.

She sauntered over to a trunk while I was still thinking about how to respond. Don't get me wrong, I'm usually quick on the quip or sarcastic remark. Something about this lady radiated a cold, deadly, primal power that squelched any inclinations to disrespect.

For a rare change of pace, I was very careful with every word coming out of my mouth. For that matter, there was a serious effort going on to curb stray thoughts. She encouraged that idea with her next words. "Yes yes, you're a careful and cautious cub. Now get some clothes on before you make my appetizer list."

She threw me a simple outfit of tunic and trews with rough boots and a belt. In short, it was something I would have worn for work clothes in my original lifetime. It also fit me surprisingly well. Or maybe it isn't so surprising. I had yet to work out whether this was a real place or just a handy tool for examining my damaged psyche.

I put the tunic on first since it covered up anything from neck to mid-thigh that she might want to pull off and eat. The pants went next and in short order, I was fully dressed in woolen clothes that were much less comfortable than I remember from my youth.

The stuff itched abominably. There was also a persistent ache in my knee, unlike anything I can recall. It was the knee that I hit on the cave floor while sprawling ever so gracefully from the cauldron. That was also a knee that had been whacked, shot, carved on, and burned/exploded a few times.

Yet still, this ache was new and distracting. I heard the bone mother chuckle as I turned around. She didn't voice whatever had her grinning to herself though. Instead, she sat in a rocking chair and bade me sit at her knee on a low slab of rock. "So cub, what brings you to my demesnes this day? I should say I am surprised to see you at all without a guide, but I seem to recall seeing you before and noting that you had your own difference then. No?"

I wanted to answer her in the worst way. Elder primal powers in their own domain are not things with which to trifle. Even Stige had proved very formidable in his recently established home. Imagine what power and security this eldritch lady had after an immeasurable number of years or even centuries. Maybe this wasn't real and it was all my imagination. But, there were tales of the Bone Mother across cultures and across eons. Even if it was my imagination, nothing was hurt by some diplomacy.

The problem was, I had no idea what had brought me into this other world. I was assuming that another near-death experience was taking place with my corporeal body. Maybe that was the cause for this unscheduled change to my spiritual itinerary.

"No boy, you don't pop into my cave just because you're bleeding out, or dehydrated, or a troll is sucking your life-force away." She was answering my unspoken thoughts again. That was probably a strong argument for the fantasy realm or "it's all in your head". Alternately it meant that this woman was possessed of godlike powers in this place, and I should beware screwing around with the old lady.

Apparently, I wasn't guarding my thoughts well at all. She cackled again with outright jocularity. "A lady is it? Old yes. I do not know if the Lady is a proper description. And I do like the accidental double entendre with *possessed*. Don't you?"

I gave up trying to school my thoughts. Either everything going on was in my imagination, or this crone was much too powerful for my mental defenses to expel. Instead, I laughed with her at the weak joke and then spread my hands in bewilderment.

"Honestly Mother, I don't know why I am here. I assume that the magick and life force I'm losing on the other side has me hovering near death. But I was concentrating on solving some problems and utilizing my somewhat lazy gray matter for preemptive measures rather than my typical "*wait for action and respond with furious outbursts.*"

She slapped her hands together and rubbed them briskly then leaned forward with her elbows on her knees. "Oh goody! A puzzle. I love puzzles, even the kinds that are too elusive for thick-skulled thugs. Let me see then…" It was the damnedest feeling. If she weren't still sitting across from me, I would have sworn the old lady had her fingertips inside my skull, flipping through the pages of memory.

Flip! There was a brief glance of Maureen on the stretcher where I had last seen her waiting for Mexican authorities.

Flip! Eachan's boat flew through my memories on fast forward. She paused when Pedro Perro, excuse me, Coyote showed up. She spent a few minutes on scenes that didn't seem to mean much to me. The rental house Nev had first provided was followed by the bar with Raphael. The house where Bobbi had taken me was followed by the doomsday bunker and then the arrival of the white van and finally our trip to seek computer assistance from Stige.

When she was done she leaned back and I felt the release of invisible fingers on my jaw and inside my skull. In a flash, I was on my feet and a blade of pure vermillion flames came out of the sheath that had not been behind my belt an instant before. My voice came out low, and as cold and unyielding as the rock around us. "Don't do that ever again."

I got the Vulcan Eyebrow treatment for my endeavors. "Good! You still have fight in you boy. If we could get that muscle between your ears as strong as the ones in your arms and chest it would be a grand foe and masterless man you are wouldn't it?"

She paused and I saw her eyes focus on me and then past. It was as if she was looking down a tunnel with its mouth in the middle of my forehead.

"Did you bring allies lad? Or do you have visitors of your own?" She pointed to a tunnel I hadn't already seen. At first glance, it was more of an archway, and past it was the familiar snow-swept scape of my dream home. The hall still stood in the distance. Now though, the stoop and cross beams above the longhouse door were shattered and open to the elements.

Two or three of the huts were but charred ruins now. These I recalled fighting to enter and access memories that had been locked away. That wasn't the biggest change to the home of my lost memories though.

The newest and more noticeable phenomenon was a stranger moving from hut to hut and stepping past the unresponsive guardians over my dreams. When I had been in that place last, I fought dire hounds, magical wards, and Draugr, or strong zombiesque creatures out of Norse myth and folklore.

Whoever was strolling through my mental playground and obstacle course now, was immune to, or at least avoiding the perils I had to face for those same memories and visions. That's enough to make a saint angry. And I ain't never been accused of being saintly or even particularly pious.

15

"WELL HELLO THERE! Pleasure to meet you. What are you doing inside my freakin' head!?" As much as I wanted to charge straight into the fray, there was enough logic still in residence to caution against that. The straightest line between this stranger and my own position would place me perilously near some of those guardians of my lost memories.

The last time I'd been inside, I had barely survived. It had taken help from a Shaman overseeing the ceremony as well as my girlfriend at the time to get me out more or less intact. I had also been just this side of a near-death experience right then. Except for a couple of brawls, I was relatively fresh as a daisy. I mean, a daisy having its essence and color removed to freshen up a dried out bunch of weeds or something, but still, oh never mind.

I strode forward with purpose but not without some attention to my surroundings. Never did I get closer than two or three yards from the various lumps, bumps, and hummocks that I knew concealed guardians of this landscape. It helped that my voice had brought the intruder to a halt. She turned just far enough to look me in the face over her shoulder.

I would have returned the favor, except it was impossible to see her face deep within the hood of her cloak. The only reason I knew that it was "her" face was that an intriguing number of curves and contours shaped the cloak that enveloped her. I got a brief flash of light or maybe color from inside that deep cowl before her voice stopped me cold.

"There you are my Strombjorn. Or are you a walking memory inside this place?" Kara's voice did not radiate the same rage and chilling menace it had just outside of Stige's home. That didn't mean I had forgotten the danger. My lack of reaction was not a matter of choice either. At her voice, my feet had simply locked themselves to ground at the same moment my spine became completely rigid and unbending.

I quickly discovered that nothing was obeying my commands, not even my vocal cords would respond. That last bit might have been a blessing. My mouth often leads the way in situations where it should mind its place and maybe let the old eyes work or, hey, maybe the brain could take a turn?

The lack of movement or comment seemed to catch Kara by surprise. Judging from her next words, the absence of a snarky comment or rebellious demeanor did not meet expectations. "How disappointing. I had meant the walking memory as a joke but perhaps that really is all you are. Tell me, ghost, who are you? Who am I? And what is this place?"

It seemed like an opportunity worth investigating. "Mistress of Storms! You are my Valkyrie!"

I almost dropped to a knee. None of my memories showed that kind of behavior though. At least I don't recall ever doing it with our clothes on and no "*extra-curricular*" activities taking place. Instead, I took a weak-kneed step forward. The weakness was not feigned. It had taken a major effort just to get the damned leg to move.

"I am The Strombjorn. Storm's Bear and her trusted sword." The adulation in my voice came from somewhere. I fully intended to try and fool this visitor in the dreamworld. I had not, however, planned the surging adoration and nauseating sound of my compliant voice. That had to have come from before. Maybe I had been more under her spell than even I could recall anymore.

It seemed to strike a note with my intruder though. Kara pushed the hood back and looked at me with a hint of affection. That affection was laid lightly atop a foundation of amusement, and maybe scorn. I don't know how I never noticed that her smile always built itself around a sneer of disdain. It was there. Her teeth were lovely. Her lips curved invitingly, Everything a smile should be was in plain sight. Underneath though, if you really looked, was something ugly, malicious, and mocking.

"So my Bear. You are lost in this place and looking for your mistress? That is good. Your mistress has been looking for you as well Bear. For a very long time." She took casual, confident steps towards me. The same humps and mounds I avoided meant nothing to her. She stepped on them, around them. One such hump did not even seem visible to her. She stepped through it without leaving a mark of her passage.

I could not let her know how much I was noticing though. Maybe I could get some information while I tried to think of a clever escape. "It is good we have found each other then Mistress. But what is this place? And what are these things hidden near the buildings? I saw one of those mounds move as if it were alive."

As if my words brought her further into the place, I saw

Kara glance around and take notice of the huts, the long-house, the bonfire, and even the snow-covered hiding places of those guardians I had encountered before. With her attention to those details, the world shifted around her. The mound she was standing in, firmed up until her feet rested atop it.

I watched her sway easily from side to side as whatever was under her feet moved in response to the shift in its reality. She ignored that movement to answer my questions. "This is a shadow-world my Bear. It exists as a mirror to other places and times. It is someplace we can shed memories and pain so that they do not torment us for the centuries and eons of our existence. Those mounds hide guardians to keep the monsters of memory from springing on us at inconvenient times. But I ask again, what is the last thing you remember, shade?"

I was momentarily stunned. Had I been wrong about the theft of my memories? Was my random affliction of amnesia actually a boon rather than a curse? The smooth and caring tones of Kara's voice confused me. I dimly felt the surge of her aura extend to surround me and urge my compliance, my trust, my love. Did this lovely woman, this divine creature who was practically a goddess, did she deserve my distrust and anger? I wanted to fall at her feet and confess my deception, apologize for my absence and my suspicions, even my infidelity with other women over the past half a century.

But there was one little resistant, treacherous, hard-headed part of me that wanted to punch her in the throat and then stomp her into a much less invitingly curvaceous shape on the ground. Almost as if that very small voice had summoned it, I saw a wraith-like tiny figure stalk from the shadows of a hut behind Kara.

Was it my imagination? Or was there a fox, inside the dream, stalking silently closer to sit with its tail across its feet and a smirk on its furry vulpine face? A cream and red fox that looked just like the "imaginary" fox that shadowed my friend Eachan. That same friend who was being held hostage just for associating with me. The professor also was known to firmly deny the existence of any otherworldly fox, while defending the pranks of said non-existent fox in the next breath.

The shock of seeing the creature again, in here, when he shouldn't exist at all, was the discordant note it took to break Kara's enchantment. The need to prostrate myself at her feet diminished to a mere whisper, while the desire to kick her chest in ballooned to *almost* irresistible proportions.

I did manage to resist both urges. It took some major effort though. The whole struggle only took a second or two. The fact that Kara did not seem suspicious of the delay in my speaking or actions just reinforced the idea that she was intentionally bespelling me with her come-hither whammy.

Now I like a good old fashioned come-hither, but the whammy part just annoys me. It didn't seem like the right time to display my open rebellion though. I let my knee bend until I was kneeling in front of her. That came close to working against me. Even just pretending to give in seemed to have intensified the effect of whatever power she was using. I felt the urge to worship her grow. That urge got stuffed back down behind all the anger I had stored up over this psychotic demi-goddess.

"I remember being in a jungle Mistress." I decided my best bet was to go with my earliest actual recollections from the current time-line. "We were using the rifles you had us trained on. The rules were to protect anyone in the same uniform we wore, and kill anyone else on the mountain."

I turned my face to hers with a grin almost as predatory as could be expected from someone like Lorcan. "We slew them by the dozens Mistress. They charged into the riverbed with us. It was an error in judgment. From a distance, their numbers would have won the exchange. In melee though, we are Einherjar, they were small and less trained. They did not have the wolf-hunger. Then a thunder from the skies smote us. It was as if Thor himself or one of the Jotun of Muspel fell upon us."

As I dredge up that memory, here, in a place where memories were real, it became clearer than I had ever recalled. The smell of the jungle rotting slowly around us, the sounds of cries too soft to be called screams. A person has to have enough breath to scream properly, and none of us were exerting ourselves lightly. There was the clash of arms all around us. I felt my feet slipping in the mud of the riverbed. It wasn't because of water though. The riverbed was dry before the attack and seemed to have been that way for a while. Now it was churned into the mud with all of the blood spilled.

I felt a dozen small wounds and a few deeper cuts or even bullet wounds. The worst though was that bomb. When the colonel called the strike in, we were one tangled, bleeding ball of death and pain. We were stabbing and cutting and cursing in a mix of languages from English to Norse to Vietnamese with a few others sprinkled in. The napalm got us all.

The description, or maybe it was my reactions to the memories, seemed to intoxicate the Valkyrie. She stood poised up on her toes with one hand reaching out and grasping while her nostrils flared and her eyes hooded themselves half-closed. Kara moved closer.

She was practically in my arms when she spoke again.

"Yes, I can feel the pain with you. The rage and joy of battle, the warm blood spray in your face. Here, so close to the source, your memories are like wine or mulled mead. They entice and intoxicate me."

She snapped her head and locked eyes back on me. I felt the mental manipulation double itself. She wasn't paying attention though. Her spell was no longer affecting me as it had. I felt the extra exertion but it did not influence me. If she noticed, she didn't mention it as she continued speaking. "Come though my warrior. Such memories are both sweet and bitter. Here is where I brought you to rid yourself of such pains. Let us erect a new house to hold this bitter memory."

At her gesture, the shadows around us all seemed to slither along the ground to be gathered in her twisting hands. She spun them into a ball which grew until she spread it on the ground and watched it solidify into one of the sod and thatch huts that dotted the mindscape. "There we are, my hero. A place for you to rest. Since you are but a shade of a memory, you will rest and be guarded by one of my pets."

No sooner did she speak, than the ground in front of her bubbled. I thought another mound would form with a zombie-like Draugr, or maybe one of the warg style wolves. Nothing like that happened though. Instead, a small pond bubbled up and spread until it completely surrounded the hut except for the very small area where my feet were planted at the doorway.

"There my bear, a moat to protect your rest." She was obviously pleased with herself. That made my guts clench. Kara was always at her worst with that reasonable but pleased with herself look. It meant she'd thought of something truly vile. Kara had a lot of anger now that I thought about it.

At her further gestures, a small boat bobbed up from whatever depths might be in such a small and spontaneous pond. Although for all I knew, in the dream world, that pond might reach an entirely new dimension before you touched the bottom. The bobbing boat drew my attention when Kara hissed a word at it.

In a mesmerizing instant of blurred and sinuous motion, the boat became a beautiful maiden standing on the water with her arms out to me. Kara spoke for both of them. "She is lovely is she not? And will offer you a surcease such as men dream of. She will hold you in her arms and lull you into the most peaceful sleep a man can have."

I watched as the features on this water spirit shifted and melded. It was as if the thing was seeking for the perfect features that would entice me the most. They never approached the face of Maureen though. Nor did they shift into the face of my first wife whom I barely remembered because of these huts and the memories trapped within them.

I had taken a step towards the allure of this seductive water spirit. My foot slid on the slick muddy surface but I caught myself and stepped back to regain my balance. That seemed to disappoint the water maiden who had taken her own step forward to join me. Out of the corner of my eye, I saw Kara's smug smile. That reminded me of how dangerous this situation was.

Once more I broke free of one of her enchantments. This was more subtle. Instead of beckoning me to worship her, the Stormy One had lulled my caution and made her illusion seem more reasonable. I was tempted to play along. Not enough to actually enter the water, I was betting that if I stepped into that, I would sink and disappear into what passed for the depths of this netherworld.

The temptation to play along only grew when Kara murmured to the creature and caused it to appear as a duplicate of my wife Frejarafn. One minute she was lovely but not irresistible. The next she was the wife I had not seen for a thousand years. Even worse, my memories of her had been stolen for years as well. It had only been a couple of weeks since, in this very place, I had stolen back one of those memories, of Frejarafn as a young girl and the day we first met.

The longing for our lost love and the family we never had struck me like a body blow. I drew my breath in and ached from the urge to go to her, to step out into the water and accept her embrace whether there was land to stand on or not.

A barely audible whine reached me. It was the fox, just barely visible to me around the corner of the hut. That meant the beast was still hidden from Kara by the building. Was the water the problem for the fox as well? Could it not cross back to firmer "land"?

I tried not to look too closely. It would not be a good idea to direct Kara's attention at this odd being until I could figure out why it was here. The thing showed me it's purpose almost immediately. With eyes still on the water nymph, the fox padded over to the water's edge and kind of patted the ground there with both paws.

I watched in amazement as the mud shifted under those paws as if the beast were working clay like some furry little sculptor. It shaped the shoreline into a bay and on one long peninsula at the far edge, the fox patted a road into existence followed by the warehouse buildings and dock that the road led to.

I had the distinct impression it was about to show me which exact building the professor was being held in. Given enough time I think the beast could have drawn me a decipherable likeness of Eachan and his captors too. That was not to be. I did not hear the water so much as rustle when the water nymph appeared beside me.

This time the shift was violent and almost instantaneous. One minute a lovely young lass with intriguing curves was there. The next, she had ripped her form apart in a spray of liquid, to reveal a larger and much more menacing looking figure. For one second it was a tall and very muscular man holding a violin of all things, but an instant later the form was more trollish or even demonic with curved rams horns. The violin turned into a club which struck down at the fox. It obliterated part of the elaborate sculpture but missed the fox.

For its part, the little creature seemed to almost laugh and skipped lightly aside. That went on for all of one or two long breathless seconds before the water-demon struck with the club, but intercepted the dodging fox with the other open hand. In an instant, that watery hand closed over the faerie fox. The smaller beast struggled and bit, but that hand became the coils of a large snake in the blink of an eye. The entire troll-like creature spun like a vortex until the snake was man-sized and squeezed tightly around the smaller fox which drew into the water and sank into its depths.

I gasped in horror at the same instant Kara was laughing her delight. She found her voice first. "Oh, dear Magnus, what unusual visions haunt your dreamscape! Was that a pooka or some sort of brownie before it was dragged down to drown in the icy deep?"

In the water between us, the snake could barely be seen

thrashing and striking at the figure buried in its not quite transparent coils. Suddenly there was a much larger commotion in that thrashing, and then the pond slowly settled itself as a small blood pool spread under the surface and bits of reddish fur floated upwards.

I was stunned and unable to react. That only increased when a leathery old hand shot into the water and seemed to extend almost to the bottom before it closed and drew back out of the pond. In it was the fox, dripping wet and limp in that grasp. But the Bone Mother just cackled again and leaned over to blow at the vulpine face with breath so fetid and reeking of decayed flesh that I caught it from all the way across the water. I wanted to gag. The effect must have been much worse up close.

Eachan's furry companion convulsed in her hands and then sprang up and staggered upright. It stood facing both of the women with all four feet spread and head lowered in a growl. It might have been cute if I hadn't noticed that the shadow being cast by the tiny creature, was not fox-like at all. That shadow belonged to a prehistoric horror that resembled modern wolves like an enraged emu resembles cornish hens.

Let's clarify that for people who might be confused. A cornish hen is small, quite tasty, and is most dangerous to humans via the transmission of disease. They can hardly scratch or peck viciously enough to ward off a sickly kitten. Emus were fierce enough to require military and machine guns in an attempt to stop their depredations of farmland in Australia. The military was not successful despite multiple attempts over many months.

That shadow beyond the fox resembled a dire wolf that our ancestors would have barely recognized because the wolf usually ate any witnesses to its appearance. The resuscitated fox slowly let the tension out of its posture as the two women faced each other rather than present any further threat to dogs, cats, foxes or Magnuses.

That caused me some concern. Had Kara just called me Magnus? Because as far as I was aware, she had never been told that was the name I used in this day and age. It was most definitely not a name that would be recognized by a shade or memory created out of the Ia Drang conflict.

"Why are there so many people in my domains?" The voice was old and cracked, but it was also laced with steel, and it belonged to the Bone Mother. She had moved to make Kara put her back to me if she would face the arrival of an older threat with a deeper knowledge of this shadow realm. Kara responded with a sound that was part hiss and part low growl.

That was a development with the potential for mayhem. One powerhouse of magical knowledge and strength was scary enough. Kara was just a pale shade of power beside what I suspected about the Bone Mother.

Somehow the thought of watching those two throw down in a place reserved for my own mental sanctuary seemed, well... Nobody says things like *"Fraught with Peril"* anymore. But right now, it felt pretty accurate.

"This is not your realm old hag." Kara's reply gave me an inkling of where I'd learned my own diplomatic skills. I was sure the "old hag" thing wouldn't be as severe in this situation as it might be in the "real" world, but it wasn't designed to win friends either. "This is just a little pocket portal I made to work with my chattel here."

Mother's wheezing laugh was not evil, but it weren't exactly cheerful. "You made? Pumped up strumpet with her flashy light show and shiny bondage gear, you couldn't make a window to see into this place. I suspect your houndmaster, the old one-eyed whoremonger made it for you, little bitch."

Okay, that response wasn't going to go down well just about anywhere I could think of, netherworld, upper world, Asgard or even nirvana. Maybe it would pass muster in the seedier parts of muspelheim, or a comedy show in the Christian Hell, come to think of it, I'd heard of a bondage sex show right in New Orleans that might accept that one.

As I suspected, Kara went about proving the old woman right, at least about the light show bit. Lightning flashed and weird blue-purple flames shot up from the armor around my old boss, and I guess you could kind of call her my ex. And there I was thinking my day couldn't get any worse. I had to admit, that the psychotic, twisted, evil, murderous spear-maiden that had everyone up in arms, used to be my main squeeze.

"You arrogant old witch! How dare you speak ill of the all-father! You are not worthy to utter Odin's name!" I watched the anger ratchet up through a visual meter. The flames and lightning grew brighter and larger until I actually had to look away, from a constructed vision, in my head. My life is really weird sometimes.

If I had to look away from the burning rage of Kara the Stormy, the Bone Mother seemed immune to it. She laughed almost joyfully. "I didn't Utter his name, little Miss Sparky. I called him a whoremonger and your houndmaster, because you are his bitch, no?"

This time there was no verbal response. Instead, Kara unleashed those coils of lightning that had been growing around here. A thunderbolt of searing light, flames, and noise shot from Kara's spear, aimed at the frail-looking old woman. That arcane, elemental, raw furious strike of energy was as big around as my torso, or about twice as big around as your average dancer or swimmer. It flashed forward, not necessarily at the speed of light, but probably faster than sound, judging from the sonic accompaniments.

One minute there was a smirking old lady, an instant later a blinding horizontal column of violence and noise, and then nothing but smoke and a small crater where the old woman had stood. I was stunned. Even Kara seemed surprised at the astounding success of her strike. Surprise bled over to disdain with barely a pause. Kara sneered and strolled over with hips swaying in a manner both arrogant and seductive. She was usually at both her best and her worst when all of that smug hubris came to the surface.

For my part, I was too stunned to move at all. Kara was under no such constraint. She stood over the crater from her vicious attack and cooed to herself while she stirred the little pile of ash and dirt at the center of the hole. "And who is weak and arrogant now, feeble old woman?"

16

KARA REALLY NEEDED to get out in the world and watch a few suspense movies or horror flicks. Never give a foe a straight line like that. The ground erupted at her feet in answer to the supposedly rhetorical question. Out of that exploding cloud of dirt and dust, a hand rose. At least the bones of said hand rose from the ground with the wrist still buried.

It is possibly worth noting, that the hand in question, was larger than anything I ever expected to see on say a largish troll or even a Jotun, the giants of my own people's legends. The mightiest of frost giants, Thrym might have a hand like this. Considering Thor had beat him to death at a feast ages and ages ago, his hand would have been about that boney too.

Kara tried to leap aside while the cloud of dirt was still in the air. The problem was, she came right back down still within the arc of those titanic fingers. The hand closed with a rather final sound of bones locking together. From the strain and color in her face, Kara found the fit of her new ossified overgarment to be a little tight.

She was struggling with the creative little prison cell

when the other parted again. This time there was no explosion of dust. The ground just rippled and bubbled as the Bone Mother rose from it as if it were water or maybe quicksand.

If Kara's grunts and thrashing revealed some of her predicament, the appearance of her foe was even more revealing. Parts of the Bone Mother were simply missing. The meaty bits around one whole side of her were cooked, scorched, or in some places just, absent. Most glaringly, her entire right arm was missing at the elbow. In the other empty places, you could see a lot of air and the aged bones of a being old enough to have taken father time to prom.

She turned that ravaged and horrifying gaze on Kara. "Is that your best shot girl? I had higher hopes. There are so many stories about your psychotic rage and immense power. You get that worked up and just inconvenience me with a little damage to the meat?"

She drew a deep breath and shook all over something like a wet dog or one who has just woken and needs to stretch. That act, of shaking her shoulders and twisting about, caused the very "earth" beneath us to shift and tremble. It was worst around Kara. Cracks split the ground running away from that titan's claw that imprisoned her. The giant bones themselves creaked but did not loosen their grip.

From my angle, only a portion of Kara's face was visible. That little portion was turning purple from rage, or exertion, or maybe just from having her body crushed in a giant skeletal fist. She still had enough air to hiss out her anger, "You withered shadow from a forgotten past!"

The fist around Kara tightened enough to stop the flow of her words. She struggled for perhaps fifteen seconds before the futility or lack of oxygen started slowing down the efforts. Finally, Kara went still. She was standing upright and glaring at the older being with more scorn and hate than I thought was advisable considering the crushing grip around her.

There are reasons Kara was my boss and not the other way around for so long. While she stared and glared and otherwise kept her face to the Mother, she was also apparently playing puppet master. I just didn't realize until too late which one was pulling these particular strings.

A movement behind Kara caught my eye. I turned to see her spear rise up from where she'd dropped it. The deadly point came to hover behind her with the tip almost at the back of her head. I thought it was the Bone Mother preparing to unleash a horrible execution-style death on Kara.

That idea was conflicted within my head. On one hand, there was still some lingering traces of affection or devotion, or maybe it was her enchantment skill. Part of me didn't want to see my Valkyrie killed. I just wanted her to leave me alone.

On the other hand, Kara had been my worst nightmare since I woke up in that medical tent in Vietnam. She had also been the puppeteer to my actions and those of dozens of my kind for centuries. Some of the memories I had managed to recover, seem to suggest that we weren't always nice even by the standards of warriors and raiders.

My gut tightened and wanted to empty itself at a memory we found on my first foray into this dreamscape. I clearly recalled every detail from the moment I caused the young Indian to fire my rifle and start the massacre at Wounded Knee. The video in my head stopped at the artillery fire that ended the battle for me. In particular, the face to face image of a dying woman with her innocent babe still snuggling close haunts me at any given moment.

The images and memories were sharper inside wherever I was. Whether it was a product of my mind or some other dimension or realm, memories and emotions had more bang for their buck in such a place. That was demonstrated forcefully just a second later.

The moments of my inner reflection were packed with changes outside of that potent memory. The Mother had somehow regrown a great deal of her wasted anatomy. I was starting to think that she could use the "earth" and dust of this realm to regrow flesh or at least shadow flesh since Kara seemed to think we were all just shades of ourselves.

The Bone Lady shook out her hair without looking to see if anything important fell out along with the dust, dirt, a maggot or two, and something that looked like an ear belonging to someone else. Snacks for later maybe? When she looked up, the Mother's face was practically unmarked again. Or rather it was unmarked by anything other than centuries of age and experience along with some barely noticeable scorching and a tooth or two peeking out.

"So you have stopped your futile tantrum child?" Her voice was that of a grandmother talking to a particularly troublesome offspring called Kara. There was no fear or anger, just some amusement and the faintest inkling of irritation.

When her question got no answer, the Mother let out a dry "clucking" sound. "So are we sulking as well?"

It was a pretty good straight line. Maybe that was what Kara had been waiting for. I had just decided to plead for the mother not to kill her here, where the fallout inside my mental space was pretty incalculable from my experience. It turned out I was asking the wrong person for mercy.

"Not sulking, *plotting*." Kara twisted her head at the same time her shoulders surged within those bony fingers. The spear sped through her dark tresses, which hid it for a split second longer. She cut it close enough, that the edge of that spearhead grazed her cheek and threw a thin spray of red droplets into the air.

That was nothing compared to what it did to the Bone Mother. The spear was starting to flash and twist along with a howl as if it had awakened. All of those combined in a detonation that began in the Mother's chest, it lifted her up and carried the exploding pieces over the water and dropped it in.

What fell was not a woman, but a blackened skeleton with raw red gobbets of meat dangling here and there. Even before it hit the water, her corpse was breaking up into a pile of bones which sunk towards the bottom of that pool.

Kara snarled and kicked the wrist bone sticking up to hold her "cage" in place. The whole thing crumbled to dust while she stretched her arms overhead and then cast a wickedly self-satisfied smile at me. "I felt that you know? Felt you start to warn me or beg for mercy. You're much easier to read from inside your own head my bear, or is it Mouse?"

She turned and stalked towards my little moat, crossing one ankle in front of the other in that seductive, hip-swaying stride. She stopped well away from me to pout and softly purr. "Oh, how I wish things were like they used to be. When you were *My* bear. You do remember how I get after a satisfying win or creative kill?"

With her standing just out of reach, one hand cocked on her hip and the other leg stretched out to the best advantage, I could barely help remembering other such occasions. Occasions when there hadn't been a moat between us, or anything like clothing, or inhibition. When your love-making is like riding a storm, the term "unbridled passion" is both apt and wildly inadequate. Maybe she was right about the strength of memories in this place.

"So, my bear, that was not a bad performance. If I could not feel the resonance of you here in your own head, you might have fooled me with that dimwit impersonation. Frankly, it almost worked except for the fox and the old woman. They gave you away even if I had missed the signs of your actual awareness." Kara's seductive pose did not fool me for longer than a single hearty dose of my hormones. She was too calculating even in the act of evil overlord gloating.

"I do not have time to wipe your mind now." She turned her head from side to side studying me before she continued. "I can see you have broken my molding anyway. It would take a great deal of time and effort that I fear I am just not willing to invest. You should not have fled me Bear. And I can not risk your return if you are not properly controlled. You would be little more than an embarrassment. So I'm afraid you will have to stay here."

With her verdict rendered Kara stood watching me for a little while longer. Maybe she thought I would beg or argue. As far as I could tell, neither would do me any good. The actions might entertain her, but they would not change her mind.

I went with a recent tactic that had begun to impress me with its effectiveness. I kept my mouth shut. Standing in a pose that would indicate neither subservience or defiance, I shifted my weight from one foot to the other and dropped my thumbs to the woven belt provided by now scorched and evaporated hostess, the Bone Mother.

Kara knew me better than that. I guess a few centuries together will do that for some people. Then again I've known couples that were so far apart, even an eon might not do the trick. She showed me how much I was fooling her with a chuckle. "Oh, you've barely changed, other than loosening your leash and collar. That's too bad. I liked you the other way, domesticated but not pacified. Much like keeping a wolf at your side rather than a dog. Are you sure you don't want to come back and be my trained wolf again? Or trained Bear at least?"

She knew me well enough to require no answer on my part. She just shook her head and answered her own question. "No, of course not. You've been allowed to run wild again. I doubt the training would take without making mush out of your head. Which I'm afraid is the ultimate ending here anyway."

She turned to the pool and said a name just low enough to avoid my ears. At her call, the water bubbled and the snake rose from its depths and transformed into the muscular-looking water-man. "He does not leave alive, my pet. If he tries to leave that memory cell, then drown him. And that shall be that. The Storm Bear will be no more. Just another zombie for my ranks."

She turned to face me with the oversized snake slash warrior looming behind her.

" Make no mistake, Magnus," she hissed my newer name as if just the sound of it made her furious. "Your Hugr, the awareness within you, shall remain here, trapped within itself. To the outside world, you will be breathing but not alive. What they call comatose today. To escape this fate, you will have to sacrifice yourself. And when you die, you shall find yourself powerless against me back in Valhalla. I will shred your Hugr to its most base form. Your will shall be gone, replaced by my own whims. So enjoy your memories while you can."

With that, she waved her hand and suddenly a dozen or more of the smaller huts around me burst into an almost colorless flame. As the buildings burned away, I was flooded with memories all at once. Things I had done or seen that had been hidden were made plain. It was as if every memory from dozens of years slammed into your head with stunning realism, immediacy, and detail all at the exact same second.

I felt like my head was going to explode. I could picture the moment alongside all of the other visions clamoring for attention. Eyes swelling until they exploded out of the sockets in a technicolor rainbow of images and sensory information. For the first time in a very long time, I was knocked completely unconscious without a punch being thrown or any kind of impact from a blunt object or high caliber round.

It must have been no more than a minute or two before I woke up. My head was pounding. It wouldn't have surprised me if there was blood running out of my nose, or maybe my ears. Hel, I wouldn't have been surprised to find an eye or two laying at the water's edge after all of those memories had their way with me.

When I rolled over to my back, I received a close-up vision of the snake-creature looming over me. It was more of a hybrid than before. There were beefy arms and shoulders with the head of a cobra sticking up in place of a man's neck and face. It even had the hood spread out around it.

Normally such a sight would be cause for alarms and immediate action. I might scream like a toddler, wet my breeches, or leap into a life and death grapple when confronted by such an image at any other time. This was my head though and in my experience, these things just kind of lurk around in there. Or at least they did for both excursions I'd had recently.

Kara's instructions helped quell any instinctive fear as well. She's specifically told the thing only to drown me if I tried to escape. I don't think falling over under mental assault qualified as an escape plan. Given that much information, I felt confident that it was just checking me over for later abuse. It didn't have permission to indulge its favorite choices in violence yet.

Speaking of people with a whole portfolio of favorite violence, where was Kara? I sat up with my feet carefully drawn back from the water's edge. There was no need to test the thing's instructions too much was there? A casual look around didn't spot any immediate dangers. That led to a more careful scrutiny that showed just as few threats, but also the tracks that led away from Kara had been standing.

That trail only went a few steps and then disappeared in a churned up chunk of dirty flanked by two scorch marks. They were just about as far apart as the lightning bolts Kara had manifested to open her portal back at Stige's abode.

My situation was improved by at least that much. Now I just had to figure my way out of a coma while a vicious guardian in his own element waited to drag me back to a Valhalla that sounded less appealing than ever. The creature in question gave me reason to suddenly question my own logic. Instead of looming around and being threatening, it spun in the "pond" and then charged straight at me.

I didn't see any way it could stop before crashing onto the shore. With my luck that would leave it enough substance to lock onto a weak and bewildered Magnus. The drowning part would be much easier on the Nokk, or Nordic Nixie than it would on me.

With the limited amount of space on my little island, I wasn't spoiled for maneuvering room. The best option I came up with was to scurry back into the little hut that was just like those that had released so many of my memories. They weren't all back though. I could still see dozens of the little huts. There was also the huge Long-house still standing intact despite the shattered entrance. I had no doubt that the memories in there were still shielded from my prying.

I retreated into the hut ahead of the rushing water-snake-man-hybrid-monstrosity. In fact, it never even made it to land. Instead, the water exploded into droplets and a furry red fox landed amidst the shower. Other than a few spots of fresh water, he didn't even look damp despite appearing to be made out of water just second ago.

To say I was surprised would have been an understatement. Somehow I had completely forgotten about the damned fox during the little scuffle involving two women scrapping it out within my mental confines and utilizing serious juice behind their mojo. Then again, I suspected that fox had its own mojo with a much more subtle flavor to it.

On the heels of that thought, the water erupted again and spun a small but fierce waterspout that swept up bits of the nearby shore and spun them into a muddy vortex. I was forced to shield my face, and most importantly my eyes, from the splatters of mud, water, and magick that suddenly resolved itself into the Bone Mother standing before me with a smirk.

"She's certainly more arrogant than she is bright, isn't your ex-flame boy?" At least she hadn't commented on my own lack of wits. It was probably too easy to make fun of the lackwit standing there with his jaw gaping at a creature that he had already suspected was something of a divinity herself. I mean, honestly, had I really thought Kara was going to just casually knock off an eldritch power that was probably as old as the human race itself?

She didn't say anything out loud, but her eyes sparkled with a merry amusement at my surprise. There was probably some sarcasm and smug disdain lurking within that look too. She didn't voice them though, instead, she took a careful step forward and swung her bare foot like an American Field Goal kicker. The fox never even saw it coming. He went from sitting with his tail over his front paws to sailing out over the horizon and out of sight.

"What the Hel!?" I was almost as surprised as the absent vulpine nuisance. "That fox belonged to...or rather, he belongs *with* a friend of mine!"

"What fox?" Her response was enough to make me want to bang my already confused and aching head into the wooden hut a few times. That's the same way I usually felt when Eachan did the same thing right after we had both seen or even interacted with the spectral, spiritual, magical, or otherwise mysterious creature that followed him about.

"Oh dear, the boy really is not much smarter than his ex is he?" She shook her head mournfully while kicking dirt out in a sheet which covered the pond as if it had never been there. "He doesn't know that one does not acknowledge Pookas, or Brownies or half a dozen other fae creatures does he?"

By the time she stopped shaking her head, the little hut was no longer surrounded by a moat but was instead sitting on the same ground as the rest of the scene about us. Snow was even beginning to dot the surface of that new "ground" despite there being no snow in the air at the moment.

"There we go now. That inconsiderate child should not

leave traps and terrible creatures in this world. Even if it's in your own 'scape." The Mother stood and looked around at the other buildings and the damage I myself had done previously.

"Your head really is not a tidy place young warrior. Perhaps you should start working on ordering it, no?" Her head spun around to look at me suddenly. "But what are you still doing here, Idler? We've solved your riddle. You've freed more memories. That is quite enough for one visit, isn't it? Don't you have things to attend to now that your mistress isn't expecting you?"

This time she didn't use her foot. The mother gestured and I felt myself falling backward until my spine impacted, with a hard stone table in a lair somewhere beneath the streets of New Orleans.

17

THE FIRST THING I felt was the stone slab under my back. It wasn't as hard as I had first thought it, because there were now linens and a blanket between me and the table itself. That took the sensation from harsh, to mildly uncomfortable.

The second thing I felt was a strange wet, warmth around my hand. That was replaced by the grazing sensation of something hard and jaggedly sharp. If that hadn't brought me instantly awake the whining voice I heard next would have.

"Enough! It's my turn! I want a taste!" I jerked my head around in time to see my hand passed from the mouth of one small horror to another. Both had jagged, sharp, uneven rows of teeth that looked like smaller and less hygienic versions of Stige's shark-teeth. The first one seemed to be pouting as the other larger creature relieved him of my barely responsive hand.

I say barely responsive, because as much as I wanted to jerk the appendage free, and possibly smack these little carnivores about, all I could force my hand to do was flop weakly at the end of an equally limp forearm.

"Stop that!" My voice cracked with a hoarse urgency that did exactly not ring with authority. But it must have been unexpected enough to catch the greedy little beasts by surprise. Both of them darted backward, although the larger of the two got in one decent nip of those nasty dental nubbins on the way. It didn't do a ton of damage, but the mere presence of a bloody trickle made me worry about infection. Those really were some nasty mouths.

My voice also drew a movement on my other side that I barely caught with my peripheral vision. I tried to flail out a defensive fist, or at least wave in a vaguely threatening manner with fingers that would not answer any commands. What I got was a mass of soft hair and an indistinct female voice.

After a long and strenuous effort, I got my head turned to see the head pillowed on a rolled-up blanket by my wrist. It was the wrong color to be Maureen or Bobbi-Lee, so I was guessing it had to be Neamh Ange. That was confirmed when her wheelchair scooted back and then forward again at her sleepy movements.

My voice might not have been enough to wake the exhausted girl in the wheelchair, but it was enough to summon the Amazonian looking Lola from a door that opened in what had appeared to be a blank wall. The troll-ess looked as unamused as her voice sounded. "Be quiet Einherjar. You will wake the girl or perhaps my other patient."

To the other two smaller creatures she devoted a silent scowl and shooing motion. Both little horrors were smart enough not to test the formidable female troll's mettle. They slouched away with barely a whine. One of them did pause long enough to shoved Nev's supporting hand out from under her head. That resulted in a small gasp and a thud when she hit the hard surface beside my bedsheets.

That small victory gave both of the small "men" some enjoyment. They left the room snickering to themselves rather than bickering about who was going to taste my fingers. I made a mental note to extract a little amusement of my own at their expense, provided the opportunity presented itself. Not so much for my fingers, as for the petty maliciousness towards the lady.

Nev Ange stirred and lifted her head to rub at the impact spot and blink sleepy eyes. That's when I realized she'd been cuddled up with the laptop computer Stige had made and never got through dickering over. That seemed to warrant a comment or warning on my part.

I pointed at the computer in question. "You planning to sneak that out past security? Because people from this side of the block tend to do things differently. You steal from certain alt-naturals and it leaves a kind of psychic stench. Lets them track you and then gives them a free trip past any defenses someone might normally have. I've heard of priests and saints getting into a sticky situation through such misunderstandings."

The girl had the grace to blush. It was subtle due to her caramel cream skin coloring, but I spotted the pink tones. Even her voice held a trace of embarrassment, "I haven't stolen it, but I did plug it in and do some research. The...people, down here wouldn't let us leave. They wanted to wait for you to wake up or die. I'm not sure what would have happened then. Chances are it wouldn't have been good. But the point is, with nothing else to do I got on here and started looking into the things we had talked about previously."

We were both shushed by the troll. "Did I not tell you to be quiet? And that goes for your companion as well."

Her tone was cool but professional as she started looking me over through a vizor like device. It looked like something from a sci-fi movie as envisioned by elves. There were stone and wood but mostly it was crystal lenses. There also did not seem to be any battery compartment or power source. "Well, you seem to be past the worst of it. I still don't understand why you slipped into a comatose state anyway. Perhaps I drained more essence from you than I would a normal human. At least one I expected to survive. However, everything I've heard of your kind indicated that you were hardier than this."

Abruptly she stopped and snapped the vizor off of her heard with a growl. "I thought you told people that you have not talked to your Valkyrie or that other fellow for years. So why are you enveloped in the aura of a Valkyrie and one as strong as Kara? There are not many that are strong enough to leave such a signature."

I could see her cruel-looking talons curl and cut into the stone table like a normal person might peel an orange. That made it pretty plain that she could peel me even more easily. In my current weakened state, well I'd have to hope for divine intervention. Considering the gods most likely to respond to me, the cure might be worse than the disease. I refrained from any rash prayers and opted to try and answer her.

"Would you believe your little extraction services sent me across the veil? I don't mean I died, but I did slip into a shamanic vision. Probably a factor of a near-death experience courtesy of spiritual exsanguination. Anyway, Kara ambushed me there and locked my psyche away. That's why I was in a coma and that's why you smell her magick all over me." I shrugged. Why not tell the truth for a change? Secrecy hadn't been doing me a lot of good lately.

It seemed like the only people inconvenienced by my secrets and paranoia were the people I probably could have trusted the most. The ones that I should really be guarded against seemed able to pop in and out of my personal space at will. I mean c' mon, Kara had been in my freaking head, unless my mental fruitcake had wandered to the fruitier and nuttier side of the recipe.

Lola the troll dropped her jaw and stared at me, probably a reaction to my unexpected candor. She caught up though and responded with a unique sound that shared traits with sultry laughter and the growl of something large and face-eatingly hungry. Considering the source, that was probably to be expected.

"Well, your sense of humor seems to be on the rise. Or else all of the life force I took came from your head. That is a very nice tale. It is not something our community will probably accept at face value though." She still had a hint of amusement behind her voice, but it didn't make me feel much better.

I started to get up. Rather, I tried to get up. All I managed was to push myself off balance with nothing below my face but the stone floor. It was a good thing that the troll was close enough to jump in and support my shoulders with one spade-sized hand. Her other hand rearranged my pillows and even stretched uncomfortably far enough to open a closet and drag out a couple more of the soft supports.

She chided me while tucking me in like a child. "Yes, it seems I drained your brain to mush. Why would you think it is a good idea to get up so soon after recovering from a comatose state?"

I barely took notice of her question. I had some of my

own. "Son-of-a..." I had to catch my breath before I continued. "I'm weak as a sparrow hatchling. My head is swimming, and everything attached to me is aching. I think I feel
the table throbbing. And that's enough to make me want to
lose breakfast if I had anything in my gut to lose."

For a creature with her size and appearance, Lola had a
fairly good bedside manner. She lowered me, one-handed I
might add, to the sheets beneath me. As she did so she
seemed to fiddle with the crystal lenses before putting them
back on. I barely noticed all of this because of the uncountable multitude of aches and pains.

I couldn't help hearing a very novel and unheard-of
hitch in my voice. I prefer *hitch* to *whine*."Lola, why do I hurt
so much? I've had multiple mortal wounds that didn't feel
this way. As a matter of fact, even some of those old wounds
ache as much as a fresh stab with a dull knife, soaked in
lemon, or battery acid, doused with salt."

While I talked she was giving me the once over with the
glasses. By the time I finished whining, I mean "speaking
with a hitch", she was ready to deliver her diagnosis. "Well,
Einherjar, this is probably the first time in ages that your
protective and healing magicks are not ahead of the damage
you blunder into. I can see inflammation and radiation from
several old injuries. To add to that, you have a low-grade
fever, inflammation of the upper respiratory tract from a
viral infection, and congestion from the same infection."

Nev Ange raised her head and cocked it to one side. I
definitely heard more entertainment than concern in her
question. "That wouldn't be a rhinovirus would it?"

Lola discarded concern entirely and laughed out loud.
"That is a good guess, little woman. He has a man-cold."

It's hard to remain dignified while your body is trembling with pains it hadn't felt in centuries, all while being

laughed at by two women. I tried to retain my composure by reconciling the aches and tribulations with her diagnosis. Everything fit except for the newest generalised ache around my knee, the one I'd wrecked climbing out of a cooking pot in the dreamworld.

Great, I get to try and save all my friends, a couple of allies, and even a few people that wanted to kill and eat me, not necessarily in that order. And while I was doing all of that, I need to remember to "get enough rest and remain in a warm and humid environment". I guess it's a good thing that New Orleans is almost always warm and humid.

Lola finally wound down to dry her eyes from the laugh tears. "Oh, that felt good. I've been so worried about Stige, I think I really needed a good laugh. That's enough though! You, little human girl, visiting hours ends in ten minutes. Say your goodbyes and go back to the room you and your friend were assigned."

That reminded me that I hadn't even asked about anyone. Stige, Luis, Bobbie-Lee and even Heather had all been at risk of one thing or another when I agreed to my possibly ill-advised mission of mercy. "Did the treatment work for Stige?"

I didn't get the answer I wanted. Lola just looked at me with the smile fading from her face. Her final answer seemed to be a weary shrug as she turned away. Just before she left the room she added to the shrug by tossing a few clipped words over her shoulder. "He's still breathing and his heartbeat is stronger. That is all for now. Don't forget, ten minutes."

Nev and I silently watched the door close behind her. I cleared my voice and started first. "How is Bobbie-Lee and have we any word on Luis or his Valkyrie or any of the others at all?"

Nev leaned over to pat my hand. "I'll let Bobbie tell you herself. Nothing to worry about there. As for the others, well, I picked up a couple of facial recognition hits with this little wonder-box the troll made. Did you know it has some kind of satellite level wi-fi that I can't even figure out? If the dark elves made his cooling system then maybe the signal adapter came from Area 51."

I tried to wait patiently while she scooted about and turned the laptop so I could see the screen when she powered it up. "I can't find anything on your other chosen buddy. Same goes for the psycho witch with the weather fetish and her sasquatch flunky. We did, however, get a hit on the SUV carrying the other guy's girl, Heather. That led to the second hit."

She punched a couple of buttons and switched to more photos of a facility built along the water. It was isolated and left to look abandoned, except for the shiny new cars and the very edge of a boat docked inside the warehouse. Subsequent photos zoomed in until I saw a face I knew.

I was stunned and missed the first few words when Nev continued what she was saying. "While they were escorting this Heather from the vehicle, we caught a shot of another female being led around inside a fenced-in area. It reminded me of *yard time* in prison. The red hair was visible from a mile off but I had to zoom in to confirm the hit. It's your lady friend Maureen."

I lost track of a minute or two right then. I was just so glad to see that at least one of my "people" was still alive. I could hardly breathe because it happened to be Maureen. We'd had a rough patch and some misunderstandings, mainly because I thought she'd run away to get some space.

It turned out that she was actually sold to the same

Cartel guys that I was on a collision course with. I freed her at the same time I was dealing with the real bad guy. A body-skipping semi-divine entity was using the drug runners and gunmen until I left him locked in an ancient storehouse of knowledge and weapons. That was the favor Freke required of me in order to erase his memories of seeing me in Austin. He seemed pretty certain that I didn't want anyone going back to tell Odin or Kara where I was. He was right.

I hoped to get some time with Maureen and straighten things out. We'd been together a few months that felt like much longer. She was the first woman to really get under my skin since I woke up in Vietnam.

Until I met her, it hadn't seemed fair or prudent to get involved with a mortal woman when I had so many secrets and potential enemies of a supernatural flavor. From the amount of trouble and damage she'd seen since then, it still wasn't fair. Now, whether we could fix things or not, I owed it to her to get her out of this mess. Maybe I owed it to her to come clean about a number of things too. Or else she deserved to be free of me, and safe from the kind of chaos that I was finding myself in.

I finally found my voice about the time Ange stopped talking about the software, hardware and even satellite links she used to get her information. "When were these taken? And do we have the location for sure?"

I caught Ange studying my face too intently for my own comfort. She cleared her throat before answering. "The photos are a couple of hours old; a little longer for the first shots of this Heather character. I kept the satellite focused on the warehouse as long as I dared. Any more and they might have caught onto our snooping on agency spooks with their own government's hardware. Still no sign of either of the guys. No sign of your biker buddy, my equipment handler, or the white shirts in white vans."

It seemed like a daunting task. For some reason, I suddenly felt okay about some of it. Or at least energized enough to do some planning. "Fair enough. I think we need to move sooner rather than later though. I might be able to get the white van to show up for us anyway. Then we have to worry that the government goons could be thinking about cutting their losses and disposing of witness soon. If that wasn't enough risk, Kara will be looking for Heather and can find her fairly easily with her own Einherjar to use as a tracking device."

With her eyes still oddly intent, Nev Ange cocked her head to one side as if studying a strange alien creature. "You aren't even that scared are you?"

The door opened on her last words, well before I could answer. Lola provided an answer of sorts for me. "If he isn't that scared then he should be."

She bustled into the room with an old woman behind her. At first glance, the figure in worn and tattered clothes appeared to be just another homeless derelict of a person living off the streets and trying to survive one more day. A closer look at her face was enough to change all of that and leave me lurching back while my face cycled through all of the attempts I made not to show fear, or alarm, or disgusted horror.

It wasn't so much that she was hideous. Although that might have been a factor. Her eyes were both milky white and darkly opaque. That is, one of them was a featureless white, while the other might have been an obsidian ball. The rest of her features were out of proportion in so many ways it was impossible to catalog them all. Her nose was too large, hooked in the middle and bent sideways at the end, it was also quite noticeably out of the mid-range placement in a human face.

The effect was to make one side of her face look much smaller than the other, though her eyes were roughly the same size and her mouth might nor might not have been normal...well, you get it. She was a dying cancerous leper of a hag painted by Pablo Picasso while he himself was dealing with hallucinogens and a world-class hangover.

Oh, and it was all painted in black and white. She was devoid of color. There wasn't even a hint of peach, or cinnamon, or even brown in her skin tones. They were mottled grey, just like her hair and even her fingernails. The overall effect was that of a ghost brought to terrifying solid form.

Her voice didn't help. When she spoke it was a croaking moaning sound that was difficult to focus on. "Scared you should be. Your fate is uncertain now. How long has it been since you fought without the Shield of your Power? You should be frightened indeed. Frightened of your destiny, of the fate of your friends, and of the creatures that seek your end."

It was refreshing. After listening to the Bone Mother's line of insults, this eldster's formal speech was a new flavor. It reminded me of other times and places. The message, however, was unwelcome and more than a tad annoying.

"Right, doom and destruction, yadda yadda, blah blah blah. Let me guess, you're a voodoo queen or some song of the south oracle? Nice contacts, by the way, they really sell the whole package." I knew even as the words came out of my mouth, that it was the wrong thing to say.

She chuckled in a voice that was oddly appropriate there, in a room surrounded by rock and earth well below the open air and light of day. It was a voice that belonged below the ground, about six feet below on average. Her next comment confirmed that notion,

"You do not suffer from cowardice. It takes a brave warrior indeed to taunt the Tenebrae." She grinned at me through dry and cracked lips that revealed uneven grey tombstones of teeth. I tried not to grimace as I was racking my memory for what a Tenebrae might be. Nebulous? Shadowed? It sounded Latin but I had only an inkling, the word Umbra came to mind as well.

She offered a new hint while I was pondering. "The daughters of Nyx do not suffer insults lightly. If I were not delivering important news, then I would strike thee blind and fill thine sleep with nightmares to gray hair and rend minds."

That did it. Tenebrae was originally a Latin name for semi-divine beings. It was the formal speech pattern as much as the names mentioned that did it for me. Truly ancient creatures and beings tended to slip into archaic communication, especially when they became agitated. Say by a mouthy guy who had temporarily forgotten that suddenly, he wasn't bullet-proof or even mildly bullet resistant.

Creatures of the night, Keres in Greek myth were called Tenebrae in Latin. They were daughters of Nyx, the Greek Goddess of night. By either name, they were a bloodier and darker version of our own Valkyrie. Where Valkyries were drawn to the glory and honor of battle, Tenebrae reveled in the violence, the horror, and bloodshed of the battlefield. They weren't the kind to invite over for tea and crumpets.

"What news do you bear then, elder spirit?" Okay, so maybe I come from a different time period too. The important thing was to try not to annoy her anymore, at least not while I was as mortal as anyone else and weak as the proverbial kitten.

She cocked her head to the side and then spit out more dust with that dry laugh of hers. "So perhaps not as stupid as it first seemed? Very well, just this morn, as I returned here to slumber in safety, I saw the snowy chariot of the death-wizard arrive. His minions spilled forth and surprised Stige's normal watchers. Why would the watchers worry, when always before the white wagon only took humans?"

She shook her head while I did a little freelance interpretation. I didn't for a minute believe some wizard in a white chariot was running around. But a modern car might look like a magical chariot without horses, or a van might look like a wagon. We knew someone with minions that drove around in a white van too, didn't we?

"Most of the little folk fled while a scant handful gave a fight. They dealt horrendous wounds." her voice seemed to almost purr at the thought of those gaping wounds and splatters of blood. "The minions overwhelmed them though. The dead were left for their companions to deal with, but no fewer than three of the shrouded watchers were taken in the wagon. As they rode away, one of the minions yelled out of the window that they would trade, our folk, for the humans we sheltered."

By that point, the little horrors who had been tasting me were back to peer around the doorframe. That meant that Nev Ange and I were pinned down by glares from eight eyes, including the ebony orb and its milky counterpart.

18

I COULDN'T HAVE BLAMED any of them for blaming us. My first instinct was that Ange, Bobbie and I were all in a worse fix than even I had ever imagined. Considering how active my imagination had been, that hardly seemed fair at all. The jury was still out on whether my mind had slipped inside the dreamworld, or was suffering from fever dreams. I had an eggplant of a knot on my knee that didn't fit either scenario.

People don't normally get bruises from an accident in their dreams or inside a dreamworld either one. Swelling and broken blood vessels usually require a physical source. I say usually because I'd heard of other tales involving shaman and witch doctors. One report even talked about finding a fellow in the middle of the desert who had drowned and then fallen far enough to break most of his bones. And all with nothing taller or wetter than a cactus for miles around.

The trolls and Nev Ange would probably have mentioned if my body had been on walk-about while I was talking to Mother Bone though. That was not the immediate concern though.

No, my top priority in worries was echoed by a whining voice from the doorway. "We were doing just fine before they showed up. I say we give one to the bokr Papa Beaufort, and we tell him the other one was already under the butcher's knife before we heard his deal."

I glared at the larger of the two tiny menaces who had awakened me. He glared back and then lifted a hand tipped with grimy claws. It looked as if he might intend to wipe the ropy drool from his chin, but instead, he stretched his oversized lips around the disgusting fingers and made a sound as if sucking the meat off of a chicken bone.

That was enough to reaffirm my feelings about a good pummeling if circumstances permitted. It also brought up a question though. He only mentioned two of us. Surely they hadn't forgotten Bobbie just because she wasn't in the room. I looked at Ange for an answer, but her glaring eyes were locked on the nasty little finger sucker.

My answers came from elsewhere. Lola cleared her throat to get my attention. "Your other friend is not here. She took the motorcycle back to her steading to get more supplies. She gave her vow on a geas stone though. I have no doubt she will be back before morning. Even a foolish human will not fight the geas for long."

I had no idea what a "geas stone" was. I had heard of geas or geasa though. They were the old Celtic version of a vow on my Thor's hammer. The Celts swore by them, (pun intended) believing them capable of anything up to and including death or lineage curses. If I had to guess, Bobbie would find herself heading back without thinking too much. If she fought it, she would get uneasy, then it would get worse the longer she resisted. Eventually, anxiety, pain, or even physical illness would drive her back to be relieved of the vow.

But that also meant she was out. We had an operator outside of the lair. These people would be cautious about doing anything to harm us while there was a free agent. It gave us some time.

I decided to make the most of it. "Before anyone jumps to any conclusions, remember, I was asking questions about the same guy in the white van already. He isn't an ally, but someone else sticking their nose in other peoples' business. I already wanted to bust that nose for him. Now I can do that and get your people back at the same time."

It was hard not to turn and watch the two smaller menaces. I could see furtive movements from the corner of my eye. The authority in that room was right in front of me though. If I could convince Lola, then she would hold the others in check. Without her, I was just another line on the menu. *Special of the day, Chosen Warrior, free-range, extra tenderized and free of enchantment or protections.*

Her closed body posture did nothing to encourage me. In fact, I decided we might need to plan a break, provided the little horrors didn't drop me before I got some of my strength back. I was terrified by the thought that I was so weak. I refused to show fear to these little turd muffins though. For one, it would be counterproductive. For another, I'd chew off my own fingers before I gave them the satisfaction of seeing me afraid or begging.

"They could have been lying from the beginning. It is always easier to get into an enemy's camp if you claim a common foe." The Tenebrae's voice was either contemplative or the flat tone was a side effect of being a billboard for death and drab attire.

Lola, on the other hand, had not moved. She still stood

silently, arms crossed, staring at us. She barely seemed to listen as the little goblinoids and their haggard gray ally argued against Nev and me. Instead, she looked Nev full in the eye. Then she did the same for me.

Only after a long pause to consider whatever she found there did the elongated troll matron speak. "I never liked Beaufort anyway. If you can save our little ones then do so. If you can hurt or inconvenience the bokr at the same time, then it would be the icing on the cake, no?"

She turned to glare at the little menacing goblinoids. "Didn't I evict you once? Go find something useful to do. Our guests will not go into the stewpot. Perhaps you should find food before you become dinner."

Lola clapped her hands sharply to send the smaller monstrosities scurrying. Then she turned her attention to the gray horror in stringy hair. "You do not require any such encouragement, do you? I respect your sisterhood. But we do not fear you, and you will abide by the community rules as long as you stay with us. Correct?"

"Yours is just another place for me to rest Mistress." The Tenebrae did not bow, but there was a hint of a nod or barely perceptible inclination of her head. "However this decision is yours to make."

She turned to leave, but at the last minute stopped to face me again. "I almost forgot, warrior of old. I meant to ask you why you have hobbled the tongue of your fetch? He has quite the stories to tell. A keen wit as well. He has entertained me well, so I thought perchance to return the favor. What would it take to convince you to unhobble the voice of your totem?"

I leaned back as if to avoid a slap to the face. She'd caught me by surprise. I knew that the birdcage had been in the motorcycle. In all the excitement though I'd forgotten all about my longtime pet and sometime friend Rafe. The recoil was not from surprise though, so much as a denial of what she implied.

Wizards, Shaman, Vitkis or Gothis of my timeline sometimes talked about a Fylgja. It was what other workers or witches might call a fetch or a familiar. To me, it represented a spiritual being of fate or maybe a helpful ancestress. The problem was, I hadn't done any rituals or tried anything special to summon Rafe. In fact, I'd bought him from the same shop I used for Grimmr's food. The whole purchase had been on a whim, and there was definitely nothing ritualistic about it. The only sacrifice I'd made was a couple of nights worth of tips from subbing as a bartender.

That was my first reaction. My second was to cringe at all of the fodder we'd just given Nev Ange to pester me with questions about my obscure origins. Warrior of old, and with a fylgja at that. I didn't even want to consider how I was going to answer those questions.

I needed to answer the scary lady in her fashionable death shroud first. "I will consider it elder mistress. It was through ignorance and not out of spite."

That seemed enough to placate the nightmare creature. She nodded solemnly and then had the last word just before the door closed. "Consider quickly. The fetch deserves better. Best not to anger a creature of your own spirit."

Well, that was ominous enough if I believed for a minute that Rafe was more than a bird that caught my attention with his antics in a shop window. I put that question out of my mind momentarily. Lola gave us both one more long, hesitant look. Then she left through the same door as the others. I tried not to make anything out of her hesitance, or the way she shook her head as she walked away.

"Warrior of old huh?" Nev Ange didn't even take me by

surprise. Maybe it was a touch faster than I expected, but I *did* expect the interrogation.

I had a dandy excuse to avoid the questions. "That's hardly important right now. We have more important things to worry about. Maybe you missed it, but there's a certain level of threat implied in the alt-natural decision here. We've got a chance to get out of this, but only if we add three little dark-elf cousins to our list of rescuees. If we fail that task, then these particular folks are literally nightmares that will chase you down."

Something about that last statement got to Ange. She bit her lip and tried not to look scared. The pale skin, wide eyes, thready breaths and trembling weren't exactly subtle clues though.

I ignored that for the time being. She might be scared but she was holding it together. That didn't keep me from remembering the mess she'd turned into while Stige was pretending to be the main course in an old fashioned luau and pig roast. I might not like it, but I had to depend on her. Not just for me, but to keep her and Bobbi alive as well.

I had little choice but to continue planning. "I don't know about you, but I'm starting to feel more than a little outnumbered. We have so many hands turned against us, or ready to turn in an instant. It's kind of daunting. But, I think I have an idea to even the odds a bit."

That didn't seem to help her trembling or the wide-eyed stare. If anything it made those eyes even bigger. It didn't stifle her voice though. "You? Have a plan? Is it better than fighting to the death, with the guy we needed for this computer? Or maybe on a par with getting bled dry or whatever you want to call it, right before the big gunfight at the Big E-Z Corral? Why don't you run your plan past mama Knave here and we'll iron out the bigger wrinkles?

Then we grab Bobbi as soon as she gets back, and go get our people."

It wasn't hard to see the skepticism on Ange's face. Nor was it particularly difficult to understand. Even I might be forced to agree that I reached a bad decision or two over the past couple of days. That didn't mean all of my decisions were bad though. At least I hoped that wasn't the reality of our situation.

I just had to convince Ange of the same thing. "Ange. This once you're going to have to trust me. Just like I trusted you to get me off that boat. Or when I jumped in the truck, left my bird with you, let you lock me in a high tech root cellar. Yea maybe some of my plans go a little sideways, but we're still in the game, so trust me once more. I don't even want to breathe a hint of what I'm planning. But if anyone pays, it will be me."

That got a sharp and appraising glance as well as a heated word of an earthy and fragrant nature. There might have been a bovine included. "I repeat, that's a load of Hereford dung. You're planning to set yourself up as a target, or maybe run in and hope your luck digs you back out. Well, mister, I don't understand everything I've heard, but I do understand that you ain't exactly superhero material these days."

Sharp glances somehow morphed into angry and bitter glares. "You getting a bad case of dead ain't exactly going to further my agenda here chief. So why don't you give up some details? Otherwise I'll..."

I could see why she paused. About the only threat she had was to turn me in. She could rat me out to the trolls and hungry little monsters that wanted to eat us all. Or she could try and involve the authorities, which would just alert the people we were after and get me nice and locked away.

Her buddy Rafael was being held by the same guy that I had to face in order to avoid ingestion by various fairy tale bad guys. She couldn't go to anyone really. Finally, she had to face it. There wasn't a whole lot left to threaten me with.

"You're going to wish me luck on the way out of the door, that's what "you'll do". Until then, I'm going to rest and see if there are any shortcuts to getting my energy back. You might keep digging on that mongrel machine of yours and see if there's any more info to give me any kind of edge. And if you wouldn't mind, could you get someone to bring my duffel, all of my belongings, and maybe carry Rafe and his cage in here for me?" I wasn't sure why I wanted that last part.

My instincts seemed to be doing a lot of guiding now. Which didn't bother me since I had no idea what to do and instincts might as well take the lead for a while. My usual "damn the torpedoes and full speed ahead" approach might not be the best idea this time.

I managed to flex my fist, raising my arm off the table for more than a few seconds was about as hard as lifting a small car might be normally. Lifting the car, or immediately springing out of bed, either one was theoretically possible. But neither one was as likely as filling an inside straight. I had some ideas about that though.

In due time, a small troll with dimples of all things showed up. She peeked around the door just as shy as any other young and uncertain kid. It was kind of charming. She had the pigtails, the awkward smile and wide eyes, and a couple of the cutest little goat horns sticking up over her ears.

After determining that I looked too weak to pounce and eat her, she darted in and put a familiar duffel bag on a chair that she then shoved towards the bed. I noticed she kept the chair between us like some kind of shield.

It was almost insulting. I mean we've all heard of the Billy Goats Gruff. Whoever heard of a troll-eating man though? Nope, that invariably went the other direction. Then again, she'd probably heard stories her whole life about the kind of guy that would set up an entire family of her kind for an impromptu barbecue where they were both guests, entertainment and main course. Maybe the Paris trolls weren't eaten, but they were certainly cooked thoroughly enough for the pickiest health inspector.

It seemed like a good time to start some damage control and mediation. "Thank you, sweetling. I very much appreciate your help. You go play now and be safe okay?"

She bit her lip and shook her little head vigorously enough to risk tangling a pigtail on a horn. With a determined look smoothing out the dimples, she strode back out only to return carrying a cage as big as she was.

I wasn't exactly surprised at being glad to see my old buddy Rafe in the cage. The intensity of the emotion was surprising though. Oh, it wasn't a weepy scene or some cardiac-related event. I mean my heart didn't race or skip a beat or anything. I was just glad to see my bird. For his part, Rafe hopped from foot to foot and cranked his head around to watch me from one and then the other. The whole time, his head bobbed up and down on feathered shoulders.

At least he wasn't calling me a dumbass. The troll child set him carefully on the chair with his cage supported by the back of the seat. That left my duffel within easy reach. So instead of fishing the bird out, I flopped a clumsy hand over and dug out the pouch with phones in it.

One pouch held both my rune shielded "burner" phone and the more technologically protected device a well. Without the bag to clutch weak and numb fingers around, I'd never have got the damned things on the table with me.

They were finally there, and I had no idea how I was going to dial and then hold them if I couldn't trust my hands any more than that.

There was a "cawing" sound from the cage. If I didn't know better, I'd say it was colored with disgust or at least derision. Maybe just dull disdain? Anyway, the bird squawked and then shuffled over to work a claw around one of the bars. Perched there, Rafe leaned at an awkward angle and then worked his beak through the bars around the lock. I wouldn't have believed it if I hadn't seen the next bit. The bird, whom I thought just a simple pet from the shop, used his tongue to blindly seek a button and release the bolt that he slid back with his beak.

While I was still dealing with that improbability, he hopped from the chair to my slab and then shuffle-jogged along the edge until he was by my ear. In a curiously gentle motion, he nibbled at my hair and rubbed his beak on my ear. Then my curiously sweet and smart pet, let out an absolute air-raid warning of a squawk with his beak approximately one micrometer from my eardrum, or maybe less.

The effect was both immediate and dramatic. My heart rate shot up to bullet train speeds, at the same time my spine levitated to sit me straight up with the bird hopping out of the way. My eyes were probably saucer-sized and my breath came in a long gasp. But the most dramatic improvement was in the energy with which my previously useless hands gripped the table and held me in place.

I sat like that for what felt like a long time. In truth, it was probably less than a minute before I gingerly turned my neck to look around. Whether it was adrenalin, fear, or avian joojoo, something had given me back just a fraction of the strength I was missing.

I mean, I still wanted to avoid a fight with anything

tougher than a newborn lamb. But at least I might be strong enough to get pants on. If they didn't resist. So that became my first task. Fortunately, it was a task that seemed to amuse Rafe completely. He hopped back into his cage and courteously pulled the door shut. I noticed he didn't relatch that door though.

Getting dressed took longer than it should and was not without its adventurous moments. I almost fell more times than I care to recall. There was also a minute when I thought I might have to call for help before my pullover finished me off via strangulation. After a while, I was dressed and ready for the next step.

The phone only rang three times before I heard a weak voice. He was worn out enough that Luis actually had a trace of the Spanish accent I'd never heard before in his perfect west coast diction. A worn voice on one of us means more than we missed a nap though. I was willing to bet that he'd been left to entertain Lorcan. That weariness came from using huge amounts of energy just to keep his spirit anchored to his body and this plane. If they kept it up, he might just fall over and wake up in Valhalla.

At least that's where he would go if his Valkyrie had any say. Chances were, she had no idea what kind of trouble he was in. Heather was just too new to know the ins and outs of her job.

At some point, the Valk can learn to sense their charges from miles away. Some of them even set a kind of alarm mentally. At least once I saw Gondul stand up in the middle of a feast and go rushing out to get one of her guys out of trouble. Heather wasn't Gondul though.

Besides, from what Luis had said, she was too busy playing at infiltrator. She was probably enjoying herself to no end. It might not even occur to her to check back with

Luis until it was too late. Because judging from that voice, he didn't have a lot longer.

"Hey bro, I Can't really talk right now. I'm kinda tied up with something." Even in that much pain and trouble, he was trying to be funny and comforting to me. I guess he had me in his contact list or something.

That guess was proved true by a new voice on the line. "It's more tied up with some*one.*"

Lorcan erupted in that dry, croaking growl that he called a laugh. "So is this the Bear? I've missed you Bear. But I won't miss you the next chance I get. Or are you calling to beg mercy?"

Even if I had been inclined to ask for mercy, there was no chance in Hel's hoary halls that I would ever beg to that dickhead. "Sure thing Argr, if your mouth isn't busy playing mare for some of Kara's stallions why don't you see if she wants to talk to me."

Back in the day calling him unmanly, cowardly or effete, (which were all things implied by "Argr") would have resulted in an immediate challenge to holmgang, or a duel, probably to the death. In fact, he could probably kill me in front of a whole village and nobody would object. We took our insults seriously. Living in Austin had changed my old-world views about such things. But I knew it would set off Lorcan The accusation that he was playing the submissive role in a little homo-erotic entertainment was just that dire.

I heard a bestial roar followed by some enthusiastic thrashing and crashing. I'd like to think he was battering his brains out on the walls or something. Truth is, I'd never been sure how much of his skull was brain and how much bone, or shite for that matter.

A few seconds after the auditory storm settled down, Lorcan was back. "I was already planning on pulling off some of your favorite bits and pieces slow and easy. Maybe do you like a fly, take the legs and arms off of one side and watch you spin around in your own juices til you just stop eh?"

Maybe it seemed like I exaggerate his cruelty and sheer glee for mayhem. A fly is really the least tortured thing I'd seen him play with. I don't even *want* to remember some of the pets, or horses, or people. That just made me want to piss him off more. "Hey, why don't you stop drooling over other guys and their juices and go get your mistress. If I get bored and hang up she'll probably find out and take out her ire on you. You know she can always ferret out anything you try and hide from her."

I heard a new sneer in his voice when he answered. "She never ferreted you out, did she? And it's been at least a few years hasn't it? Maybe she's loosening her grip. Maybe I can deal with you myself and she never needs to know."

That just reinforced some of my own theories about time and Einherjar. Lorcan truly thought I'd been out of the fold just a few years. He had no memory of the intervening decades. Maybe he'd been put on ice, so to speak. Or maybe she'd drained his memories just like she'd done mine.

I still remembered enough and had enough mental power, to push his buttons some more. "Has the shite finally shoved the rest of your tiny brain aside? If you kill me, I'll just go back to the fold. I doubt you've figured out how to erase my memories first. So I'd almost have to be a good warrior and tell my worshipped mistress that one of her hounds had slipped his leash and gone rogue. Now wouldn't I? Speaking of her, go get her before I hang up and take off for the backside of nowhere."

This time I identified the sounds as a fist striking flesh repeatedly and brutally. From the accompanying grunts and wet sounding curses, I had to guess Luis was paying a price for my attitude.

Lorcan stopped and came back to the phone though. "You're not being a very good friend Bear. I barely pulled back in time to keep him with us. But I'm good at that remember? I can always judge how far to take it without killing someone unless I want to. So what makes you think I'd kill you? Maybe I'll hide you someplace to play with you for a good long century or two. Do it without the Stormy One's notice. Just keep you all to myself and solve everyone's problem at once. Everyone except you that is..."

He might have said more, except I heard a new impact of flesh on, metal? Followed by a splat and thud that coincided with each other. Then came the most beautiful and terrifying voice I knew. "Hello, my bear! I am surprised to hear from you. You have either gotten better with runes and dreamwork since I lost you, or you had help. Was it the old woman? After I got out, I started wondering at how she easily she went down. It was a mistake. I was just too excited at seeing my old love I guess."

A tiny scared voice in the back of my head wanted to run screaming. I ignored the little voice though and put some steel into my own. There was no need in letting her know how I felt about this whole situation. In fact, not giving away my thoughts and emotions was key to this plan. It was hard to keep my voice casual though with that idiot in my head gibbering and running around to bang fearfully on the inside of my skull.

I managed the casual tone anyway. "Evening Kara. Do I take it that Lorcan is taking a little nap to think about his mistakes and your displeasure?"

Her laugh was just as husky, enticing, and gut-wrenchingly terrible as I remembered. "Oh Bear, nobody talks to me like you always did. So many times your mouth walked you right to the edge of oblivion. And so many times I recalled in the nick of time, just how many other uses I had for you, and that mouth."

"Well Kara, I won't say we never had a good time." There was no trouble letting a tremble of longing enter my voice. We had spent way too long together for me to ever rid myself completely of her spell. But I'd also been out from under that enchantment long enough to know what it might mean to go back. "Then again we did some pretty damned horrible things together too didn't we?"

Just saying those words almost dropped me flat again. I had forgotten that little moment where she unleashed some of my housed memories. They came back in an avalanche to remind me. For a minute, my head was reeling and seeing a montage created from horror movies, pornography, the winter Olympics, and the best war cinema all in one tangled ball. Interspersed in just a few places, were scenes of people and places from before I died even the first time. There were so very few of those images compared to the rest.

Her voice brought me back. I don't think I missed more than a few words. "So, no matter how entertaining this has been, you didn't call me to reminisce. What is your purpose my Bear?"

That brought me back just enough to fumble out the parts she needed to know. "A trade Kara. I turn myself in, you let Luis and his Valkyrie go with a promise of amnesty."

Her laugh was nowhere near as dry, croaking, and unappetizing as Lorcan's. In fact, it snuck in my ear and slithered down my spine to do inappropriate things around my core, about where the Reikki people look for your Root Chakra. I'm pretty sure that's where the cerebral brain interfaces with the smaller brain that people say we keep alternately in our asses or our "little head". Either way, that core pricked up its little ears and started lobbying for some serious negotiations with the owner of that eldritch, primal, seductive laugh.

I shoved that lobbyist down and waited for Kara's reply once she stopped laughing. It didn't take *that* long. "Oh Bear, or maybe I will call you Magnus now? Somehow it suits you. But no, you are my Stormbear. Which means I know you Bear. Why would you give yourself up for someone you've met once or twice. Even if you shed blood together, it is not like you to be so sentimental."

This was the important part. I had to sell her on an excuse she'd accept."Debts, my lovely Storm, I owe his Valkyrie for my life. Even worse I uttered that debt aloud. You of all people know how a broken vow or an unanswered debt can curse me. You tried hard enough to break me of that, didn't you? And how often did it come back to haunt us."

By her silence, I knew Kara was actually thinking about it. She hadn't cut me off yet so I kept playing my hand. "Besides, Mistress, I am tired. It has been so long. So many years and decades of looking over my back. Waiting for the trap to spring. Waiting for someone to stumble on my hiding place, or one of the wolves or ravens to spy me. It wears on me beloved. I would end it all and be yours again."

That was a mistake. I felt it stealing over me as I uttered what I thought were lies. Maybe some of them were deceptions, but some were not. I was tired. Part of me did want it to end. Maybe I would have if there was a chance to go to Hel's frozen halls, to lay in slumber, covered with a gentle sheet of rime. An end to pain, and worry, and stress. To never feel the stress of her anticipation or my own guilt, that would be worth it, almost.

Apparently, it made sense to her too. "But Bear, you have to know, I can not leave you as whole as you have been. I can not even leave you as free as you were when last you road at my side. There is too much risk. If you come back, I will crush your will to it's dimmest spark. But I will keep you with me and love you for what once was. That much I can promise you. You will remain my loyal servant and I shall see to you from time to time."

The sad part is, she really thought it was a good deal. The even sadder part is once I would have agreed with her. The years away from Valhalla had left their mark though. If anything, my stubborn streak had grown. I liked the freedom to make my own decisions. The simplest choice of what to wear, what to eat, when to get up or call in sick to work, those were freedoms that I was used to. They were not freedoms she would let me keep.

That was a chance I had to take. "Just meet me at this address. Tonight, midway between sunset and midnight. Bring Luis and your promise. Oh, and try to keep Lorcan off the boy for now. Maybe someday he'll be up to that asshole's level of thuggery. Then I'll gladly watch the fight. Not like this though."

The rest of the negotiation was unremarkable. Every indication was that she bought my story. She probably couldn't conceive of a chance that I would ever not want to come back and be her loyal little wolfhound. We firmed up a few details and hung up. By the end, she sounded convinced that I would willingly submit to her again. I was fairly certain that she would bring Luis and stop anyone from doing anything else to him for the moment. I was *more* than fairly certain that she'd have Lorcan there as a backup or to ambush me before the actual trade.

After that the other calls were easy.

19

THERE WAS a knock on the door and then a long pause before Lola's voice came through the stone door before the rest of her entered. "Warrior, are you able to receive a visitor?"

When I looked up, she had her eyes covered with one hand the size of two of mine. She probably put a hat over her ramshorns and went out to teach NBAers how to palm basketballs for a side-job. Those extra jointed fingers would do well at a number of sports and competitive tasks. I recalled how well they worked with needles and thread in addition to glowing sigils. It was really something to see this competent and intimidating woman going out of her way to avoid embarrassing me.

"Not only can I receive a visitor, but I'm also not sure I could stop one. Even that little poppet of a trollish child that strolled through wasn't at any risk. Provided I intended a risk anyway." I was trying to be lighthearted, but there were bitterness and self-mockery under the jokes.

Lola accepted the invitation, but ignored the more

depressing tones. "You look better than I expected. Did you have reserves I did not know about?"

Her tone wasn't quite accusing, but it didn't miss it by far. I had to try not to look guilty when her question reminded me of some things. I might not have used reserves to get up and struggle my way into regular clothing, but that didn't mean I was without them. I had all but forgotten about some of the fun little preparations I'd made in Bobbi's bunker. But something told me to slip that extra ace back up my sleeve for now.

I covered my reaction by pointing at Rafe's cage. "The bird. It seems I might have been wrong about having a Fylgja. He hopped up and screamed a tiny burst of energy into me. Not that I understood any words or intent, but I can't ignore the extra tiny boost. Now I only feel like death warmed over. Before it was roadkill rolled in crud and pounded into crapcakes."

For a minute I wasn't sure she bought it. But Lola stepped over to give the bird the once-over with her fancy star trek elven vizor. "Odd. He does not look like a familiar, but there is something decidedly odd here."

She probably wanted to keep poking at that mystery, but I cleared my throat to get her attention. "Did you come to give the bird a physical exam then? Or was there something you needed with me?"

Lola had the grace to look mildly embarrassed. But she cleared her throat back at me and then cast her eyes downward. "I feel bad about what we're asking you to do after I took so much for Stige."

"What was that?" I wasn't sure I was hearing her right. Was this the same person that had all but cracked my skull, threatened me with a roasting spit, left me in the care of finger eating little monstrosities, and threatened the girls that I was responsible for bringing here?

Lola's eyes came up defiantly and her voice began with a little growl that turned into a rush of words. "I said you are in no shape to fight this fight. If you are to save our little people, then you must be stronger. So take this. We all chipped in. It's not too much from any one of us, but it's a little from almost all."

What she handed me was a small, crystal vial, except that the stopper was part of the rest of it. There was no seem and no apparent means to unstop the thing to get at what appeared to be a swirling pearlescent hued liquid or partial liquid inside. The most intriguing thing though, was that it seemed to be incandescent or maybe fluorescent. Whichever scent it was, it glowed.

I stared it at it for a good half a minute before it became clear. "Lifeforce? This is bottled life force? Strength, power, mojo and joojoo all rolled up squeezed out and stoppered in a bottle??"

Lola perked her ears and nodded eagerly. "Oh, it's not a bottle, but you got everything else just right. It is our offering to return to you a fraction of what you gave up. You are still not as strong or as tough as you were before. That was beyond us. This should help though."

"Not a bottle, so how does it work? Do I break the top off and drink it or what?" I was still looking for some opening or seam or some means to access the remarkable gift inside.

Lola answered with a weak laugh. "There is no opening nor any liquid. It is energy. You simply place it against a chakra. I would suggest your crown Chakra or root chakra. Envision being recharged by a battery and the energy will do the rest. It is made for just such a request. All of the energy inside can be drained into you in less than ten seconds."

I clutched that little bit of crystal-like the lifeline it was. "Thank you, Lola, and thank all of your people for me as well. This might just make all the difference in getting your own people back."

I got a smile and a much more cheerful exit than Lola's arrival had been. Since Rafe was being unusually docile, that left me more or less alone to think and plan. The little gift from the alt-naturals in Stige's lair made all the difference. Now, this wasn't as desperate a mission, at least not necessarily a suicide mission. The end result might be the same, but now I had a chance.

I was tempted to suck down all of that marvelous mojo right on the spot. I didn't know enough about it though. For instance was this a short boost, a permanent loan, or would there be some price to pay? I hadn't thought to ask before Lola left.

Well, without stumbling weakly down a lair full of predators possessed of a penchant for man-eating, there was nothing to do about missed questions or lack of foresight. So I got back to work on what I could manage instead of regretting what I couldn't.

I was still working on my limited amount of gear when someone that could have been the little troll child's big sister showed up. This one was about the right size and shape for a teenager. That meant she might be younger than she looked or might actually be a lot older. Trolls are weird like that. I was betting that her appearance was in direct proportion to her age though.

This one was slender but well-muscled. She had long legs displayed below short cut-off jeans. It was a great look back in the seventies. I hadn't seen anyone wearing it since then except maybe Daisy Duke in that movie. It looked good on her. She even had the crop top t-shirt to go with it, and those sandals that wrap up the calves like roman's used to wear.

She walked in with an exaggerated roll of her hips, and a subtle shift in the muscles of her abdomen. The arch of her back was just as familiar as the flirtatious smile. She ruined that though by a seductive lick of her lips, which showed off those wickedly sharp teeth. Just enough to remind me this wasn't a human no matter how flirty and normal she acted.

Maybe that's why I took the tray of food from her and in return only gave the youngster an affable thank you that didn't hint at anything more. She must have got the point because she pouted, it was actually very cute, and then told me Nev Ange was sleeping but they'd feed her when she woke up. They were also expecting Bobbi Lee back any minute.

That was the first of a procession of visitors. Young and old, large and small, harmless-looking to nightmarish, the denizens of New Orleans alt-natural world came out in droves to give me a word of encouragement or some other small gift. Not that all of the gifts were small or insignificant. One, *thing*...brought me an axe that was about as large as the slab I'd been laying on. It probably weighed about as much too. That was the predominant theme.

Weapons and armor were the mainstays of my gifts, but there were a few baubles and even gems too. Those offset the occasional clump of feathers or gnawed on bone. Some of it was quite lovely though. I shoved my greed down and carefully set aside all of the valuables. I wasn't doing this for pay. Really I was doing this for several reasons. The buddies of these folk were just a little extra task added on top of all the others.

There were a couple of small carvings and semi-precious stones I kept. Other than that, it was the armor that I had to consider taking. Not the old Spanish style breastplate. Someone had taken care of it and polished it to a shine. It wasn't something I cared to wear out in public though. But the simple chainmail shirt was something else.

I got the maile from an honest to goodness real old-world dwarf. Not like you see on fantasy movies and posters. This guy was almost as tall as I was and might have even been wider across the shoulders, thicker through the chest. That was a real novelty for me.

He was articulate and soft-spoken unlike one of his kind from Tolkien. His appearance went the other direction though. He didn't look like a squat, broad, bearded human. This fellow had huge eyes that seemed to have their own light source somewhere. At least they glowed faintly depending on the angle. His brow looked more like a neanderthal, as did the oversized arms that reached to his knees. But the armor was exceptional.

"Did you make this yourself?" I was busy turning the fine lightweight links over in my hands and looking for any sign of weakness or maybe a bad patch job. It was a waste of time. I think I probably knew before I started that I wasn't going to find any flaws with this work. It felt lighter than iron or steel but was easily as durable. I looked up for his answer to my question while my hands were all but petting the stuff possessively.

"I did not. At least, I did not begin the work. This was begun by my great grandfather a very long time ago. It was commissioned as a gift for a young warrior. But he died." The unnamed dwarf bowed his head and appeared to truly mourn this man that had died centuries ago.

With his head still down, the dwarven craftsman continued. "He went out in substandard armor and took a spear that this shirt would have stopped. The armor slept in a chest back in the old world until we came to these new lands. Even then it rested until I found it again not that long ago. But I finished the work. Perhaps your Norns sent me a dream or spurred me on."

The unnamed dwarf paused to toss a thin shift-like garment at me. "It is not a gambeson, but this gift came from the Dokkalfr cousins of those you will try to rescue. They say it will even stop a bullet, as long as it is not too large or fired from too close."

That last bit drew a deep rumbling chuckle out of the depths of a chest just as thick and barrel-shaped as mine. "I have never had occasion to test the bullet resistance. I could fetch my handcannon to do so if you wish?"

I got a mental picture of that beefy gray hand holding a revolver with a barrel big enough to fit my fist. I shook my head vigorously to deny any need for a ballistics test that might include my tender flesh inside this thin material. He pulled the cloth over my head in the meantime and barely gave me time to settle the matte black material around my shoulders before he followed it with the metal rings.

"This Byrnie fits me, albeit tightly. It should fit such a man as you." His words were interspersed with grunts and growls as he jerked at straps and buckles. All of that elicited grunts and gasps of my own as he cinched the armor tight around my chest and waist. When he was done though, the armor felt like it had been made for me.

Of course, I wasn't sure how useful it would be on a covert op. As good as that mail felt on my shoulders, it wasn't going to get me through all of the obstacles arrayed against me. Even with all of my recuperative gifts at full power, I wouldn't have wanted to make that bet. There were just too many black hats and too many variables. Besides, I didn't have those healing factors at all from what Lola had said.

Considering the fact that all of those abilities came courtesy of Kara, I didn't think I could count on an impromptu boost. She wouldn't help me unless she saw no other way to achieve her goals. I was also under no delusions that her goals hadn't changed that much just because I offered to make a trade with her. If Kara got the chance, Luis, Heather, any witnesses, and her favorite mislaid warrior, Magnus, would all disappear quietly and without a fuss.

Still, it was exceptional armor, the kind of mail only dwarvenkind can pull off quite so well. "Many thanks, good craftsman, but I do not know a name to praise for this gift?"

As I said, I'm a product of an ancient era too, don't judge me. It was the right tone though because it got the fellow to throw back his shoulders and lift that shaggy maned head to show a fire in his eyes.

His voice held even more fire and pride than his gaze. "I am called Andvalin, of the house of Nabbi. My line has long been friendly to mankind and has crafted weapons and armor for some of the greatest heroes. Thus are you honored with the work of craftsmen out of legend itself. It is good that you know this and offer praise to my forefathers, though I had but a small part in finishing the good byrnie."

He reached up to scratch through the scruff of his beard before he continued in a thoughtful tone. "If you succeed in your quest, then at feast, a thankful word about the help of my family would be appreciated."

It sounded formal, but I also recognized an advertising campaign when I saw one. Dwarves don't have people beating down their cave doors for work anymore. Being tied to rescue and an underdog fight against creatures such as

Valkyrie and Voodoo sorcerors would be good marketing. The dvergr have always been keen about treasures and profit. It seemed that hadn't changed.

Unfortunately, he was cunning enough to word that request in a way that I would have a hard time refusing. The crafty little con artist had all but tied my hands and forced me to wear the damned armor out into modern New Orleans. That or I could risk revenge or even a curse from his kinfolk. If I recalled, Nabbi was a lesser-known dwarf, but one with lots of rumors about his magical aptitude. It wouldn't be past such a fellow to toss some negative magick my way. Even if he wasn't alive, some of his descendants probably had a similar gift. It did tend to run along bloodlines for the stone folk.

I was still trying to figure a way out of the manipulation, but a response was in order immediately. "A fair request good Smith. Fulsome praise shall I heap on the name of Andvalin and the house of Nabbi for their skill and generosity in this endeavor. I would make my preparations though, in order that there might be a victory feast. So, I bid you a fair eve and many thanks again."

I wasn't fond of all the formal palaver, but I had been expected to maintain standards back when Kara kept me on a tighter leash. The words still flowed in a manner to do the old psycho proud, if I do say so myself. They seemed to appease the knotty old dwarf who beamed a smile and then bowed from the waist until I thought he might tip over.

After that, I was left alone. The dwarven smith had probably appointed himself as a guard while his "hero" prepared. It would give him opportunities to both associate himself with the quest, and brag about his part in it, if anyone came to "bother" me again. Then again, maybe he was just the last visitor.

I say the last visitor, but really there was one more. The smaller of the two obnoxious little beasts who had been tasting my fingers had appeared earlier with an offering of "meat to make you stronger". Since I had no idea when, where, or from whom he had gotten that particular gift, I had politely declined then settled down to dicker with him.

It had taken a couple of small gemstones from my pile, as well as most of the less savory totems and prizes like jagged bones and feather bundles. After the bargaining though, he had agreed to keep watch and alert me when Bobbi Lee got back.

I wasn't sure when that would be, so I hurried to get everything together before she came back with extra fire-power and who knows what else? From what I'd seen of Bobbi so far, an anti-tank weapon or two might be in order, maybe even an armored personnel carrier. For my part, I had the knife I had worked on from time to time since the dangerous little southern battle belle had given it to me.

Along with that piece of armament, there were two pistols between my own and one I had retrieved from where Bobbi and Nev had stacked their weapons earlier. I debated taking Bobbi's sniper rifle. If I had been going into a normal battle, it wouldn't have been a debate at all. I've always liked watching my foes fall from far enough away that they can't find me to shoot back.

Nev Ange's shotgun was something else. I checked it over, the beast was street legal but not by much. If I bent the barrel just a tad it would be short enough to qualify as a crime. She had bullet loops in a snug accessory that fit over the buttstock. Between those rounds, the ones in the gun, and a few I found here and yon, there was enough firepower for a decent firefight, provided I got close enough. It was hard leaving that sniper rifle where it was, but I just didn't see where it was worth the extra encumbrance.

And of course, I had the dwarven ring byrnie over the oddly comfortable black undershirt. I hedged a little by slinging a plate carrier over the armor with the buckles let out as far as they would go. Between the armor, the armored plates, and the supposedly magical cloth, I ought to be about as protected as Bobbi would have been in the fictitious armored vehicle. At least I hoped it was just in my imagination.

20

Bobbi made it back about the time someone brought me a bowl full of mystery meat stew. Despite an absolute conviction that eating the stew was a bad idea, I thanked the little troll girl for her help again. She really was just as cute as a pup in her own way. She was just too damned young, even if I did ever decide to try some interspecies dating. She did me another favor and took Rafe and his cage back to wait in Nev Ange's room. Apparently, the day had taken its toll because my electronics and intel guru was reportedly sawing logs to beat Paul Bunyan.

I had pushed the bowl aside when the door opened silently and the little finger fetish horror from earlier slithered in. His misshapen nose bobbed up and down in response to the stew, but I managed to get his attention with a snap of the fingers.

He barely managed to finish the entire brief report, while staring intently at the food. "Wha'? Ah yea. Th'other girl just rode up outside. So there ya go. Deal done and the goodies is mine. But, umm, you gonna eat that stew?"

I left him running his filthy paws through the stew to

fish out chunks of whatever had died to give up some protein. The timing had to be just right. I also had to count on a little luck. I mean, in most neighborhoods, there wouldn't have been a chance. But Stige and his people had this locked down tight and had proven it.

Bobbi was going to be in a hurry. She had packages she'd want to get inside. If I was just a little bit lucky…

Maybe Kara wasn't watching over me anymore but someone was. Otherwise, my quest might have ended before it ever started. I darted out of the back tunnel so quickly that I almost screwed up and ran into Bobbi before she was in the front door. Fortunately, she didn't hear me sliding to a stop. I watched her backside recede down into the lair while I padded over to her truck as quietly as a thick man wearing a lot of protective gear can manage.

That was the second bit of luck. The keys were in the ignition of the Comanche pickup. I guess the sidecar wasn't quite large enough or maybe secure enough to hold all of the combat veteran's firepower needs. The worn silver bullet camper she was towing had enough space in it that I decided I didn't want to know what she considered adequate firepower and equipment.

The third bit of luck came in the apparatus on her trailer tongue. It just took a few seconds to snap the leg down, ratchet it up a couple of notches and slap a cotter pin in to hold the weight of the camper while I released it from the truck. That ought to give me just enough time to make my escape without involving the girls in something that might get them a bad case of shot-up-itis and bleeding out syndrome.

Jerking the door open I slid in and then had to waste more time adjusting the seat so my shorter legs would reach the damned pedals. Finally, I fired it up and just barely resisted the urge to stomp on the gas. Spinning wheels and revved engines would have just caught her attention sooner.

It was immediately apparent that I might as well have spun the tires. A meaty splat on my driver side window had me turning from the rearview mirror to look into some very pretty eyes if you're into the kind of blue eyes that go stormy and a burning violet color when the girl behind them is both confused and steamed.

I cocked my head sideways and did my best to widen my eyes like a bewildered and innocent schoolgirl. Bobbi smacked the window again and gestured for me to roll it down. But I shrugged a lack of understanding and started to step on the gas.

That was a mistake. Bobbi apparently cared more about getting her answers than the cost of replacement glass. The side window came spraying into the cab of the little pickup with a little assist from her rifle-stock. I was glad it was safety glass and more annoying than dangerous; like sharp glass, or bullets.

The barrel of the gun followed the glass into the cab a second later. It stopped a few inches from my left eye. "You want to explain why you're stealing my truck? Or how you're up and moving? Or where Nev Ange is? Or maybe just start with a good reason for me not to see if I can get your brains out of the other window by repeatedly firing this weapon?"

I looked back to see eyes that had gone cold and deep blue instead of violet. That prompted an attempt at self-preservation via some logic. "Now Bobbi, you can't shoot me. If you do then I won't be able to save the alts being held, hostage. If I fail to save them, then the alts below us will kill and eat Nev, and you as well if they ever catch you. So if I were you, I'd either try and get Nev out, or get the Hel out of dodge myself. Because your buddy Magnus has some iffy odds of pulling this off. But his odds are a lot better if you don't shoot him, right?"

That earned me a thump to the side of my head with a gun barrel that was only slightly softer than the abused cranium. "What? Did you just say Nev Ange, my friend, to whom I owe my pea-picking life, is caught up in this scheme of yours and will be killed by fairy tale bogey monsters if you fail?"

"I didn't come up with this deal Bobbi, I just accepted their price for keeping us out of the stew pot. And while part of me wants a hotshot sniper and combat scout on my flank, the other part doesn't want anyone else dragged into this." I very slowly and deliberately lifted an open hand to push the gun barrel away from any accidental lobotomies by gunfire.

She pulled the gun out of the window and laid it her chin atop it and her crossed arms in the busted window frame. "Well Bucko, I don't think it's your say about who goes or doesn't go. If you take my vehicle then I can either try and escape the bogey-men on foot, or trod down there like a good little sheep to wait for the shears."

Her voice was almost as tired as her facial expression when she continued."I'm more of a sheepdog than a sheep, so why don't you fill me in on the way and I'll keep an eye on you from out in the boonies? Never can tell when a timely shot could change those iffy odds of yours."

I hesitated. I couldn't really deny that her help might make a difference. The last time I found myself in a spot anything like this, a sniper turned defeat into a hard-won battle. One shot at a crucial second, had, without any trace of doubt, changed the end of the fight. That previous fight looked absurdly manageable compared to my current situation.

My head fell almost to the steering wheel with that realization. "Bobbi, if I take you with me, you promise to follow my lead? No independent actions or cute little plans that never get shared? If there are going to be secrets, then I just can't afford to take you."

She quirked an eyebrow at me while her mouth curved into a cute little smirk of triumph. I wasn't falling for it though. "I'm serious Bobbi. I can't risk having you along with any surprises."

She let the smirk straighten itself into something more serious. There was a faint twinkle in her eye that I didn't like though. It was still there when she nodded and put her fingers up like a Boy Scout. "Scout's honor chief. I'll follow orders like good fodder. But sitting here and waiting to see if Nev and I get eaten, I just couldn't take that. Let me go tell her I'm going though so she won't worry."

She waved me off before I could start protesting. "Don't worry. I'll hide her chair and her leg before I tell her. We'll be long gone before she can make it. Besides I doubt those critters down there would cut her loose anyway."

I kind of doubted that they would cut either one of them loose if Bobbi was naive enough to go back into the lion's den. Fortunately, that worked well with my plans. If she was stuck down there, then she couldn't complain about me leaving her behind.

Then again, if she went down, got held, and I failed...Was that something I was willing to risk? I honked the horn twice to make her turn around just a few steps short of the underground shelter. As soon as I knew she was looking, the truck went into gear and this time I didn't resist the urge to floor it.

I saw her start to whip the gun around. At the last second her common sense exerted itself and she swung the scope back from where she probably had a very nice close up of my left profile. Instead of spreading that face all over the windshield, she swung the rifle further behind my head and fired three shots as quickly as she could work the bolt.

I didn't actually feel the bullets hit. But the power behind those rounds made the whole pickup bed ring like a demented bell as holes magically appeared just low enough to punch their way through both sides of the truck. After that, the bullets were free to wing out into the night until they finally dropped somewhere far out into the gulf.

That wasn't the brightest thing she'd probably ever done, but I felt pretty happy about her opting for vandalism over brain surgery via high-velocity extraction. From the sound of those shots, I don't even know that she had to hit me to stir up my brains and leave me less sense than I even normally exhibit. I think a near enough miss might have pulled some gray matter out and tossed it through the window just like she had previously threatened.

I made it around a corner and out of sight before she reduced my mental capabilities further. Once I was certain she couldn't catch up and reacquire my head as a target, it only took a minute to pull up the encrypted phone and fire up it's GPS application. Then it was just a matter of following the little digital map to my destination, or at least close to the destination. I pulled over in a parking lot beside an abandoned building that the sign identified as having been Visitors Quarters.

Even a serial idiot can make a good decision every once in a while. That's why I chose a parking lot on the opposite side of the ex-military-base and well outside of the fence or any visible camera. There were mounts on some of the buildings that testified to previous surveillance. With the base being decommissioned though, most of that equipment had gone into storage or else padded some far-sighted supply sergeant's bank account.

I had no doubt that the surveillance would change once I got closer to my goal. Which reminded me that I didn't want to take any chances. I was pretty sure that I knew how the voodoo faction had tracked me. For some reason, I still trusted Nev Ange's encryption. I pulled out the phone and dialed the number she finally plugged into it earlier.

"You *MULE*-headed shit for brains...." she had to pause while even her wit searched for the proper noun. "*MAN*"

I had never realized exactly how much condemnation and unreasoning stupidity could be audibly associated with what I had previously thought was just a gender identifier. It was there plain as day now. Something about that Y chromosome rendered me slow of wit, unreasonable, infuriating, disappointing and incapable of unsupervised action. I wanted to apologize for carrying that absurd chromosome. There wasn't time though so I got to the point.

"Nev Ange. I'm about to dump one of these phones in the gulf. I figured out that my burner phone was never a problem but I can't take a chance. I made it to the docks and will be heading in shortly. You don't have time to find a ride and get here so don't even try. If Bobbi..."

"Is that him! Is that the worthless son-of-a-bitch on the phone? Give it!" From the demand in her voice, it seemed that Bobbi was going to give me a chance to tell her myself not to try and join the party. I should have known better. Nev Ange answered the demanding tones with her calm and honey-sweet and reasonable voice. It was a sound that I was beginning to correlate with intense anger and possible repercussions.

I risked doom and destruction by loudly interrupting their own conversation. "*LADIES!* I don't have time for this.

I'm at the Naval base and I'm heading in. Ange, I'm leaving your phone in the truck. No doubt you two can find the phone and truck easily that way. The other phone I am about to dump in the water. If it's any consolation, I don't think they were using either one to track us. I'm pretty sure I have most of that figured out, with only a wrinkle or two left to iron out. I think you might want to call the cops though. Dixon may be able to flash a badge and make it go away. But it might get enough attention to keep him from doing anything extreme to our people if I fail. Enough attention makes it hard to get up to quite so much mischief. That's why cockroaches scurry when the light comes on."

I was aware that both ladies were trying to interrupt my little speech. At the moment it didn't matter. I just wanted to say my piece and get on with it. The adrenalin had really started to kick in. My muscles were tight and my blood pumping hard. It was time to, as some of those Texan Oldtimers called it, "get to the nut cuttin'."

I left the phone open and tossed it onto the truck seat while the girls jabbered at an empty vehicle. At least I thought it was empty until I slammed the door on my way out. That was when I heard the whimpering from the truck bed.

My response was fairly quick. I pulled the shotgun out of the shattered window and swung around until it's large-bore barrel all but enveloped the bulbous and dripping nose of Nik or Nok or whatever their names were. It was the smaller of the guys who wanted to eat my fingers. He didn't seem to have any appetite at the moment though.

I understood his response when I saw the gaping bullet holes from Bobbi's temper tantrum. He was on the opposite wall from where the rounds had entered. That meant he had been stung by flying shrapnel and then got to watch through jagged holes as big as his fist while I drove along the gulf.

"What the Hel do you think you're doing?" I might have understood his fear and even sympathized. That didn't mean I wouldn't scatter green or purple blood all over that truck depending on his answer and what fluids pumped through the little menace.

"I came...to help" He actually sniffled. Maybe these guys had been watching old Tim Curry movies or something. He had some of the whinier goblins down perfectly. I always preferred Blunder for actually standing up to the villain. Come to think of it, his plan worked out just slightly worse than some of my own.

"How exactly did you plan to assist? And *why*?" I can't help it. Skepticism is my first reaction to helpful faeries. It's even worse for helpful goblins and such. I mean they're *supposed* to be malicious and conniving. It's their schtick.

"Because those were friends of mine. We grew up together, some of us at least." His sniffling had slowed and he got out that whole statement in one breath, unlike the previous statement.

Then he added the clincher for me. "And I know something you don't. Noxur snitched on you. He's working for some of the people inside there. Been feeding some humans in fancy clothes information for *meat*."

The way he said *meat*, really bothered me. It was almost as if he'd called it long-pig like Stige, or man-meat like any number of movies. I had no doubt that's what he meant, even if he didn't come out and say it. It was enough to ruin any amusement I might have had at hearing the taller gobbie's name was so close to my guess.

The rough part is where my imagination immediately went to find a source for that illicit protein. After all, did the spooky agent guys in their suits and ties have a number of my friends held someplace? The only one we could be sure of was Maureen and even that information was hours old. For all I knew, the prof, and Bill, or maybe even my lady fair herself, were all gob-food by now.

"Okay. Let's say I believe you. That doesn't mean I trust you." My words were not what he wanted to hear. That was apparent from the narrowing of his eyes and an angry expression that overlaid the resting homicidal face he was born with. He started to sputter a denial but I cut him off with a poke of that shotgun barrel he'd forgotten.

I didn't have time to sugar coat it though so I didn't. "You get one chance. Get out of here. Fade into the shadows and find one of those nifty tunnels I hear your little community has all over New Orleans. Go down that rathole and don't come out. Because if I see you again before this is all over, well I'm gonna have to assume you're as big a snitch as the buddy you just ratted out. And I don't like rats. But a shotgun takes care of that kind of problem beautifully doesn't it?"

He was still sulking when I saw him slip around a clump of weeds and just disappear as if he was no more than a figment of my abused imagination. I wasn't sorry to see him ago. But I was maybe just barely a hint regretful that I didn't thank him for the info about betrayals.

No help for it now though. Things were already in motion and I had to go ahead with the plan or give up and watch the fireworks from afar. That would just mean my friends and loved ones were enduring the show up close and personal without any help from me. And that would not do at all.

21

THE SUN DIPPED down to squat on the horizon as I darted to a chain-link fence in a stooped jog. The fence was no longer patrolled, but I checked for electricity by letting my grounded bolt cutters fall against the links.

No flashing sparks meant no scorch marks. Within minutes I had one whole side of the fence cut away from one a pole. The peeling back of that fence was a little more tedious. The damned thing kept wanting to recoil and jab jagged pieces of metal at me. With the amount of armor I had on, there was no risk of injury, but they were playing hel with the cloth bits of my ensemble.

Next came the hard part. I had weapons, a small-arms vest, and mole gear, and old-world chainmail all on top of a body made more for hibernating than swimming. It's almost sad when you are envious of a polar bear's agility.

To forestall the embarrassment and pain of my swim, I moved into the shadows between buildings and took my time crossing empty areas. I stopped in each shadow and scanned rooftops and nooks and crannies for surveillance gear, cameras, motion sensors or anything like that.

It was the third dock that did it. Even from a couple of buildings away, I saw the newer antennae and a little black globe that would hold a rotating camera. There was little doubt that other cameras and more gear would be hidden around the place.

That water was some of the nastiest stuff I'd ever found myself in. With cameras watching so carefully though, well, I wasn't spoiled for choices. One of the pieces of gear I'd been "gifted" turned out to be a heavily decorated scuba mask. Somebody probably used it for a Halloween costume, a disguise, or a holy mask in ritual disembowelment for all I knew. What mattered was that it was intact and only needed some elbow grease to put in working order.

I spat into the mask and rubbed it in then rinsed the excess goop out. It sounds unsanitary but divers have done it for decades. Something about a good dose of saliva prevents fogging. Considering how foggy my brain seemed to be, excess obscurement seemed risky.

I had to drop the chainmail coif down around my neck to get the mask on. Then I let go of the dock piling and sank. It must have been thirty feet to the bottom of that old wharf area. Most of it was cluttered with everything from blobs of congealed motor oil, to old engine parts. Once on the bottom, I started a hopping march across the mud and crud that floored that waterway.

The hard part was not letting my feet settle too much. If I sank too deep into any of the muck, I'd just stand there like a very unhappy fixture while I drowned. The second consideration was avoiding all the debris that loomed out of the darkness. I didn't dare wear any kind of lighting, or the guards I expected above would spot me before I got close. My first detection of them would probably come from the bullets smacking me as I surfaced.

It took about a week and a half of subjective time, or most of a minute of real-time, to reach the pilings under my target dock. Normally on a dive, you would just adjust your buoyancy and float gently upwards at that point. I didn't have space for a diving vest on top of everything else, and to be honest I'd never heard of a diving vest rated to lift an armed and armored gorilla.

That meant I spent another suspenseful moment or two haulings myself up on the rough and slimy pilings. The condition of that dock was confirmation that this part of the base had spent some time neglected. No fancy steel or concrete kept the buildings above water. Nope, this one still rested on cypress that was coated with years of pollution that might have been the only thing keeping the rotted wood together.

I broke the surface well back from any edges above me. The last thing I needed was to be spotted and dealt with before I even got started. Of course, that also meant I had to work hard at controlling my breathing after the hazardous underwater stroll. Gasping would have been as bad as the underwater spotlight. I could clearly hear footsteps and something else walking back and forth above me. I just prayed that it was a good old fashioned Doberman or shepherd, maybe even a malinois. The last guard animals I'd run into were trained jaguars. I doubted spooks and spies would have anything that noticeable.

By the time my chest had stopped heaving and I was able to breathe through my nose again, the footsteps were out of hearing range. That didn't mean I could blithely pop up and saunter around topside. Instead, I made a brilliant revision of my plan.

Considering the age of everything else, I found it unlikely that there was some state of the art James Bond-level secret lair and drydock for the yacht. That meant I could get in from there. I found it within three-minute search, accomplished by moving from piling to underdock to piling and even one unidentified chunk of metal that probably didn't belong underwater there.

From the dubious security of that metal pylon, I watched the yacht and the inside of the warehouse around it. Patience has never been one of my gifts. That was compounded by the knowledge that Nev and Bobbi might have police swarming the place any minute.

And the cherry on top of that big anxious sundae of anticipation was the instinctive certainty that my friends were in danger nearby, as well as my paramour, or someone who might be, or had been, or...yea, Maureen was in there. She had to be.

I stuck it out for several minutes anyway. It was long enough to be certain that there were people on the boat. There was someone in an office that looked out from above the warehouse itself. Then there were the doors in both side walls including a big loading area with an overhead door on the shoreline side of the building. There was a similar overhead door at the back of the big open bay.

Finally, in the enclosed slip, was the yacht moored close to a concrete wall and the rubber padding that protected both boat and dock. And of course, there were the guards patrolling outside with a dog.

The smart move would have been to check the office. It was the most likely place to have computers and monitors and a communication center. The boat seemed more likely to be housing the guards, or cells for the prisoners, or maybe both.

I cast a careful and considering eye at the cameras scanning back and forth. Then switched the same careful attention to the elevated office. If I timed it right, I could just possibly make it from the shadows near the boat, to beneath the office without the cameras seeing me. After a minute of waiting, I would then be able to scramble up the ladder like some mad capuchin monkey and enter the office to disable their security and any guard. It would also give me an elevated position from which to scout and disable further guards more effectively.

I suspected Maureen was in the boat though. That fact alone had me ready to try and drag all of my armor and the bonehead beneath it up the stern-line rather than follow the safe and secure plan in the office.

I was saved from making that choice when the door of the office opened to show none other than Agent Dixon himself with a bulky-looking walkie-talkie to his mouth. He was excited enough to make himself audible despite an attempt at whispering.

I clearly heard his orders, "Incoming down the main dock. It looks like a vehicle with multiple hostiles. Use Non-lethal means until I can ID our targets. Once I mark any subjects of interest, you may switch to lethal means for everyone else. Repeat, Non-lethal until I give the order."

I heard no fewer than eight people respond with a call-sign and "affirmative". That was a lot of people with a lot of guns and even more bullets. Toss in the dogs and I might have my hands full. That was without considering any stray bullets from outside sources. I had to consider whether Bobbi had time to procure transportation and make it to the docks.

Simple math said that it was possible. My instincts told me it was someone else. In fact, I had been betting on this distraction. It was working too. Guys crashed through door-ways and ran down stairs to line the front of the warehouse area. As soon as the overhead door went up, they would have a full firing line out onto the dock area.

Anyone out there would be stuck with whatever cover they brought with them. If my guesses were right, that would be a white van they could all hide behind. I heard tires approaching outside followed by locking brakes and doors opening.

The same sounds repeated themselves on a more subtle scale. Maybe I was hearing the difference between an approaching van and an approaching luxury car. That fit my expectations. As did the exotic islander voice that rang out a moment later.

"You were warned not to interfere. Now it is too late. Come out of the warehouse or I shall burn it down." That was definitely Papa Beaufort. He sounded arrogantly sure of himself. I couldn't help but look forward to how that was likely to change.

It wasn't going to happen immediately though. I heard Dixon whispering into his radio again. This time it was only because he had taken up a position only yards away from me. I could see his legs and lower back where he crouched behind a barrel. All he had to do was turn around and duck his head a few inches to look me right in the eyes. He was too excited and focused on his own assumptions to even worry about that though.

"Hold position and maintain silence. Scanning targets now." I didn't understand what he meant until he turned enough to show me the glow of a portable device of some kind. I had to guess he was tapped into the security system of the whole area on that little machine. Good thing I hadn't made any bold moves as soon as he appeared.

I held as still as possible. Even my breathing was shallow enough for chest rise to be barely perceptible. Everyone was focused on the doors and walls on the shoreline though. Everyone except Dixon, who had more tricks up his sleeve than I had planned for.

That was apparent when he spoke again, "We have positive aura hits. Everyone outside that door is a viable target. Use Non-lethal means only. Take special care with the largest subject and the one standing behind the smaller vehicle. Auras also emanating from the trunk of a smaller vehicle. On my mark open the door, release the dogs, fire tear gas canisters and follow with bean-bag rounds."

I was still mulling over exactly what he was seeing for auras. Had the good ole U S of A developed technology to detect magic? And if so, what the hel was out there that *all* of them were radiating? I mean a couple of the "hits" were obvious. The biggest one would be Freke, the one behind the car would be Papa, and the ones in the trunk were probably my kidnapped alt-natural watchers, the ones I had to keep alive for Lola and her mob. What was with all of the other hits though?

I found out an instant later. There was one instant of warning when Dixon yelled. "Watch it they're charging! Raise the overhead and deploy!"

One of his boys must have been primed for action. Before the words were out of the agent's mouth, the motorized chain to the doors started to move. That was as far as Dixon's deployment got before there was a hellacious slam of meat on the door closest to the dog handlers.

The dogs went berserk. They couldn't seem to decide if they were killers or cowards. One would snarl while the other whimpered and then they'd switch roles, and the whole time, that slamming continued as if a hyperactive gorilla was pounding on the corrugated metal. He was pounding hard. Huge indentations began appearing on the wall and the door itself, that is until the door burst into the room.

From the sheer strength and violence behind that assault, I fully expected Freke to follow the door into the room. Then we'd see just how effective dogs, and bean bags and teargas were against an ancient killing machine that was only borrowing the human form for kicks. There was a sadistic part of me that wanted to see the immortal old wolf dispense some karma to these assholes who had been holding my people hostage. Mostly I wanted to see Agent Andrew Dixon on the receiving end of that kind of rough justice.

I was right about the ineffective ability of bean bags to stop what was coming. I was wrong about the source of the karma though. Instead of seven feet of biker, I got just barely six feet of polo shirt and khaki pants. The guy that stood in the door took two bean bags without faltering. There was something wrong with the silhouette too. I was still trying to sort that out when he lurched back into motion and fell on the slavering dogs.

It was his shoulder, that's what was bugging me. It became evident when that arm dangled uselessly from a shoulder that was obviously dislocated and probably pulverized. The anatomy was misshapen enough that I suspected a number of shattered ribs and collarbone were part of the equation. That didn't stop his attack.

He got a grip on one dog's throat as it snapped at his forearm, the good one. The other dog latched onto his disabled arm and started literally ripping it from the socket. That ended when the averagely muscular black man, lifted one dog off the floor and dashed the two canines together with a sickening crunch that ended in two yelps and a spreading puddle of scarlet. He also managed to pull the damaged arm even further out of place. It almost looked like the only thing holding it on, was the sleeve of his polo shirt.

That didn't stop him from lurching forward at the dog handlers who were frozen in disbelief. Most people are properly afraid of attack dogs. I doubt either handler had ever dreamed of, much less seen, such an instant solution to the dog problem. One of them stepped forward to receive the charging attack. He got a grip on his foe but didn't stop him so much as fall to the ground in a grapple.

That gave his buddy time to drop the useless shotgun and draw a much deadlier handgun from his belt. It took four rounds to stop the attacker. Those last two had pretty much ruined the head of the wiry juggernaut. That was fairly terrifying but not as bad as the sight of a half dozen more of the things charging through the doorway. The combined bean bag fire was about as deadly as birdseed at a wedding. The minions of Beaufort ran through it like they were headed for the honeymoon suite.

The last one through the door did not charge. He walked in with a leash that led back to the collar on seven feet of menace busy wrinkling his nose and curling a lip in distaste at the creatures around him.

Right behind Freke, came Papa Beaufort himself. He held the cane in front of him like a fencing foil. If so, he was a better fencer than Basil Rathbone himself. Maybe Rathbone was good enough to win army championships and make Errol Flynn look like a badass swordsman. But neither Errol nor Basil himself were capable of swatting bullet-fast bean bags out of the air. The cane and attendant hand did all of that seemingly of their own volition. Beaufort had all of his attention on the final member of their little invasion.

Raphael didn't look fresh at all. He was a bloody mess from toe to top. Judging from the severity and frequency of wounds, old uncle Nimrod had endured torture for the better part of the last day or two. Which also jibed with my most recent suspicions.

"Where is the Viking!?" Beaufort yelled loud enough to lose some of that soft islander accent. I knew I had no intention of answering, and it looked like everyone else in the room was busy dealing with "people" that didn't respond to subtleties like subdual rounds or teargas. I got a close-up of the action when one of the attackers tackled a g-man into the water not that far from me.

The gunman had lost his shotgun during the scuffle. I heard it clatter to the docks above me. In retrospect that might have been for the best. On the way into the drink, he managed to clear the pistol from his holster. I heard four muffled explosions as the gun went off underwater and then a cloud of red spread over the surface. A few seconds later the g-man's body floated to the surface. A few seconds after *that* so did his head.

That's when I became acutely aware of action on the metal scrap that I occupied. I felt it shuddering as Papa's minion swarmed up it. Which meant that I was expecting him more than he was expecting a hidden einherjar on his "ladder". The head cleared the oily slick atop the water and came further upwards without noticing me.

It was probably a movement that caught his attention. I found myself looking into eyes that were all white, with no visible color to them at all. That's when I made the connection. Old Papa Beaufort was making voodoo zombies. I'd heard of them and read an article about how it was all just fancy pharmaceuticals made from blowfish poison or something.

Whoever wrote that article had never faced a zombie fresh after the kill. This one had a number of contact range bullet holes in him. Any one of them would have made me sit back and think about what I had done. The zombie ignored them all, even the mortal looking wounds. He did not ignore the shotgun barrel that had caught his attention by swinging to bear on that otherworldly, blank, dead gaze.

Those eyes really creeped me out. So I felt a lot better when the shotgun ripped them out in a spray of matter that included not only eyes but everything attached to them. The muzzle blast from a large-bore gun at mere inches, is not something to underestimate. Thankfully the whole mess recoiled away from my nook and sank slowly beneath the sludgy water.

If I was lucky, everyone above was too busy to notice that the shotgun didn't sound like the pistol shots that had preceded it. But I was pressed for time anyway. With all of the excitement above and around me, it was time to move. I managed to spider-crawl across a few feet of the dock by digging my toes and fingers into the rough underside of the dock. Just those two or three yards had my arms and legs aching as if I'd run a triathlon.

I hadn't gained any extra time in the crawl. It didn't seem like a great time to rest and recuperate. But I had my backup. I pulled out the little crystal full of community mojo and sucked just a few sips of life force out of it. There was no indicator or dial on it to tell me how much was left. I didn't dare take it for granted that there was much juice in there for me.

What I got was enough to scramble onto the dock. The Norns must have been watching me with a kindly eye. Not only was I unseen, but I also came to my feet with the shotgun dropped by the deceased agent in the water. It had been almost in my fingertips when I clambered up to dry footing.

There was still movement in the boat. They didn't pay any attention to me though. I shrugged my shoulders and discarded ideas about hauling myself up lines or anchor chains. This wasn't a pirate movie and I wasn't exactly myself. I walked across a swaying gangway with the purloined shotgun at my shoulder and tracking for targets.

Nobody popped up asking to be shot. I could hear movement and murmuring below decks, but nobody confronted me topside. With the gun still tracking, I went down to the cabin deck. The first cabin I came to was open and a gunman stood at the little round portal with his back to the door.

That was very poor form. He'd probably learn a lesson from the beanbag that took him in the back of the head and left a red smear where his nose bounced off the glass. The noise was loud enough that it snapped up the heads of two bedraggled fellows chained to a bed. Eachan was manacled to one side of the headboard, and Wild Bill was attached to the other.

Both of them stared at me in silent disbelief. Which was too good an opportunity to pass up. "Is this a bad time? Do I need to come back when you two are finished playing out bondage fetishes?"

Eachan recovered first. His head dropped but an instant later his shoulders started shaking with laughter. "I believe I am quite done with this particular scenario Magnus. If you would be kind enough to remove these bonds and get me the hell out of here I would be terribly appreciative."

For his part, Bill just stared and seemed on the point of tears. I looked away to avoid embarrassing the poor guy. I needed to get the keys for the handcuffs anyway. They were on one of those belt snaps I found on the downed government man. The professor seemed more composed so I unchained him first and handed him the keys.

"Hunker down for now. It's a major warfront out there right this second. Let me get the other prisoners. To be honest though prof, I hadn't thought much past this stage. I didn't really expect to succeed. So if you come up with an exit strategy then go for it old boy." My words were supported by the noise outside. Shots still rang out above the battle on the docks. There were also the inhuman cries of the zombies and the sheer terror in the voices of people who weren't adequately prepared for what they were facing.

Eachan had already started on Wild Bill's handcuffs. I could also see that their legs were zip-tied. For that, I retrieved a pocket knife off my unconscious victim and gave that to the Scottish educator. "Try not to slit any blood vessels. You might want to take care of Bill's ties too. He doesn't look that steady."

I got a flash of the professor's old spirit out of his eyes and a roguish smile. "As you wish my friend. I shall endeavor to get the twain of us afoot and then we shall see about our escape. As for the other prisoners, they are not on the boat. I heard they were being held in a separate part of the warehouse for...testing, I believe the agent called it."

Bill finally spoke for the first time, though it wasn't very constructive, his voice was completely heartfelt. "Jesus Christ Magnus. It really is you? How did you..."

I cut him off with a wave. "Not now Bill. We'll have time for that later. Or else it won't really matter eh? I have to go get the girls. Listen to Eachan, the old man is cannier than most. Who knows? Maybe he can figure a way out of here and past all the baddies outside."

While I talked I also "secured" the unconscious agent with his own handcuffs for which Eachan no longer had a use. I found a government issue handgun on him but no subdual gun like the other had carried. Eachan once pulled a venerable old Webley .454 on me, so I was confident of his firearm handling. He caught the .40 caliber pistol that I tossed him in a holster.

It was when I stood up from all of the securing and relieving of firearms that a casual glance through the portal arrested my attention. What I saw was pure chaos. The agents had fallen into clumps. Most of them were employing their sidearms while a few furiously reloaded the shotguns with more appropriate ammunition. Dixon or somebody had finally wised up to their disadvantage in the current fight.

The zombies were milling about at the far end of the warehouse while their leader stood and surveyed the situation at the head of his tiny army. Beaufort the Bokkr stood with his feet at shoulder width and his hands crossed atop the cane that rested precisely midpoint between those Italian leather shoes. No more firearms were aimed at him. Which was a shame. I was keen to see if he could slap bullets aside as easily as bean bags. Even more intriguing was the thought of how he'd deal with a bunch of buckshot coming at him.

At his terse word over a shoulder, Freke was led forward on a leash that glowed faintly with contained energy. That much was visible even from where I stood. It was a sickly mauve color that sprang from the leash on the wolf, as well as Beaufort's cane, and another leash around Raphael's neck. Raphael didn't look strong enough to need a real leash, much less a magic one.

At another command from the voodoo sorceror, one of the less zombified minions took Freke's leash and began leading him towards the nearest cluster of gunmen. Some of the others weren't paying close attention or they would have noticed how often Freke raised his head to sniff the air and then look directly at the part of the boat that was hiding his old buddy Magnus and some prisoners.

That was the missing puzzle piece I'd figured out. Beaufort wasn't using a phone to track me. He was using the wolf. Freke could easily track me across a county or two if he was left with enough faculties and energy to employ those skills. It didn't explain who had told Beaufort about the ad, but sketchy people like him had contacts in the oddest of places. Any one of the ads I placed might have caught the eye of someone that reported to the old voodoo practitioner.

I had another hunch about that wolf and the leash. It made me direly regret leaving that sniper rifle back with Bobbi. Still, it wasn't an impossible shot with my current weapons. I just had to make a choice about whether the potential risk was worth the potential gain of making an attempt.

If I missed, there was little doubt that they would turn the wolf on me and anyone who got in his way. Even on my best day, I didn't stand much of a chance against one of Odin's immortal, divine, primal entities. Freke would gut me like a fish and smile down at me the whole time. But he wouldn't do that without being commanded.

That was the potential benefit. If I took out the leash holder, then it might give the wolf time to shake off whatever enchantments were on him. I lined up the shotgun with flechettes. There was little chance of missing with that weapon. There was also little chance of getting a full disable at the range I had to work with.

With a sigh, I lowered the weapon and turned my back on the carnage. I was barely in time. The gunfire and screams began a second later. With that chaos ringing out behind me, I put some iron in my backbone and walked stiffly past the two newly released prisoners. "Find us a way out Eachan. I'll go get the girls. If I'm not back in just a little while, you two get the Hel out of here and locate Nev Ange. She'll help you. Provided you pick up the dark elf creatures in the trunk of a BMW outside. Otherwise, she will be just as screwed as I am if I haven't made it back."

Bill lurched to his feet and stumbled across the room to intercept me. His hand on my bicep wasn't enough to spin me around. His voice, however, was. "Angie? She's here? She found me? But...she's not out in *THAT* is she??"

His concern and affection for the girl were enough to soften that iron rod I was trying to hold in my back. I didn't want to bend too much. Otherwise, I'd be back there risking us all on an unlikely gamble to free the wolf before he killed everyone in the warehouse. Bill deserved an answer though. A pragmatic little voice also reasoned that he wouldn't be worth a damn to us if he was too worried about this handicapped kid sister.

"She's someplace safe for the moment. If we don't get those critters out of the BMW though she might get hurt. That was the deal to let me come rescue you folks. Just get out, get the creatures, and retrieve the phone out of a Comanche pickup right outside the fence. She'll probably still be talking on it when you get there." I gave him a gentle push to clear the door and left him staring in disbelief.

That was his problem though, not mine. I'd given him plenty of ammo to start looking for things. A guy as smart and hooked in as Bill should have figured out about the shadows in his world easily. If he hadn't done so, it was because he didn't want to. Some people have a hard time with unexplainable things in their nice orderly world.

The boat seemed secure. I didn't see or hear another

soul on my way down the decks or across the gangway. Once I put a foot on the shoreward side of that dock though, all Hel was apt to break loose. Zombies still fought although there were only two or three left combat effective. The agents had consolidated again into a tidy firing line behind barrels and partitions. They were facing almost directly opposite of me.

That's the only reason I made it from the ship to the doorway that Eachan had thought the girls were behind. I considered hitting the door at a full run with my already considerable mass augmented by all the hardware and protection I was carrying.

Prudence made a rare appearance about then. I skidded to a stop and checked the doorknob which turned easily in my hand. I stepped through, once more with my shotgun at shoulder height and sweeping the room. There was only one target though. An annoyed and mildly disheveled looking blond with her side-pony-tail looking worse for the wear. She was sitting in a steel-framed chair with zip ties restraining her ankles and I assumed on her wrists behind the chair. "Oh, Em, Gee. Like, get out, shut the door and like totes go away Storm Bear."

"Glad to see you too Heather. Keep it down." I stopped whispering and reinforced the idea with a finger to my lips. "Shh."

She rolled her eyes but complied for a few curious seconds while I checked the room for everything from cameras to booby-traps. All I found was yet another door. I took a few steps towards the door then turned back at a hiss from the tied up Valkyrie. With a sigh, I reached down and pulled the Kabar from its sheath to free her.

Once more she gave the eye roll and a smirk. At her smirk, a stray bullet came through the wall beside me and hit her with a "snick" sound. But of course, it didn't hit her. It hit the ties holding her wrists together. With an imperious gesture, she urged me forward and took the knife from me while I shook my head.

"Fer sure Moose, did you like think I needed your help? As if. There's like way too much going on out here. Too many random factors that I can totally use to shift odds, like however I want. You totes need to like listen though. Don't. Go through. That door." I almost missed the girl from our last encounter, right up to the point when she broke out the valley girl dialect.

"Okay, I am like listening to you. Like *in another life!*" Okay so maybe my imitation was pretty crappy, but it was hard not to poke fun. Besides, I *expected* to have a gut reaction to whatever tests they were doing on Maureen. For the sake of whoever was with her, I hoped she was better than I feared.

I sighed and started towards the door again accompanied by a flurry of hissing and finger-snapping behind me. Personally, I thought she'd be better off cutting herself free in case things went south.

As they did a heartbeat later. The door in front of me flew open and Maureen came out at a fast walk. Behind her was a guy in a suit with his shotgun held casually upwards. In his right hand, he held one of those law enforcement tasers. The kind that fire little darts that carry a stunning electrical charge into whatever exposed flesh they contact.

He started to lift the thing, but a sharp. *"Nuh-uh!"* discouraged him. Maybe it was the shotgun instead of the words. He froze in place regardless of the incentive.

"Magnus!" Maureen was almost as immobile. The look on her face screamed confusion and surprise. It seemed enough to keep her tongue-tied while I closed half the distance to her. It was going to prove difficult to embrace her without taking my gun off of the target behind her. I was damned if I wasn't going to do my best though.

The banging of the door behind me put that notion to rest. "Freeze dickweed!" That would be agent Dixon himself, overflowing with eagerness and the milk of human blindness. Blind to anything but his own opinions that is.

I stopped moving, but my gun stayed trained on the guy behind Maureen. Showing hesitation at this point was likely to get several people shot. Without turning to face him, I greeted the spook in a loud confident voice."Howdy agent Dixon! I've been looking for you man. I think we need to work some things out."

"I'm sure we do Mr. Gustaveson." All of his attention was on me. I saw that when I turned just enough to watch both of Uncle Sam's finest. He never even spared Heather more than a glance, which was a gigantic tactical blunder. The girl could walk up and chop him to pieces without breaking a nail. She was pretty good at the hand to hand stuff. Plus she cheated. Let's just say the odds were never going to go against her as long she had her head in the game.

He ignored her anyway as he side-walked in an arc until we could see each other without the drawback of taking my eyes off his man in the doorway. "What is your play here Mr. Gustaveson? You have two guns on you and I still have a hostage. You can take one of us maybe. But the other will drop you a split second later."

I decided to be candid. "My current plan, is to keep talking and stalling while I try to come up with a plan."

That got an ugly laugh from Dixon. "That's good Magnus. Very droll. I forget that you aren't quite as stupid as you look. For instance the thing with my cameras. I'm not even sure how you did that. You'll have to explain that to me before things get too rough, later."

He made a gesture at his guy behind Maureen, who took a quick step and placed himself directly behind the girl. The shotgun hit the floor and a knife appeared in his left hand while the right aimed that stupid taser at my face over the girl's shoulder.

I wasn't that scared. First, he would have to get a couple of yards closer for the thing to reach me. That was one of the reasons he was still standing. He was far enough away that I couldn't be sure of missing the girl if I shot him. I didn't even want to think about what flechettes would do to her.

His return shot with the taser would have been disappointing anyway. My armor and gear were good, but there was a whole extra layer of defense right on my skin. Since I heard Kara was in town, I put a little extra work and energy into the tattooed runes that might protect me from electrical violence, like from her spear or an itty bitty battery-operated taser.

I needed to keep them talking though. That knife behind Maureen's back had me more worried than either of the weapons aimed at me. "No idea what you're talking about Dix. I did my best to avoid your cameras but didn't do anything to them."

His laugh was incredulous and scoffing at the same time. "Really Gustav, you snuck in here past my cameras without disabling all of the views that I watched go out one by one? Next, you will tell me you didn't summon the hellspawn that were tearing my mean apart. Which reminds me, move it. Get through the door and we will be right behind you with the girl, and our guns. If he doesn't move in five seconds, please remove one of her kidneys agent Winston."

I turned to look at the other guy. He didn't brandish the knife. It was concealed behind Maureen while he gestured with the taser. "You heard the man. Get out there before I carve her for thanksgiving.

It seems that people just don't understand what it means to up the ante with people like me. I switched the grip of my left hand to the stock of the shotgun. Since it was Nev Ange's sawed-off I could easily manage it one-handed so that gun oriented on Dixon while my right hand produced the compact handgun I took during the great yacht escape. At our present range, my handgun trumped his taser and was a helluva lot more precise than the shotgun.

Winston knew it too. Despite the new pallor on his face, he gave Maureen a push. From the color that drained from her face along with a gasp of pain, he must have stuck a little bit of the knife in her. That moved him up to the top of my list for karmic pain and retribution. He probably knew that as well. If anything his face went paler when I split his eyes with the blade of my gunsight. "Hurt her again and they'll be scraping the compost in your head off the floor."

"Magnus, please." There was a catch in Maureen's voice, it sounded almost like a whimper. That tore me up worse than the gasp. My Maureen was not fearful. She was strong and fierce and would have been itching to administer her own reckoning to the guy with a knife at her back. I could only guess what they had done to make her this way.

"Let's start over with our countdown, Agent Winston, Mr. Gustaveson. One...Two..." The shotgun stayed on target with the source of that voice while I started backing for the doorway. I discovered that while I hated the thought of flechettes ripping up Maureen, I was quite pleased with the mental image of tiny razor blades ripping Dixon to shreds.

"That's better. Mouse is what everyone calls you right

Mr. Gustaveson?" Dixon kept a wide enough angle that I was having a hard time keeping track of both him and the guy holding my redhead. I backed straight out of the doorway and waited for them to advance as well.

That made this a game of careful observations and maneuvers. I couldn't lose sight of either of them. They didn't want to lose sight of me and they *thought* it was a good idea to get that taser within range. Dix still wanted me alive. Even if the taser could work on me though, I most likely would squeeze some triggers and make a mess of Dixon and one or two others.

A surge of hope tried to betray itself on my face. I fought down the urge to break out in a wide grin, despite the natural response to seeing an ignored Valkyrie lean over to remove a zip tie that had somehow become unlocked. Her motions must have *accidentally* slid the teeth of the thing out of line with the locking mechanism, on both legs, at the same time.

22

"SECRET AGENT MAN, you have forgotten to secure your rear."
I had forgotten about Papa Beaufort in all the intensity of
the current exchange. Apparently, he hadn't forgotten me. "I
assure you that your Viking will not escape this way. Why
don't you secure the other girl and we will all come out here
for negotiations."

I wish I had a picture of Dixon's face. He was surprised
and angry, confused and terrified all at once. I guess he had
to use his own eyes once the cameras went down. The sight
of Freke making hamburger of his agents would not have
been easy.

It wasn't any easier for me to leave my back to that softly
exotic island voice. For all I knew there was an oversized
biker-wolf stalking up to remove my head from behind. I
probably wouldn't hear a thing before the vertebrae
snapped. Maybe I'd be lucky enough to reflexively blow
Dixon to dog chow on the way out.

Dix almost set off the fireworks. The new voice made him
jump. He probably associated it with the death and dismem-

berment of much of his team. The fact that these guys were close behind me amidst a depressing abundance of silence, indicated that most of the normal troops were down.

I didn't pull the trigger when he jumped. I might have gently patted the trigger with my finger, not enough to send dozens of nasty bladed projectiles at him though. The same reaction occurred when he took a half dozen steps to put himself behind Heather. By then she was completely unbound so Dix just jerked her to her feet and back against him. So much for Dix. I'd seen somebody else make that mistake. It hadn't ended well for them.

That gave me an opportunity to swing around and divide my attention between the knifeman with Maureen, and the newcomers; which included Beaufort, a handful of his minions or zombies, and Freke still on a leash held by the central flunky in a white polo. So far the leash-holder had always been more human, and less undead. There was no reason to think that had changed.

I watched everyone I could see as closely as possible without giving myself whiplash. It was a steady but rapid scan from one room to the other until Agent Winston and Maureen stepped through the door and immediately backed away from me. Winston still had the girl as a shield and pulled her along close enough to deprive me of any shot. Not that I wanted to start the ball rolling anyway. Not yet.

That thought was reinforced when I saw movement back behind the zombie squad. In the low-light, I wasn't certain, but it looked like a toy helicopter carrying a cargo net or toy rescue basket. It was hard not to stare as the thing carried it's load over and tucked it on top of the rails to support the waterside overhead door. After that, it darted back into the shadows and I lost it, not before I got a brief glimpse of its payload.

Dixon stepped through the doorway, right behind Heather whom he held with one aggressive fist wrapped around her bicep. I was only glad her Einherjar wasn't around. Luis had some serious attachment issues with his boss. I couldn't say much, Kara and I had not kept a professional distance either back when I did her dirty work.

Some of that was still ingrained. I wanted to take care of Dixon for Luis. Or maybe it was to get even for Maureen, or some of the others. Or just maybe because this guy had been a pain in the ass since the day he decided I was behind the disappearance of his uncle Rawlins back in Austin.

Nope, I refocused on the situation and goals. I mean I had more or less arranged this since the minute I figured out how everyone was keeping track of my movements. At the time it seemed like a good idea to get everyone together and hope they dealt with each other while I picked up the pieces.

Now it wasn't looking so good. Dixon and Beaufort upped my tension when they began "negotiating" like I wasn't even in the room. "We haven't been introduced, sir. My name is agent Dixon. Those men you were fighting on government employees. This does not look good for you at all."

Beaufort didn't faint in terror at Dix's invocation of the ever-vigilant Uncle Sam. In fact, he even bowed like the belle of the ball at an antebellum cotillion. "And I am Papa Beaufort."

His wide grin and cocky smirk didn't show that any potential trouble with the government phased him. "Your government needs to invest more in teaching their men how to protect themselves. I do not believe many of them will survive the night. Which brings us to a curious situation."

"And what situation is that?" Dixon answered the other fellow as if they were two CEOs in a business deal. I wasn't sure if I was part of a hostile takeover or the product the takeover was all about. I suspected that neither of them felt I was great employee material. That made me the package.

"Let us be frank agent Dixon." Beaufort was so confident that it irked me. "I could easily finish this whole night with all of you dead. But it might cost me more than this debacle already has. I would prefer that you let me have the one person in this room that I came for. What you do with the rest is up to you."

Dixon thought for maybe half a minute. "That is an interesting offer. I might be inclined to consider it, except I'm pretty sure we're both after the same person. Unless you came for one of the women?"

"That is most unfortunate Mr. Dixon. Leave now and you can keep the women and anyone else. That is my final offer. I assure you that I will leave with the Viking. If I have to walk through the scattered pieces of everyone else, then so be it. I believe you saw how my large friend deals with obstacles?" The voodoo priest gestured with a graceful wave toward Freke on his leash. For his part, Freke stared around at everyone with a look of disgust tinged with anger.

It didn't take much guessing for me to know how little the wolf liked being controlled. There was little chance that he would object to killing a bunch of people merrily and messily. But that would have to be his idea, not someone else's. I'd heard he even balked at Odin's wishes sometimes. Maybe there was something I could do to shift the odds.

Dixon didn't give me long enough to finish that plan. "You might not walk out of here as easily as you think, Beaufort. I still have a few surprises in the building. As for the women..."

He shoved Heather away from him to fall between himself and the zombies. "Take that one if you want. She's got an aura like the rest of you but she's been nothing but trouble. I don't have any use for that one."

"Then you won't mind if I take her."

It was a completely new voice entering the negotiations as a figure stepped from a swirl of shadow against the steel wall. The fact that there was no doorway or even sufficient shadow to hide someone approaching should have made everyone wary. I'm pretty sure my eyes were the only ones showing fear.

"Both of you preening peacocks can amuse yourself with the other girl. I'll take the one on the ground, and my own dear Storm Bear." Kara had a level of confidence that made both of the "bosses" seem like real shrinking wallflowers. Then again, she could back up every bit of bravado she exuded. Unless you were a helpless looking old hag in another pocket dimension, right?

She didn't enter the fray alone either. From the same section of shadows, and the portal undoubtedly hidden within those shadows stepped my old frenemy Lorcan. He barely took two or three steps before he tossed a sluggishly moving burden of his own to the ground near Heather. The entire time his eyes never left mine.

He didn't speak either. It was Kara whose smug voice reached out like a slimy caress. "There now Magnus. Just as promised. You are here and I have brought the other Einher-jar. You should have told me you had this other gift for me though. I might have brought you a parting gift of my own."

She prodded Heather with her own fur-clad foot. Kara always liked furs and leathers where she wasn't wearing metal. I suppose she'd fit right in with the goths, metal-heads, and death metal rockers at the bar back in Austin. Then again I'd never let her through the door at Helstyx if I had my way.

"I thought the deal was him for me?" My own voice had been silent so long that it got both Dixon and Beaufort's heads to swivel towards me. Kara just laughed and ignored them. I was pretty sure that wasn't going to help keep things on a nice even keel.

"My precious Storm Bear. Have I truly taken so much of your mind that you did not see this coming? I've brought them. I've exchanged him. You are now mine. It isn't my fault if Lorcan has plans for the Valkyrie and her neophyte is it?" she nodded at Lorcan who produced a weapon I hadn't seen in a very long time.

I wondered where he'd gotten a good old fashioned flame-thrower. Somebody once told me they were designed to clear terrain. I knew from personal observation that they were great for clearing personnel too. He probably "found" this little toy on the same day that Kara "lost" her favorite pet enforcer Strombjorn.

A cleared throat got us all to turn back towards Dixon. He had shown a surprising amount of prudence and stepped back towards his own ally and the human shield with her mass of flame-colored hair. Behind him, I saw that same barely divisible disturbance in the air as the stealthy drone made another passage carrying yet another load. I hoped it wasn't another claymore. That would be just like Dixon to blow up the building and everyone in it just because he didn't get his way.

Since he had all of our attention, the agent had his counter-offer to make. "How about I take the girls, Mr. Gustaveson, and everyone with Mr. Beaufort over there?

You, miss whoever you are, can settle for the two on the boat. One of them has an aura but he's old and rather brittle. I doubt he'd survive the testing long enough to be worth my time."

That brought dueling evil overlord laughs from the sorceror and psycho storm valkyrie. Beaufort beat Kara to the question on both of their minds. "And why would we do that?"

It was a good straight line. I'll give Dix that. He set them up to ask a perfectly timed question for his own dramatic response. He raised something that looked like the handgrip on a tool. If said handgrip had a cap you twisted to expose a button that Dix depressed. "Because if you don't. I'll release the deadman switch here and send the whole place up in a ball of fire, followed by a long nap for all of us in the muck of the harbor."

23

ANY SATISFACTION I might have felt about my accurate guesses was outweighed by what a mess the claymores would make. Nobody would survive if he had more than a couple of them set up with overlapping cones of devastation. The fact that the quiet little drone was still ferrying them around told me he probably had plenty of the boomboxes.

While we "negotiated" the whole crew seemed to instinctively circle clockwise. That put Freke and the Zombie trio at the door Dix had been standing at initially. I was between that door and the yacht, with Kara on my right and Beaufort on my left. That also left me one too few hands to keep everyone covered.

Lorcan had the zombies covered with the flamethrower, although the blue-flame-tipped barrel of that weapon kept swinging towards me as if on a string. The brutish chosen warrior managed to get it back on target every time his aim strayed but not before earning a sharp frown from his mistress and my ex-mistress. She might have been less worried about the zombies than Heather and Luis. To get the undead, Lorc would have to wash flame right across where the other Valkyrie an Einherjar were sprawled.

Beaufort was fixated on Kara while his zombies wanted Dix and his buddy. The two g-men were watching everyone at once. Then again I'm pretty sure everyone spent a bit of their fascinated attention on the hand with that deadman's detonator too.

That left me free to wake up the hamster and start the wheel spinning in my own head. A few hours ago it had seemed like a good idea to toss all the ingredients in a pot and watch it bubble. I hadn't planned on being part of the stew myself though.

That plan had depended on them taking some time to merrily beat away at each other while I got in, got my people and got out. Obviously, I had not counted on the efficient butchery of a chained wolf-godling. I was also hoping to have Maureen, the Prof, and Heather backing me with their own individual tricks by the time I faced Kara. Might have messed up on the timeline too.

So now I had the whole enchilada to take care of in one messy bite. That wouldn't bother me so much if I had at least managed to get all those friends and allies out first. Even the toothy buggers in the boot of the BMW were supposed to be out before I had to deal with Kara.

I was wracking my brains for a trick, a ploy, a diversion, anything to give me that least little edge. My wracking was interrupted by a flapping and a squawk that turned into the coherent word, yea. "Dumbasses!"

At least I wasn't alone in his derision. That was fresh. All of those guns and steely-eyed gazes and flickering mantles of power just kind of froze for a minute and watched as Rafe winged in to scrabble awkwardly at my shoulder. The modern vest did not provide him much of a landing pad.

Thankfully the older armor gave him someplace to lock his claws in without going through muscle and scraping against my ribs or collarbone.

Kara adjusted first and quirked an eyebrow to mirror the incongruous smile that threatened her warface. "Your bird? You brought your bird to battle all the forces arrayed against you?"

"I wanted to keep it fair. I started to bring my dog but he has a larger brain capacity than your hound over there." I had often suspected that my mouth was unattached to my brain. That just about proved it. I hadn't even decided if I was offended by Kara's remark before I was shooting off a sarcastic rejoinder. "Besides, doesn't your pet over there know if he kills them they'll just beat you back to Valhalla to talk to your All-father?"

Kara just laughed, while Lorcan let out a grunting growl. Which he followed up by enough rumbling profanities to let me know he caught the joke and was properly offended.

"Oh my precious Stormbear, you used to be so bright. Always doing my research, knowing the terrain, scouting out my enemies. Have I taken too much of your mind to remember? Fire cleanses."

She took a deliberate step to the side as if the thought of that "cleansing" made her more aware of the weapon her minion was carrying. It didn't stop her lecture though. "Even a strong and ancient Valkyrie is careful of fire because we must use so much energy to heal it. The simplest burns can leave one of us drained and weak for days. That is true for most things of the supernatural world. Fire is a great bane. That child is too young to save herself and her charge. And now you've gone and insulted my dearest Lorcan. I imagine he will be glad to demonstrate for you? Won't you, my pride-wounded warrior?"

"Insulted, yea. Can I roast them all mistress? Stupid bird too?" He didn't sound insulted, just eager.

That was okay though. Because I was plenty offended. That bird had been around and listened to my crap for a lot of years. Nobody got to talk bad about him without earning it. I reached up a finger to rub his beak just in case he understood enough to be offended as well. For once he didn't try and remove any pieces of said finger. Instead, he rubbed his head on it then rubbed his head on my cheek and nibbled on my hair.

That made me want to wince. Last time he did that I had an eardrum rendered into a special torture device by his squawking. This time he didn't squawk at all. Instead, the bird freakin whispered. "Bright Light, go Night Night."

What the Hel? I couldn't help myself. I took my eyes off of the standoff to look at that weirdo bird. He just repeated the same words softly, and then blinked both eyes at me three times in succession. And then I'll be damned if the bird didn't start counting, in Norse, backward. With every word, he would squeeze both eyes shut. They weren't perfect pronunciations but I got the words. "Fimm, Fjorir, Trheir, Tvei..."

That's when I got the meaning as well as the words. I got my eyes shut just before the world went bang and got the party up and rolling. The blast was not exactly negligible. It would have been worse if the claymore had been pointed at us instead of the walls and ceiling. I got shoved several feet by a titanic feather duster. I caught my balance just before the force bowled me over. I could just imagine rolling to my back in all of that armor and gear.

Lorcan would be all too happy to come over and gut me while I wallowed like an upside-down turtle. That was provided the zombies didn't find the sight irresistible. None of them got to see it though, because I got a hand down and shoved off in a stumbling run before I actually hit the ground.

With all of that, I was better off than the rest. Zombies were bouncing around like blinded pinballs. Dixon and his guys were knocked back against the wall blinking furiously, and Lorcan was down on one knee with his eyes screwed shut. Only Kara and Beaufort seemed to have some kind of eyesight. Rafe might have been okay too. He was spiraling through the air but got his wings spread before he hit anything like steel or concrete. The last I saw of the raven he was shooting upwards and on a diagonal away from the fight. Because it was a fight, of sorts.

That explosion had triggered a frenzy of activity even if only a minority of share of it was visually directed. The whole building shook and rang like a gong while one entire wall fell outward. It let a lot of light *in*, and cleared the way for the yacht to get *out*.

The rest of us were too busy to worry about escape just yet. I should have known Lorcan would be first to initiate violence whether he could see straight or not. He triggered that flamer and shot a scarlet and smokey black cloud halfway across the warehouse. It went over Heather and Luis at its widest point and then reached further towards Freke and the Zombies.

I didn't even think it through. I suppose I instinctively knew that there was nothing I could do for the two of my brethren in the middle of our bull-ring. The best I could do was join them in the pyre, or maybe put them down before the flames finished them. That wouldn't help them. Likewise, all I could see of Maureen and her two bad-guys was movement on the other side of the billowing smoke and flame. But I did have a chance to help a different ally. The captive wolf was only a weapon as long as he had that leash on.

I spun to the side and fired three blasts of flechettes that ate into the minion holding Freke and the zombie closest to him. I got the leash too. It exploded into brilliant sparks all tinged with that mauve and inky blackness. Freke burst into action an instant later. His sweeping arms caught the entire pack of Beaufort's minions and undead. Even the shredded and dying man was lifted off his feet and driven back over the edge of the pier to vanish underwater with the wolf.

Beaufort spun in a complete circle. He had been trying to line his cane up on Freke but gave up on that as the other disappeared from sight. Rather than wait for him to reappear, the sorceror completed his spin completely around and aimed the cane at Dixon. A single sharp word was all it took to release the same energy he previously used to subdue Freke outside Bobbi's cabin. This time it shot across the room in a bolt and jolted the boss G-man up onto his tiptoes before he fell like a bunch of rags. Wet rags. Wet stupid arrogant rags that I really wanted to set on fire.

I only got to see that activity because Lorcan paused with his own weapon to survey the results. The first thing we both saw was the huge hole in the floor between us all. There were no smoldering corpses of Valkyrie or their chosen, just shadows and the faint ripples of blue waves and dark floating crud. Her luck had held and made the floor collapse with the explosion. It had to have been a split-second before the flames would have roasted Heather and her chosen. That was all in the instant before we saw Beaufort's light show attack at Dixon.

Then Maureen appeared from the smoke cloud, with nothing but a face and taser over her shoulder. I thought about warning the Winston fellow. Tasers rarely have a full effect on one of the chosen as old and toughened from wear as Lorcan or I. It would probably piss the old warrior off. I just hoped he wouldn't resort to the flamethrower in retaliation. Then again, this was Lorcan. He'd want to get up close and personal with the guy who stung him with fifty-thousand volts or so. At least I hoped so.

That left Beaufort for me. I figured I could take him a lot more safely than Kara would. She might finish blowing the warehouse down. It wouldn't matter at all to her if she did. I dropped the empty shotgun and drew my backup. At our present range, it was easy as pie. I put one round into his head and watched the island sorceror fall just as limp as Dix had.

Everyone stopped moving for a couple of heartbeats. We were down to the real fight now. The humans and even the zombies had been risks, but they were nothing compared to Lorcan and he was just a small symptom of the kind of plague Kara could be. Even worse, I had no idea if I could do more than cut her a little bit, even with the firearms and rune enhanced blade.

That didn't change my prime mission anyway. I never thought I'd make it out of this one. One way or another my time was up on this particular trip. The main thing I had come to this warehouse for, was to free Maureen. I couldn't do that if Lorcan fried her.

"Lorcan stand down. You too Winston." I swung my gun from one to the other of them while Kara stood with an amused smile. I thought maybe she'd take control of the situation. When I gave her the quizzical look though she deliberately smiled and took a step to the side. It put her closer to Lorcan but was also a statement. It went with the wave of a hand to tell me "All your big guy. Let's see how you get out of this one."

"Shut up, mewling cub." That was Lorcan for you. His hate was probably two or three times as big as his frontal lobe. "I will take care of this upstart mortal. Then I will gut you and celebrate with the girl. Who knows? Maybe she'll even like it. A few have."

That's probably what made Lorcan have such a huge Hate-On. I know his voice had that effect on me. If I had to walk around hearing that all voice day I'd probably want to maim and kill as much as he did. Or maybe I hated him for so much as looking at Maureen, much less salivating over her potential rape.

"Not gonna happen, bitch." That was my own voice gone raspy and raw with emotion. "I'll take you with me even if you kill me. No celebrations for you. Hey, I got an idea. If Kara's right, would she bother repairing your junk if I burned it off? Left you with an overcooked cocktail weenie?"

"Shut up both of you." It was surprising to hear Winston. With his boss out of the fight, I figured he would be in a panic. But no, he was up to shouting down two guys with centuries of killing experience and magick he couldn't even fathom behind them.

"You dare talk that way to me? I am Lorcan, chosen hand of the Stormy Kara. If you weren't so ignorant you would be groveling instead of blustering." Lorc was getting behind the idea. He apparently planned to toy with the human before he got down to business. "That little toy of yours is useless. It will barely slow me down before I get my hands on you. Maybe I'll disable you. Save you for some entertainment after I've dealt with the bear. A warm-up for my fun with the girl. Or you can drop the sparkly toy and run. I might not even chase you."

If I had my way Lorcan wouldn't be chasing anyone. I could at least do that much. But that was a minor concern.

"Kara call him off and I'll go with you. Let the mortals go. At least let the girl go."

"The girl is it? I wondered how they got you here. You were always a sucker for the lady in distress Bear. So maybe I will teach you a lesson. Lorcan, roast them both."

"I warn you! If I have to tase you then you'll wake up on a lab table. You don't want to know what Dixon has planned for all of your kind." Winston was a cooler customer than I had given him credit for. Not cool enough though. I saw his hand move convulsively behind Maureen's back. It was the same hand that stuck the tip of his knife blade into her just moments ago. It made perfect sense to me that he was getting rid of her to free up both of his hands at once.

I barely had time to shout a warning before she was falling away in front of him. *"Maureen!"*

.

My heart lurched as she fell. The entire warehouse seemed to freeze just out of focus for me. All I clearly saw was Maureen's falling body and the barrel of my gun swinging from Lorcan to the bastard that had stabbed her. His taser went off just as I started pulling the trigger.

Now I've only seen those things on television and movies. Maybe the cameras weren't up to catching the whole light show. Normally all you saw was the lines appearing in mid-air about the time a junky or carjacker jerked like a marionette whose puppeteer was sneezing. This was the first time I ever saw the emerald green and sky blue flickers of lightning that went with the lines.

It was also the first time I saw the target get a completely poleaxed look as he was lifted off the ground and flung into a stunned and smoking pile of stupid. That didn't make any sense at all. I've been hit by the handheld stunners and they feel like I've hit my funny bone. I'd heard of people standing up to two or three shots of even the police version. And I know for a fact that Kara would have prepared her boy to counter any tricks I might have planned.

She looked just as stunned as I felt about Maureen. For her, it must have been the spectacle of Lorcan arching his back in pain only to collapse unconscious.

Then I fired three shots as quickly as I could work the trigger. All three shots hit Winston in the chest. Even if he was wearing a vest, that much firepower that quick was going to put him down and out of breath.

Kara's attack almost did the same for me. Her favorite tube of purple lightning hit me at the hips. That same attack that had blown the Bone lady to pieces once or twice hit me like a roaring bolt of sheer seething violence and lightning, and disappeared in a cloud of swirling sparks around me.

That damned dwarf hadn't been lying. He did some hellacious work. Or the night elves had done it with their cloth. It didn't matter which was responsible. It just mattered that I was still in the fight. Right up until I heard the swish and sizzle and felt fifty-thousand volts of magically enhanced man-made lightning toss me to the ground.

I was down. I was just a few blinks short of out. My heart was pounding uncontrollably along with a very unsettling flutter in my chest. I had enough training to know what I was feeling. Without my normal enhancements in place, I was just as vulnerable as anyone else who had been abused extensively and then had his heart shocked out of rhythm. If I had the breath, I would have laughed at one of Kara's feared enforcers dying from a heart attack.

It was just a little bit of energy from a toy that shouldn't have touched me. There was no chance it was stronger than Kara's spear-bolt. But it was enough to send me back to Valhalla. Just a little energy...energy?

Like life energy? My fingers were twitching and didn't want to work. I kept mentally yelling at them until they dug the little phial out. There was still a spark in it, but how much was left? I "sucked" at it like a man dying in a desert. The ensuing surge of magick kicked me like a defibrillator. A single second was enough to jar my heart back into a less terminal rhythm. I let the phial fall out of my hand to dangle from the thong around my neck. I still couldn't move more than those few fingers, but I wasn't going to die. Maybe if I just lay there and rested a bit.

That's why I wasn't sure if I was dreaming or awake when I rolled my head on a rubbery neck just far enough to see Maureen and Kara circling each other. Kara had her spear out but was using it more as a shield than a weapon. Her eyes were locked uncertainly on the blocky plastic weapon in Maureen's hand.

Kara licked her lips and then smiled at the redhead. "You show courage little Celtic lass. For that, I shall let you go. You know your toy can not hurt me though don't you?"

My Maureen shrugged and casually glanced at both Lorcan and I. "That's what they thought too, isn't it? Do you want to try your luck? I bet I can get some more help in here before you wake up. Then you won't wake up until I let you, on a cold steel lab table, right before they start the saws and drills."

"Courage indeed." Kara might have been muttering to herself rather than Maureen. But we all three heard it. "So what do you propose? You go your way and I go mine? The first of them to wake up will slaughter the other. That might be your Mouse, and it might be my Lorcan."

"I'd put my money on my Mouse to win that one...Stormy was it? Like a stripper name? No matter. Let's change the odds. I go my way with Mouse, and you go your way with Lorcan."

Kara was starting to get her confidence back. She still kept her eyes on that taser but she didn't look as wild-eyed. "I have too much invested. The bear is mine. I won't have him telling anyone else his stories."

"Or Odin will hear them?" We'd all forgotten Freke. He climbed out of the water and stood regarding the scene with keen interest. He didn't show a hint of fear to Kara. He never had shown any kind of fear. It's just possible that he was strong enough to practically be a god himself. He certainly seemed to think he was more than equal to one of the strongest Valkyrie around. He was also just as curious as any wild animal.

"I have oft wondered where he was. So you lost him, Kara? How long ago?" He cocked his head to the side, like a dog, or a wolf I guess.

"Mind your own business mutt." Kara was not best pleased with the wolf's observations. If she thought for a minute that she could take him, he'd be dead already.

"Odin *is* my business girl-child." Trust an ageless primal force to put even a thousand-years of Valkyrie in her place. "Take your minion and be off. Maybe I won't tell Odin about all of this when next I see him, and maybe I will. Or maybe I won't have to go back at all just yet. What say, you girl?"

He stood to his full height and stretched his hands over-head to crack a yard or two of the spine while he waited for her reply. She never spoke though. Instead, she strode over to Lorcan with her back rigid and her hips showing none of the customary seductive roll. She struck the dock with her spear while her other hand lifted Lorcan by his belt like a slab of meat. They both paused just at the edge of the plane of flickering electricity that sprung up like a doorway summoned by her spear.

When Kara spoke, it was to Maureen rather than Freke."Don't think you've won anything. Even if the bear survives this, I withdraw my protections. He will be as vulnerable as any other mortal, and just as uncertain where he will go after death."

Maureen didn't back down or look uncertain. She took a step forward and brandished her taser again. "Enough with the pretty speeches. Take your sparkly ass through yon sparkly doorway and sparkle back to wherever ye came from bitch. Before I fry your teats to a crisp."

The doorway closed behind Kara, her burden, and a scream of rage.

Freke laughed and looked over at my Maureen. "Would you truly have fired your toy lightning at one of Odin's strongest and most favored swan-maidens?"

She let her mouth shape itself into a cracked smile and lifted her taser towards the ceiling rather than in any fashion that might seem a threat. "Can't. These things are one shot."

The grizzled old wolf of a biker laughed so hard I thought he might shake the rest of the building down. It was still standing when he squatted down near my head though. "You do pick some of the best ones Strombjorn. She's as fine a catch as your little black-haired Refn so long ago. I'll leave you in her care now, eh? And maybe I'll just try and forget everything myself rather than seek out a mortal wizard this time."

He was still laughing as he disappeared through the shattered wall of the warehouse. I could see emergency vehicles speeding towards the docks. There must have been some kind of firehouse close enough to hear the explosions. They wouldn't take long to get to us.

I was right. They did take long enough for Eachan to back the boat out and point it towards the open gulf. The firetrucks appeared only a few minutes after that.

I guess the old scholar was a bit of a sailor after all. If I recalled, Wild Bill got seasick in anything larger than a paddleboat. He wouldn't be much help sailing the big yacht. I saw both of them look at the ruined building. They couldn't see into the shadows as well as I could see out. I guess that's why they waited as long as they could for some of us to emerge before Eachan used the motors to power the boat out into the waterway and away from the approaching sirens.

Maureen had been busy in the meantime. She didn't seem too worried about me. Instead, she checked on her captor Winston and then Dixon and Beaufort. Winston woke up with a start and a groan. The beanbags would leave some beautiful bruises. Maybe he had a broken rib or two to go with them. I kind of hoped so, especially when he started jerking multiple zip ties around my wrist while I was still too weak to stop him.

Maureen ignored his actions and my predicament. That was bewildering until I saw the tasers still in Winston's holder. All of them had odd little scratch-marks on them. They were something like old gunfighters used to carve in their revolvers for each man killed. They were even more like the Ogham staves I'd seen Maureen use for divination and magick. That would explain the emerald and blue light show. Those druidic and Wiccan types always liked the more nature-oriented magick.

That's why I wasn't surprised when she greeted the first responders at the door with a badge she produced from a hidden spot in her belt. It must have been a helluva an identification. Firefighters, paramedics, and cops alike hung on her every word and made order out of chaos. She turned command over to Winston once he was through tying everyone up.

Then she hunkered down beside me. "No murder charges for you Magnus. Though I thought m'heart would choke me to death when ye turned that blunderbuss on agent Dixon. It's nice to warn a lass, ye ken?"

Her weak smile and attempt to lighten the mood didn't get much response from me. I wasn't even upset when she bit her lip and let a fake tear or two slide out of the corners of her eyes.

She gave up and continued her little speech. "Everyone you shot was either just bean-bagged or already dead apparently. They might be able to make a charge of abusing a cadaver for the zombies, but my bosses will get that all taken care of. For now, why don't you take a nap."

I mumbled her name despite any intentions I had not to do so. She shushed me with a weak smile and a hand on my forehead. "Not now mo chroi. Just rest."

Maybe it was her words or the abuse and neglect I'd been subjecting myself to. Or maybe it was more of her magic. Mostly I think it was the sick feeling of betrayal that made me want to curl up and cry. Turns out maybe she wasn't "My" Maureen at all.

24

I WOKE up in the back of an ambulance. This one was much newer and nicer than the ones I worked in twenty or thirty years earlier. The medics were an upgrade too, of sorts. The red hair was as thick and lustrous as ever. The face beneath it looked just as provocative and lovely as my most cherished memories. Even the concern in her eyes was enough to catch my breath. But I wasn't too out of it to remember that it was all a lie.

"There you are Mo Chroi." Even the name was a lie. Who was I to interrupt the woman though?

" I've given ye nary a drug. We both ken how well that body of yours heals on its own aye? This wee bit of a shock will fade in no time. My magicks dinnae make it stronger so much as they make it slipperier. It just made the shock go around your protections and get into where they need to work." If she was expecting an answer to that she was in for a big disappointment.

I couldn't think of many people I wanted to explain the history that gave me my protections and enhanced healing. There were even fewer people that needed to know I had lost it. Maureen wasn't on either list. In fact, she was just on one list for me; a long list of people I regretted meeting and wanted to forget.

She must have seen it in my eyes. Again she tried the tearful ploy, and again it failed. I'd fallen too hard for her to let that happen again. "I had little choice Mo Chr...Magnus. I was on the trail of the witch back in Austin when we ran into you. One thing led to another and when I filed my final report they made me start a case file on you. I didn't try very hard though. My reports were always vague as if I didn't really know you."

That must have been a pretty neat trick for someone living in my home, in my bed even. For all, I knew she got her orders to cozy up to me before we ever slept together. For some reason that made a difference to my aching heart. I didn't tell her that. But I did have questions I couldn't keep bottled.

"So the tracking spell was part of the job?" I wanted to ask her whether everything was part of the job, from the shortest kiss to the longest night we shared. Her mute nod at the first question choked those questions still in my throat.

"I guess this explains how you kept getting captured by the bad guys. You were never in that much danger, were you? Just sitting there gathering your evidence while I ran around getting shot and blown up or worse in my frenzy to save you." Again she gave me the silent nod for an answer. That silence was starting to piss me off more than her lying words had earlier.

"So now we're headed to Dixon's secret lab so he can test and torture and cut me up to look at all the bits and pieces." My voice showed my disgust and disappointment, but I kept the smug satisfaction hidden. They might get me there but without Kara's protections I wouldn't last long enough to give up any secrets.

Maybe I should have been worried about the uncertainty of my afterlife. I distinctly recalled Kara telling Maureen that I was no longer her chosen. Not in so many words, but close enough for me to believe her. The fact that I was still down was confirmation enough. The only need for the straps holding me down inside the ambulance was to keep me from falling. I barely had the strength to lift my voice, much less an arm.

Maureen didn't answer my previous statement about labs and experiments. No, that voice came from the front of the ambulance where I was vaguely aware two people were sitting. From the voice, Winston was driving and explaining at the same time. "Dixon is still back there in the warehouse. Emergency services will transport him to a nearby hospital shortly. It should be a day or two before he gets sorted and heads to Washington with his report and samples."

"Samples huh?" I could only begin to picture how much of my hair or how many tubes of blood he'd gathered while I was unaware.

"I couldn't leave him empty-handed. Not after all of that. If he woke up with nothing to show for it our cover would be blown. So I left him a dead zombie and the zombie over-lord." That was Winston again. I knew I was following the voice but somehow I got lost in the words.

"Wait. Your cover? And you in plural...you said our." I turned to Maureen then. "So if you don't work for Dixon, who in Hel's name *DO* you work for?"

Winston answered for her again. "She works for me. And I work for people that you don't need to know about. At least not now."

"Great, politics and infighting between agencies in D.C.

How novel." It was bad enough being played by a girl I'd allowed to get close. But I really hate authority figures jerking my strings. When you make that *heart* strings tangled and yanked on by warring spies jockeying for favor it just makes it worse, dirtier.

This time it was Maureen. Somehow that didn't feel any nicer or sweeter. "We decided it would be better if you did not end up in Dixon's hands. That had nothing to do with politics and rivalries. As far as he knows, we are as much his people now as he thought we were in Austin."

A third voice joined their side of the conversation. "He never was able to see much further than his own plans and wants. Boy was a trial for the whole family."

That voice almost gave me the strength to get up. Or it might have if I wasn't strapped down three ways from Sunday. "Rawlings!? For all that's holy, I thought you were dead!"

The old retirement age cop cracked a bright smile in a face that looked like dark old mahogany. "Got that impression myself for a while there kid. Fact I was prob'ly more dead than alive for a while there. Had the damnedest dreams while I was on that machine too. All that talk of german folktales I 'magine. Cute little girl with a fine little butt kept coming by in my dreams and askin' if I was ready to go. Said her name was Gondul."

I was shaken enough that I missed some of the next few moments. The three of them spoke softly while I sat wondering if the old man really had survived. Gondul doesn't show up for sick people. She shows up to collect dead warriors, or in this case brave old men who got involved in things beyond their pay grade.

Something Rawlings said brought me back into the

conversation. "Wait you really aren't taking me back to some lab?"

That drew a great deal of uncomfortable silence until Winston slowed the vehicle and brought it to a stop. He turned in his seat until we could all see each other. Of course, he and Rawlings were both upsides down in my field of vision since I had to tilt my head back to meet his eyes. "You people have your conversation. I need a smoke and I can't do it with that oxygen hazard sign in my face. You've got one cigarette of time. Maybe two if my nerves don't settle down."

The gravity of his voice didn't exactly go with the conversation. He meant every word though. A second later the door closed behind him as he walked away fishing in his jacket for some cigarettes, or maybe a secret decoder radio to call in his strike team.

Maureen shook me out of those thoughts by springing into action. She started removing straps and buckles so quickly that she was getting in her own way. The strap over my chest took her three attempts to get off. I wanted to hope this meant what it looked like. But I'd spent a good part of the last few weeks wanting to hope she was my soulmate. I might make a bunch of mistakes, but I try not to keep making the same one over and over again.

I let her know I wasn't falling for it this time. "You got me, lady. I'm confused here. Am I supposed to try and escape and get shot in the attempt? Or is this just another experiment to see what I do?"

Rawlings added to the conversation with a snort of disgust and another of the lectures I'd almost missed when he was "dead". "Boy, you ain't got no sense at all. The girl is sticking her neck out for you. She has orders to bring you in. I heard the conversation myself. But she's about to get overpowered and fail to stop her prisoner from escaping. Guess when it comes down to it, so am I. How embarassin'. Had my badge back for less than a week and my first prisoner is going to escape."

This time my voice wasn't as harsh. "Okay, maybe I'm off base. But I still don't get it. Winston said you aren't feds. But all of you have badges and IDs. How am I supposed to believe this?"

Maureen gave a mildly more delicate snort than Rawlings. "We can't be both, boyo? The badges are for Dixon's special task force. But Rawlings and I answer to Winston and he answers to a secret group or cabal or whatever you want to call it. According to him, most of the people who do the same thing we do, work for the private sector. Oh, there are a few government squads like Dixon's. Some Russians, a handful of Scots. I heard there are special forces in India and Argentina too. Most of us are freelancers, esoteric cults or religious groups. There's even a rumor of some old-world Templars somewhere in the Mediterranean. Look. Just trust me that we aren't all like Dixon. Get up and get out of here. Winston can only stall for so long before this place busts into a spy anthill all to look for you."

I was struggling to sit up when I remembered the little vial. Was there anything left in it? I tried my best to pull it dry when my heart was about to stop. But did I get it all? Maybe I had been too weak and unfocused. I lifted it to my lips and imagined the energy rushing down to warm the energy node or chakra at the pit of my stomach.

If a normal energy drink gives you wings, then this stuff gave me anti-gravity pads. I all but floated off the gurney while various aches and pains tried to sort themselves out. Maureen gave a sharp nod and smile of approval. "See? I knew you're magic would kick in. There's a bus station two blocks over. Here's a wad of cash we all chipped in. Get out of here. You run and you run far. Austin won't be safe. Dixon has tentacles deep into the shadowy places of that city."

We caught ourselves leaning in for a goodbye kiss. It was aborted before we even touched lips. Instead, I let the girl wrap her arms around me while I patted her shoulder. "Goodbye, Magnus. Stay out of sight for a while. We'll try to get a shorter leash on Dixon. The dead agents and blown up warehouse should help. Your professor got away too. He'll be able to start a stink with his clout and money aye? You just don't come out of hiding until you're sure."

Her concern was touching. I just wasn't sure how real it was. I couldn't let her go with just a pat though. She was still My Maureen somewhere in the back of my head, or maybe it was my heart. I gave her a kiss on the forehead and ducked out of the ambulance.

I looked back once before I rounded the corner. Maureen had the rear door open and was matching me. She lifted her hand in a half-wave at the same time her boss met my gaze with his own. He nodded once and flipped his cigarette into a puddle before stepping in to start the van. I never saw them drive away because I was heading the other direction on a different street.

It took me three or four minutes to get to the Comanche pickup. I was almost to it when I saw the boots sticking out of the driver's side window. That was almost enough to make me sprint off in a different direction. A shadow falling like a rock from overheard changed my mind when it resolved into a raven that landed on the roof of that pickup cab. "Hurry, Dumbass."

That was enough to get the boots out of the window and replace them with a familiar face. Bobbi tucked a few errant hairs behind her ear and gave me about half a frown. "Made it did you? I lost ten bucks. Nev Ange had faith in you but I figured you were as gone as Caesar's ghost. You sure are a disappointment to me to show up after that shit-show down on the docks."

I couldn't help myself. A grin split my face and my laugh split the air. "I love you too Bobbi Lee."

"Whoa, there cowboy. We still ain't even been dancin'. You can't tell a girl you love her before you done spooned a little bit and showed her your two-step. Ain't no time for that right now though. Get in the truck. Your crazy little stunt has folks in an uproar. You gotta get outta town about breakfast time of last Sunday. I mean fast." She went so far as to open the door for me before she scooted out the other side.

I scooted past her and laughed at her phrasing then answered with one of my own. "Crazy stunt? You mean *crazy like a fox!*"

I got another laugh out of the look on her face before I wound down and apologized. "I'm sorry Bobbi-Lee. It's been a stressful day. I might have sprung a gear or two in my head. Besides, I've always wanted to say that line. You'd be surprised how rarely it fits a situation."

She rolled her eyes without laughing. "With you cowboy? I assume the crazy part fits on a regular basis. It's that "like a fox" bit that's hard to tag you with on most occasions. Get out of here now. Keys are in the ignition. Nev had me drop off a goody bag for you too. Coffee, sandwiches, cookies, maybe some explosives and cuttin' edge electronics. You know, a picnic basket for mercenaries. I recognize some of it from that trailer of hers, but there's a bag or two that come from inside the troll's caves. Don't bother explainin' it. I'm just a simple messenger girl." She was outside and leaning on the window by the end of that explanation.

Almost everything she said begged a question. I opted for an obvious inquiry first. "The trailer? How did you get it here without the truck."

Bobbi flashed another roguish smile and then spread her fingers into a downward V and simulated walking along the windowsill. "Would you believe a four troll hitch? The big ones must be stronger than a Clydesdale and a touch faster. And that Lola troll? She sat up top of the trailer like it was a stagecoach. She sang the entire way to a parking lot just over yonder. Ran us straight through traffic without a hiccup or a second glance from bums, cops or meter maids. Seemed like we was all but invisible 'long as she kept singing."

The parking lot she gestured towards was in plain sight of the docks and a couple of hundred yards away. Now that I knew what to look for, I could see the bullet trailer there plain as day. They'd tucked into a row of older cars that looked like they hadn't moved in a decade. The trailer fit right in. "Why did they let you go? I didn't get the little dark elfkin out. For that matter, they must have released you before I even got here. Is Nev in there? I need to ask her some questions before I go."

"Don't you even think about going in there, boy. We got it from a good source that you are persona non-freakin-grata in these parts. Not exactly dead or alive status but I get the idea nobody's getting in much trouble if you turn up with a dozen accidental bullet holes. The trolls decided you might need some help. Nev Ange convinced them we'd be an asset. And I snuck Raphael out during that little hoe-down y'all was enjoying. He got the boogeymen out of the trunk and is takin' em back. Seems he has connections with those kinda folks that he never tole us about. Just get in the truck and get out." she circled the vehicle and was by the driver door by the time I had it started.

Bobbi grabbed me by both ears and gave me the kind of kiss that made you want to hang around a while rather than drive off. "That's from Nev."

Then she gave me another one that was almost as surprising and nice. "And that one's from me. To say good-bye. You can take me out for Steaks and dancin' next time you're in town."

She pushed herself off of the truck and gave me a lazy smile and lazier wave. "Bye dipstick. All your old gear is in your bag. We put your friend's cage in the floorboard." At her words, Rafe jumped through the window and shuffled over to dip his head under the cage cover. I heard the rustling of feathers and clinking metal followed by the ritual I'd always used to put him to bed. *Lights out, Night Night, now close your eyes.*

25

THE TAILLIGHTS of the beat-up old Jeep pickup were barely out of sight before people stepped out of the darkened interior of the nearby valet shack.

"Did he go along?" The professor looked like he'd been on a diet and desperately needed a shower and a change of clothes. His normal dapper outfit was spattered with blood and the wrinkles that came from sleeping in them for days at a time.

Wild Bill right beside him was in a similar state, though his clothes hadn't been so nice to begin with. His eyes might have been a tad more alarmed as well. He didn't answer Eachan's question though.

The answer came from the girl in the wheelchair who held Bill's hand while Bobbi Lee strolled over with a crooked smile. "He didn't seem inclined to question me. I figure you're right though. If he knew we were all here he'd sit around and chat until the spooks came and knocked him on the head. My question is, do you trust the fellow that told you what was up?"

This time it was Eachan who fielded the question.

"Rawlings was a good cop and a better man. If he said they would be after Magnus then there is no reason to question it. I do wish I knew why he suggested the fast goodbye and as he phrased it a *clean cut of the umbilical*."

Bobbi nodded once then cast a sideways glance at her best friend. "And you didn't hide any trackers in the gear you packed up for him? I don't mind lying to the idiot a little. He sure as shit played fast and loose with us a few times. But I don't wanna think I'm setting him up for those government yahoos to latch onto."

"Nope, no bugs in the gear. Though I might have another way of tracking him." Ange shared a look and a giggle with Bobbi Lee. "Good thing there's nobody as good as me in that bunch of penny-ante hackers the spooks were using. Hell, they never even noticed when I used my drones to knock out their cameras and subvert that stupid final option plan with all the claymores. They won't be able to follow the few bread crumbs I left for myself alone."

Wild Bill cleared his throat and spoke for the first time since they all emerged. "So what is he going to do now? You don't think he can escape the feds do you?"

"He'll head for the back hills," Bobbi said it as if there was no doubt at all. "I 'magine that boy's been over the crick and past the pasture. He'll get someplace away from people and cell phones and set himself up to lay low a while. You give an old hunter like that a few days and he'll have some mountain trapped to Hog Heaven. I pity whoever they send after him.

From the silence and the thoughtful look on all four faces, everyone agreed.

The End

APPENDIX OF WYRDNESS

(MORE OR LESS IN ORDER OF APPEARANCE)

Freke and Gere are the wolves who sit at Odin's feet at times. Otherwise they are out and about in the world. They are curious, wild animals, duh. But their main purpose is to teach mankind about teamwork, family, packhunting, that kind of thing.

Ia Drang is a valley, by a mountain, in Vietnam, where a bunch of Americans rounded up way more vietcong than their daily limit. One of my uncles was there. He suffered from some pretty severe social effects but towards the end I got him to talk about his time in the service. Troyce Ray Stacker was the seed for much of Magnus' backstory. The battle was made into a movie "We Were Soldiers".

Runes The runic alphabet of the Norse has several variations. Magnus uses the elder futhark of twenty-four runes. It can be used to write a message, carve a marker stone, or depending on who you talk to they are tools to divine information, or cast magical effects.

Valkyrie There are a number of "choosers of the slain" named in various stories. Kara, Brunhild, Gondul and more. Alternately called Swan Maidens or Wolf Maidens, they are under the direction of Freja rather than Odin. Odin does have control of them when attending to his warriors in Valhalla though.

Trolls, goblins, dark elves and dwarves- unlike many fantasy works, trolls and such within Valhalla AWOL are often able to pass as humans with a little help. Many of the "alt-naturals" I use are based on Norse beliefs, feel free to look up what a Nordic troll was compared to the traditional dimwitted thugs. They were often considered fair of form and magically adept.

Pookahs Brownies and others for once, someone tosses Magnus a clue about that damned fox. The bone lady's revelation about not discussing it coincides with Scottish folklore about such creatures. For instance, a brownie might work for no more than shelter and some milk and bread. If they are paid more, they disappear. In this instance, the Fox demands that he not be acknowledged for the most part. At least there's a clue there though!

Shamanism and the bone lady. There is one extended sequence within a dream world, or perhaps it's Magnus imagination, subconscious, or something else entirely. This scene comes from various shamanic beliefs. The Bone Mother, Bone Lady, or any number of other names, is a crone-like figure that often greets initiates to Shamanic journeys.

Tenebrae this one fascinated me. The Tenebrae, or daughters of Night, were typical of Greek myths in that they were a force of nature that was humanized. They were also very close to a nastier version of Valkyrie. The Daughters don't look for heroes to claim though, they use the battlefield as a feeding ground for their insatiable appetites focused on pain and terror.

ABOUT THE AUTHOR

Steve Curry is a fledgling author just beginning to use a wide array of experiences and careers. His current forays into writing are Urban Fantasy infused with Culinary tidbits from a decade as a Le Cordon Bleu chef. Military weapons and protocols plus realistic medical and physical descriptions abound from his work with Uncle Sam's Army NBC branch and time as a Licensed Respiratory Therapist in ICUs across the nation. Toss in lots of mythology, new age religion, supernatural goodness and real-world history along with a soupcon of Jim Butcher's humor, and a few pinches of Robert Parker's character-building traits to see how he'll entertain you. He currently resides in West Texas under the management of a yellow hound dog with claims on most of a large bed. Others in the hierarchy are an imperial princess and rainbow unicorn riding granddaughter, his wife, the imperial queen and mistress of eyerolls, and an uncountable horde of invading mongrel cats. You can join others interested in his work at Steve Curry's author pages

https://www.MyWyrdMuse.com

https://www.facebook.com/MyWyrdMuse/